PLAY

OR

DIE

JEN COLE

Published by The Happy Mac
PO Box 5, Darling South
Victoria, Australia 3145

First published by The Happy Mac, 2012

ISBN: 978-0-9873612-0-2

ACKNOWLEDGMENTS

Thanks to John Garnett for his wholehearted and unflagging support during the writing of this novel.

Thanks also to Jane Smith, whose desire to see it published resulted in a great adventure for the author.

To my family, for their willingness to read and critique, and to the friends who enthusiastically provided feedback, I am forever grateful.

CHAPTER 1

They watched her walking along the city street, and wriggled in anticipation.

Jo flowed with the crowd, barely aware of it. The thoughts playing over in her head reduced the traffic's blast to white noise. Was she mad going to this interview? She had a farm to run. How could she even think of becoming a student as well? Her dad would have said, "Forget the farm, you're eighteen. Don't tie yourself down. Sell up, get your degree and have a life." She bit her lip. It wasn't that easy letting go. Maybe I could put a manager on while I study, she thought.

"Are you ready, my dear?"

The question, spoken in her ear, snapped Jo back to the present and she whirled. A man of about thirty with slicked-back ginger hair, was smiling at her wolfishly. His lime-green trousers and candy-striped jacket looked ridiculous but there was nothing funny about him. He flicked the tip of his tongue over his lip and his grin broadened.

"Ready to play the game of your life?"

Her response was immediate. "Get lost!"

She pivoted and strode down the bustling street, senses alive for the presence of a follower. My God, did something about her cry out, country girl? Well she'd shown that pervert she was no easy mark.

A minute of brisk weaving through the crowd and Jo risked a glance back between the somber business suits. No lime-green or pink in sight. She gave a short laugh. There hadn't really been anything to worry about. This early in the morning, with so many people around, someone would have stopped to help if that creep had tried anything. Besides, she was a Shep girl and Shep girls could handle themselves.

Concerns about how she'd manage the orchard while she studied came crowding back, but Jo pushed them away. She wasn't ready to let go of the farm. The answers to her father's death lay there and selling up would mean she'd never learn what really happened.

A wave of sadness washed over her. Strong coffee helped at such times, and her interview wasn't for an hour. The narrow street coming up on her left looked promising. Turning into it she stood on tiptoes, straining to peer over the moving heads. Was that a cafe halfway down?

"Jo Warrington," the oily voice spoke in her ear. "You really *do* need to know the rules of the game."

Gasping, she turned to face the toothy smile. How had he caught up with her? Fear vied with anger and she allowed anger to win.

"What the hell! How do you know my name?"

He bowed, arms widespread. "Allow me to introduce myself. Danny Fitani, world-renowned Game Show Host extraordinaire."

"Right." Jo could not help a snort. "So renowned I've never heard of you."

"Yes, sadly." He brought one hand to his heart. "Because the world in which I'm renowned is not this one. That is to say, it *is* this world, but many years into your future."

A loony then, but not harmless. He knew her name. She'd only arrived in Melbourne last night and he hadn't been at her hotel. Could he have followed her down from Shepparton?

As Jo stared at the grinning face something clicked. She'd never doubted that the coroner's verdict – *Accidental death due to improper maintenance of machinery* – was wrong. Her father had always been meticulous in maintaining his equipment. Yet the idea of someone deliberately tampering with the giant tree shaker seemed equally absurd. Her dad had been well liked. His sole annoying habit, a tendency to jump rather too readily onto his anti-globalization soapbox, was hardly grounds for murder. The only other possibility was that some lunatic...

And now standing before her was a stranger who knew her name, claimed to be from the future and wanted to play games.

Jo adopted a soothing tone as she eased open the zipper of her shoulder bag and slipped her hand towards the phone. If things got out of control, she'd pull it out and threaten to call the police.

"I'm sorry, Mr. Fitani. I'm not into game shows, but I'm sure you'll have no trouble finding someone who is."

He laughed. "Call me Danny. I can see you don't believe me, but you will."

He half turned away and then spun back, swinging an open hand at her face. Instead of connecting, it passed through her head like a shadow. Jo gave a choking cry.

Fitani laughed. "See? I'm an avatar, or hologram if you will. In my world we can't *physically* travel in time, but we can gain *electronic* access to any year in the past that has sufficient microwaves. Microwave photons are different from other electromagnetic radiations. As they hit curved space-time, they gradually lose energy and change to secondary photons. It's a very slow decay, which leaves a trail across time. The right kind of signal can follow the trail back. I hope my translator is helping you make sense of this."

"Your translator?" was all she could say.

"Sure, language changes rapidly – a grandmother only two generations removed could tell you that. My world's English would sound like gibberish to you."

Jo exhaled as she worked it out. No lunatic could orchestrate this. She was being set up by one of those TV shows that put unsuspecting members of the public through bizarre ordeals. She hid her anger at being picked as their stooge on this of all days, and realized there was no point in walking away. They'd only keep following and taunting her. To get it over with she'd have to play along.

"Okay, Mr. Fitani." Jo spoke coolly as she glanced around for hidden cameras. "Tell me about your game."

From the corner of her eye she noticed a white van parked opposite. Could the hologram projector be inside? If so, would she be able to see dust motes dancing in its projection light? She couldn't detect a light stream coming from the van and the Danny Fitani hologram seemed solid and real.

"The game is quite simple," he said.

"Wait a minute." Projecting a hologram onto a street and even moving it along the pavement might be doable, but getting it inside a building? Perhaps there *was* a way she could shed these people. "I was about to have a coffee." Jo indicated the tables outside the cafe ahead. "Can we sit down while you tell me about your game?"

Fitani nodded. "If you like."

She set off towards the tables, but at the last minute leapt for the cafe door and slipped into a world of smothering warmth and clattering dishes. A coffee machine screamed as Jo looked back through the fogged window. No sign of the hologram. They'd have to get themselves another sucker.

A waitress approached, tucking back a wave of dark hair. "Will you be having breakfast with us this morning?"

The melodious Irish accent made Jo smile. "Just a coffee," she said. "If there's a table at the back."

The waitress twisted through the close-set tables where customers sipped coffee over newspapers and tablets, and Jo almost bumped into her when she pulled up.

"I'm sorry, I thought there was a free..."

Beyond her the game show host sat waving his arm.

"Over here, Jo. I found us a table."

The waitress cocked her head and Jo sighed, slipping into the chair opposite Fitani. She ordered a short black.

"And for your friend?"

Well, Jo thought, I'm not hallucinating. How are they doing it?

Fitani waved dismissively. "Nothing for me." He was lounging in his chair with one hand resting on the table.

Could they have guessed she'd run for the nearest cover and planted the real Danny Fitani in here to wait for her? Jo grabbed for his hand. He made no effort to withdraw it and her closing fingers became an empty fist.

He smiled. "Still an avatar."

"How are you doing this?" Exasperation put a squeak into her voice.

"I told you. This era's abundance of microwaves enables us to send and extract data anywhere on Earth."

The waitress returned and Jo gratefully sipped the strong coffee, preparing herself for the upcoming laughter and calls of "Surprise!"

Instead Fitani continued to speak, adopting a lecturing tone. "To explain the game I'll need to fill you in a little on my world. It's a harsh place, only bearable because our technology, too advanced for your understanding..."

Jo lost patience. "Can we do this without the patronizing attitude?"

Fitani beamed. "That's the spirit! Here it is, then. In my world, people rely on entertainment to get them through each day. We at *Fun 'n' Games* bring our viewers the very best in entertainment, and I can tell you, after a four-hour shift at the Edge, there's nothing to beat a real, life-and-death drama. That's where your world comes in."

He leant forward, holding Jo in a magnetic stare. "From this *dark era* we choose contestants for the ultimate sporting event – a five-day struggle for... LIFE ITSELF!"

Jo broke free of his gaze and strove to keep her voice steady as she extracted coins for the coffee and put them on the table. "Sorry, that's not my kind of game. I wouldn't play for any prize. I have to go now. I have an appointment."

"Ah yes, your university interview for the agricultural degree course."

Her knees jellied and she found herself unable to rise.

"Don't think you were chosen at random, my dear. Only special people become candidates for *Play or Die*. Prey must have few family members and be unable to procreate. You've just lost your last close relative and your medical scans, taken after your mother was diagnosed with cancer, show you cannot bear children. That means your premature death won't cause any significant changes to the future world."

Jo clenched her fists to hide the tremble in her hands. How had they found out about her medical scans? She'd told no one – not even Tayla, her best friend. She went on the attack. "Surely *any* change to the past would affect the future. Just *talking* to me must be changing it."

"Ah, a thinker. We like that in our Prey, but no, small changes in the past peter out, leaving no important impact. The world's too big. Too much inertia to overcome. Our mathematicians assure us that only a great change involving masses of people could significantly alter the future."

Jo spluttered and Fitani held up a hand. "You would theorize that an *important* change in the past could begin a domino effect, but our mathematicians insist a domino effect from a single event can't be sustained. Status quo will always be re-established with no great change to the future. Still, nothing is certain and we prefer to play it safe at *Fun 'n' Games* by avoiding what *we* deem extreme changes, such as prematurely ending a family line. Since your family line has already ended, we classify your death as an insignificant change."

"But if I'm killed, people will ask questions!"

"Who, your one old aunt in the Adelaide Hills? How much impact do you think *she'll* have? People die every day in all sorts of ways – take your father. After a brief kerfuffle, the world rolls on. By the way, you needn't worry about your interview. We sent an email from your account to the university administration explaining about your father's recent demise, and requesting some time to settle his affairs. The reply we intercepted was most understanding. They've pushed your interview date forward a week. So you see, you now have five days free in which to play the game."

Jo couldn't hide the horror in her voice. "Are you saying you killed my father to set up a game?"

Fitani raised his eyebrows. "Come now Jo, that would hardly be sporting, and didn't I just tell you we don't prematurely stop family lines? Your father's death was simply an event we recorded during our search for candidates. It shot you to the top of our Possible Prey list."

"You recorded his death?" Jo momentarily forgot all else. "So you know if it was an accident?" The minute the words were out she mentally kicked herself. *I must look like an idiot falling for their Back to the Future crap.*

The game show host looked amused. "I could get one of the crew to check our recordings, but why should I waste my time?"

Jo laced her words with sarcasm. "Are you waiting for me to say I'll play your game if you give me the information?"

Fitani guffawed. "Good heavens no. You're already playing, my dear."

"Like hell I am! I'm not co-operating with this."

His expression became serious. "It's a brave person who's willing to sit and wait to be killed. Before you make that decision, let me explain what you're up against. The Hunter was given your dossier this time yesterday and so has a head start on you – a twenty-four hour head start of planning and preparation."

Fitani paused to let his words sink in, and then went off on a tangent. "Believe me, choosing a suitable Hunter is no easy task. The same parameters of few family and an inability to perpetuate their genes apply. On top of that, the Hunter must have sufficient sociopathic tendencies to be open to the idea of hunting and killing someone for money. Hunters cannot be professional assassins – that would give them an unfair advantage. Likewise in the spirit of fair play, the Hunter and Prey are physically matched as closely as possible."

Jo blinked. "If this is no joke, that would make the people of the future completely evil."

"So other Prey have mentioned."

"Other Prey?"

"Oh yes, our show's near the end of its third year. We run three seasons a year and your Hunt is our ninth. By the way I should tell you that crack about us being evil got lots of ironic laughter and lost you several points."

"What?"

"This is an audience participation show. The viewers' emotions as they watch how you deal with your situation are continually uploaded, decrypted and converted algorithmically to join a scoreboard tally. Accusing us of evil was a bit much, coming from a member of the most evil age of all."

Jo spoke hotly. "What's *that* supposed to mean?"

Fitani flapped his arms in mock dismay. "Oh Jo, drop the outraged innocence, before you lose all the points you've gained so far."

"I have no idea what you're talking about. What's my world going to do that's so evil?"

"It's not what you're *going* to do. It's what you're *not* doing right now. It's your criminal neglect."

"Neglect?" Jo thought of the issues she'd studied at school. "Sure we have problems, but we're dealing with them. We're fighting pollution, deforestation, water shortages, third world starvation..." She faltered under Fitani's continuing sneer.

"You're citing symptoms," he said. "You haven't even mentioned the problem. You do know what I'm talking about don't you? Only one country in your time is making any real effort to do something about it."

As Jo hesitated, he pronounced a word at a volume that attracted frowns from nearby tables. "Over-popu-lation. How can you possibly believe paltry conservation plans will more than briefly delay the outcome of your era's multiplying millions? Your world is on a fast track towards global depletion and widespread wars, leading ultimately to a nuclear holocaust, which will wipe out nearly all life on Earth."

Jo stared. "But *you're* here."

"Only because of The Company. There would be no future without them. After the holocaust they will piece together the remnants and painstakingly rebuild our world." He patted the gold embroidered logo on the pocket of his jacket, adding, "Praise The Company."

Jo narrowed her eyes. "So this game is a kind of retribution? A punishment for our sins?"

"Glad you understand."

"I don't. If you feel so strongly about this, why aren't you contacting my world's governments? Get them to change their policies and prevent the nuclear holocaust from happening."

Fitani gave a harsh bark. "The people of my era have suffered and struggled greatly, but we have survived. Would you have us sacrifice ourselves to save your selfish world?"

"Okay," Jo spoke slowly. "But if you're not prepared to change the past, then surely you have to accept your situation. Get on with your lives and leave us alone."

"Enough! You think your world should get away scot-free? It's responsible for our pain and a price must be paid. *You* have been selected to pay it."

"But why me? As you pointed out, *I* won't be adding to the population."

Fitani put a weightless hand on hers and smiled as she jerked back with a shudder.

"Expediency, Jo. Don't take it personally. This game enables us to achieve a small degree of justice. Though your whole era is to blame, for practical purposes it's only safe to punish a few carefully selected representatives. I've already explained the circumstances that made you a suitable candidate. Now allow me to finish the rules of *Play or Die* before you run out of time."

Jo sucked in air. "What do you mean?"

"At 8.00 a.m. when you agreed to hear about the game, we sent the *Play* signal along with your geospatial coordinates to your Hunter's phone."

"My geospatial coordinates?"

"Indeed. The Hunter knows you're in this area, so it's lucky you moved out of the open for your briefing." Fitani winked. "Some Prey in the past have been bagged before their briefing even ended."

Jo looked round the cafe. The Irish waitress was edging between tables balancing a latte on a saucer in one hand and a plate of scrambled eggs in the other. Customers chatted together or hunched over their reading. Coat-muffled shapes passed by the misty front window. Everything looked normal but her stomach was a knot.

"So." She kept her voice flat. "The game ends when I'm dead?"

"Oh, not necessarily." Fitani broke into a radiant game-show smile. "You can never say the people of the future aren't sporting. Your Hunter, in order to win his or her – let's use 'its' to keep things simple, stupendous prize money, has to bag you within five days. If it hasn't bagged you in that time the game is over. You go free and we arrange for a professional assassin to kill the Hunter. Hunters aren't informed of this penalty, so the unsuccessful are quickly dispatched. Do you see the beauty? Whether it's the Prey or the Hunter who dies, the viewers are always guaranteed a kill."

Jo found herself asking, "Why don't you tell Hunters about the penalty?"

"Hunters tend to get emotionally involved in the game and some continue trying to bag their Prey after the five days have elapsed. If they were aware of the penalty clause, they'd take steps to avoid their assassin while still coming after the Prey. They might even succeed in making a kill before they themselves were eliminated – hardly fair to Prey who'd earned their reprieve."

"So if I can escape the Hunter for five days I get to walk away free?"

"Absolutely! But don't think those five days will be easy. Every three hours we will send your coordinates to the Hunter. It also has your photograph, so it knows exactly what you look like."

"What? Do I get to see what the Hunter looks like?"

"No, you don't." Fitani chuckled. "Isn't it fun? But don't worry, to keep things sporting, you have an advantage it doesn't. Remember you have a scoreboard. By coming up with inventive ways of avoiding the Hunter, you can win approval points from our viewers. For each thousand points you gain, I will appear and you get to ask me any three questions, except about your Hunter's identity.

"Some of the Prey in past seasons have thought up quite ingenious questions. One asked whether his Hunter was allergic to anything. The answer was yes – to bee stings, so the Prey found a large commercial apiary to hide in until the time was up. That Prey's Hunter wasn't prepared to risk its life going in after him, although it probably would have, had it known the penalty for failure."

"I don't suppose my Hunter is allergic to anything?"

Fitani smiled. "No."

"If I'm only allowed three questions after every thousand points, why are you answering all my questions now?"

"Ah." Fitani leant back, lacing fingers behind his head. "This is your briefing. It began when you sat down and will finish when you leave. You may ask as many questions as you like during your briefing. But I should mention that two previous Prey have been killed mid-question, perhaps mistakenly imagining my presence would somehow protect them. Still, not all Hunters are smart enough to head straight for the Prey's coordinates as soon as the start signal is sent. Many waste precious time choosing weapons or employing assistants."

"Assistants?"

"Hunters may use any means short of professional assassins to bag their Prey, and given the substantial prize on offer, most decide employing help is a worthwhile investment."

"Can I also get help from others?"

"Certainly, though you may not use a hit man either."

"But I could try to kill the Hunter myself?"

"You could, although be sure the person you're trying to kill is actually your Hunter. If either you or your Hunter kills bystanders, whether deliberately or accidentally, the game is cancelled and the one responsible for the bystander's death has a professional assassin sent after them. Hunters are informed of this during their briefing to prevent them from getting unsporting ideas such as setting off explosives in the area of a Prey's coordinates."

Jo didn't know at what point she'd given up hope this was a joke. She only knew it was taking all her will not to jump up and run. The more information she could get from Fitani, the more hope she had of surviving.

"Can we move this briefing to a restroom?" She recoiled as a waiter swept by.

Fitani shook his head. "The moment you leave the table your briefing is over. You won't see me again unless you reach a thousand points."

"How far away is my Hunter right now?"

"About two hundred meters."

Dear God! "Is the Hunter moving towards or away from this cafe?"

"Good question. That won you a few points. Your Hunter is currently moving away from this cafe, though it could turn around at any moment."

"Tell me quickly then, is there a back way out of here?"

"Yes." Fitani's reply was unhurried. "Through the kitchen."

"If my Hunter enters this cafe, will you tell me?"

The game show host looked bored. "Only if you happen to ask me at that exact moment."

A dozen questions raced through her mind, but the words that burst from Jo's lips were, "What really happened to my father?"

Fitani rolled his eyes. "The viewers don't care about your father. You're losing points and wasting valuable time."

"You said you would answer any question."

He sighed. "If you insist." His gaze drifted away and seemed to freeze for a moment. Then he looked at her. "My technicians tell me that a man called Simon Brooks hired another man called Morris Blatman to kill your father. Blatman accomplished this by sabotaging the tree shaker."

Jo could barely hold onto these facts. Simon Brooks, Morris Blatman – neither name meant anything.

"Why?"

"How should *I* know? We can see what people of the past are doing, but we can't read their minds."

"How close is the Hunter now?"

"Fifty meters."

"Is it coming towards this cafe?"

"Yes."

Fifty meters! Jo watched the door. She had time for maybe two more questions – but what to ask?

"Is the Hunter alone?"

Fitani smiled. "Yes it is."

"Is it carrying a weapon?"

"I don't see one."

"Is it carrying anything?"

"An umbrella."

Jo picked up her shoulder bag, putting it over her head and across her body like a sash to keep it secure. Stay calm, she thought. The tables will slow up anyone trying to get back here. I'll have time to take a look at whoever comes through the door with an umbrella before I race out the back and merge with the city crowd. It's cutting it fine, but worth it to know what the Hunter looks like.

She glanced at the game show host and caught an odd expression on his face. The doorway was empty – no customers with umbrellas, but something in Fitani's look made her skin crawl. The words tumbled from her lips.

"Is the Hunter in here now?"

"Yes."

Shit! Jo pushed her chair back so fast she collided with a passing waiter and both went sprawling. She rolled onto her knees but was off-balance and wobbled backwards, just as a sharp spike poking from the end of an umbrella jabbed past her face. Instinctively, Jo grabbed the umbrella and pulled it in the direction it was already travelling until the stiletto end speared into the wooden floor. She heard a muffled curse as the person holding the umbrella tumbled forward with it.

The waiter she'd collided with had regained his feet and was reaching down to assist her. Jo grabbed his arms and pulled herself up. Then she spun him around and pushed him on top of her assailant, who was rising with the freed umbrella. Waiter and Hunter went down and she raced for the kitchen door.

CHAPTER 2

On his back, the real Danny Fitani stretched and added a pillow. The smart mat adjusted to his new position as he checked the time display. He'd been in his tube five hours. Seven more until it opened, allowing him to visit the studio Playroom in person. He could send his avatar in the meantime, but it wasn't the same as being there in the flesh. Recording, editing and broadcasting an event in the past was hard work. Personal encouragement was vital to keep his best people coming back each Play-Time.

A communication light blinked. With a gesture, he reduced and slid the virtual hunt-screen to one side before opening a second screen onto the smiling face of Angela Karpin, his chief programmer and a partner in the studio Playroom.

"We've had a great viewer-response to the start, Danny," she said. "They do love the way you terrify the Prey with your sleazy Game Show Host persona."

Fitani waved away her words. "Without the loyalty of our technicians and programmers, we wouldn't have a show." His tone became confidential. "I'm kind of glad I don't get much sleep during a game. Every time I do, the old nightmare rears its head."

Angela laughed. "The one where you go to the studio Playroom and find none of the crew's turned up? That'll never happen. They can't resist our Playroom. Where else can you operate the tools for dealing out justice to the Ancestors?"

"Speaking of the tools of justice, how's that new camera software behaving itself?"

"Like a dream, thanks to Mavis and Garal. They're brilliant programmers."

Angela blinked out. Against the checklist in his mind, Fitani ticked off *Hunt Begun*. Later, to hold the audience over the slow bits, his crew would add a separate feed, where people could tune into a commentary on the unfolding events, and watch interviews with viewers, but the chase was too fresh for that yet.

CHAPTER 3

Jo hurtled through the archway into the compact kitchen. A boy with a frying pan tottered and his pancake landed on the bench, but she had no breath for apology. The back door was almost in reach. As she stepped towards it a mountain moved to block her.

The not-so-white apron she bounced against was stretched across an enormous stomach. The face above it was purpling. A meaty hand landed on her shoulder. Another lifted to point back the way she'd come.

"Staff only. Out!"

Jo looked back. The hooded figure was coming through the archway, umbrella held low. Her cry was drowned in an eruption from the mountain, who stepped towards the Hunter.

"You again!"

As the chef moved forward, Jo ducked under his hand and slipped past him. She reached the door, heaved it open and leapt through. It closed behind her, shutting off the chaos in the kitchen and she found herself in an alley lined with rubbish bins. With a gulp she ran their putrid gauntlet to a busy pedestrian laneway. Going left would take her down to the street on which the cafe fronted, so she turned right, joining the crowd.

There was little room to move in the narrow laneway. Along the sides low stools and rickety tables rubbed against hole-in-the-wall bars offering coffees, juices, homemade soups and sandwiches. Those not edging towards the offerings, stayed with the slow-moving press in the middle. Jo joined them and eventually reached three steps to a higher level.

Leaping to the top, she turned to look back over the heads. There! The hooded Hunter was just entering the pedestrian way. It must have been forced to leave the cafe through the front. Had it seen her? It looked up and she turned and ran.

This elevated part of the lane had a single row of tables down the middle, forcing people to surge along the sides and dodge waiters heading out towards their customers. Jo surged with the rest, her heart thumping wildly as they all spilled out onto Collins Street. The pedestrian lights were green and across the road the Australia on Collins shopping arcade seemed to open its arms to her. She ran towards it, but at the last minute, baulked. Hardly anyone was going in. She needed the protection of a crowd.

On impulse she turned left but quickly realized the wide walkway of Collins Street was too exposed. Ahead on her right was another shopping arcade – the Block. Desperate to get off the open street, Jo ran into it. Another mistake. This arcade was high-end, its exquisite mosaic-tiled floor whispering, class. Antique orbs hung from the vaulted ceiling, illuminating nineteenth century plasterwork. The store windows displayed expensive jewelry, imported chocolates and crystalware. At the prices they charged they didn't need many customers, and this early it was empty apart from a strolling Japanese tourist with a bulging plastic bag, and a pair of grandmothers inspecting the cakes on display in the Hopetoun Tea Rooms.

It was too late to turn around. Jo ran, her heels clacking disrespectfully on the tiny mosaic tiles. At the end, the arcade looped sharply. Oh God, she thought. It's delivering me back to the Hunter. Then she saw the side lane splitting off, and veered into it, sprinting past mahogany sidewalk tables with cane-backed chairs of patrons enjoying breakfasts under heat lamps.

The lane ended at a narrow street. A stitch bent her over, and moaning, she forced herself to straighten and look back the way she'd come. No sign of the Hunter, but it wasn't safe to rest here. She turned left onto the street and then right into a new arcade – this one light-filled and delicate. Its polished black and white diamond-checked floor flowed under an arched glass ceiling supported by iron lace. As Jo staggered through it, her stitch burning, bright colors flickered at the edges of her vision – a lollipop shop, shelves of Venetian glassware and a window of multi-colored babushka dolls. Finally she burst onto a wide pedestrian boulevard and found what she'd been seeking – a department store. Hope sped her through its wide doors, past the perfumes and cosmetics displays to the escalators. She leapt on, momentum helping her to weave up through the standing shoppers patiently ascending. At the top she peeled off to the restrooms, staggered into a cubicle and locked the door.

Jo collapsed onto the toilet seat, sucking in deep breaths and waiting for her heart to stop its painful pounding. When it did, waves of uncontrollable shaking swept her and turning, she vomited into the bowl. Finally this too passed and she knelt exhausted, her eyes closed and mind and emotions drained.

Gradually she became aware of noises around her. Women were moving in and out of the cubicles, washing their hands and using the electric dryers. Jo flushed the toilet but wasn't yet ready to leave her haven. She put the lid down and sat, pulling out her phone. The blank screen stared back at her. Should she call the police? What would she say? Someone I don't know is trying to kill me for a prize offered by people from the future? Even if they bothered asking her to come into the station, they'd have trouble hiding their smiles as they took her statement, and by the time she was through, the Hunter would be waiting outside.

Her phone pinged and she jumped. A text from Tayla. *Good luck with the interview. Call when it's over.*

What could she text back? Interview cancelled, running from killer? Tayla would think she was joking... or that she'd had a breakdown. How could Jo convince her when she hardly believed what was happening herself? If Tayla panicked and contacted the authorities, Jo could end up being held by the police or men in white coats until the Hunter picked her off, or worse, Tayla might come rushing down to Melbourne and end up getting killed in the crossfire. Jo's heart sank as she realized she couldn't involve her best friend.

She typed, *Boring mixup. Interview now Friday. Staying here till then. Fill you in on wknd.* She sent the text and checked the time... then checked again. It couldn't be. Just 9.15 a.m. It felt as though a day had passed since she'd met the game show host on the street, yet it was little more than an hour. That's good, she realized. It means I have almost two hours before the Hunter gets my new position... and I need every second.

Jo shivered. That Hunter is smart – or maybe I'm just stupid. I knew there was a back door to that cafe. Fitani told me so, but it never occurred to me the Hunter might come in that way. If I hadn't followed my instincts when I saw Fitani's expression, I'd be dead right now. The memory of the lethal spike flashing past her face brought a renewed surge of terror but she fought it back. To survive this she needed to keep her wits about her.

What else have I learnt about the Hunter, she thought. It's bigger than me but not by much. It could be a small man or a large woman. Still, that bold murder attempt in a crowded cafe, feels masculine. Wouldn't a female be more cautious about her own safety, preferring to set a trap? The average female perhaps, but a sociopath – who knew?

Hell, all she knew for sure was the Hunter was dressed in navy track pants and a hoodie... *was* dressed that way. If it had changed, she'd never recognize it, and changing was exactly what *she* should be doing. If the Hunter was wandering this area hoping to spot her... or had employed people to look for her!

Heart racing, she slipped out of the cubicle. Two women were just leaving the wash area and for the moment Jo had it to herself. She was surprised the full-length mirror reflected so little damage from her wild run. Her blonde shoulder-length hair was slightly mussed, her tights had a ladder, and her new high-heeled boots were scuffed, but the rest of her outfit looked fine. Tayla had helped her put it together for the interview: a white shirt and red jacket paired with a pleated charcoal mini.

"You'll distract them with your long legs in this," Tayla had said, holding up the skirt. "They'll forget all their hard questions."

The girls had laughed, but Jo now felt she stood out a mile. Covering up was essential. She turned to a basin, wincing at the blister forming on one heel, and rinsed her mouth. She gulped some of the cool water and then pulled open the door a crack, peeking out. This floor was devoted to Women's Fashions and although it was July, with the cold weather at its worst, winter sales had already begun.

Though no one was loitering in navy track pants and a hoodie, Jo couldn't get her legs to move. The decision was made for her when a woman, obviously in a hurry, pushed in and swept past Jo to the cubicles. Exposed in the doorway, Jo darted out to the hanging garments and grabbed a trench coat, scarf and beret, before retiring with her booty to a change room. With the long coat buttoned, the grey wool scarf wrapped around the lower part of her face, and her hair pushed up under the black beret, the former Jo was hidden. Now she was just one of the shoppers lured into the city by the sales.

The instant disguise boosted her confidence and she headed to the counter in the center of the store. A young assistant, wearing an oversized badge that announced, *Hi I'm Cheryl*, stood waiting. Cheryl's smile wavered when Jo began removing items and dropping them onto the counter. It disappeared completely when Jo pounced on the beret as soon as she'd scanned it, and returned it to her head, twisting her hair up underneath. Cheryl removed the electronic tag from the scarf and rang up the price. She'd barely released it before Jo snatched this back too. Lips now thinned, the salesgirl scanned the coat.

"I don't suppose you want this bagged?" she asked.

"No thanks." Jo pulled it from her hands and slipped it on. "It's cold this morning."

Cheryl took Jo's credit card. "The store's quite warm."

"I don't feel it," said Jo, already sweating under her disguise.

As she signed the chit for an amount she tried not to think about, a nasty thought occurred. Can't people's movements be traced by their credit card transactions? If the Hunter's hired a detective agency to locate me, they'll know where I am every time I use it. Not only that, she realized, my transaction history will reveal all my disguise attempts and escape plans. I need cash.

Jo headed for the escalators and then remembered she hadn't changed her bag. She hesitated, hating the idea of wasting any more time. In sudden inspiration she took off her coat, slipped the bag on like a sash, and buttoned the coat over the top. It didn't feel too bad, and now she could walk with hands in her pockets, which would change her look even more.

By the time Jo had scurried down between customers on the escalator and across to the exit doors, she was light-headed from the heat, but as she staggered outside the rush of cold air brought back her senses.

A businessman veered to avoid her and she put out a hand.

"Excuse me, do you know where I could find a Bendigo Bank?"

Jo could never say that name without feeling a rush of pride for the resourcefulness of farming communities. After the betrayal of the big banks who had pulled out of country regions pronouncing there was no money to be made, Bendigo farmers had proved them wrong by setting up a Community Bank, which had been so successful it now had branches all over Australia.

The businessman pointed down the boulevard. "Go to Queen Street and turn left. There's a Bendigo Bank on the corner of Collins."

"Thank you *so* much."

Jo heard a faint, "You're welcome," as she hurried in the direction he'd indicated. But at Queen Street her heart sank. This wide street would be taking her back the way she'd come.

You'll be fine, she told herself firmly. The coat and beret have totally changed your look. Except, she realized with a jolt, for being alone. Wouldn't her pursuers be homing in on females walking by themselves? Jo looked around. Pedestrian traffic was thin. A group of students ahead might provide some cover. If not, this wide street would be a trap.

CHAPTER 4

In a Queensland motel room BEAM agent, Richard Sayers, was emptying drawers, having completed his assignment.

Setting up another farming community to resist the H Group had taken nearly a month – longer than usual. He'd had difficulty finding the right person to lead the northern mango growers, and he hoped the man he'd chosen would work out. So far his leader had needed a lot of handholding.

Too bad he wasn't more like Bill Warrington, who preferred minimal direction and was a respected, natural leader among the Shepparton apple growers down in Victoria. Richard felt confident Bill would keep the Shepparton community strong and force the H Group to withdraw from that area. No one was perfect though, and Bill's most infuriating flaw was his casual attitude towards protocols.

"I can't be bothered with all the cloak-and-dagger stuff," the apple farmer had said. "My priorities are Jo and my orchards, in that order."

Richard had to agree Jo deserved top billing. He smiled, re-living his last visit a month ago. It had been mid-June and Jo had come striding to greet him through a tunnel of bare-limbed trees. She'd been helping her dad with the pruning and her cheeks were glowing. Even in dungarees she was a stunner, though there was always a little knife twist in knowing nothing could happen between them. The stumbling block wasn't so much their six-year age difference, as the lie he was living. To Jo, he was a seller of farming equipment. In the spy business you could forget about starting normal relationships.

Six months ago BEAM had discovered the H Group was targeting Shepparton apple growers and they'd sent in Richard. As a travelling salesman, he'd gone from farm to farm with laptop and brochures, making a few sales for the farming equipment company that fronted for BEAM, while searching for the right person to lead an organized local resistance. Jo's father had quickly become the obvious choice.

"I can't afford new equipment right now," Bill Warrington had told Richard. "Not after this latest squeeze from the supermarkets." He'd then gone on to complain about the whole globalization trend, which he saw as putting ever-increasing power and resources into the hands of ever fewer people.

Over time the two men had built a rapport, and Richard had finally told Bill about the H Group and their plans for Shepparton. The apple farmer had been stunned, then angry, and finally cautious. He'd taken his time examining Richard's evidence, but in the end had concluded his community was indeed under threat.

"The only way I can see of battling the H Group is to take a stand against the supermarket chains," Bill had said. "I'm going to organize a meeting of the independent growers."

"Do that," Richard had agreed. "But remember to stay focused on the supermarkets. Don't let anything slip about the H Group."

The meeting had been hugely successful. Outraged at the latest low buy-price the supermarkets were trying to force on them, the growers agreed to unite in refusing to accept it. When the supermarkets found they couldn't play one farmer off against another they'd be forced raise their offer.

The meeting had ended on a feeling of optimism, but Bill had suddenly become worried about Jo, concerned at what the H Group might do on finding their plans threatened.

Richard tried to reassure him. "The H Group uses *economic* means to break you. When communities hold a united front against the supermarkets, they invariably pull out. Behaving like gangsters would draw attention, and they don't need to do that while there are still plenty of vulnerable communities they can move on to. The H Group's modus operandi is quiet acquisition."

"All very well," Bill said. "But when they run out of easy targets, won't they be tempted to try a little 'overcoming' of the resistance?"

Richard shook his head. "So far they've only resorted to violence when their secret was threatened. Then, it's true they've acted quickly and ruthlessly. Anyone smart or perhaps unfortunate enough to discover an H Group connection with farming communities, and start asking questions, rapidly meets with a fatal 'accident'. That's why it's vital you give no hint of your knowledge of the H Group, but act as though the supermarket chains are your goal. As long as you take that approach you have nothing to worry about."

Bill grunted. "Battling the supermarkets *is* our goal. If we win that fight, and you're right about the H Group, they'll move on. Your lot can follow them and good luck to you. But what if you're wrong? If the H Group decides not to leave, I don't want Jo around here. She wasn't planning on further study, but her exam results were good. I think I'll try and convince her to apply for an agricultural degree course."

"Do what you have to, so we can move forward," Richard had said. "The longer we wait, the harder it will be. An outsider has already made an offer on the Davies' farm and I believe they're considering it."

"Is this outsider connected with the H Group?"

"That's how they operate. He's Jack Murray, a thirty-something inner-city teacher. Ostensibly an uncle left him an inheritance and he's decided to leave the rat race and become a gentleman farmer."

Bill gave a laugh. "Sounds like the kind of fantasies city folk have."

"It's a good cover. He asked a local estate agent to go to Mitch Davies with an offer. It's no coincidence the Davies' are the weakest link in the community. BEAM will keep digging," Richard promised. "We'll find Jack Murray's tie to the H Group. Unfortunately, our resources are negligible compared to theirs and worldwide experience has honed their strategies."

Richard frowned at the memory of that conversation, wishing his assigned communities weren't so widely spread. At the moment he was two thousand kilometers from Shepparton. Protocols were the only way to keep in touch but getting Bill to follow them wasn't easy and Richard hadn't wanted to put his community leader offside by nagging. Now he wished he'd insisted. Almost four weeks without a word from Bill was too long.

Richard opened his laptop and logged onto 'Patti's Blog', scanning for comments by Suze, the online persona BEAM had set up for Bill. Patti's was one of thousands of open weblogs whose owners were happy to let the world read and comment upon their postings, and BEAM used such blogs to communicate with its agents.

Patti's most recent entry, dated yesterday, was another tirade against her mother who had grounded her last Saturday for some minor infraction. Richard skimmed through the archived history of comments. The last from Suze had been exactly a month ago, when she'd agreed with Patti that all little brothers should be shipped off to some faraway island.

As Suze, Bill could leave seemingly innocuous comments on Patti's blog, which would be meaningful to Richard. Suze agreeing with something Patti had said, was code for 'everything's fine'. If Suze asked Patti a question, it meant Bill needed to talk and would be turning on the safe mobile phone Richard had given him at nine each night for an hour, until Richard called him. Finally if Suze disagreed with Patti, it meant a big problem had occurred and Richard needed to get down to Shepparton fast. So far Suze had never found cause to disagree with anything Patti had said.

Suze was supposed to write a weekly comment, but Bill often let an extra week or two slip by, complaining the Internet made his head ache. Richard knew the farmer found it distasteful pretending to be a young girl on Patti's blog, but all the same, Suze had never before gone as long as a month without posting something.

Richard closed the laptop and finished packing his suitcase. It was high time he took a trip to Shepparton.

CHAPTER 5

Jo leapt forward to gain camouflage among the students. They ignored her, engrossed in their own conversation, and she drifted alongside, trying to look part of the group. Meanwhile, she watched intently for the navy track pants and hoodie, and wondered how much money to withdraw. Ten thousand? She might have to hire cars or take planes, and she'd also need places to stay. That could get expensive and she didn't want the Hunter tracking her through bank withdrawals. Twenty thousand then? It was all the money from her mother's bequest, which had been slowly growing in term deposits over the last two years.

She'd planned to use the bequest to buy a car when she turned eighteen after her final exam, but then her father's accident had occurred and she'd been caught up in the inquest and funeral arrangements. Instead of withdrawing the money, she'd allowed the term deposit to roll over and now the twenty thousand lay intact and waiting in the bank.

How bulky will 20,000 dollars in cash be, Jo thought. She did a quick calculation. If I got the highest denomination, hundred dollar bills, I'd have two hundred notes. Would they fit in a money belt? I'd need a big one, and if it makes me look bulkier, good – it'll help disguise me. She glanced at her watch. Hell! Although the first hour had taken an eternity, the second had flown. It was nearly 10.15. In just forty-five minutes her coordinates would be sent to the Hunter.

Jo fought the urge to run, and stayed with the slow-moving students. Ahead, a rack of suitcases outside a doorway signaled a travel shop. Should she get a money belt now? No, the bank transaction could take a while. She'd do that first.

At Collins Street, Jo spotted the Bendigo Bank and broke off from the group to cross the road. The queue inside, though long, was feeding to a number of tellers and moving quickly. She used the waiting time to anticipate questions she might be asked, and to unbutton her coat and ferret in her bag for the kinds of identification they'd no doubt require. As she reached the front of the line a chime sounded and a number three lit up.

The teller at window three wore the bank's tailored, maroon blouse with a starched yellow kerchief in the pocket. She flashed a professional smile, and Jo returned it with what she hoped was calm confidence.

"I have 20,000 dollars in a ninety-day term account that I'd like to withdraw." Jo gave her name and the account number and the teller's polished nails clicked at the keyboard.

"That account doesn't mature for two months. There'll be a penalty on the interest for early withdrawal."

"Yes, that's okay."

The car she'd planned to buy was a fleeting regret. She was just glad the money was there to withdraw.

"Shall I transfer the sum to your cheque account?" asked the teller, moving the mouse as she scanned the screen in front of her.

Jo answered casually. "No, I'd like to take it in cash please."

The woman's head turned sharply. "That's an unusual request."

"My father died recently and I've been settling his estate. I've come to Melbourne to make a number of payments, and it's easier to do them with cash."

The teller looked skeptical. "I don't know if we even have that much cash available for a single customer. I'll have to check with the manager and I'll also need three forms of identification."

Jo handed over her new driver's licence, along with her national healthcare and credit cards. The teller indicated the chairs provided for customers.

"Please take a seat. Shouldn't be long."

Sitting, Jo caught sight of the bank's wall clock. Ten-thirty. Her heart jumped, but she steadied herself. Don't panic, she thought. Use this time to plan. My coordinates will be sent at 11.00 a.m. so where's the best place to be? The train station's just down the road from here. No, if the Hunter's using a detective agency, operatives could be lurking at the entrances with photos of me. Where then? Jo bit her lip... Back at the department store! With luck the Hunter would imagine she'd got so involved in shopping for survival gear, that she'd lost track of time. The store had four levels, covered two blocks and no doubt had a myriad of exits. To trap her there he'd need to send everyone he had, including any agents at the station. So if she went straight to the station *after* 11.00, she should arrive just as the Hunter's assistants were surrounding the store. Jo shivered excitedly, and then sobered quickly.

I'm not safe yet, she thought. Say she made it to the station, what then? She'd need supplies. Unbidden, a name came to mind. *Chadstone.* It was where she'd gone on her last girls' trip with her mother. That day, two years ago, had been an unexpected treat – an outing in Melbourne. A small part of it had involved visiting the specialist, who had rooms in the sprawling Chadstone shopping center, and who would do some tests to solve the mystery of Mum's tiredness. The tests had not taken long, and afterwards they'd seen a movie, had lunch, and spent a carefree afternoon shopping. Three days later, Mum's doctor revealed what those tests had found – a particularly virulent form of cancer. Just eight months after the diagnosis, a few days short of her sixteenth birthday, she'd held her father's hand at the funeral.

Jo threw off the memory and glanced at her watch. What's happened to that teller? Why is she taking so long? The numbers on the dial changed to 10:36, and she closed her eyes. Keep planning, she told herself but flashes from the weeks following her mother's death were now filling her mind. Her father had been devastated and had relied heavily on Jo for emotional support. She'd been forced to drag herself out of her own grief and grow up quickly. It had been a natural progression to take over her mother's role on the farm, learning to do the books and tackling the endless string of chores each day after school and on weekends. Between them, she and her father had kept the orchard afloat, but at the sacrifice of much of her social life. There were times, such as when she saw a group of girls at school giggling over some magazine, that she felt a hundred years old.

"Miss Warrington?" the teller had returned. "Our manager, Mr. Singh would like a word with you. Could you come this way?"

Jo sprang up and followed her into a side room where a dapper, serious man sat behind a desk. He half rose as she entered, and indicated the seat opposite. On the desk between them were her driver's licence and health and credit cards, which he pushed towards her.

"Miss Warrington, I understand you wish to make a cash withdrawal of 20,000 dollars."

"Yes... did the teller explain my situation?"

"She did, and please accept my condolences on the passing of your father. But I wonder if you fully understand the risk you take in carrying such a large amount of cash?"

His forehead was wrinkled and Jo noticed several prematurely grey threads running through his hair.

"I do, but I have a number of cash payments to make this morning, so I won't be carrying the money for long."

"I see. Unfortunately, we require some notice for a withdrawal of that amount or we wouldn't have sufficient notes to provide for our other customers over the day."

"Oh. How much can you give me?"

"We could give you 10,000 dollars now and the other 10,000 tomorrow."

"I won't be here tomorrow!" Jo caught herself as panic bubbled up. She breathed deeply and reached for the idea forming in her mind.

"I'll be at Chadstone later today. Is there a branch in that area I could get the remainder from?"

"We have a branch around the corner from Murrumbeena station, which is near Chadstone," replied the manager, scribbling down the address for her. "Let me give them a call."

Jo returned her identity cards to her wallet and slipped the card with the bank's address into her pocket while the manager spoke on the phone. His desk clock showed 10.42. Her fingers and toes clenched in agony.

Finally he hung up and pressed an intercom button. "Mrs. Norris, could you please join us." Then turning to Jo, "You're in luck Miss Warrington. The Murrumbeena branch can supply you with the other 10,000 dollars. I've told them to expect you."

Jo stood and extended her hand. "Thank you Mr. Singh. I really appreciate it."

"I'm glad we could help," the bank manager said as he stood to shake her hand. "I hope things go well with your father's affairs."

Though desperate to get going, Jo forced herself to nod and smile. "Thank you."

The teller put her head through the doorway. "Yes Mr. Singh?"

"Please give Miss Warrington 10,000 dollars in cash and transfer the balance to her cheque account. And Miss Warrington… do take care."

"I will," she said, before following Mrs. Norris back to the transaction window.

As the teller counted and bundled the money, Jo became aware of a disturbance about halfway down the waiting queue. A man and woman were arguing, and she could hear a rising note of hysteria in the woman's voice. The two were facing each other so Jo could only see the back of the man's grey coat, but she observed that his sparring partner was a neat blonde in a short black skirt and crimson top. As Jo watched, the man took hold of her arm and she gave a scream. The queuing customers were turning to observe the drama, and another man entered the argument, loudly telling the grey coat to calm down and let the woman go.

Jo's teller coughed discretely, and turning, she saw the counted money waiting for her. With a quick 'thank you', she thrust the bundles to the bottom of her bag, noticing peripherally that the drama in the queue was escalating. Others had joined in the shouting and she heard the words, 'Citizen's arrest,' and saw a grey-sleeved arm waving an open leather wallet. A police car was pulling up as she left the bank, and she moved on quickly, not wanting to be caught up in whatever was happening.

With less than ten minutes to get back to the department store, Jo adopted the half skipping weaving run of a city woman late for an appointment, or so she hoped it looked, and reached the store panting, but with two minutes to spare. *I've got to get right into the middle. It must look like I'm engrossed in shopping, not just about to leave.* As she plunged through the milling shoppers, Jo wondered if a sauna could be any hotter, and was glad she only had to endure the department store for a few minutes.

At eleven by her watch, she reached an area displaying sunglasses alongside racks of cheap magnifying eyewear for the ageing population. She decided to stay two minutes longer to allow for any time discrepancy and eyed the sunglasses. They were tempting, but no. *Sunglasses with a coat, scarf and hat in the middle of winter just screamed I'm trying to hide.* Better to buy something completely unlikely for someone in her situation. Across the aisle was the answer – artificial flowers.

She grabbed a bunch of long-stemmed lilies and took them to the counter. As the sales clerk rolled them into a paper cone, Jo pulled the last fifty-dollar bill from her wallet. There'd be little change, but she waited for it, re-buttoning the coat over her bag. She didn't want the woman calling out to her from across the store. As soon as the notes were proffered, Jo thrust them into her pocket and lifted the flowers so they partially hid her face. Then with a thumping heart, she headed for the exit. The doorway loomed... she was through.

Now she faced several blocks' walk down the very street pursuers could be travelling up, on their way to the department store. Jo didn't want to risk that close an encounter. She paused indecisively before spotting a solution. A city tram was approaching. A quick sprint got her to the island stop in the middle of the road just as it pulled up. She boarded and took a seat near the door.

The tram sailed on and Jo laid the flowers across her knees and undid some coat buttons. She felt around inside her bag and her fingers brushed one of the reassuring bundles of money, but she was looking for the transport card she'd purchased that morning to travel from her hotel to the city. Ah, there it was, next to her phone.

She slipped the card into her pocket, and suddenly felt sick. Her phone – it had been on in her bag the whole time. Couldn't its GPS chip give away her location? Would the Hunter's hired help have access to tracking equipment?

With horror she remembered the woman in the bank queue. *A bit shorter than me,* she thought, *and older, and her crimson top wasn't quite the same shade as my jacket, but her hair was the same color and length. She certainly looked a lot more like me than anyone else in the bank, and if I'd been out of sight with the manager when the operative came in, he could well have assumed that woman was me.* She yanked out her phone and started to turn it off, then paused.

The tram squealed to a stop opposite the station and Jo left with a group of passengers. Her phone lay on the tram seat. With luck it would be a red herring. She hoped whoever took it wouldn't manage to crack her auto-lock. Bad enough to lose an expensive phone without having to pay for someone's long distance calls. Still, it was worth it to steer the Hunter in the wrong direction.

At the station's entrance, Jo pulled the transport card from her pocket and held it against the sensor. The barrier opened and she stepped through. Smooth as a regular, she hoped. Thanks to the bank manager she had a station name, but the myriad of platforms and signs inside set her heart fluttering.

Calm down, she told herself. Murrumbeena Station has to be listed somewhere. And there it was – on the Pakenham line, platform six. A train would be leaving in three minutes. Keeping the flowers up, she made her way to the platform, found a bench and collapsed onto it beside a scruffy student reading a textbook.

Strands of sweaty hair stuck to her face and she pushed them back. The blister on her heel stung and her feet were throbbing, but she'd succeeded, and when three minutes later the train approached, she almost sprang to meet it.

CHAPTER 6

Angela Karpin patrolled the studio Playroom out of habit, but after eight seasons she was able to leave most of the problems to her programmers. The fact that so many kept coming back reinforced the heady feeling of being part of something worthwhile.

When three years earlier, Fitani had proposed a partnership in a blank Playroom, she'd been simultaneously flattered and suspicious – flattered that he'd thought the programming skills of a nineteen-year-old up to his project, and suspicious that his real interest was in her investment contribution – her highly acclaimed tube games had won her a great many Personal Points. There was probably some truth on both counts, but Fitani had ended up surprising her. She'd known he was a showman, but he'd also turned out to be a skilled motivator and organizer. Moreover, he never seemed slowed by doubts and this, she'd come to realize, was because he had something she lacked – faith in The Company and its path for them.

Their broadcasts from the *Fun 'n' Games* Playroom had gained an instant following, but *Play or Die* was to become their greatest success. It may even have saved her, she admitted. At the time, Ben had just turned two and had gone into the children's silo, and though she was pregnant with Sandra, compulsory sterilization followed the second child, so after Sandra, she would never again have the comfort of a baby to banish the creeping despair so many were succumbing to.

Somehow *Play or Die* had turned things around for everyone. People had become reinvigorated when they'd discovered they could dispense real justice to their hated Ancestors and the rising suicide rates had dropped. Angela was proud to play a part in bringing this healing to the people of the Safe Places all over the Earth.

As she glanced at the action on screen, her attention was drawn to the Hunter, who was with one of his agents, sorting out the debacle that had resulted from Jo leaving her phone on the tram. This Hunter was like a snake, she decided – both repellent and fascinating. He worked his charm to bring others under his thrall, while never losing sight of his goal. His preparation for the game had been faultless, especially given the mere twenty-four hours he'd had before Jo's briefing. Since the game had begun however, arrogance had led him to make a mistake, and the Prey had slipped through his fingers in the city.

No doubt he would catch her, but Angela found herself hoping it wouldn't be too soon. Something in the Hunter reminded her of Scott Marshall. Their paths had last crossed a month ago, in the Congregation Playroom at the Spring Season Raging Festival, when he'd come up behind her during the effigy burning, and squeezed her breast. She'd struggled from his grasp and called him a filthy Ancestor before giving him a shove. In retaliation he'd pretended to lose balance, stumbling against her, and stomping hard on her instep. For the surrounding crowd, whose heads had turned at her scream, he'd apologized with mock humility, all the while enjoying her pain and anger.

This Hunter, Angela decided, was a Scott Marshall-type, and she felt an unexpected twinge of sympathy for the Prey. Not, she told herself, that she really cared either way. They were both vile, selfish Ancestors, and one of them would soon be getting their punishment.

CHAPTER 7

Jo boarded, swept a glance around the carriage and took a seat in an empty section. As the train pulled out, she sighed, feeling tension drain away. Her eyelids began to droop until the shock of nearly falling asleep flipped them back open.

Don't let your guard down, she told herself and scanned the carriage a second time but the occupants continued to look completely ordinary. It was 11.15. For sanity's sake she had to assume she'd given the Hunter the slip and would be relatively safe until two o'clock.

How best to use her time until then? Make a list of the things she needed. Jo pulled a pen and notepad from her bag and wrote, Passport? Never having travelled overseas in her eighteen years, she didn't own a passport, but guessed the process of acquiring one could take some days.

She crossed it out. I'm stuck in Australia but that's not so bad. It's a big country. As long as I move fast to a different place every three hours, I should be able to avoid the Hunter, shouldn't I? With a sick feeling, Jo admitted to herself that keeping ahead of the Hunter would become increasingly difficult the more tired she got.

I can't afford to sleep through a coordinates posting, but the Hunter can if he has others tracking me down. That means he'll always be fresher than me. Jo realized she'd been thinking of the Hunter as male for a while now, but it felt right so she didn't fight it.

Okay, since I have to be awake at each posting, I'll need a watch that has an alarm. She wrote it down. And a money belt, oh and a decent pair of walking shoes! Just thinking about them made her feet start throbbing again. Should she get a haircut? Going short would change her appearance and make it easy to use wigs as well. Jo added *wigs* to the list but put a question mark after it. How much appearance changing would she need to do? Fitani had said they were sending her new coordinates, every three hours, but he hadn't mentioned, and she hadn't thought to ask, whether her photo was also being updated.

The Hunter's briefing, according to Fitani, had taken place yesterday. How much personal information about her had Fitani given him? How many arrangements had the Hunter been able to put into place in those twenty-four hours before she'd received *her* briefing?

For the first time, Jo wished Fitani back so she could ask those questions, and remembered two things – that he *would* reappear if she gained a thousand points, and that she was now on constant show for the TV viewers of the future.

Her face grew hot as she realized these strangers had already watched her vomiting into a toilet bowl and she cringed at the thought of the personal, private things they would continue to see over the coming days.

You can't care about that, she told herself. To these people you're nothing but a circus chimp performing for their entertainment. Never give them the satisfaction of showing embarrassment. Concentrate on what's important.

Important – she found herself scribbling down the two names Fitani had given her. *Simon Brooks* and *Morris Blatman*. Simon Brooks had hired Morris Blatman to kill her father. These future people thought they were using her, but Jo realized with amazement that she'd already used *them* to discover the names of her father's murderers. This *using* business can be a two-way street, she thought with rising hope.

The train pulled into Southern Cross station. Jo knew its undulating roof and steep escalators well. This was the terminus for all Victoria's country lines. She could get off right here if she wanted, and catch a train home to Shepparton. Her resolve of barely a minute ago wavered. The word *home* felt so sweet and she was so tired. But home would be no haven. The Hunter probably already had people stationed around her house, and if he didn't, he'd quickly send some when her 2.00 p.m. coordinates put her there.

Estate agents were also waiting to pounce. One had phoned yesterday as she was leaving for Melbourne. A buyer, he'd said, had approached him about her farm.

Jo sighed. Only three weeks ago she and her dad had been sitting over mugs of tea at the breakfast table discussing the usual week's tasks. Then the first change had started. Out of the blue her father had said, "Jo-cat, the university has a mid-year intake. Why don't you apply for their agricultural degree course?"

"Huh? Since when do you need me to have a degree?"

"We should keep up with the times."

Jo had laughed. "Is this the great skeptic of new-fangled ideas I hear talking?"

"I'm serious, Jo. Qualifications make you saleable, should we ever have to let the farm go."

"What? No Dad," she'd protested. We grow the best apples in Shep!"

Her father had held up a hand. "And the supermarket chains, with their three and four hundred percent markups are grinding us into the ground. It's harder than ever to cover our costs. That new tree shaker alone will take another five years to pay off. The Davies have just sold up," he added.

She was scornful. "Their kids are to blame for that. They abandoned the farm to get jobs in Melbourne and Mitch and Fran were too old to keep up the place on their own. The new owner, that city bloke, Jack Murray, seems to be doing alright."

"Maybe, if things really are as they seem… and don't forget, I'm no spring chicken myself."

Shocked at hearing him speak this way, Jo had responded vigorously. "Dad, you're barely middle aged, not old. *And* as fit as a fiddle. No city farmer could hold a candle to you."

That had made him smile. "I hope not. Fiddles are made of wood. In any case, while I'm *barely* middle-aged and still have the energy to run the orchard on my own, you should take the opportunity to head off to university."

He'd had answers for all her objections and gradually the frightening thoughts of losing the farm had given way to a growing excitement over what she could achieve armed with up-to-date techniques and scientific knowledge in agriculture. That same night she'd filled out the university's online application form and when the invitation to attend an interview had arrived, Jo had been thrilled and optimistic.

How had things gone so wrong? A man she'd never heard of had ordered her father's death, and now people from the future were using the opportunity provided by her new orphan status to order hers. Well if they thought she was a goner they had another think coming. She was far from helpless. She'd avoid their damned Hunter *and* bring her father's murderers to justice.

The train moved on and Jo shifted in her seat, catching a waft of her own body odour. The morning's repeated combinations of terror, exercise and overheated city stores had taken their toll. She thought of her Richmond hotel room. Could she risk going back to have a shower and collect her gear? Better not, she decided grimly, but at some stage she'd have to let them know she wouldn't be returning. No point in running up unnecessary bills.

She already missed her phone. How easy it would be to call the hotel right now. And how stupid, she reminded herself. Every time I turned it on, I'd be telling the Hunter where I was. She wondered if Tayla had been texting. Before much longer she'd need to let people know her phone was out of action, or first Tayla and then other friends would start worrying about her lack of communication. What I need is a pre-paid phone that can't be traced to me. Jo added "phone" to her list.

They pulled into Richmond Station and a new group of passengers boarded – a woman with a small child in tow, a group of teenaged schoolboys laughing at an off-color joke as they dropped their sports bags in the aisle, a sad-looking middle-aged man with a briefcase and a twenty-something woman dragging a fat romantic novel from her bag as she sat. None of them looked like agents, except perhaps the man with the briefcase, but he hadn't even glanced at her.

Tired of making notes, Jo thrust the pad and pen back into her bag and caught another whiff of her BO. I've got to find a place to take a shower, she thought. Otherwise people are going to start remembering me. Her lids dropped, and she let them rest for second.

"Next stop, Carnegie Station." The singsong voice of the train's PA system woke Jo and she jerked upright in shock. How could she have fallen asleep? Carnegie – it was the station before Murrumbeena. She'd memorized it in order to be ready for her stop. Her watch now read 11.45. She'd been on the train for half an hour, twenty minutes of it asleep!

Maybe that "power nap" was a good thing, she thought as the train pulled out. I do feel a lot better for it. Jo took the bank manager's card from her pocket and peered at it, trying to decipher his scrawl. Looks like Neerim Road. What strange names they have in Melbourne.

At Murrumbeena station, she abandoned the flowers and stepped out, walking briskly through the exit gate to the street beyond, which indeed turned out to be Neerim Road. On the corner was the Bendigo Bank.

CHAPTER 8

Feeling disheveled, Jo shook out her hair and then re-twisted it up under the beret. She unbuttoned the coat for quick access to her bag and entered the bank, hoping the transaction wouldn't take long. It didn't. The money was waiting for her, and on proof of identity, the teller handed it over without a fuss.

Now back on the street, Jo eyed the taxi rank outside the station. With no idea where Chadstone was a taxi seemed the obvious choice. She walked to the first car in the rank and climbed into the back seat.

"Chadstone Shopping Centre, please."

"No worries." The heavy-set driver spoke with a Middle Eastern accent. "Which entrance?"

"Um…" Jo hesitated.

"You want groceries, clothes, see movie, what?"

"Clothing," said Jo.

"Okay!" The driver pulled out into the street. "You been to Chadstone before?"

"A long time ago."

He laughed. "My wife she hates Chadstone. Too big, she gets lost all the time."

"I guess it's grown since I was last there."

"Yes, very big! Last month my wife has to go there – doctor appointment. She walks in from carpark and sees Coles Supermarket. She thinks, "This is my way out." After appointment she ask someone, "Which way to Coles Supermarket?" You know what they say?"

"What?"

"They say, "The old Coles or the new Coles?" There are *two* of them!" He laughed so hard the taxi began veering into the next lane and the car behind tooted loudly. Unconcerned by this and still chuckling, he turned into the lane feeding off to the shopping center.

As they drove between rows of parked cars, Jo extracted several hundred-dollar bills from one of the bundles and slipped them into her empty wallet. Nervously she eyed the seven-dollar meter charge for the brief trip and wondered whether the driver would be able to change a hundred. She'd have to ask and risk his possible wrath, but when the taxi pulled over near the entrance, Jo realized this potentially embarrassing moment was in fact an opportunity. The driver's ID card said his name was Hassan bin Evhad and when he turned she said, "Hassan? Is that how you say your name?"

"Yes, Hassan," he said.

Jo held up the hundred-dollar bill. "I only have a few things to buy, Hassan. Will you wait for me?"

"For hundred dollars I can wait an hour," he said with a grin, taking the note. Jo checked her watch. It was just after midday.

"Okay," she said getting out of the car. "I'll expect you back here at one o'clock."

He waved acknowledgement and drove off, leaving Jo beside an outdoor cafe. In her heavy coat and scarf, even the weak noon sun felt hot. Surely she could lose some of this gear. The Hunter and his agents were most likely still in the city. Jo unwound the scarf and took a grateful breath as the cool air reached her face. Yanking off the beret as well, she stuffed both into a nearby bin. Though she'd like to have shed the coat, she settled for leaving it unbuttoned, not prepared to fully expose her outfit.

As she entered the shopping center, Jo remembered the taxi driver's story and paid close attention to the stores around the doorway. On her left was a kitchenware shop, displaying racks of gleaming saucepans hung with red and white sales signs. On her right the cafe extended indoors. Hassan hadn't been kidding. The place was vast... and so different from the city, with its narrow streets and old buildings. Each of these spacious corridors could fit three city arcades and the displays in their enormous windows were fresh and vital. Light flooded through the curving transparent roof, and strategically placed cycads and giant palm trees created a sun-drenched oasis.

Beautiful perhaps, but so extensive that Jo immediately became paralyzed, realizing she had little chance of getting all the items she wanted and finding her way back to this spot in an hour.

In marked contrast, a girl of eleven or twelve ambled loose-limbed along the walkway towards her. In ripped jeans and skimpy t-shirt, she seemed unconcerned by the winter temperatures, and appeared to have all the time in the world, stopping to inspect the fashion shoes in one window, before moving on to the nightclub gear in the next.

Without waiting to consider, Jo took a hundred dollar note from her bag and approached her. "Excuse me."

The girl looked up, not quite meeting Jo's eyes. She had three rings spaced down one ear and her dull brown hair, held loosely in a fraying scrunchie, was crying out for a wash. She looked ready to take off and Jo blurted out her question.

"Do you know Chadstone well?"

The girl's voice was tinged with caution. "Yeah."

"Then if you have time," Jo held up the note, "I'd be willing to pay you a hundred dollars to be my guide for an hour."

Now her eyes lifted, and her hand shot forward. "Okay."

Jo paused in the act of passing it over. How reliable would this urchin be? She looked as though she hadn't had a decent meal in a long time and she certainly must be skipping school right now.

"Payable on getting me back to this spot by one o'clock with the things I need," said Jo, putting the note into her pocket.

The girl looked disappointed. "What do you need?"

"Not much. Shops that sell sports shoes, cheap clothes, travel gear and mobile phones."

A smile lit her face. "I can do that. I'm Danielle."

"I'm J.. Judy," said Jo. "Let's get started."

Danielle turned. "There's a sports shoe store on the level below."

She set off at a smart pace and Jo hurried to catch up, wincing as her blister seared. At the shoe store a hunky assistant strolled over and flashed Jo a cheeky smile, which triggered a pleasurable tingle, until she remembered her 'hat hair' and BO. Embarrassment, however, was not an emotion she could afford and she straightened her shoulders.

"I need a good pair of sports shoes." She glanced at her badly scuffed boots and again felt her face grow hot. "But I don't have any socks with me."

"No problem." The guy cheerfully indicated the racks at one side of the store. "We sell a wide range of sports socks."

He walked across and selected three packs, splaying them for Jo as he returned. She pointed to one and he popped open the plastic casing. While she removed her boots and pulled the socks on over her tights he brought out a metal measuring device.

"I know my size," she protested as he slipped it under her foot.

He adjusted the metal width slider. "Ah, but we like to measure to ensure we get exactly the right shoe for you. What activity will you be using them for?"

"Mostly walking and possibly some running." Jo hoped the latter would be minimal.

He rose confidently. "I have just what you need."

As he headed towards the back, Jo checked for Danielle and saw she was happily engaged in trying on shoes from the sale tray at the front of the store. Hunky guy returned carrying two shoeboxes.

"These are both good brands," he said removing the lids. "They give excellent side and arch support as well as overall cushioning."

Jo peered into the boxes and rejecting the pair with fluorescent stripes, indicated the more conservative ones. The salesman laced them on and she stood and took a few steps.

"Fantastic! I feel like I'm walking on air."

He smiled. "Reasonably priced too."

Jo glanced at the price sticker and had to look again, having never spent so much on shoes in her life. She gave no indication of her shock. "I think I'll leave these on. I can't face going back to my boots."

Hunky guy was unfazed. "A lot of people do that. Those shoes are great for shopping. They put a spring back into your step."

Jo paid for them, bought two extra pairs of socks and accepted the bag containing her boots. At the front of the store she collected Danielle, who cheerfully abandoned the sale tray asking, "Where now?"

"Clothes, mobile phone, travel store, and if you know of a shop that sells wigs…"

"Oh sure! There's a hair warehouse here. They have extensions, wigs — you name it. Wigs are so cool. Do you want real or fake?"

"Maybe both!" Danielle's enthusiasm was infectious.

By five minutes to one they were back at the starting point. In addition to the hundred dollars, Jo had given Danielle her boots, which the young girl willingly accepted before heading off with a happy wave. Jo felt uneasy watching her go. Danielle seemed neglected, but what could she do? At least the girl now had some money for food… and no one was trying to kill her.

At the outdoor cafe, Jo wolfed down a thick sandwich and reviewed her purchases while she waited for Hassan. She was now wearing a new watch with an alarm function and hefted a day-pack containing: a money belt, a packet of Band-Aids minus one, which was covering her blister, a four-pack of undies, deodorant, wet wipes, a mini tube of toothpaste and a toothbrush.

In the disguise department, she'd acquired grey track pants with a matching hoodie, a pair of jeans, two loose shirts — one black and the other a more tailored beige, and a casual lightweight khaki jacket. She was particularly pleased with her purchase of a real wig that closely matched her own hair color and length, and two artificial wigs — one a mop of light brown curls and the other a black spiky cut with dark red highlights.

One failure had been the phone. When she'd asked about a pre-paid mobile, the assistant had been happy to sell her one, but had passed over a clipboard with a form attached. It required her to fill in personal details and provide several types of identification.

"What's this?"

"Government regulation to prevent criminal use. We can't sell you a wireless communication device unless you fill it in."

So much for being untraceable with a pre-paid phone. For a second Jo had considered asking Danielle to buy one, but at her age they'd no doubt require a parent to fill in the form, so she'd given up on the phone idea for the moment.

The taxi pulled up and Jo gathered her purchases and jumped in.

"Good shopping?" grinned Hassan.

"Yes, but now I need a motel at least twenty minutes away."

The driver considered. "Dandenong is twenty minutes." he said. "Many motels there."

"Great, a Dandenong motel then."

A twenty-minute drive, she figured, put her far enough away from Chadstone that her two o'clock coordinates would not link her to it, for she intended to return.

CHAPTER 9

In the back of the taxi, Jo swallowed the last of her sandwich and considered the next hurdle. The motel would want a name and address. She'd stick with Judy, the name she'd given to Danielle, and choose a surname starting with W, like her own, to make it easy to remember. As she toyed with W surnames, the taxi passed a billboard displaying tantalizing glimpses of a golf course estate behind the vertical bars of a burgundy gate.

Winegate, she thought. That will do. An address now... interstate is less likely to be challenged. A childhood memory surfaced of Saturday walks to the postbox with her mother. Mum had written regularly to an old friend who lived in Church Street, Canterbury, in Sydney, and little Jo had been entrusted to push the weekly letter through the slot. It was perfect – a real street in a real Sydney suburb.

Relieved, Jo allowed her mind to slip into blank mode for a while. Fortunately Hassan seemed over his chatty streak, and peace enveloped them as the uninspiring scenery flashed by: fast food places, car yards, furniture outlets, and warehouses.

Sooner than she was ready, they reached Dandenong and passed through the main street of rundown shops, several boarded up. The motels that began appearing also seemed on the sleazy side, but Jo didn't have time to be picky.

She leaned across to the driver. "Hassan, that one with the vacancy sign coming up."

He swung into the entrance and drove to the reception area.

Jo flipped the handle. "I'll just be a second."

She pushed through the glass door into the tiny office where a battered desk took up most of the space. Behind it stood a tired looking man wearing a white nylon shirt and a limp tie. He flicked her a glance, which she took as an invitation to speak.

"I'm on my way to another town. I just need a room for an hour or so to wash and freshen up."

His lip curled. "We don't rent by the hour. Minimum room hire is a day."

"How much is that?"

"Hundred and twenty-five."

Jo glanced at her watch. It was close to 1.30. With a sigh she extracted one hundred and twenty-five dollars from her wallet and pushed the notes across the counter.

The man eyed them suspiciously. "We prefer credit cards."

"Don't believe in them," said Jo. "They make people spend beyond their means. The room's one hundred and twenty-five. There it is, in advance."

With apparent reluctance, he dragged the notes into a drawer on his side of the desk, scribbled the payment and date into a small receipt book, tore off the page and handed it to Jo. Then he opened a large registration book and stood poised with pen in hand.

"Name."

Jo was ready. "Judy Winegate."

"Address."

"48 Church Street, Canterbury, NSW."

"What's the postcode?"

Shit! After a slight hesitation, she recited 2137, knowing that for New South Wales, the two was right at least.

"Car registration," the man continued.

"I'm in a taxi." Jo indicated the cab waiting outside the door.

The man grunted and turned the book around, handing over a pen.

"Sign here."

Jo picked up the pen, wrote JW and caught herself in time to finish with Winegate, rather than Warrington. Another good reason to have an alias with the same initials, she realized.

Dourly the man handed her a set of keys. "Room twenty-eight, up at the end."

Feeling no surprise this motel had vacancies, Jo returned to the taxi and directed Hassan to the parking space outside room twenty-eight. The meter read thirty-four dollars.

"Can you keep the meter running, Hassan? I'm just going to clean up and I'll be out in half an hour."

Hassan nodded. "I wait."

The motel room was dark, cold and stuffy, but Jo barely noticed. She stripped off her coat and flung it over the back of a chair, then upended the bulging daypack onto the luggage bench. From the pile she grabbed the deodorant, money belt, jeans, black shirt and jacket. She had less than half an hour till her next coordinates posting and a lot to do.

Hurrying into the bathroom, she glanced at her watch, happy about being able to leave it on. It was water tested to fifty meters, which the saleswoman had said was the minimum requirement for being able to wear it safely in the shower. She'd set its alarm to go off three minutes before 2.00 p.m.

Jo used the toilet and then turned on the shower, stripping while the water heated. The gushing stream felt so wonderful she managed to quell the thought of the watching TV audience and concentrate on getting cleaned up as quickly as possible. This done, she wrapped one towel around herself and rubbed at her hair with another before finishing with the motel's hair dryer.

In the main room Jo applied the super plus deodorant, which promised to keep her fresh and dry for twenty-four hours, and slipped underwear on beneath the towel. Then she pulled on the jeans and eyed the money belt.

"Get a quality belt," the salesman had said. "My sister travelled to Bali a few years ago with a cotton one. During her first day of sightseeing, she dipped into it and found her sweat had made the notes so wet they tore in her hands. When she took the belt off that evening, she had a black ring around her waist where the ink had leeched through onto her skin."

Jo had laughed dutifully while privately thinking it would hardly be a problem with Australia's plasticized notes. In the end she'd bought a large, six-pocket belt. The side worn against the skin was chamois to minimize chaffing and absorb sweat and the pockets had a waterproof lining.

Tipping out her shoulder bag onto the bench, Jo separated the bundles of money and removed their elastic bands. She put five notes into her wallet and began arranging the rest into six even stacks. She'd already spent close to 1500 dollars, which left around thirty notes per stack. By the time she'd stuffed each stack into a pocket, the belt had swelled to twice its size.

Jo clipped it on, ignoring the discomfort, and finished dressing. She inspected herself in the half-length mirror above the luggage bench. Not too bad. In shopping with Danielle, she'd grabbed items more generous than her regular size 8, with the thought of accommodating the money belt. It had been a good move. The loose black shirt, which she wore over her jeans, concealed the treasure beneath. As she slipped on the jacket, Jo decided her look was that of an ordinary, albeit rounded young woman with no greater worry in the world than deciding whether to order the chicken or bacon burger. If only that were so.

She checked her watch. Seven minutes until her coordinates were broadcast. Should she use it to rinse out some things? No. Silly to carry damp clothes around. She'd stick with cheap and disposable while on the run. But it would be smart not to leave evidence she'd changed her outfit.

Jo gathered up the discarded clothing and carried it to the wardrobe. The warped plywood door was stuck. A yank set the four wire hangers inside clinking forlornly. The rod they hung from was fixed beneath a high shelf that housed a couple of folded blankets and pillows. Jo grabbed a chair and climbed up with the bundle. She thrust the clothes to the back of the shelf and arranged the blankets and pillows in front to hide them.

Mid-step down from the chair she heard the cough. Terror loosened her joints and she ended in a heap on the floor.

"Not to worry," the oily tones of a hatefully familiar voice assured her. "Only me."

Shaking with relief and anger, Jo scrambled to her feet. Fitani was leaning casually against a wall. He was now wearing a bright purple blazer, eye-searingly paired with a green shirt and orange trousers. With the wide smile splitting his narrow face, and his slick ginger hair, he looked ready for a visit to grandma's house.

"Knocking would be nice." Jo got out between clenched teeth.

"Oh, Jo," exclaimed Fitani. "Hologram remember? I *can't* knock. I can however congratulate you on a marvelously entertaining chase so far."

"Since you're able to project your voice, you can surely project a knocking sound," said Jo. Then Fitani's words sank in, and she added with a huff, "I hardly see how it could have been *that* entertaining."

"Are you kidding? From the moment of your brilliant escape at the cafe, you've had us all on the edges of our seats!"

"Really? Apart from the cafe I would have thought it had all been pretty boring for your viewers."

"Au contraire – nothing boring about your being nearly apprehended on at least three different occasions."

Jo sat heavily on the bed, the blood draining from her face.

"The first was at the bank," said Fitani gleefully. "Your big mistake as you later realized, was leaving your mobile phone turned on, continually broadcasting your position. Fortunately for you, your Hunter made mistakes also. It was so confident about its ability to catch you without help, it failed to mobilize its agents early enough. Had it done so, you'd certainly have been apprehended in the department store.

"By the time your Hunter gave up trying to find you by itself, and contacted its agents, you were on your way to the bank where you had another lucky break. Because you were out of sight in the manager's office when an agent entered, he homed in on a woman who looked like you. What a comedy that was! The agent ended up being carted off by the police. The woman he'd accosted turned out to be a respectable boutique owner, known and vouched for by the banking staff, instead of being the fugitive he claimed."

Although Jo continued to sit silently, the last snippet of the host's commentary had not been lost on her.

So, she thought, the Hunter has made me out to be a fugitive of some kind. Well that makes sense. He'd need to provide a reason that would seem credible to a detective agency.

Fitani was enjoying himself. "When you headed back to the department store, we all thought the Hunter had you for sure. Its assistants were closing in on your GPS signal but your disguise prevented them from easily picking you out in the crowd. They needed to get near enough to look carefully. Buying those flowers was a smart move. They not only helped to hide your face, but made you look so much like an ordinary shopper that you actually walked right past one of the agents searching for you."

Jo gulped.

"The next nail-biter you gave us was on the street corner. Two agents in the crowd were just ten meters from your coordinates when you crossed the road and jumped onto a tram." Fitani chuckled. "The consternation on their faces when the operations' agent guiding them by phone, informed them that your coordinates were now moving at speed down Swanston Street! They soon realized what you'd done and sent agents to chase the tram, but by then you'd debarked and your phone had been pocketed by one of the passengers – an opportunistic young thug who rode to the next stop, then jumped on a tram heading north. While you were calmly boarding your train, the Hunter and its assistants were engaged in a wild goose chase, which again ended up with hilarious results. Nicely done."

"Thank you." Jo spoke coldly. "I take it I have now racked up enough points to ask three questions?"

"You have," declared the game show host. "And because I'm feeling generous I won't even count that as one of them."

A loud beeping sound interrupted their conversation. Jo pressed a button on her watch to turn off the alarm. Three minutes till crunch time.

"Question one then," she said urgently. "What are all the ways in which you're helping the Hunter?"

"Excellent question," said Fitani. "Firstly, at its briefing, we filled it in on you. The Hunter knows where you live and all about your current situation. Secondly, we made it our usual offer of an advance on its winnings as a float fund. It accepted and so has a million dollars to play with."

Jo gasped. If a million dollars was an *advance*, what was the prize?

Fitani continued. "During the course of the game we will send the Hunter your coordinates every three hours, as I told you earlier. As well, it will also receive an updated photo of you. Our cameras will take a full body shot from a couple of meters, or an upper body shot from a closer distance if obstacles are in the way. Finally, Hunters are entitled to one request for technical assistance. Your Hunter's request has already been made and fulfilled. It was to construct a false identity for you. On the police database you are now listed as Kylie Marshall, a drug addict with priors for theft and assault. Kylie is wanted for kidnapping her baby son after the court awarded custody to the father. Your photo and fingerprints match those on the database. Don't worry though," Fitani said reassuringly. "When *Play or Die* is over, we will expunge that record."

Shit! As Jo digested this, her gaze wandered across the mirror. The sight of her pale image, sitting frozen on the bed, reminded her that Fitani's cameras were about to snap her new disguise. She sprang up, jerked back the bedspread and dived under the blankets, pulling them up around her neck and closing her eyes.

Now the only clue the Hunter will get, she thought, is a false one of me asleep in bed. And that, along with my coordinates at this motel will hopefully make him think he can take me at his leisure. I just have to stay here until I'm certain they've taken the photo.

In her mind she counted slowly to sixty, and was repeating the count when Fitani called out. "Rise and shine. It's all been sent, and you'll be pleased to know your quick thinking has again raised your point tally."

Jo leapt out of the bed. "You said this game was sporting!"

Fitani adopted an innocent air. "What's not sporting?"

"For a start you're lending the Hunter a million dollars. I should get a million too."

Fitani laughed. "And how would you repay us? We take the Hunter's million off its prize. In any case Hunters must be equipped. This is our way of equipping them."

"Well there's the technical assistance," said Jo. "If a Hunter receives technical assistance, so should the Prey."

The host stifled a yawn. "You get three questions every thousand points. It evens out."

"What? That barely "evens out" the Hunter getting my photo and coordinates every three hours. I appeal for a ruling on this."

Fitani sighed. "Complain, complain, that's all you Prey do, and all you *can* do," he added with a grin. "*Prey* can't alter the rules."

"But the viewers should be able to," cried Jo in sudden inspiration. "You have to keep *them* happy or it will be *your show* that dies."

Quickly she spread her arms in appeal to the unseen audience, and addressed the walls. "Danny says you people of the future believe in fair play. If that's true, shouldn't the Prey, like the Hunter, be allowed a technical request?" She paused, then added, "And wouldn't you like to see how I'd use it? If this is an audience participation show, let the producers know how you feel!"

Fitani, she observed, seemed momentarily frozen with his mouth hanging open, but he quickly regained his wits and gave her a wink.

"Good ploy," he admitted. "No one's tried a direct appeal to the audience before. The Emoto Board's gone wild. It may take a minute to calculate what our viewers have decided. Wait here."

He disappeared and Jo hurried to the bench and swept all her bits and pieces into the backpack. She looked at the black coat draped over the chair. She'd planned to take it, but there was no point now. The Hunter would have received a photo of her wearing it at 11.00 a.m. Instead she grabbed the empty shoulder bag, and was heading for the door when Danny reappeared, adopting a pompous stance for his pronouncement.

"The people have spoken and we have listened. The rules have now officially been altered as follows: On a *single* occasion, Prey may elect to substitute their three questions for a request for technical assistance so long as this request is possible for us to grant and does not counteract their Hunter's request."

Jo felt a thrill of hope, not at having gained a questionable advantage in the game, but at having successfully communicated with a vast number of people in a future world. They had listened to her and been persuaded. She wondered if it would be possible to bring them onto her side.

Danny continued to speak. "You've already used up one of your questions on this round, so you won't be able to make a technical request until you've gained your next thousand points. Therefore, you might as well ask your remaining two questions."

Jo fidgeted, her hand on the doorknob. "I need to get out of here. Can I ask my questions on the move?"

"Absolutely," replied the host. "You've earned your questions and it's my job to stick with you until you've asked them. You have one left."

"Wha... *Now* you decide to be literal!"

"You asked a fair question and got a fair answer." The insouciant reply hung in the air as she strode to the waiting cab. Jo climbed into the back and saw Hassan's welcoming smile freeze as he looked at Fitani seated beside her. Oh no, she thought. He probably thinks I'm a prostitute.

"My brother caught up with me," Jo said lightheartedly as though this had been the plan all along. The driver removed his glare from the game show host and shrugged.

"Where you go now?" he said gruffly, starting the ignition.

She hadn't convinced him and realizing she'd lost an ally, Jo sighed. She'd planned on going straight back to Chadstone, but now she couldn't trust Hassan not to give her away, if the Hunter's assistants tracked him down. Would they do that? Of course they would. The motel clerk would tell the assistants she'd arrived by taxi, and they wouldn't be worth their salt if they couldn't locate the driver of the only taxi parked in the motel at two in the afternoon.

"To the nearest station, please," she told Hassan.

"Dandenong station closest," he said, and without further talk, pulled into the traffic.

Fitani cleared his throat. "You have a question for me?"

44

She spoke softly, indicating the driver with her eyes. "Not yet."

He squirmed. "Don't think I can stick around all day."

"Now Danny," her tone was musical. "You've just finished telling me that's *exactly* what you have to do until you've answered all my questions. I guess I *did* get my money's worth from that second question after all." She gave him a wink and settled back into the seat, closing her eyes.

Five minutes later a loud tooting from an annoyed driver, accompanied by a swerve and sudden stop, indicated they'd reached their destination. Hassan had kept the meter running at the motel and the total now read eighty-six dollars and fifty cents. Jo drew a hundred dollar note from her wallet and passed it over, smiling warmly.

"Thanks Hassan, you've been a great driver. Please keep the change."

Hassan nodded, looking somewhat mollified but ventured no comment. Jo grabbed her backpack and shoulder bag and exited the cab, her companion having already slipped out unnoticed.

Without a backward glance, she strode into the station, thrusting the empty shoulder bag into a nearby rubbish bin and freeing both arms by slipping the backpack on properly. Ignoring the automatic machines, Jo stood in a short line at a station window. She pulled another hundred-dollar bill from her wallet, hoping it would provide enough of an inconvenience to make the clerk remember her. When her turn came she pushed the note with her travel card under the grill.

"I'd like a ten dollar top-up on my card please."

The ticket clerk, a surly heavyset woman, scowled at the bill. "Don't you have anything smaller?"

"Sorry, that's all I have."

Pursing her lips, the woman swept up the note and card and went out a door at the back. Jo waited calmly. She had plenty of time. It was unlikely any of the Hunter's agents would have been closer than fifteen minutes to the motel when her coordinates were sent, and it was only now 2.15 p.m. by the station clocks. Even if agents were pulling into the motel at this very moment, they'd need time to question the desk clerk and check her room. Then they'd have to contact the taxi company to get the name of her driver, and track him down and question him. By the time they learnt he'd dropped her here, she'd be long gone. With luck they'd question the surly clerk, who would send them on a false trail back to the city.

Jo's thoughts were interrupted by the return of the clerk, who was moving slowly, clutching a mountain of change in coins and small notes – her petty revenge. Jo took the money and shoved it into her jacket pocket. Then picking up her card she asked, "Which platform do I need for the next train to the city?"

"Number eight," said the woman shortly. She looked around Jo and called out, "Next!"

Jo made her way to the sparsely populated platform eight. A lit board indicated the next train was due to arrive in seven minutes. She sat on an empty seat and Fitani appeared beside her.

"Ready to ask that question now?"

"I am." Jo took her notebook and pen from the backpack. "I would like to know who the Hunter has hired to help him."

Danny flashed his smile. "*It* has hired," he corrected, "not one, but two of the foremost detective agencies in your country. They are *Eagle Investigations* and *SIS — Secure Investigative Services.*

Jo wrote down the names with a wrinkled brow. "These must be competing organizations. Why would they both agree to work for the Hunter?"

"Though I'd love to answer that, you're out of questions. However I look forward to speaking with you again on the accumulation of your next thousand points."

At the last word, he vanished, momentarily replaced by letters hanging in the air, which spelt out *SHOULD YOU BE SO LUCKY* before these too disappeared.

A biting blast of wind lifted dust and litter on the exposed platform and cut through Jo's lightweight clothing. Above, rain clouds were gathering, causing the winter afternoon to grow prematurely dark. Much as she loathed Fitani, Jo felt strangely abandoned.

CHAPTER 10

Danny Fitani sent his avatar straight to the studio Playroom and was greeted by a spattering of applause from the twenty or so people in the room.

"You've got your hands full with this one," said Angela, weaving through the equipment to greet him. "I liked that you changed the rules to give Prey technical assistance. Can't wait to see how she uses it."

Fitani grinned. "The viewers decided." He turned to Mani. "Great job collating their responses so quickly."

"Thanks Danny. The ratings have soared since the audience got its way… oh, and I've arranged for you to interview a couple of viewers with opposing bio-feedback."

"Excellent." Fitani surveyed the Playroom. A halo appeared around a camera technician's head at eye-level. On it, a time display began counting down from eight minutes. "Sven, you need to get out of here."

"Under control, Danny. I'm just finishing off now. This new camera software is brilliant. I can record and select from multiple angle shots twice as fast."

An attractive dark-skinned woman entered the room. "Hope I'm not too late for some action. Where do you want me, Danny?"

"Hi Sima, good to see you. Could you help the crew covering the Hunter's agents? And you're not too late. I'm betting there'll be plenty of action coming up."

"Sven," Angela called. "Your countdown's at six minutes!"

"I'm going, I'm going." Sven was rapidly tapping one screen on his left, while his right hand made gestures at another.

"Garal." Fitani spoke to the man beside Sven. "Take over from him, will you."

Garal reached for Sven's controls. "I've got it. You just go."

"Yeah yeah," said Sven. "I just need to..." His halo transformed into a black cloud that completely enveloped his head. Its display continued counting down from five minutes.

"Flaming Ancestors!" Sven dropped his hands and two people nearby rushed over, taking an arm each.

"Come on Sven, walk fast," said one of them. "We'll get you to work on time."

CHAPTER 11

The train rolled into the platform and Jo rose stiffly, hunched against the cold. She walked to an empty carriage and pressed numb fingers against the door button. Inside she took a window seat and stared out unseeing at the afternoon gloom. Three stations rattled by. Gradually the warmth thawed her frozen limbs and she blinked, forcing herself out of her stupor.

Come on Jo, she thought. Don't go all zombie now. You've done well so far. Use this traveling time to think through your next steps. She looked at her watch. 2.35 p.m. What was the plan? Leave at Murrumbeena station and walk to Chadstone. Get her hair cut short and use the Internet lounge she'd spotted with Danielle, to study street maps and work out escape routes. Maybe there'd even be time to check out the names of her dad's killers! And while she was doing all that, the Hunter and his agents would be off searching for her in the city – if they'd fallen for her trick. But even if they hadn't, they wouldn't know where she was. The final thing she needed to organize was her 5.00 p.m. exit strategy, such as a taxi ready on the spot.

Jo gave a little gasp of realization. If I make sure I'm in a taxi for each coordinates broadcast, I'll be able to relocate instantly and stay clear of the Hunter. Then between broadcasts I can work on tracking down those responsible for Dad's murder.

As her confidence returned, Jo began to relax. She had things under control. When the train pulled into Murrumbeena station ten minutes later, she jumped up and strode to the gate. Taxi cabs waited in the rank and on the spur of the moment she decided to save time and take one, rather than walk to Chadstone. She certainly now had enough change in her pocket to pay for a short trip.

A young couple seemed to have bagged the first cab. They were talking with the driver through the window. She'd have to take the second. As Jo stepped forward, she found herself doing a classic double-take. The driver of the first taxi was Hassan! As if her mind had screamed his name, he looked up and saw her.

His mouth dropped open and he began raising an arm to point in her direction. Jo turned and sprinted back into the station. The train was still there but its doors were closing. With every sinew straining at the effort, Jo hurled herself forward, leaping through what remained of the opening. The doors crunched on her backpack, but with a great wrench she freed it and staggered into the carriage. As the train pulled out, Jo ran to the window in time to see the young couple standing on the platform. The woman had a phone to her ear and was speaking urgently into it. The man, his face tight, stood watching the carriages pass.

"You're a silly girl," said a white haired old man sitting near the door. "You could get yourself killed pulling a stunt like that."

Jo barely heard him. She collapsed onto the nearest seat, pressing hands against her pounding heart. How *could* she have been so *stupid?* Murrumbeena station was where she'd first caught Hassan's taxi. This was where he waited for fares and he'd returned to his usual spot. The Hunter's agents must have just arrived to question him and she'd walked right into their arms.

If only she hadn't shown herself, those agents would now be on their way to Dandenong to grill the station staff. Instead they knew she was on this train and would be sending operatives to every station along the line.

I have to get off right now! As the train pulled into Carnegie station, Jo leapt out and sprinted across the platform. The exit path took her to a busy road. A hundred meters up on her right, the road crossed a highway. To her left, the footpath dipped under the railway track and came up into a shopping strip. Jo ran left, slowing to a brisk walk as she reached the shops.

A variety of cafes, along with food shops selling roast chicken, fish and chips, cakes and pastries, bread, fruit and Asian takeaway, vied to entice the passing trade. Between them, keeping the peace were the occasional newsagent, optometrist and real estate agent.

Jo looked for a place to retreat and hide her flowing blond hair. An open area between the shops turned out to be a walkway leading to a setback public library. She hurried along the path to the tinted glass doors and pushed through into a large foyer decorated with posters and advertisements for children's competitions and literary events. To her right, double glass doors opened into the library proper. On the left, framed by posters, two doors displayed the childlike cutout symbols of a man and a woman.

Jo pushed through the ladies door and entered a small washroom. It was empty and she shrugged off her backpack. Bending to untie the flap, she noticed one of the shoulder straps was half ripped off. Damn, the train doors had wrecked it. Still, she thought, I couldn't keep the backpack anyway. By now those two agents will have updated the others on my new outfit and everyone will be searching for a blond in jeans with a backpack. I need to change my look again.

She pulled out the light brown wig and twisting her hair up, put it on and studied the effect in the mirror. Definitely odd, but maybe that's because I'm not used to myself as a curly brunette, she thought.

Wispy strands of her own hair were already escaping and Jo knew she had to find a hairdresser fast. Grabbing the pack by its good strap, she headed back to the shopping strip before fear got the better of her.

In her short time away, the thickening rain clouds had caused the automatic streetlights had come on, though it was barely three. The first shop Jo passed was a novelty store and calling out to her from its window was a large V-shaped straw bag with red poppies sewn on the side. She backed up, entered the shop and leaned over the items in the window to inspect the bag. It was spacious, but didn't seem very sturdy. Instead of a zipper, just a thin ribbon tied the top halves together. Still, it was only five dollars and would do. She walked over to the pink-cheeked grandmother knitting behind the counter, and had barely opened her mouth before the old lady spoke.

"The straw tote bag? Yes, you can take it dear. It's our last one. They've sold like hotcakes."

Jo extracted the bag from the window display and pulled a five-dollar note from her jacket pocket. She was tempted to ask about a hairdresser, but decided such a question would make her too memorable to this on-the-ball grandma. Instead she ducked back to the ladies room in the library foyer and this time in the privacy of a cubicle, transferred the contents of the backpack to the straw bag, tying the pink ribbon to keep it from gaping.

Back on the main street, Jo threw the empty backpack into a rubbish bin and continued until a sign told her the shop ahead was *A Cut Above the Rest!* A pair of scissors formed the offbeat exclamation point.

Jo hurried to the salon, remembering to pull off her wig and stuff it into her bag before entering. A young apprentice sweeping the floor immediately set aside her broom and came to the counter to inspect the large open appointment book. Two hairdressers busy cutting and chatting with their clients, paid her no heed.

The apprentice smiled at Jo. "Do you have an appointment?"

"No, but I was hoping you could fit me in."

"Oh." The apprentice looked doubtful. "We're pretty busy. What did you want done?"

"Just a cut," Jo was nonchalant. "I've washed my hair, so I won't be needing a shampoo."

"Well… if it's a quick trim," Jo didn't correct her, "perhaps we can fit you in."

The apprentice went over to one of the hairdressers and had a hurried conversation before returning.

"If you can wait twenty minutes, Nadine can do you," she offered.

"Thanks, that'll be fine."

Jo crossed to the waiting area and settled into a chair in front of a huge potted aspidistra. Screened from the street, she selected a magazine and opened it on her lap. It was just after 3.00 p.m. by her watch. She set a new alarm for two minutes before five and jumped as a flash and boom signaled the arrival of the storm. Rain pelted down and what was left of the daylight, vanished. It was going to be, Jo realized with a sinking heart, a long night.

Nadine wasn't happy when she discovered the 'trim' was to actually be a whole new style, but she warmed to the project under Jo's profuse and laughing thanks for fitting her in, and before long the two were chatting like old friends while Jo's golden locks piled up on the floor. At 3.50 a very shorthaired Jo stepped out into the cold. The shopping crowd had thinned dramatically and cars already on their homeward journeys swished by with the slanting rain in their headlights.

Cutting her hair had been a good move, Jo decided. The sophisticated, ultra short style made her appear years older and would dry in a minute. More importantly, she could wear wigs without having to worry about her own hair slipping out. Grabbing the brown one from her bag, she pulled it on and ducked into a cafe to check her blind adjustment in their restroom. It looked fine, she decided, teasing out the curls a little, and sat better than it had before – or perhaps she was just getting used to it. Jo decided to stay for a coffee and a bite to eat. She was hungry and realized it would be wise to refuel when the opportunity arose.

Now cutting into a slice of microwaved quiche, the only thing the cafe had left at that hour, she considered the night ahead. It was Monday. Shops would close in an hour, but cinemas would be open, so movie watching could kill some time. Maybe she could also find an Internet cafe open till late.

The big problem was where and how she would get any sleep during the night. She *had* to find ways to sleep or her thinking and reflexes would rapidly deteriorate and the game would come to a quick end.

Jo shuddered, remembering a documentary she'd once seen. In it, a camera crew had followed a Kalahari bushman hunting a kudu. The bushman had carried only a spear, water bottle and the calm knowledge that he would eventually run the big antelope down. At first the kudu had raced off easily, barely concerned about the puny human follower, but the bushman, setting himself an easy jogging pace, had followed its tracks relentlessly. The hunt had gone on for eight hours until both hunter and prey were exhausted – the prey, with no water, a little more so. When the kudu finally collapsed, the hunter had been able to walk almost up to it before throwing the killing spear. As she'd watched this riveting scenario Jo had wondered at what stage in the hunt the kudu had realized it could not outrun the hunter, and how long it had been forced to live with the terror of that knowledge before finally being overtaken.

The silence made her look up. She was the only customer left in the cafe, and although more than half an hour remained until 5.00, the cleaning, closing-up rituals were beginning. A passing waitress picked up Jo's empty plate.

"Anything else you'd like?" she asked with obvious reluctance.

"No thanks."

Jo stood and tucked the straw bag under her arm. As she stepped through the door, a freezing gust slammed it behind her. She shivered, regretting the thinness of the jacket, and began retracing her steps along the covered walkway. At the turnoff to the library, she paused.

Was there time to go in and use their Internet? How long would it take to check some maps? Too long, she reluctantly decided. My first priority is to make sure I'm moving fast when my five o'clock coordinates are broadcast. I should go back to the station and wait for a train.

Jo continued towards the station but the closer she got, the less the idea appealed. Although the mobs of commuters now heading home would provide camouflage, she hated the thought of being stuck in a carriage when her coordinates were sent. A taxi felt safer, but where to get one?

She reached the end of the shops and the overhead shelter they'd provided. The rain, although currently just a drizzle, would eventually soak into her clothing if she was out in it too long, but it couldn't be helped. Jo walked forward briskly and reaching the side street leading to the station, peered down it. The cab rank, she noticed, was empty. Several people, huddled under umbrellas, waited in a queue. This was definitely not where she wanted to be.

Up at the main highway, she spotted a better solution. A hotel on the corner, bearing the original name of 'The Corner Hotel', beckoned passersby with a floodlit sign advertising this week's special – a beer, burger and chips for ten dollars. If that wasn't sufficient incentive, neon lights in the outline of poker machines promised instant riches…

The hotel doors opened into warmth, light and jangling slot machines, and Jo paused to get her bearings. Beyond the down-at-heel punters glumly pushing buttons on the slots, glass doors led to a bar and dining tables. She stepped through and scanned the area for a public phone. Spotting one on the wall of a short passageway leading to the restrooms, Jo reached into her pocket for change.

Battered volumes of the White and Yellow Pages sat on the shelf beneath the phone and looking up taxis, Jo made the valuable discovery that she could dial "13 cabs' anywhere in Victoria to call one. Her watch showed twenty minutes remained until five. She drew a long calming breath and let it out slowly, then lifted the handset, fed in some coins and dialed the number.

A brisk female voice answered. "Taxi service, your location please."

"I'm at The Corner Hotel near Carnegie station. How long will it take for a cab to pick me up?"

"To go where?"

Jo's mind went blank.

"What is your destination?" repeated the voice impatiently.

Jo felt a rising panic. "I've forgotten the name of the suburb… but it's by the beach," she added in inspiration.

Rapidly the voice began reeling off suburbs.

"Brighton, Elwood, St Kilda, Port Melbourne?"

"St Kilda!" pounced Jo gratefully, as a childhood memory surfaced of walking through the mouth of a gigantic grinning face on an outing to Luna Park in St Kilda.

"A taxi will be at the front of the hotel in ten minutes. Please be waiting for it."

"Thank you."

Jo hung up and sagged briefly against the wall. While there was time she should call Tayla. Her earlier text that everything was boringly fine wouldn't hold for long. Tayla would want details about the cancelled interview and if enough of her texts and calls went unanswered, she was quite capable of stirring up a hornet's nest. Her family had known Jo since she was a baby. They might call the police and she could find herself picked up and having to answer impossible questions while time ticked by and the Hunter closed in.

Tayla's mobile phone number had been on Jo's auto-dial and she'd never memorized it, but she knew her friend's home number, and fed in some more coins. Please don't let Lyn answer, she thought as the tone sounded. It was almost impossible to stop Tayla's mum, once she started talking.

"Hello?"

"Lyn, hi. It's Jo."

"Jo, dear. Tayla told me about your interview being cancelled. How frustrating for you. What happened?"

"Just a stuff-up at their end, but they've sorted it out and re-scheduled me for Friday. I'm going to stay in Melbourne until then."

"Jo what can you possibly do in Melbourne all that time? You'll be bored and lonely after two days."

Jo glanced at her watch and spoke quickly. "I'll be fine, Lyn. Just wondered if Tayla was there."

"Tayla's out with some friends, but she's got her mobile with her. Jo I really think you should come back to Shep…"

"Normally I would Lyn, but I dropped my phone on the street and a big oaf stepped on it. So it's a good thing I'm in Melbourne. I should be able to find a repair place here, but if it can't be fixed I'll have to organize with my provider to get a new phone. Could you let Tayla know? She's probably wondering why I'm not answering her texts."

"Oh Jo," Lyn sounded worried. "That sounds expensive, or is replacement covered under your contract?"

"I'll have to find out, but it could all take a while, so tell Tayla it might be a few days before she hears from me. Lyn I've run out of coins for the public phone, and the light's blinking. We may be cut off any second." Jo put on a cheerful voice. " Don't worry about me. I'm perfectly fine."

"If you say so dear." Lyn sounded resigned. "But you're to come and have a roast lunch with us on Sunday. At least you'll have one decent meal this week…"

"Thanks, Lyn. Looking forwa…" said Jo, and hung up.

Her mouth felt dry. She bought a mineral water and took it to a window table overlooking the front of the hotel, where she watched lines of vehicles crawl up to the traffic lights, stop and move on again. A narrow strip in front of the hotel enabled cars to pull over briefly for passengers to alight, but no lengthy stopping was possible, so Jo kept a watch out for her taxi, ready to spring up the minute she saw one in the stream.

Sipping the water, she tried to remember what she knew about St Kilda. Luna Park stood out – she'd enjoyed it a child, but remembering horror movies of chases through darkened fun parks, Jo had no intention of returning there. In any case, she thought, I can't stay in St Kilda. The five o'clock photo will show me sitting in the back seat of a car, so they'll likely check which cabs were in the area of my coordinates. That will lead them to my driver, who'll tell them he took me to St Kilda. I'll need to keep moving after he drops me off. I wish I knew more names of Melbourne suburbs.

A taxi light on the roof of one of the cars in the stream caught her eye. Jo grabbed her bag and dashed for the exit. The taxi was waiting on the narrow strip, its indicator light flashing, and she ran to the open window.

"St Kilda?" inquired the driver.

"Yes, that's me."

As she climbed into the back seat Jo recognized the driver's tall slender build and deeply black skin, and nearly asked if he was Sudanese, but caught herself in time. She could just picture the conversation – "Yes I'm Sudanese. How did you know?" She knew because of the large Sudanese community living in Shepparton, but she couldn't tell him that. If he was later questioned, it would give her away. In any case, what if he asked her why so many Sudanese families had moved to a country town? What would she say? That Melbourne was a bad place for teenage Sudanese boys already traumatized by the warring in their own country? That city-life enticed many of them into American-style street gangs? Even though the move by Sudanese families to Shep and other country regions had been a great success, it wasn't a conversation she'd feel comfortable having.

The driver merged with the traffic stream, turning left at the main road, and then glanced back at her in his rearview mirror.

"Where St Kilda you go?"

Jo thought quickly. "A hotel will do, but I don't know St Kilda well. Do you know any?"

"Many hotels in Fitzroy Street."

The name sounded familiar. "Okay, a hotel in Fitzroy Street."

The driver nodded and Jo settled back with a sigh, checking her watch. She had about six minutes before her photo and coordinates would be sent. With a shock she remembered she was wearing the curly brown wig, and delved into her straw bag for the expensive natural blonde one she'd purchased in Chadstone. The Hunter and his people were looking for a blonde with shoulder-length hair, and she wanted to keep it that way as long as she could.

With an eye on the driver, Jo quietly drew out the wig and held it in her lap, untangling the long tresses. She needed to be wearing it when her photo was taken, so would have to put it on soon. However she didn't want the taxi driver to notice his passenger's hair was suddenly different. Fortunately this driver wasn't the talkative type and was watching the road.

Quietly Jo moved to the far edge of her seat, beyond the range of his rearview mirror. She tucked the bag behind her legs, out of sight of any camera shot. The Hunter's agents would now have a description of her outfit, but the straw bag wasn't part of it.

A sudden high-pitched beeping made the driver glance into his mirror and then turn his head to locate Jo. Inwardly cursing, she gave him a cheerful smile and held up her arm to display her watch. "Just my alarm." She silenced it.

A voice on the driver's two-way radio recaptured his attention and he told his dispatcher he could pick up the new fare in ten minutes.

Quietly, with a thumping heart, Jo pulled off the brown wig, and sat on it. Two minutes till the 5.00 p.m. broadcast. She slipped on the blonde wig as the driver entered a turnoff lane, and saw a signpost to St Kilda. Ahead a traffic light turned red and the cab slowed to a stop. In the relative quiet of the idling car Jo prayed the driver wouldn't feel the need to fill the silence with conversation. Her prayer went unanswered.

"Fitzroy Street over next road," he said, turning his head. His mouth dropped when he saw the new Jo, then changed to a leer.

"Good." Jo's voice was cold but she felt her face grow hot. The man's expression had triggered the memory of where she'd heard of Fitzroy Street. Apart from its fun park, St Kilda, she now remembered, had a reputation for its nightlife of drugs and prostitution in and around Fitzroy Street. When they turned into it, Jo told the driver to pull over.

The Hunter's agents would soon be converging on this area. Quickly she paid the fare and grabbing the straw bag, leapt from the taxi. As the cab took off, Jo remembered the brown wig. It was still on the seat. In her long blonde wig she once again looked like the woman they were seeking and that was something she had to change immediately.

CHAPTER 12

St Kilda had obviously lifted its game since she'd giggled with her schoolgirl friends about its reputation. Along Fitzroy Street, expensive restaurants specializing in foods of many countries, were opening their doors. Smart businessmen and women spoke into mobile phones as they walked, or perched on stools in wine bars, sipped from long-stemmed glasses.

Pleased that her fear of being stuck on a dark sleazy street had not come true, Jo slipped into a crowded bar and headed for the restrooms. In the cubicle she swapped her blonde wig for the black spiky one with maroon highlights, and wondered whether she should also don the grey track pants and hoodie. Sportswear was down-market for this area, but it *would* alter her look, so she changed outfits, pushing the jeans and jacket into her bag.

As she washed up at one of the basins, Jo examined herself in the mirror with happy surprise. The wig, which she'd originally thought the most "out there" of the three, not only suited her but totally changed her appearance. The grey track pants and hoodie gave her a "straight from the gym" yuppie image, and with renewed confidence she strode back to the street and hailed one of the cruising taxis.

The driver of this cab was an older man with short greying hair and a square build. The name under his ID photo was Bruce Herron, and his accent was decidedly Australian.

"Where to, love?"

"Wow, an Aussie taxi driver!" she exclaimed, and then blushed at how racist that sounded.

The driver chuckled. "Not many of us left," he said. "Just a few owner-drivers like me. The '13cabs' drivers are all pretty much new arrivals – Greeks, Lebanese, Pakistanis, Sudanese, Armenians and plenty from India. Driving's a good job for learning your way around a new place, but it earns peanuts and Aussies won't do it. Where did you say you wanted to go?"

"A cinema further down the coast, but I've forgotten its name."

"There's the Palace, at Brighton Bay…" he suggested.

"That's it. I'm meeting a friend there. Don't suppose you know what's showing?"

He laughed. "I don't have time to be watching movies, but then I usually get my fill of drama on a late shift."

Jo decided it would be wise to keep up some casual conversation. "Do you travel far during a shift?"

"Depends. No driver likes to go too far afield – you may not get a fare back. Time of day also makes a difference. At night the best business is around the action venues – restaurants, clubs, casinos and so on."

"Do owner-drivers have to find their own fares then?"

"No, all taxis use a dispatch service. At least half our fares are radioed in to us."

"So there'd be a lot of dispatch services?"

The driver gave an ironic laugh. "No, two of them have the industry sewn up. You need authorization to provide centralized booking and dispatch using a taxi's GPS, and in its wisdom the government has decided to authorize just two. We owner-drivers have to choose one of them to be our network service provider, and we pay a flat fee, regardless of the number of jobs they give us."

"Taxis are equipped with GPS?" whispered Jo in shock.

"GPS, security camera, you name it." Bruce indicated the camera lens on top of his rearview mirror.

"Most taxis have the latest electronic gadgetry these days in the name of efficiency and security, and recently the government caved in to a group of stirrers demanding security screens!" His voice turned to disgust. "Screens will turn taxis into prison vans. It's ridiculous. Part of the enjoyment of this job is chatting with the customers. Who wants to be isolated in a glass booth?"

Jo was still stuck on the GPS discovery. "So your dispatch service knows exactly where you are all the time?"

"They sure do. After I've dropped you off at the cinema, if someone in Brighton wants a taxi, the dispatcher will relay it directly to me. In the old days it was much more hit and miss. The two-way radios would be going all the time with the dispatchers sending out bulletins asking who was near a particular address and different drivers calling back with an estimate of how far away they were. Drivers had to be on the ball then, and they sure had to know their Melbourne streets."

Jo found herself shaking. No doubt she'd once again been much closer to capture than she'd realized. At least she now knew she must *never* be in a taxi when her coordinates were broadcast. All the Hunter had to do was find out from the dispatcher which taxi had been at those coordinates and send agents to intercept it before it dropped her off.

In fact, she realized, the Hunter's agents could also get the dispatchers to tell all taxi drivers in the area of her coordinates to radio in if they picked up a longhaired blonde girl in jeans and a khaki jacket.

"You okay love?"

Jo pulled herself together. She didn't want to arouse suspicions in this driver. "I was just thinking on what you said about the security screens. Is taxi driving really that dangerous?"

"During the daytime no, but between about 10 pm and the early hours of the morning, especially on Friday and Saturday nights, it can get hairy. Drunks can give you a hard time, and before they changed the law allowing us to take payment in advance after 10 pm, there'd always be some who'd jump and run rather than pay for their trip. We still have to contend with muggers who think taxi drivers are easy game, but I have a little deterrent with me." He patted the lower half of the seat beside him. "Cameras in the cabs have also helped to discourage robbery."

Jo hesitated and then decided to risk the question. "Do you ever get police bulletins about dangerous people in your area who might be trying to make a getaway in a taxi?"

"It happens occasionally. In fact just before I picked you up we got an alert to look out for a blonde junkie wanted for kidnapping a baby."

"That's terrible!" Jo loaded her voice with horror. "What could make someone do such a thing?"

He sighed philosophically. "Junkies will do anything for money. All they can think about is their next fix."

"I hope they find her before the baby gets hurt. The parents must be frantic."

"They'll get her." His voice was confident. "How far can a strung-out junkie go when everyone's looking for her?"

Jo thanked her stars the driver saw no connection between his expectations of a "blonde junkie kidnapper" and the "nice girl" in the back seat of his cab. Maybe the profile the Hunter had set up for her in the police database could work to her advantage after all.

For the rest of the trip they chatted on a range of topics and when the driver pulled up at the Palace Cinema, Jo was certain he'd never think to associate her with the wanted woman, should he be questioned. The tab came to forty-three dollars and she drew a fifty from her wallet, telling him with a smile to keep the change and thanking him for his good driving.

"My pleasure love. Enjoy your movie."

He pulled away leaving Jo under a rounded fifties-style archway at the entrance to the old cinema building. Inside was an open plushly carpeted lounge area with a cafe and bar to one side and a wide passageway leading to various cinema doorways on the other. At five-thirty there were few people around, and she decided to plan her next steps over a coffee.

Soon, ensconced at a little round table with a cappuccino and a shortbread, Jo began to consider the coming night. Her next coordinates' posting would be at 8.00 p.m. so continuing the strategy that had served her well, she set her watch alarm for two minutes before that hour.

She would sit in the cinema for the eight o'clock posting, but what then? Jo had noticed a railway crossing up from the cinema, so a train station must be close by, but that was no solution. As soon as the Hunter knew she was in Brighton, he'd get his agents to the station quickly, and at 8.00 p.m. she'd stand out waiting on the platform for a train. Terrified now of the taxi option, Jo pondered her diminishing choices.

What if I booked a hotel room? After the 8.00 p.m. posting I could zip out of the cinema and hole up in my hotel until the eleven o'clock posting. But after that? At eleven o'clock on a wintry Monday night, the streets will be deserted, except for the Hunter's agents closing in. How will I get out of Brighton?

Jo fought back a surge of panic. There had to be something she could do. Hitchhike? Too risky – anyone stopping to pick her up at that hour, other than some pervert was likely to be the Hunter or his agents. Bus? If any were still running, the Hunter would have the bus stops covered. Return to the cinema? Agents were bound to be waiting.

She bit her knuckles. Checking into a different hotel wouldn't do. Once they knew they had her trapped in Brighton, the agents would comb through all accommodations in the area.

The only other option was to take off on her own two feet and the prospect of running and hiding under rain-soaked bushes on a bitter winter's night, was a bleak one indeed. Even if she did that and somehow managed to evade the Hunter's agents for three more hours, she'd be exhausted and wretched and ripe for the plucking at two in the morning when her next coordinates were sent.

Tears prickled and Jo groped for a tissue, finally admitting to herself that she needed help. Should she go back to Shep after all? Phillip, Tayla's dad, would be home by now and he was a big bloke. The Hunter wasn't likely to take Phillip on, but he wouldn't need to. He'd bide his time.

Though Jo was practically part of Tayla's family, her story was just too unbelievable without evidence. They would assume she'd had a breakdown. Phillip had work to do. He couldn't stay home day-after-day pretending to guard an hysterical girl afraid to leave the house. They'd call a doctor and she'd end up drugged in some hospital, which would play right into the Hunter's hands. Jo swallowed a rising thickness in her throat. She couldn't go to Tayla or anyone she knew. Well-meaning friends would be the death of her. She had to be free to run... but where to?

Brighton now felt like a trap. At her 8.00 pm posting the Hunter would send an armada of agents. She could hide somewhere until eleven, but by then all the exits would be blocked and the agents would be tightening the cordon. Jo sat sick with dread, her coffee and biscuit untouched.

It wasn't even six yet. Maybe she should jump on a train right now while the carriages were still crowded, and get out of Brighton. But where would she go? She'd have the same problem in any suburb. Even the city would be mostly closed down at 2.00 a.m. on a Monday night and if she *could* find a club open, they'd never let her in dressed the way she was.

To stay alive, Jo thought, I have to move fast and far after each posting and the Hunter knows that. He'll send agents to every bus and train station around my coordinates and have taxi drivers in the area alerted to report in if they pick up single young females. With all the exits covered, his agents can close in on my location and round me up.

There had to be a way of escaping this nightmare. Perhaps the Yellow Pages would give her some ideas. Across the corridor was a bank of three public phones. No phone books, but maybe if she asked... Jo returned to the coffee counter and caught the eye of a pimply boy arranging cups.

"Excuse me, do you have a Yellow Pages I could look at?"

The boy reached under the counter and drew out two tatty volumes.

"A-K or L-Z?"

She reached for the books. "I'll take both."

"Bring them back when you've finished," he called as she returned to her table.

Opening to the index, she began scanning the entries, hoping something would jump out, but nothing seemed helpful. Hope faded and Jo closed the book and shut her eyes. What I really need is someone who won't ask questions and who can spend all night driving me around. She pictured herself sleeping peacefully in the back of a car. What about a limousine service? Would limos be bound by the same constraints as taxis, having onboard GPSs with dispatchers aware of where each one was? Unlikely. Limos were usually booked for several hours at a time. A car might only be hired out once or twice in an evening and that would be done directly through the limousine company, not a dispatcher!

Jo grabbed the L-Z book and flipped to limousines. There were dozens of companies. Most seemed geared towards weddings and parties, but some were aimed specifically at a corporate clientele and these all emphasized security and confidentiality.

Her heart now racing, Jo read through the most promising advertisements and picked out three possibilities. She wrote their names and numbers in her notepad and then looked up Brighton Hotels, writing down two that sounded swank. To hire a limousine she'd need to be able to give a convincing pickup address. Both hotels were located on a street called Esplanade. She wondered where that was.

Her appetite suddenly returned, Jo gulped down the lukewarm coffee and chomped on the shortbread, eyeing the other patrons. Most were queuing for tickets or buying popcorn, but two carrying glasses of wine were settling at the table next to hers.

"Excuse me." She leant across to the girl, who had just opened her mouth to speak to her boyfriend. "Do you know how far Esplanade is from here?"

The girl turned, frowning at the interruption. "It's just five minutes down the road."

"That's if you're driving," her boyfriend said. "On foot it would be closer to twenty-five."

"I *will* be walking actually. You couldn't tell me a good way to get there?"

"Turn left out of the cinema and go down Asling Street," said the girl quickly, obviously not keen that her boyfriend had entered the conversation. "Asling becomes St Andrews. Follow it to the roundabout, and you'll see Park Street branching off. Park Street will take you to Esplanade."

"Thanks," smiled Jo.

She returned the phonebooks to the counter and headed out of the cinema. It was just on six. If the boyfriend had been right in his estimation, she had enough time to get to the hotel, book a room and return to the cinema before her eight p.m. coordinates were broadcast.

CHAPTER 13

Although the rain had now stopped, the wind cut straight through Jo's thin hoodie and shirt, making her thankful for the additional padding of the money belt. She tucked the bulky straw bag under one arm and set off down Asling Street at a comfortable jog, glad the track pants made her look the part. St Andrews was a well-lit street with attractive houses and Jo began to enjoy running off the tension of the day. After ten minutes she had worked up a warm glow and reached the roundabout.

In Park Street she slowed to a fast walk to get her breath back, occasionally swapping the annoying bag from one side to the other. Five minutes of this brought her to Esplanade, which turned out to be a busy highway running along the beach. She turned left and began jogging again, breathing in the salty mist from the dark sea. A few more minutes and the Brighton Savoy appeared. Jo stopped to think through her strategy.

The fact she had neither luggage nor credit card would make the reception clerk uneasy, so a laughing, happy-go-lucky approach, like the one she'd used with Nadine the hairdresser, would probably work best. She reached into the bag and pulled out her wallet. It contained around four hundred dollars. That should be enough, she thought, looking down at her right hand. A plain gold band – her mother's wedding ring, adorned her middle finger. Jo swapped it to the ring finger of her left hand.

A husband can be a handy thing, she thought, as she walked up the pathway and through the grand entrance doors.

"Whooo, it's windy out there!" she said, crossing the foyer and smiling at the young woman behind the reception desk. The clerk, neatly dressed in the hotel uniform, with her dark hair pulled back into a smooth ponytail, returned Jo's smile.

"Can I help you?"

64

"Yes, my husband and I would like a room for the night. He'll be bringing the car around shortly, but he got so excited about being back in Brighton that he just *had* to go down to the beach! *I* said no thanks, you can drop *me* off at the hotel. *I'm* not walking along the sand in the dark and cold!"

The receptionist smiled sympathetically. "Do you have a booking?"

"No!" Jo laughed. "My husband's so impulsive, but he loves this hotel. He used to come here before we were married, so we're hoping you have a vacancy."

"Well as it happens, we do." The receptionist looked pleased to be the bearer of good news. "Number two-seventeen is free if you're happy with a standard room?"

"That's great," said Jo cheerfully. "Andy'll be rapt."

"I'll just get your details then. Name?"

"Andy and Judith Wiseman."

"Address?"

"Fourteen Bridge Street, Rosedale, NSW." Jo hoped there was a suburb called Rosedale in NSW, but was pretty sure this girl wouldn't know in any case.

"We're down here to spring a surprise visit on Andy's brother," Jo gushed, hoping to divert the girl from asking for a postcode. "He couldn't come to the wedding, so we're bringing the photos to him."

The tactic worked.

"I just need a credit card now," said the receptionist, sounding a little flustered.

Jo spoke breezily. "Andy's got the credit card. He'll have to bring it over when he comes in."

"Oh, I... I can't give you the keycard without a deposit," said the girl.

Jo adopted a surprised look and then broke into a smile. "No worries, I can give you cash. How much do you need?"

"Well the room is a hundred and seventy dollars a night..."

"Right then, here you go. I'll pay for one night and if we decide to stay longer, my husband can fix things up with you in the morning."

She drew two, hundred dollar notes from her wallet and placed them on the counter.

The girl looked at the notes doubtfully. "We'll need to record your credit card number for security, but I guess as long as your husband registers the card with us as soon as he comes in, it'll be okay."

She gave Jo the registration book to sign and wrote out a receipt for a hundred and seventy dollars, which she handed over with the change and the coded plastic card.

"Two-seventeen is on the second floor. Turn right when you get out of the elevator," she instructed.

"Thanks, if my husband turns up before I come down again, can you tell him where to go?"

"Of course," smiled the clerk, her confidence restored.

Jo gave a nod and headed for the elevator. In her room, she flopped onto the bed with a laugh. Yes, she thought in a Cockney accent, an "usband is an *Andy* thing.

That had actually been fun! Only twelve hours ago she would never have dreamed she could have done that. Now if the Hunter's agents went sniffing around Brighton hotels after her coordinates had been sent, the people at this one would tell them no single woman had checked in here tonight. The husband ploy would also be wise when booking the limousine, should the Hunter's agents think to contact the dozens of companies advertising. Now what time to book it for?

As soon as my eight o'clock coordinates are sent, she thought, the Hunter will move his agents quickly to block all exits via train, bus and cabs, and then begin searching the places I might go to after leaving the cinema – restaurants, pubs, nearby accommodation and so on. He won't worry too much if he doesn't find me in the first three hours after eight, as his agents will have surrounded Brighton, ready to converge when they get my eleven o'clock coordinates. So, I'll have to make sure I'm well out of Brighton by eleven. If I book the limo for 10.30 I'll have time to rest, eat and freshen up before I leave.

Jo's watch showed a few minutes to seven. She took the notebook from her bag, and turned to the page with the limousine numbers. The first company on the list had promised Internet connectivity and this was the one she now called.

A clear, unhurried female voice responded. "Chronis Cars, how may I help you?"

Jo adopted what she hoped was an equally sophisticated tone. "My husband and I are interested in hiring a car with driver from 10.30 p.m. tonight, until ten tomorrow morning. Is your company able to provide this service?"

"Certainly," said the woman smoothly. That period falls within a twelve hour shift, which is our maximum before we need to change the driver."

"Good, now your advertisement says you can provide Internet connectivity?"

"Yes, our drivers carry broadband dongles to enable you to connect your laptop to the Internet while in the car," came the prompt response.

"Are you also able to provide a laptop computer on loan?" asked Jo with her fingers crossed.

"I'll check for you," said the voice pleasantly. "One moment please."

Quiet classical music played over the line and Jo let out the breath she'd been holding.

The voice returned. "Yes, we can provide a laptop on loan."

"That sounds ideal. What will the total cost be?"

"Eleven and a half hours in a chauffeured Lexus with Internet access and laptop hire comes to 1,200 dollars. That includes the driver's gratuity and GST."

"Excellent, we'll book it."

"Very good," said the woman. "May I have the name please?"

"Andy and Judith Wiseman," the names now rolled off her tongue.

"And your credit card number?"

Damn! Jo put on a supercilious tone. "We prefer to do this without the use of credit cards. Your company's advertisement emphasized it understood the confidentiality needs of your clients."

"Absolutely," began the woman reassuringly, "and we won't charge the card if you prefer to pay cash, but we *do* need a record of it for security purposes," she ended firmly.

"These may be your security purposes, but they are not ours." Jo allowed her voice to grow cold. "To compensate for the inconvenience of forfeiting your security on this occasion, we are prepared to add another three hundred dollars to your fee. We are staying at the Brighton Savoy and will pay your chauffeur the full fifteen hundred dollars in cash, on his arrival."

There was a pause and Jo held her breath.

"I'll need to consult with the manager on this. May I call you back Mrs. Wiseman?

"As long as it's within the next five minutes," said Jo. "My husband and I are about to go out to dinner."

"I will call you back immediately," the woman said, and hung up.

Jo had been expecting something like this. The company would feel the need to confirm at the very least, that the callers were indeed guests of the hotel. It was now just after seven – still time to get to the cinema if they called back soon. The phone tinkled and Jo lifted the receiver.

"Yes?"

A male voice spoke. "Phone call for Mrs. Wiseman."

The girl at the front desk must have finished her shift, thought Jo. Good.

"Thank you, I'll take it," she said.

"Mrs. Wiseman," began the familiar calm voice. "Our company is happy to take your booking on the understanding that 1,500 dollars is paid to our chauffeur on his arrival."

"Very good. We will expect him at 10.30 p.m."

"He will be there. Good evening Mrs. Wiseman."

"Good evening."

Jo hung up, exhilarated by this second successful negotiation. She wasn't concerned about meeting the chauffeur alone. She could always say her husband had been called away on urgent business, but at least she'd given the impression that a married couple had made the booking.

Now she hung her jeans and jacket over a chair and checked their pockets. She pulled out a twenty-dollar note and tucked it into her bra for the cinema, regretting the lack of pockets in the track pants but deciding she'd rather pull cash from her bra than make anyone aware she was wearing a money belt.

Jo fastened her room's keycard into one of the pockets of her money belt and was on the point of leaving when she remembered the blonde wig. She needed it for her photo, so the Hunter and his agents would keep searching for a girl with long blonde hair, but how would she carry it? Not in the annoying straw bag. That was staying behind on this trip. Jo looked around. The mini bin in the bathroom contained a fresh plastic liner. She pulled it out, dropped in the wig and tied the top. Seven-twenty – time to go.

As she reached the lobby, Jo shot a glance at the reception desk. Sure enough a middle-aged man was now at the post, typing something into the computer. With luck there'd be no further fuss about registering the credit card.

Outside the frigid wind had picked up in strength, but with the freedom of no more than a plastic bag in hand, Jo moved into an easy arm-swinging run, which ate up the distance. By seven-forty she was back at the cinema, red-cheeked and glowing with warmth.

She pulled the note from her bra and walked to the counter, casting her eye over the colorful posters and choosing a movie at random.

"A ticket for Revenge of the Ninjas please," she said.

"That movie started half an hour ago," the same pimply boy warned. He'd apparently been promoted from cup stacker to ticket seller.

Jo pushed the twenty towards him. "Well, I'd better hurry then."

"Cinema three." He handed Jo her ticket and a five-dollar note in change.

Jo entered Cinema three, pausing to grow accustomed to the darkness and to slip the change into her bra. The movie was in full swing and the few patrons scattered around had eyes for nothing but the flickering images in front of them. She climbed the carpeted stairs to the top and took an empty seat on the aisle. No one was back this far and she had the row to herself.

Quietly she pulled off the black wig, and removed the hoodie. Underneath was the dark shirt the Hunter already knew. Pushing hoodie and black wig under the seat, she slipped on the blonde wig. An explosion of action erupted from the screen and Jo sat back with a sigh.

Despite all, she became caught up in the movie and jumped when her alarm sounded. Quickly she silenced it, and keeping her eyes on the screen ahead, counted slowly to sixty three times. Then, to allow for discrepancies between her watch and the *Play or Die* timer, she counted off another two minutes.

Now Jo moved fast, returning the blond wig to the plastic bag and putting the hoodie and black wig back on. She tiptoed down to the heavy exit door and slipped into the brightly lit foyer.

At five past eight, the place held a dozen or so people. Some sat at coffee tables, while others examined the posters or queued for tickets. Jo noted with relief that no one seemed interested in her.

Outside she started for the hotel, hoping to look like an innocent jogger, though few were about at this hour on a cold winter's night. No one stopped her, and twenty minutes later she was turning the knob of her room.

Closing the door behind her, Jo realized she was shaking with exhaustion, and stumbled to the bed. Though bone tired, she could only afford a short rest. She set a fifteen-minute alarm and stretched out.

She was running on a newly made road and strands of sticky tar were clinging to her shoes, making it harder at each step to lift her feet. Adding to this annoyance, a little bird on her shoulder was chirping right into her ear. She tried to shake it off but it held on tenaciously and chirped all the louder.

With a groan, Jo rolled off the arm supporting her head and silenced the beeping watch alarm. Then she grabbed the straw bag off the chair and upended it onto the coverlet. The new beige shirt had worked its way to the bottom and was now badly crumpled – hardly a corporate look. She searched in the wardrobe and found an iron and ironing pad, and soon had the shirt looking fresh and neat. A touch to the jeans as well and Jo was satisfied she would look acceptable.

With her energy returning, she unclipped the money belt and pulled off the hoodie, flinging it onto the bed, before heading for the bathroom. She stripped off the dark shirt, washed the underarm part of the sleeves and slipped it damp onto a hanger. Unlacing her shoes, she peeled off the stained, sweaty socks and dropped them into the bin. I have two packets of fresh ones, she thought.

The lancing hot water of the shower pummeled Jo's tired muscles, bringing her fully back to life and reviving not just the memory of her audience, but the realization she was starving.

She turned off the water and wrapping a towel around herself, padded into the main room, putting on deodorant and fresh underwear. The money belt went on next, followed by the jeans, beige shirt and the new socks. She was in the process of lacing her shoes when a loud knock at the door froze her in mid-knot.

Shit! She hadn't ordered room service. Could it be the management chasing up that bloody credit card? Jo decided to keep quiet in the hope that whoever it was would give up and go away. A shape materialized on her side of the door.

"First you insist I knock," he said in mock petulance. "And then you refuse to answer the door."

"Fitani!" cried Jo in relief.

"My dear Jo," His grin was wide. "Surely you can bring yourself to call me Danny by now."

The host's costume on this occasion was quite conservative for him. A pair of black silky trousers tucked into dark red ankle boots, was topped by a deep purple bloused shirt, tied loosely at the waist with a lilac sash embroidered at the ends with the familiar gold logo.

"Thousand point time." Jo made it a statement.

"And what a roller-coaster thousand they have been!" said Fitani. "My dear you are doing wonders for our ratings. People are tuning in from every pocket on Earth. Few Prey last as long as you have, and with the strategies you've been using, you're odds-on at the moment to survive right through to your second day."

"Hmm, thanks, I think."

"Now," Fitani rubbed his hands together. "Getting down to business, have you decided whether you'll be asking three questions or using your technical assistance request?"

Jo considered. If she was going to be able to appeal to, or influence this audience from the future, she needed to know more about them, and in any case, she realized with a little thrill of joy, if she could keep Fitani hanging around by dragging out her questions, she'd have a husband to show off.

"I'll opt for questions this time, but I'll be asking the first one over dinner as it's now..." she looked at her watch, "nearly nine thirty, and I need to be out of here in an hour."

"As you wish. Have you ordered food?"

"No, we'll be dining in the hotel's restaurant."

Jo finished lacing her shoes and put on the black wig. She collected her keycard and opened the door. "After you."

In the foyer, Jo made straight for the reception desk with Fitani trailing along.

"Good evening," she greeted the man behind it. "Is it too late for my husband and me to dine in the hotel's restaurant?"

The clerk glanced at Fitani, poorly suppressing a smirk at his costume.

"Are you a guest, Mrs..."

"Wiseman," said Jo. "Yes, Andy and I are in room two-seventeen."

"Well the kitchen will close soon, but if you go straight in they should be able to help you."

"Thanks." Jo turned to Fitani. "Come on Andy, we don't want to miss out."

The dining room was intimate with only a solitary elderly gentleman in one corner spooning up a dessert flummery in an absentminded way.

Jo chose a table visible from the doorway and sat with her back to the door. Fitani sat opposite. If an agent looks in, she thought, he'll see a woman with short dark hair, dining with a companion. She considered the possibility of the Hunter himself turning up. He'd certainly recognize Fitani and realize who his companion was. But there's little chance of that, she thought. With two detective agencies at his beck and call, the Hunter wouldn't be doing this kind of preliminary footwork. Brighton's too big, and at the moment he has no idea where in Brighton I am. He'll be sitting at some command post, coordinating his troops.

A waitress approached and placed two menus on the table. "Would you care for something to drink?" She proffered the wine list to Fitani, who made no effort to reach for it.

"The water's fine," said Jo, indicating the bottle on the table. She had no intention of dulling her senses with wine. She picked up the top menu. "We'll order straight away as I know the kitchen is closing soon."

The waitress stood by as Jo ran her eye down the list. "Andy will just have clear soup as he's not feeling well. I'll have the porterhouse steak, medium rare."

Jo returned the menus to the waitress, who tucked them under one arm, filled their glasses from the carafe and headed towards a doorway at the back of the room.

"Andy?" Fitani raised an eyebrow. "Couldn't you have picked a better name? Ratings you know."

Jo gave him a glassy stare and he fluttered his fingers before his mouth in an affected yawn. "Are we ready to move to the question-asking phase of this procedure?"

She answered calmly. "I'm ready. The more I play this game, the harder it is for me to get my head around why people of the future would want to see me hunted and killed. I don't want to die without understanding that, so here is my question. Can you please tell me all about your world and its people?"

Fitani coughed in surprise. "I fail to see how knowledge of my world can possibly assist your survival attempts. Your curiosity seems to have gotten the better of common sense. However, the rules of the game bind me to answer your questions, so I'll do my best. Here are our lives in a nutshell:

Twelve hours of Tube, eight hours of Play and four hours of Work, make up our day."

He paused, looking at Jo expectantly.

CHAPTER 14

Fitani's rhyme triggered a memory from an Australian history class. In 1856, Melbourne's Labor Movement had won a world-first eight-hour working day for the building industry, using the slogan "Eight hours labor, Eight hours recreation, Eight hours rest'. The next century they'd revised the slogan to attach a monetary value. "Eight hours work, eight hours play, eight hours sleep and eight shillings a day."

Fitani's four hours of work sounded like a big improvement on this but what was twelve hours of tube? Jo just stopped herself in time from asking.

Having failed to trick her into an impulsive question, Fitani continued. "I suppose I'll need to explain that?"

"That would be good," said Jo.

"Twelve hours of Tube is our resting time. We rest in our tubes." Again he paused, but now up to his tricks, Jo simply waited.

"The tubes were The Company's great survival solution. Praise The Company. When your world's failure to control its population led to the Great Destruction, billions were killed outright and over eighty percent of the earth became uninhabitable.

"In the bitter years that followed, when the sun's warmth and light barely penetrated the smoke and soot circulating in the atmosphere, additional millions died from starvation and radiation poisoning. Only a handful of places with uncontaminated soil, bypassed by the worst of the radioactive winds remained, and in each of these *Safe Places* huddled a few thousand, desperately scratching a living in their new hostile world."

Danny's voice took on a sonorous note and his eyes glazed. "Children born were few and sickly. The end was upon the human race," he intoned. "The people wailed and cursed the Ancestors who had brought this fate upon them. But just when all seemed lost, came The Great Arising! The very earth itself parted, and ascending into the light from the depths below appeared … The Company. All hail The Company!

"The blessed CEO graced my own *Safe Place* with his Supreme Presence, but no pocket of humanity was forgotten. Two sacred aircraft, preserved beneath the Earth, took to the skies, protected from the deadly radiation by *Company Science*. Over time they located every Safe Place on the planet. Then the blessed CEO sent to each Safe Place a Company Director, bearing an entourage of Family, Secretaries and Secretaries' Families, all beautiful and sound of limb and carrying with them great works of science and learning."

Jo gave a snort, interrupting Fitani's ecstatic rendition.

"Something wrong?" he inquired with annoyance.

"Well if I'd been abandoned on the surface, I know how *I'd* feel towards those who'd dived underground to safety, and were now emerging to take over my world because their own resources had finally run out."

Fitani was horrified. "You don't understand at all. The Company ascended to save us. Without The Company, humanity would have been doomed."

"Perhaps," said Jo. "But maybe those on the surface had gotten themselves through the worst and could have survived on their own."

"Unthinkable!" said Fitani. "BC, Before The Company, the people of the Safe Places were savages, living short, desperate lives. AC, our lives improved a thousand fold. We became civilized employees, cared for, nurtured and shown the way forward by our Great Employer."

"No doubt The Company helped when they finally emerged, but for how many years had they hidden, safe in their underground bunkers, hoarding their science while the survivors struggled above? I'd say they *owed* the surface people their knowledge, without any strings attached. Instead they co-opted 'the savages' into their own private workforce!"

As Fitani struggled for words, the waitress appeared and slid a consommé in front of him. The plate she put before Jo held a large steak with thick-cut hot chips and a salad.

Jo smiled her thanks and her stomach rumbled as she cut a piece from the seared meat. Spearing it, she used her knife to push a golden chip and some salad onto the back of the fork and raised the combination to her lips. Fantastic! More than five hours had passed since the warmed-up quiche in Carnegie, and she was famished.

As she chewed, Jo noticed Fitani still seemed dazed. Not wanting to alienate him or his audience, she said mildly, "You haven't yet explained about the tubes."

"Yes, the tubes," Fitani revived. "They will help you to understand the great beneficence of The Company. BC, the surface survivors had set up their dwellings in the centers of each Safe Place, for the only way they had of coping with radiation was to live as far from it as possible. This meant their housing took up good land that could have been used for crop cultivation.

The Company Directors showed the survivors how to build tall radiation-protected silos at the edges of the Safe Places.

"Today, all employees live in this vertical housing, thereby maximizing the land over which crops can be grown. Can you imagine how we house thousands of people in a handful of silos?" he asked, immediately answering his own question with, "Tubes!"

Jo, now halfway through her steak, swapped plates with Fitani and began on his soup, which she noted with approval, was also excellent. No one disturbed them. The old man in the corner had departed, and the waitress, who'd returned to the kitchen after delivering their meals, had remained there, so the dining room was theirs.

Fitani, frustrated at his failure to transfer his own enthusiasm to Jo, began to pontificate. "An unequipped tube seems nothing special – just a hexagonal tunnel, big enough to comfortably fit a large person lying down. Does that seem a cramped place to rest for twelve hours? It's not. The technology of our tubes turns them, compared with the accommodations of the original survivors, into little slices of heaven."

Jo raised an eyebrow, reserving her judgment. "Go on."

"Actually, I need to go back a bit. When the four-hour work shift ends, employees return to the silos and leave their protective suits in the cloaking room. From there they step onto a cleansing conveyer belt to be oiled, scraped, and sonically exfoliated."

"Sounds painful," said Jo, pushing the empty soup bowl back to Fitani and retrieving her steak.

"Not at all. It's a pleasant process, very soothing after a hard shift at the Edge. As they leave the cleansing belt, employees thumb-in to their twelve-hour Tube-Time, and proceed to the Ladder Check-in point."

"After having donned their civvies," Jo interjected.

"Their civvies?" Fitani's expression was pained at having been interrupted. "Oh you're talking about clothing?" he said as his translator kicked in with an interpretation. "No, no. We have no need for protective coverings in the silos. The climate is perfectly controlled."

"Are you saying everyone walks around naked?" spluttered Jo.

"Ah, question number two," said Fitani with a grin, and Jo mentally kicked herself, grimly vowing to think carefully before she spoke again.

"Nudity is not uncommon, but tends to be the resort of lazy, lower grade employees. Those with imagination array themselves in holographic clothing of great style and virtuosity," he said, spreading his arms.

"Programmed clothing drapes perfectly, never chafes, snags or stains and surrounds the wearer until he or she cancels the illusion. There are many styles to download from the catalogues. Naturally, the more elegant the style, the more Personal Points you need to spend. Some designers program wild and wonderful creations. Others gain inspiration from the styles of previous ages. Currently fashionable among some of our show's teen viewers, are variations on the outfits you've been wearing."

During his description Jo had been gaping. "For the first time," she admitted, "your technology impresses me."

Fitani laughed. "Yes, we've been amused by your concern about minimizing the times you are uncovered. What actually fascinates our audience while you shower is the sight of such quantities of pure water doing no more work than momentarily passing over your skin before being drained away. Such a shocking waste, of what in our radioactive world is our most precious resource."

As Jo absorbed that information, the waitress arrived to clear the table.

"I hope everything was to your liking?"

"Yes, excellent," muttered Jo, and then recovering herself added, "I wonder if we might pay for this meal now, rather than adding it to our room tab?" She wanted no further conversations with desk clerks about payment using credit cards.

The waitress frowned. "It's not usually done. We'd have to make up a special bill for you."

"As you do for diners who aren't guests of the hotel," said Jo firmly. "Yes please."

The waitress nodded and left with the plates. Jo knew her old self would have meekly signed the room chit rather than make waves. If nothing else this game was teaching her assertiveness.

"Shall I finish answering your first question?" asked Danny.

"Please do."

"On second thought, it might be easier to show you." He made a gesture and a vertical cylinder appeared in the middle of the table. "This is our inner silo, where the playrooms are housed." He gestured again. A wider cylinder slid down over the first. "The outer silo. You can't tell from the outside, but the wall is made up of horizontal tubes."

Jo frowned. "There doesn't seem much of a gap between the inner and outer silos."

"It's sufficient. Here's a cross-section." Fitani sliced his hand down the center of the model, and the front half vanished.

Leaning forward, Jo saw that the exposed inner cylinder was filled with rooms from top to bottom, all joined by a central lift, but before she could examine them, Fitani made another gesture and the inner cylinder vanished. She was left staring at the inside wall of the outer cylinder. It looked exactly like a giant curving honeycomb. Jo squinted into the hexagonal openings. Surely those weren't bodies inside!

"The entire wall of the outer silo is made up of tubes," said Fitani. "As you can see, it's a long climb to the top tubes." He chuckled. "Fortunately our ladders move."

Now Jo noticed the slim metal ladders beside each column of tubes. People were standing on some and moving up and down.

Fitani gestured again and the model disappeared. "You get your ladder number at the check in point," he said. "Then you walk the curving passageway between the two silos to your allocated ladder and climb on, stamping on a rung to start it rising. Ladders stop automatically when they reach the first free tube in their column so the employee, or employees in the case of a couple, can crawl in. As soon as a tube contains its allocated occupants, it is sealed for the next twelve hours."

Jo gasped, and had to bite her lip to hold back the questions.

"And now we come at last," said Fitani with relish, "to the furnishings of the tube."

No furnishings, thought Jo with a shudder, could compensate for being locked inside a coffin for twelve hours. The tubes seem like the Japanese Capsule Hotels, but at least you can crawl out of those if the claustrophobia gets too bad.

Blithely unaware of Jo's horror, Fitani now adopted the smooth air of a car salesman. "Each tube is furnished with a smart mat, which adjusts to any sized body or bodies in the case of a couple, providing support in all the right places. The mats contain hidden sensors to keep track of an occupant's health, and an inbuilt pharmacopeia to treat minor ailments. A headache for example is identifiable by specific physical changes in the body, and the smart mat can administer an analgesic through its contact with the occupant's skin. In the rare instance of a medical emergency, a signal is sent to a Med Team with authority to override the tube locks and move the employee to the hospital silo for treatment – an employee's health and happiness is The Company's greatest concern.

"I don't care how comfy and caring that mat is," said Jo. It wouldn't compensate for being in a tomb!"

Fitani was unperturbed. "It's true the walls and ceiling of each tube are little further than an arm's reach away, but a holographic environment masks that. Occupants can choose their own environments from the tube catalogue. The basic ones are free, such as the impression of being in a large, airy room, or of lying in a meadow of daisies under a vast open sky, but if you wish to spend Personal Points, there are endless surroundings to choose from.

"Fresh air circulates continually and occupants can adjust temperature and flow speed using a holographic gesture-screen. The same screen allows them to make visual calls to friends in their own or other Safe Places. They can view clothing catalogues and purchase outfits for the next day, order free basic food patties and drinks, or spend Personal Points on better quality meals, which are delivered through a food hatch in the entry door.

"A number of employees use Tube-Time to further their education. Using holographic avatars, they can attend classes and participate in discussions at any virtual location. Quite a few enroll in programming courses to learn how to program holographic clothing, tube environments, or virtual games. Employees can submit their creations to The Company and if they're deemed up-to-standard, they're added to The Company's catalogues and allocated a Personal Point value. Every time other employees access them, the designers receive a percentage of the Points paid. If you're talented, it's a great little earner. Several employees have become quite wealthy in this way.

"Most spend at least some of their Tube-Time accessing the myriads of virtual games and entertainments available. A number are free, but the best ones, like *Play or Die*, will cost you Personal Points to access. Different entertainments allow varying kinds of viewer participation. In *Play or Die*, participation is through the smart mats, which interpret viewers' bodily responses and send them to the Emoto Board. When you come to think of it, with all the options employees have during Tube-Time, it's a wonder we remember to get any sleep at all!"

"I would imagine resisting an increasingly urgent 'call of nature' might interfere with their ability to sleep," said Jo dryly.

A small cough drew her attention to the waitress who was placing a black lacquered tray containing the bill onto the table. Jo drew notes to cover the amount, along with a generous tip.

The waitress, producing her first real smile, thanked her.

"You're welcome," said Jo. "Please tell the chef we enjoyed the meal."

As the waitress departed, Jo stood. It was ten fifteen. The chauffeur would be arriving in a quarter of an hour. She strode to the doorway and found Fitani right beside her.

"By call of nature," he said, "I suppose you're referring to evacuations of the body. You don't think we'd neglect to cater for those do you?"

Jo stepped into the elevator, not bothering to answer as she pressed the button for her floor.

"An evacuation bowl is built into each tube."

"Not too close to the food hatch I hope," she retorted.

Fitani gave a sigh. "You seem determined to deride our way of life and yet we have survived the ravages resulting from your people's selfish overpopulating of the world."

Jo paused in repacking the straw bag, and looked up. "You're right. I'm sorry. Your people have done amazingly well in recovering from a nuclear holocaust, and it was petty of me to mock. I guess my ability to empathize has received a few hits lately with this whole, being hunted to the death thing."

Fitani shrugged. "You said you wanted to understand my world. Do you still wish me to continue?"

"I do," said Jo, removing her money belt and laying it on the bed. "Please talk while I get organized."

She opened a pocket of the belt and extracted twenty, hundred dollar notes. Five went into her depleted wallet and she looked around for something to hold the remaining 1,500 dollars. The plastic bag was hardly appropriate. Her eye fell upon the embossed leather folder found in all hotel rooms. Along with room service information and brochures advertising nearby tourist spots, most held hotel stationary.

Jo flipped open the folder and was delighted to find letter paper and envelopes. Taking one, she slipped in the money, sealed the flap and put it into the straw bag. Then, in inspiration she took another and wrote on the front, 'The Wisemans have checked out' before sealing the keycard into it.

I'm all paid up, she thought. I can just leave this envelope at the reception desk and then I won't have to deal with any desk clerks.

She took off the beige shirt, which the Hunter had not yet seen, and put on the black, folding its collar down low. Then she pulled the tailored beige shirt over the top. It'll do, she decided, inspecting her reflection. Her watch read 10.27 p.m. and casting a last eye over the room to ensure she'd collected everything, Jo grabbed the bag and headed for the door.

Fitani, all the while had been explaining the ins and outs of tube-life, describing how it linked to their music and arts, the special arrangements in the children's silos, and so on. Now he was starting to describe to the next step in the cycle – the eight hours of play.

"Each inner silo is filled with playrooms," he said enthusiastically. "If the Playrooms in one silo become passé, employees can take the tunnel passage to any of the other silos. No two Playrooms are the same."

"I would have thought," interrupted Jo, pressing the ground floor button, "that after twelve hours in the tubes, employees would prefer to be heading outside for some fresh air."

Fitani stared at her. "Obviously I've failed to convey what our world is like," he said, and a topographical map filled the elevator.

Finding herself waist-deep in a mountain range, Jo yelped and leapt to press the close-button on the opening elevator doors.

"This," Fitani was unable to keep the pride from his voice, "is my Safe Place."

Jo studied the holographic map. A breathtakingly vast patchwork of fields spread out from the base of the mountain range. Diverse shades indicated different crops at various stages of growth, alongside occasional fallow fields of rich brown, all perfectly tended by tiny machines, which moved about weeding and harvesting. Fitani made a gesture and the map began to scroll. Kilometer after kilometer of fields scrolled by, unbroken by trees, housing or roads.

"Before The Company, most of what you're seeing was untamed forests and wild pasture," he informed her. "The surface survivors grew few crops, having reverted to a mainly hunter/gatherer culture. They barely eked out a subsistence living. Now, thanks to The Company, we all eat well."

What happened to the animals, thought Jo, but refrained from asking. As the map scrolled on, a large area of blurriness, apparently several kilometers wide, and extending for many more, appeared.

"There seems to be a problem with the holographic projection," she said.

"Some things are not for your eyes," was Fitani's reply, and eventually it scrolled by. For the first time a road appeared, extending from the end of the blurred section and cutting through the scrolling fields, to finally reach a curved row of about forty silos dotted along the fringe of the great patchwork quilt.

Now the scene changed markedly. A somewhat hilly band of brown land extended beyond the silos for several kilometers. Moving over it were tractor-like machines. Beyond that band, everything was black. As far as the eye could see, the earth was black as though a huge fire had swept through wreaking such total devastation that nothing had grown back.

"The black land," said Fitani, "is all radioactive. Can you see the employees working at the Edge?"

What Jo had taken to be some kind of thin white line on the edge of the radioactive plains, she now saw were thousands of human beings, each suited up in a kind of astronaut's costume, bending shoulder to shoulder in unison.

"They are cleaning the Earth," he replied to her unasked question.

A loud blaring sound added to Jo's shock, and she realized she'd been holding the elevator doors closed too long.

"Turn off the hologram," she said, white-faced, releasing the doors as it disappeared.

For the first time Jo's heart cried out for the people of the future, for their compacted, restricted lives and their tiny, heroic attempt to save the Earth.

"Can you see now," said Danny as they stepped into the foyer, "why the idea of stretching one's legs in the fresh air can never be more than a fantasy for my people? All our clean ground is taken up with food production, the barren hills of no-man's land are in the final stages of cleaning by the machines and are hardly the place for a picnic, and beyond that are the radioactive plains, upon which no one can venture without a protective suit.

"We watch you people playing in parks, climbing mountains, fishing in streams, swimming in oceans, even walking along streets and feeling the weather, and we curse that you destroyed all that for us."

Jo turned to Fitani. "I'm getting it. I'm beginning to understand the depth of your anger. I'd probably feel the same way if I lived in your world, but surely it's rubbing salt into the wound, to be always looking back on something you'll never regain."

"We can't have the real thing, but you won't even let us live it vicariously?" said Danny.

"I don't know," said Jo. "I'm confused. I need time to think about it and right now I don't have that time. The chauffeur is waiting."

She nodded towards a solid uniformed man in his mid thirties, standing by the reception desk. Fitani said no more and the two of them walked over.

"Mr. and Mrs. Wiseman?" the chauffeur asked.

"Yes." Jo passed him the envelope with the money. "Could you please check the payment and provide a receipt."

The chauffeur took the envelope and turned to the reception desk to count the notes. Jo meanwhile pulled out the second envelope containing the keycard and pushed it through the slot provided for guests to drop their keycards while they were away from the hotel. The desk clerk glanced at the group, but deciding his services weren't needed, continued working on his computer.

Jo checked her watch. It was just ten-thirty. They were the only ones in the foyer. A sleek black Lexus sat gleaming in the pool of light outside the entrance. So far, so good.

The chauffeur now turned with a smile, the envelope no longer in evidence, and proffered a receipt.

"Everything is in order. I am George Vasiliou. Please call me George."

Jo took the receipt. "Thank you George, we're ready to leave."

Nodding, he led the way across the foyer, and stood aside as the doors parted, to allow them to pass through. Then he sprang to pull open the back door of the Lexus.

"After you dear," said Jo to Danny, and turned quickly to distract George. She didn't want him noticing Fitani's dematerializing method of entering a car.

"You've brought the laptop?" she asked.

"Yes Mrs. Wiseman." He pressed his key-remote to release the boot catch, and walking around, lifted the boot. He reached in and took out a small laptop with a broadband dongle already in its USB port.

"Great!" Jo took the laptop. "We have some time to spare, so let's take a tour of the city. You can choose the sights."

She slipped into the plush, leather interior and fastened her seatbelt.

CHAPTER 15

The driver turned right, towards the city. In the hush of the back seat, Jo closed her eyes and exhaled. She'd done it. At eleven o'clock the Hunter would make the dismaying discovery that he hadn't trapped her in Brighton after all. She melted into the soft leather, deciding she could ride like this for the rest of her life.

Fitani's voice shattered the tranquility. "Shall I continue now?"

"In a minute." Jo needed a break and played for time. "I have to check the laptop. George, how do I get onto the Internet?"

"Double-click the broadband icon, Mrs. Wiseman. Enter chronis3 as the password and then just use the browser."

Jo followed his instructions.

"It's very irregular to be taking this long with the questions," Fitani grumbled.

"Go with the flow, Danny boy," Jo muttered under her breath, and brought up Google Maps. Now to get some real addresses she could give to hotel clerks. For a while, Jo jumped from state to state, zooming in on streets and suburbs and writing down their names and postcodes.

I need Melbourne suburbs too, she thought, dragging the map to bring Victoria into view. The screen momentarily greyed and as Jo waited for the refresh, her gaze wandered to the toolbar and froze. The time display said 10.58. Her alarm hadn't gone off! She looked at her watch and saw the numbers change to 10.59.

"George, pull over, quickly," she yelled. "I have to get out!"

A sign revealed they were on Nepean highway and she could see no place to pull over, but the chauffeur veered into a turning lane leading to a side street. Jo clawed off her black wig and threw it to the floor. Yanking the blonde from the bag, she fitted it hurriedly. They pulled into a curb and she leapt out before the engine had even stopped, sprinting for a large tree on the nature strip. Putting the trunk between herself and the car, Jo tore off the beige shirt and threw it behind her.

Had she made it in time? The illuminated numbers on her watch read 11.00 p.m. but was that the beginning of 11.00 or the end? Panting, she watched the dial and counted. When she got to fifty-three, the numbers changed to 11.01. If her watch was accurate, the Hunter's new photo showed what she'd intended – her usual blonde self, though somewhat disheveled, in the familiar black shirt and jeans. At worst the camera had caught some part of the beige shirt and the Hunter may now know she owned clothing of this color. Well serve her right for forgetting to set the alarm.

...

In the car, George turned to his client in concern. "Mr. Wiseman, is your wife all right? Does she need help?"

Fitani shrugged noncommittally. "She does things her way."

The chauffeur scanned the dimly lit street. She'd taken off before he realized she'd even left the car. "I could go and look for her," he offered uncertainly.

"She'll be back," said Fitani, closing his eyes to signal the conversation was over.

George turned to the front. It was the party limo drivers who usually got the weirdo customers. The corporate types he drove tended to be pretty conservative on the whole. Well, these two had hired the car for a full shift and paid in advance, so if they needed to suddenly stop and leap out, who was he to argue? He glanced in the rearview mirror and noticed a blonde girl walking towards them. Darkly dressed, she was holding something light-colored in one hand and on reaching the back door, she opened it and slid in.

"Hope I didn't scare you George."

"Mrs Wiseman!" He was lost for words.

"Did Andy tell you about my little quirk? It's a bit embarrassing. Only my closest friends know about it, but since you'll be driving us all night, I'll have to let you in on my secret."

"No need, Mrs. Wiseman."

"Yes, there is George. I know my behavior can seem, well... odd, and I want to explain. I get anxiety attacks. What helps most when they come on is for me to immediately get away from wherever I am. Changing my look is something else that calms me down. I know it sounds crazy but..." Jo let the sentence drift.

"It's fine," Mrs. Wiseman, the chauffeur assured her. "Thank you for letting me know. I'm happy to pull over whenever you feel an attack coming on."

"Thank you George, and I know you'll keep this confidential."

"Of course Mrs. Wiseman. Discretion is the byword of Chronis Cars. Er, do you still want the tour?"

Jo pictured the Hunter frantically sending out agents out to surround this area. No way she wanted to hang around here. In fact, anywhere this side of the bay seemed too close.

"No, we'll go straight to Geelong," she said.

"My dear," Fitani interrupted. "I must insist we finish our conversation."

"Yes, we must." Jo leant forward. "George, Andy and I need a private word."

"No problem Mrs. Wiseman, do you see the button in the armrest? Just press it to raise the screen partition. If you need to speak to me, press the button again to lower the screen."

"Thank you George."

Jo raised the screen and turned to Danny. "I do want you to finish telling me about your world, but before that, I'd like to jump to my final question. It's what I asked you at Dandenong station this afternoon. How is it that two major competing detective agencies are both working together for the Hunter?"

"An easy one." Fitani's old grin returned. "Your Hunter realized employing a single agency couldn't work for long. The agency would quickly become suspicious if the Hunter was able to give them your coordinates every three hours, and might call off the whole deal. So, it organized a meeting with the heads of two agencies, posing as the representative of a billionaire. This billionaire, the Hunter told them, had a grandson – a baby who had been whisked away against court order, by his son's junkie girlfriend. So desperate was the billionaire to get his grandson back, that he decided to put two agencies onto the job and offer a million-dollar bonus to whichever agency caught her first."

"That can't leave much over for Hunter," said Jo.

Fitani laughed. "Oh I think the Hunter can spare a million dollars, given the prize pot is fifty-million."

Jo's jaw dropped. "Fifty million!"

Fitani brushed the air. "Easy to organize when you can manipulate data the way we can. Your financial institutions have so many holes it's a wonder more people haven't discovered them.

"But I digress. When the Hunter receives your coordinates, it contacts one agency and tells them the other has sighted you in that area. It then does the same thing with the second agency. Both are willing to believe their rival's resources could have tracked down the girl, so they ask no questions and head for that location.

"Should any of the agents catch you they won't harm you, but they *will* hold you for the Hunter, who no doubt has a plan for dispatching you without getting itself on the wrong side of the law."

Jo nodded. She had to admit the Hunter seemed to have worked things out well. But right now she wasn't doing so badly herself. She'd found a way to get some sleep, and as long as she woke every three hours and got clear of the limo before her coordinates were sent, the Hunter wouldn't know how she was relocating. Which reminded her, she needed to set a new alarm!

A five-minute leeway might be safer this time. She set the watch alarm for 1.55 a.m. and noticed Fitani was getting fidgety.

"I'm afraid I won't be able to finish answering your first question right now," he said. "It's almost time to go to my work shift."

"You mean to *finish* your shift. You've been hosting this game for fifteen hours."

Fitani spoke impatiently. "No, no. Hosting isn't work. I'm in Play-Time at the moment. When I contacted you this morning, I'd been in my tube just over five hours. Since then, I've been hosting and running commentary for the viewers, first from my tube and then from the studio Playroom. Now it's nearly time for my shift at the Edge."

"You work at the Edge!" Jo couldn't keep the shock out of her voice.

"Everyone works at the Edge. That's what we're employed for."

"I definitely need to hear the rest of your explanation then, but now you'd better go to your shift. You can finish your answer tomorrow, say 8.30 a.m." She checked her watch and did a quick mental calculation. "That'll give you around five hours of Tube-Time before you return. Wow, I could end up getting more sleep than you. Somehow, knowing that makes me feel a whole lot better."

Danny smiled thinly. "Everyone sacrifices sleep during the game, but it's seldom for more than a day or two."

As Jo swallowed, he continued. "There's no rule covering this situation, but it feels against the spirit of *Play or Die* for *Prey* to be setting my appearance schedule. On the other hand this is the first time I haven't been able to answer all three questions in a single visit."

"Perhaps you should consult your viewers." Having said it, Jo was not sure how wise that suggestion had been.

"I will." Danny tilted his head and his hologram froze. Half a minute later it reanimated.

"There are two schools of thought," he reported. "Some feel that as I failed to answer all questions in a single visit, the prerogative of choosing a time to complete my answer should be yours. Others see your stalling behavior on several occasions as contributing to my running out of time, and believe *I* should retain the choice of when to return.

"A vote has been organized and the results are... now in. You will be pleased to know your camp had the majority. *Play or Die* is moving in new directions, but viewer ratings have never been higher, so I bow to the viewers' decision. I will return at 8.30 a.m."

"You can't just vanish from a moving car," said Jo quickly. "It would be impossible to explain. Let me get George to pull over before you disappear."

"You now want to control when I leave?"

"I'm just trying to keep things sporting," Jo appealed. "If you scare the chauffeur, he could end up calling the police or abandoning me the next time I get out of the car. You'd be giving the Hunter an unfair advantage."

Danny narrowed his eyes. "Very well," he agreed.

Jo heaved a sigh and lowered the screen. "George, that service station coming up – could you pull into it? Andy and I need a chocolate fix."

The driver grinned into the rearview mirror. "No worries, Mrs. Wiseman."

He swung into the service station and parked in a well-lit space near the shop. Then he jumped out to open the back door. Jo smiled up at him, holding eye contact as she uncurled her legs slowly and took her time getting out of the car. Finally standing, she said, "Would you like us to get you something George?"

"That's kind, Mrs. Wiseman, but no thank you."

He closed Jo's door and headed around to Fitani's side, but stopped short on seeing the empty seat. Jo laughed. "When Andy gets a chocolate craving, he waits for no one."

She walked quickly towards the store, calling over her shoulder, "He'll buy up half the stock unless I get in there fast."

Inside, Jo dallied at the candy counter and bought a couple of chocolate bars. As she returned to the car, George, who'd been waiting for her, opened the door.

"I can't believe it!" she told him. "Andy just got a call from the office. They need him back for some emergency or other. He's called a taxi for himself. He thinks he can solve whatever the problem is and catch up with us later on. I sure hope so."

"You'll be continuing on to Geelong alone then, Mrs. Wiseman?"

"I have to," she replied, searching for a reason. "I have a delivery to make."

As George eased onto the highway, Jo picked up the laptop. Who could she be delivering to? What places would even be open when they got to Geelong, way over on the western side of the bay? Probably only hotels.

Jo googled "Geelong Accommodation" and found a hotel, which listed among its many amenities, 24-hour front desk.

"Do you know the Mercure Hotel in Geelong, George?"

"Yes, Mrs. Wiseman, big one on Gheringhap Street." ～

"How long to get there?"

"From here, a little over an hour – say 12.30," he estimated.

"That'll be fine."

Jo brought up a map of Geelong. To get as far from my 11:00 p.m. posting as possible, I need to find a place an hour and a half from Geelong.

Ballarat might work. She got Google Maps to plot the route and found the estimated travel time was an hour and twenty-four minutes. Perfect!

On a new page in her notebook, Jo wrote 'Route' at the top and beneath, 2.00 a.m. - Ballarat.

Now for the 5.00 am posting. Which direction should she go – east? Box Hill was an eastern suburb large enough to hide in. She checked the distance. It was only two hours from Ballarat, but further east, the housing dwindled.

What about north then? Shepparton was three hours north of Ballarat, but it was the last place she could go. Her eye fell on Seymour, an hour south of Shepparton, and an idea began to form. Could she trick the Hunter? What would he think if her 5.00 a.m. coordinates put her in Seymour?

Get into his shoes, Jo thought. Okay, here I am, the Hunter. I'm nasty and I'm arrogant. Arrogant? Yes. Other people's lives mean nothing to me. I see myself as superior. I'm chasing a farm girl, just out of school and barely recovered from her father's death – an easy target. She's confused and alone. She may know it's not smart to go home, but she's terrified. Her friends are home – maybe she thinks someone there can help. She decides to risk the trip under the cover of dark.

Yes, Jo decided. He'll be thinking that way. When he gets my coordinates at Seymour he'll predict I'm running home and will send agents to Shepparton to catch me. Meanwhile, I'll be heading in the opposite direction, back to Melbourne. Thrilled at how well this was turning out, Jo added '5.00 a.m. Seymour' to her route list.

Now for the 8.00 a.m. posting. She studied the southern suburbs and rejected those on the western side of the bay – too small and spread apart. The east side had bigger towns for hiding. What about Frankston? She checked its distance from Seymour – only two hours. Dromana was further south by half an hour and that was far enough since peak morning traffic was bound to slow them down. She wrote '8:00 a.m. Dromana'.

At 8.30, Fitani would be showing up to finish his explanation, so by then she needed to be away from Dromana and in a busy area. Jo zoomed the map and found a large nearby suburb – Mornington. Great, there should be plenty of breakfast cafes. She could eat while Fitani talked. She added it to her list.

Now Jo found herself yawning widely and badly wanting to close her eyes, but she'd learnt her lesson from the watch alarm. Prepare as much as you can when you have the opportunity.

Okay, she thought wearily, allowing around forty-five minutes for breakfast with Fitani brings me to nine-fifteen. I've leased the car until ten. Where do I want to be when I wave it good-bye? I'll need to change my look again, so I should head to a large shopping center with lots of people for camouflage and plenty of buses to make a quick getaway after the eleven o'clock posting. Frankston was the obvious choice.

She typed 'Frankston shopping' into the search field and got 'Bayside Shopping Centre' as the first hit. Street view confirmed it was a big one. Jo wrote '10.00 a.m. Bayside Shopping Centre' and flopped back with a sigh.

Her route was planned. If all went well, she'd be rested, fed, re-outfitted and on her way by 11.00 am. But on her way where? Her daylight aim, she recalled was not just to stay out of the Hunter's clutches, but to investigate her father's murder.

Jo became aware that the light level outside the car had increased while the limo's speed had decreased. The lighting was coming from the motels, streets and houses of Geelong's outer suburbs. She stretched and sighing, closed the laptop. After this stop she was going to get some sleep. There was only so much preparation a person could do.

CHAPTER 16

Five minutes later they turned into the Mercure Hotel, and Jo hurriedly straightened the collar of her shirt and put on the black wig. George pulled up outside the covered entrance and walked around to open the door for her.

She stepped out, clutching the straw bag. "My delivery should only take a minute or two, George."

"I'll wait here for you, Mrs. Wiseman," he replied, gently closing the door.

Jo entered the hotel and walked across the large, plush foyer towards the front desk. The clerk behind it was engrossed in a book. At his back, a wall of numbered pigeonholes held envelopes or gaped. Some had keys hanging in front. She made note of one without a key and cleared her throat. The clerk's head jerked up and his book slid under the counter. "May I help you?"

Pulling a wrapped chocolate bar from her bag she handed it over. "I'd like to leave this for room one-forty-two. They'll understand," she said with a smile.

The clerk took the offering, examined it briefly and looked beyond her to the waiting limo before placing the chocolate in the cubby.

Jo turned and retraced her steps. George was standing by the car and she supposed he must have seen the transaction. That validated this stop.

As they pulled out, Jo pushed the center armrest up into the cavity behind, opening up the full length of the back seat.

"Next stop, Ballarat," she said. "I'm going to take a nap during the drive."

"Very good Mrs. Wiseman."

Jo put the laptop on the floor and dragged the hoodie from the straw bag to use as a pillow. Then she stretched out and closed her eyes.

One of the diners had a bad cough. The waiters were thumping him on the back but it wasn't helping – the poor man went on coughing.

"Give him a glass of water," Jo kept saying, but no one was listening. The surrounding staff blocked her way so she couldn't get through to pour him a glass herself and the coughing got worse and worse. At last, unable to sustain its shield from reality, the dream broke and Jo opened her eyes upon a coughing George looming over the seat front.

"Sorry Mrs. Wiseman, but we've reached Ballarat."

"Oh."

Jo sat up, groggy and disoriented. She rubbed her eyes and peered at her watch. It was 1.30 am. They'd made good time.

"I've pulled into a service station with an all-night cafe, in case you wanted to use the restrooms."

"Good thinking, George." Jo realized she wanted to do just that. "You should take the opportunity too. Then we'll have a coffee break."

They walked in together and split off to separate restrooms. Now Jo sat in the cubicle with her head in her hands, trying to get her fuzzy brain to clear. What on earth can I convincingly be doing in Ballarat at this time of night? Other than this cafe, probably nothing's open. Think Jo. You've got less than thirty minutes to figure something out!

She flushed the toilet and moved into the wash area, splashing her face and neck to try to shock her brain back into functioning. In the mirror, a tired face stared back at her. Its hollow eyes had nothing to offer. A familiar knot returned to her stomach.

Maybe a cup of tea will help, she thought, without much hope. Jo returned to the main room of empty tables and booths. The sight of her driver, standing alone in the middle, snapped her back to the moment.

"How do you take your coffee George?"

"Strong black with sugar, Mrs. Wiseman."

"Okay, you find us a table," she said with a wry smile. "I'll do the ordering."

"As you like Mrs. Wiseman."

Jo headed to the counter. Behind it a large woman with greying auburn hair twisted into a bun, eyed her progress.

"Hi," said Jo. "Quiet night."

"Off and on," said the woman. "Around three I usually get a mob of truckers wanting their eggs, bacon and sausage for breakfast."

Jo gave a laugh. "Well, all we want is a strong black coffee with sugar, a cup of tea with milk for me and…" She pointed to a luscious fruit Danish under a glass cover. "That pastry."

"That'll be ten seventy-five," said the woman, and Jo handed her a twenty dollar bill. Waiting for the change she said casually, "I guess you're the only place open in Ballarat at this time of night."

The woman rang up the cash register. "I think the McDonalds has a 24-hour drive-through, but if you're wanting to sit down, we're it," she agreed.

Damn! The night outside was pitch dark. Where on earth could she tell George to go that would seem legitimate?

"I don't suppose you have a Mercure Hotel here do you?"

The woman handed Jo the change. "Sure, do. It's the resort and convention center opposite Sovereign Hill. Now you go sit down dear, and I'll bring your order over."

Saved! Jo floated across to where George sat at a window table overlooking the limo. Geelong's Mercure had a twenty-four hour front desk, and being part of the chain, Ballarat's probably did too. A visit to this one would give consistency to her actions. George would be satisfied and it was a much safer place to be for the two o'clock coordinates posting than standing in some dark park or alley.

She took the seat opposite her driver and asked, "Do you know Sovereign Hill, George?"

"The gold rush theme town? Sure Mrs. Wiseman. We passed it on the way here. It's a couple of minutes back down the road."

"Well opposite that is the Ballarat Mercure, our next stop. I need to collect something there."

A presence loomed at her shoulder and a cup of hot water with a teabag on the saucer was placed in front of her. A small jug of milk followed. George was given the coffee, and the Danish pastry, sliced in two, was put in the middle of the table.

"Here you go love."

"Thank you."

Jo dropped the teabag into her cup. It was hardly the way to get a decent cup of tea, but right now anything warm and soothing was welcome. "The Danish is for you George. I had a late dinner so I'm not hungry."

"Thanks Mrs. Wiseman." He picked up a slice. "I'm a bit partial to a fruit Danish."

As she sipped her tea, Jo considered the Seymour stop - a small country town. No resort hotels, but they'd arrive well before her 5.00 a.m. coordinates broadcast, which should give her time to work something out.

"Have you been driving limousines long, George?" she asked to break the silence.

"A few years now, Mrs. Wiseman. I'm a part owner of this company. My father-in-law set it up."

"And you're the night-shift man?"

He laughed. "Cassie, my wife, would soon have something to say about it if I was never home in the evenings. No, this is a family business and luckily it's a big family, so we share the night shifts. I do one week in five."

"Do you enjoy the work?"

"I do. I started off driving taxis and eventually bought a taxicab licence with two friends. It wasn't cheap. Back then we each put in eighty thousand dollars. On top of that we had to buy the car."

Jo choked on her tea. "Two hundred and forty thousand dollars for a licence!"

George smiled. "You can't operate taxis in Victoria without one. The government only allows a certain number to be in circulation, so you have to wait till a licence comes up for sale and bid for it, like buying real estate. The current going rate is close to five hundred thousand dollars."

"Wow!" Jo remembered Bruce's words. "So all owner-drivers have made that huge investment?"

"That's right, and believe me, even as an owner-driver it's a hard way to make a living. When Cassie and I got engaged, I sold my share of the taxi business and bought into her family's limousine company."

George polished off the last of the Danish and Jo checked her watch — about seven minutes until the two o'clock posting.

"Have you ever been to Seymour George?"

"Can't say I have Mrs. Wiseman. It's somewhere north isn't it?"

"Yes, on the way to Shepparton, about two and a half hours from here. That's our next stop after the Mercure."

"I'll look it up while you're in the hotel," he said, and they both stood.

Back in the car Jo retrieved her blonde wig and used the driving time to put it on and comb out the worst of the tangles. As they drew up to the entrance, her watch beeped. Five minutes to go. She turned off the alarm and immediately reset it to five minutes before five.

"This could take a few minutes," she said. "You can wait in one of those parking spots over at the side."

Should the hotel not have a twenty-four hour desk, Jo didn't want him to see her locked out. She opened her own door and waved him back. "You check the map George. I'll see you soon."

When the glass entrance doors slid open at her approach, Jo breathed a sigh of relief and stepped into the brightly lit foyer. The front desk was unattended and as the doors closed behind her, quiet descended. This is great, she thought. All I have to do is hang around here until a couple of minutes after two and then bring something back with me to the car, so it looks like I got what I came for.

A rack of brochures stood on the desk and Jo tiptoed over and carefully extracted one, taking care not to bump the little brass bell beside it. The glossy pictures portrayed single-level, resort-style accommodation with beautifully laid out conference rooms around a tranquil lake and garden setting.

She glanced at her watch. One minute till the broadcast. An inner door opened and a giant emerged. Closer to seven than six feet tall, he had a broad chest and square jaw. A blond crew cut and neutral expression completed a look more bouncer than hotel clerk. Jo guessed that on the graveyard shift he might have to act as both.

"Can I help you?" he said, making it sound like, "What are you doing here?"

Feeling like a naughty schoolgirl, Jo caught herself flinching, and quickly straightened.

"Yes you can. I'm glad this stop wasn't wasted. We were passing through Ballarat when I remembered a friend recommended this resort to me. I asked my driver to stop so I could get some information. I've been looking at your brochure," she said, holding it up. "But it doesn't have any prices."

The bouncer/clerk moved behind the desk and reached down, pulling out a white printed sheet.

"This lists our room types and prices across the year," he said, a little more graciously.

"And your restaurant?" Jo asked, taking the price list.

He rotated the brochure rack and extracted a glossy card, which he handed to Jo. "We have two quality restaurants madam."

Jo noticed that the brochure described them as "inspired". It displayed samples of artily arranged dishes.

"We also," he said, warming to his subject, "have a day spa, gym, squash and tennis courts, and a heated outdoor swimming pool."

"Sounds great."

Jo fanned out the brochures she was holding. "Would you have an envelope for these?"

When the clerk bent beneath the desk she risked a glance at her watch. Exactly 2.00 a.m. She needed to keep him occupied for another couple of minutes to be on the safe side. As he surfaced with a large envelope Jo took it saying, "Just a couple more things I need to check. Internet access?"

"We have wired access in our guest rooms and wifi to cover our conference rooms."

"Do you have non-smoking rooms?" She fed the brochures into the envelope, starting to feel desperate. What else could she ask?

"All of our rooms are non-smoking."

"And times for checking in and out?" Jo feared she was losing credibility with these silly questions, which were no doubt covered in the brochures.

"Guests may check in anytime after 2.00 p.m. Checkout is normally at 10.00 a.m. but can be extended with additional payment."

"Ah, that's good to know."

A new avenue for questioning popped into her mind. "I guess a lot of your guests visit Sovereign Hill?"

"Yes, many families come for that reason," the giant replied, now quite amiably. "We offer package deals that include entry to Sovereign Hill and access to activities over there. Other nearby attractions are also available – an 18-hole golf course, bicycle trails and so on."

"Wonderful," said Jo enthusiastically. "Thank you for your help."

"You're welcome madam."

She turned and walked leisurely to the doors, which parted silently for her. A glance at her watch showed 2.02 a.m. Spot on. Jo hopped into the car, flashing the envelope so her driver would notice she had indeed collected an item at the hotel.

"Have you worked out a route for us George?"

"I have Mrs. Wiseman. It's pretty straightforward."

"Okay, well I'm going back to napping while you drive. We'll arrive well before my meeting, so I suggest you find another service station with a restaurant and have some breakfast. Leave me asleep in the car. I have a watch alarm, so I'll wake up in time."

"I'm not sure I like to leave you alone in the car Mrs. Wiseman," George objected.

"You can open the windows a crack and lock the doors. I'll be fine, and you'll need a break by the time we get there. I insist."

"Very well Mrs. Wiseman, you're the boss."

Jo stretched out on the back seat but this time sleep did not come instantly and she wondered, as the Lexus rocked her gently, what the Hunter would be making of her extreme location changes. Again, she tried to put herself in his shoes.

He would have been expecting to catch her in Brighton at eleven o'clock. Instead her coordinates had placed her near the city. He probably assumed she'd slipped through his net by hitchhiking, since her 11.00 p.m. photo showed her on foot, and his agents would now be spread around the area of those coordinates. Having just learnt she was in Ballarat, he'd be madly contacting them with new instructions.

Jo smiled grimly. What would he have thought when her 2.00 a.m. coordinates put her in Ballarat? That she'd struck it lucky and managed to hitch a ride this far? That she'd hired a car? Would he think of a limo service? Perhaps. In any case, he'd be nervous about sending all his agents up to Ballarat. It would take them at least an hour and a half, and by the time they arrived she could have moved on to anywhere – further north to Bendigo, west to Horsham or even back down to Melbourne again.

What he *might* do, she realized, is send them to watch all the main roads out of Ballarat, but they'd be looking for a woman – either driving a rental car or as a passenger in a vehicle she'd hitched a ride in. Even at this time of night plenty of cars were travelling the main highways, and nothing about the black Lexus stood out particularly. It was the kind of car successful businessmen drove, and if any agents looked through its windows, that's what they'd see – a lone male driver. As long as she lay out of sight on the back seat, she'd be safe. Satisfied, Jo allowed sleep to retake her.

The sharp beeping shocked her. I must have set the alarm wrong, she thought, squinting blearily at the dial, but the illuminated numbers said 4.55 a.m. Jo pressed the button to silence the beeping and in the absolute stillness that followed, realized they were in Seymour. The car was no longer moving and she was alone. Warmth was something else that had departed.

CHAPTER 17

Angela Karpin snapped her fingers. The musical alarm turned off and she moaned, wishing she'd got more sleep. Of the nine hours she'd been in her tube, the first four had been spent captivated by Jo and the Hunter. After that she'd tossed sleeplessly with Jo's words about The Company dancing in her head. Why *had* The Company stayed underground for so long after the Great Destruction? Had the Arising been heroic or opportunistic? Though ashamed of these thoughts, she couldn't stop them bubbling up and in the end had managed only four hours of sleep. Now in the three hours of Tube-Time remaining, she had to catch up with her children before they went to their Playrooms, and review what she'd missed of the game.

Because Sandra, just turned two, and Ben nearly five, were too young for the work cycle, they alternated between shorter, more frequent tube and play cycles. That made it tricky to organize time with them. Right now they were both near the end of a tube cycle, so she put through a group call.

"Hi Mummy." Ben was already wide-awake and doubtless eager for Play-Time to start. He enjoyed working on the challenges in the learning Playrooms and earning Children's Personal Points. These could be used to buy treats, holo-clothing, tube games, and access to some exciting Playrooms. Ben cared nothing for holo-clothing, but he loved his tube games and the sports Playrooms, so he strove hard to earn points.

"Hi Darling, what are you doing today?"

"First I'm collecting Sandy. We're going to have breakfast together in the alphabet food Playroom. She loves doing the *Awful Ancestor* jigsaw puzzles while we eat. After that I'm going to the junior construction Playroom to have another go at the bridge challenge. If I get it, I'll have enough Points for the rock-climbing Playroom."

"Mummy!" cried Sandra, rubbing sleepy eyes and appearing on the split screen.

"Hello Sweety." "Hi Sandy!" Mother and son spoke in unison.

"Hey Benny." She flashed her brother a smile before turning back to her mother. "When can I hug you Mummy?"

"Today my darling, I hope. I'm going to try get over to your Playrooms during my Play-Time to give you both a big hug!"

They all blew kisses at each other and then the children's tube doors opened and they scampered out.

Angela's lips trembled as she closed the connection. Sandra had only recently turned two, the age at which children stopped sharing their mother's sleeping tubes and began living full time in the children's silo. Her daughter seemed to be adjusting well, but she herself was finding the wrench hard. Still, she should be able to see her children today, unless the Prey was still alive and kicking and *Play or Die* started getting frantic.

If she didn't make it to their Playrooms, the children would at least get a visit from Collis. He was so good with them. Angela closed her eyes. She missed Collis. Everyone knew it was a big mistake to choose a partner on a different cycle from yours unless you were just after a quickie in one of the fantasy Playrooms. But when you knew that person was *the one*, what could you do? She'd been in her first hour of Play-Time when she'd met Collis and he'd been in his fifth. It meant their times together were intense but always brief.

Sometimes Angela would lie in her tube with tears of regret streaming down her cheeks, but she'd never wanted anyone except Collis, so they got together as often as possible during the three-hour overlap in their Play-Time cycles. Collis was a wonderful father and the children adored him. For them, at this time in their lives, it was better their parents weren't on the same cycle, since at least one of their parents was able to visit them on a daily basis.

She sighed and opened her eyes. No time for self-pity, she thought. *Play or Die* needs you. With a gesture she called up the Hunt screen and began scanning the archived files of the action she'd missed, starting with the most recent event. She was a little surprised to see that Jo had survived the night and was now waking up from her own sleep in the back of a car. This Prey was more resilient than she looked.

CHAPTER 18

Jo sat up. On either side of her were empty parking spaces. Ahead was a paddock of some kind. She twisted around and peered through the back window. Petrol pumps stood under the yellow and orange roof of a Shell service station. A couple of buildings behind them must be a garage and the cafe, where George would be eating breakfast. He'd be annoyed that the parking area at this end of the service station was out of view.

Shivering, Jo zipped her jacket, straightened the blonde wig and scooped up her bag. She needed to get her bearings. Quietly she opened the door, climbed out and closed it with a gentle clunk.

She walked to the divided road and recognized it instantly. When it ran through Seymour, it was called Emily Street, but it was in fact the Goulburn Valley Highway. Followed north for an hour, it would take you to Shepparton. They were on the wrong side for heading north – George must have turned around, but that was fine. She had no intention of going to Shepparton. On the other hand, Jo wanted the Hunter to think she did.

She jogged to the median strip dividing the road and then across to the other side. In the pool of light under a streetlamp, she checked her watch. One minute to five. The Hunter needed to see a frightened young girl. She tightened her face into a pinched look and took up a typical hitchhiker's stand, her thumb pointing towards Shepparton.

Holding that pose for a minute turned out to be harder than she'd expected. Her leaden arm swore that two minutes had gone by, but her counting said it had only been thirty seconds. A container truck came lumbering along the road towards her. Was it slowing?

Oh God, don't *stop* for me, she thought. Keep going. Isn't it illegal for truckers to pick up hitchhikers?

There was no longer any doubt the truck was pulling up. As it drew level, the driver leaned across and opened the passenger door. In the light of the streetlamp Jo noticed his eyes were red and sunken. Lack of sleep, Bennies, or both? One side of his mouth lifted in a leer.

"Hop in beautiful."

"Are you going to Melbourne?" Jo asked innocently.

"What? You silly bitch, you're standing on the wrong side of the highway!" He pulled the door closed and accelerated, leaving her in a cloud of dust.

Jo watched his taillights receding and checked the time – 5.02 a.m. Maybe that encounter had been lucky after all. If they'd taken her photo while she was talking to the truck driver, the Hunter would be telling his agents to watch trucks coming into Shep. On the other hand if the photo had simply shown her hitchhiking on the highway, and if the Hunter already had agents waiting in Shepparton in case she headed home, he'd be sending them down the road right now to pick her up!

Jo turned and ran back across the road to the cafe. Inside a few customers were tucking into breakfasts but George, she saw with relief, seemed to have finished his and was draining the last of his coffee. As she made her way over he looked up and raised a hand in greeting.

"Hi George," she said, a little breathlessly, "I've just had a phone call from Andy. My meeting here has been cancelled and relocated to Dromana, for would you believe, 8.00 a.m. Do you think you can get me there in time?"

Her driver looked taken aback but rallied quickly. "I'll do my best, Mrs. Wiseman. I just need to settle up here…"

"Please," she picked up the bill on his table. "It's on me."

George protested, but didn't reach for his wallet. She smiled, glad of the opportunity to keep him happy.

Two minutes later they were heading for Melbourne, with Jo again down low on the back seat. Though the Hunter's agents would probably be concentrating on vehicles heading *towards* Shep rather than away from it, she'd be crazy to take any chances.

She set her next alarm for 7.55 a.m. and lay thinking about her father and the two names she'd been given. She should begin by googling them, but the warmth, darkness and gentle rocking of the car were making her eyelids heavy and the thought of retrieving the laptop and starting it up seemed too great an effort. Jo slept.

Sunlight on her face woke her, and rising, she saw they were travelling on a busy highway with the traffic flowing well. Her watch read 7.15 a.m. and Jo did a quick calculation. She'd had six good hours of sleep over the night and she'd needed it. Reinvigorated, she dived for the laptop and as it started up, George's eyes flicked to his rearview mirror.

"Good morning George."

"Morning Mrs. Wiseman, did you have a good rest?"

She smiled. "I did. I'm feeling human again. Are we on track for Dromana?"

"If the traffic's not too heavy through Frankston, we should make it in time."

"Great. I'll let you concentrate on the driving then, while I do some work on the computer."

In the search window of the browser Jo typed, 'Morris Blatman', the man who'd been hired to kill her father, and got a couple of thousand hits, but some of those were just Morris or just Blatman. She did the search again, this time enclosing the name in quotation marks. Now she got six results, only two being actual people, both deceased Americans. Well, she hadn't really expected to find a hit man on the Internet, but she'd had to give it a try.

Perhaps she'd be luckier when it came to the hirer, but no. Simon Brooks, even in quotation marks, gave her over twenty-five thousand results. She narrowed the search to Australia only, which reduced the list to three hundred and sixty-seven. These included writers, politicians, teachers and scientists. None of their occupations or interests seemed to have any connection to her father.

Was that *it* then? Was she stuck? Neither of the Hunter's detective agencies will be giving *me* a job anytime soon, she thought. What about the phone book? She brought up the *Australian White Pages* and selecting 'Victoria', tried 'S Brooks' followed by 'M Blatman'. She got a hundred entries for S Brooks, but just one for M Blatman.

Jo wrote down the address and phone number and chewed her pen. Now what? Call the number and ask for Morris? What if a Morris answered? Having the same name didn't necessarily make him the hit man. In fact, what self-respecting hit man would have a phone number under his real name? Still, she'd have to investigate further, follow him and find out where he worked – *if* he worked, all the while, dodging the Hunter's agents. And if this guy turned out to *be* the hit man and realized she was onto him, she'd have another hunter coming after her – a professional. Jo swallowed. Concentrating on S Brooks might be easier. At least it would be if there weren't a hundred of them!

She sighed. What she needed was a tangible lead and the best place to find it, Jo reluctantly admitted to herself, was back home. Her father had a filing cabinet full of correspondence and if she could find a Simon Brooks amongst it, she'd have her man.

But wasn't going home tantamount to madness? Even after the horde of agents sent there last night had departed, the Hunter would surely leave one or two behind, just in case. And by now he probably had her house alarmed and booby-trapped.

If she *won* the game, she'd be able to go home and check out Dad's papers in complete safety. Perhaps she should just put all her efforts into avoiding the Hunter for the next four days.

Jo considered what those days would be like – always worrying about how close her trackers were getting, and constantly running and hiding, all the while alternating between varying states of terror. If the Hunter didn't get her in that time, insanity probably would.

And what if after all that, she didn't survive? Fitani had said her chances were minimal. If the Hunter did 'bag' her in the next four days, then she *and* her father would be dead and their murderers would have gotten away with it. But if she could find proof of Dad's murder before the Hunter got to her, at least *someone* would pay a price!

At a deeper level Jo also knew that conducting her own hunt would help to distract her from the terror of being hunted, and give her back some feeling of control. She did not care to be cast in the role of victim.

I might be forced to play this game, she thought, but I won't let it divert me from finding Dad's killer. And while the game's on, I have access to Fitani. Who knows what useful information or technical support he can give me?

Her doubts settled, Jo turned her mind to getting hold of her father's papers. The trouble with travelling to Shepparton, whether by bus, train or car, was that the trip took from two to two and a half hours. That didn't leave enough time to find a way of sneaking into the house and getting the papers before the Hunter learnt she was in Shepparton. Approaching gradually wouldn't work either. Any coordinates posting that placed her within an hour of Shepparton would send up warning flags. If only she had a teleportation machine, she could jump straight into her house, grab the papers and be away before the Hunter was even aware she'd arrived.

Jo's eyes widened. She could do it. Not with a teleportation machine, but the next best thing. Shepparton had a small airport – not large enough for commercial aircraft, but commercial aircraft weren't an option anyway. They flew out of Tullamarine, Melbourne's main airport and the Hunter was bound to have agents there. But Shep's airport was designed for little planes and little planes flew out of training airports.

One of her friends, Jack Hudson, a year above her in school, had been mad about planes. He'd taken weekend lessons on a Piper Cherokee and at the tender age of sixteen had gained his Private Pilot's Licence. His mum used to take him to the airport when he wanted to go flying, because in Victoria, though you can get your pilot's licence at sixteen, you have to be eighteen to drive.

Jack had his sights set on a Commercial Pilot's Licence and needed to build up flying hours, which wasn't easy. Hiring a plane, even the tiny single engine variety, was expensive. Consequently he was always trying to get friends to go flying with him to share the cost. She'd once gone along despite her mother's panic, when he'd flown a group of them to Swan Hill for a picnic. They'd chatted about the places he flown to in building his flying hours and he'd mentioned Moorabbin in Melbourne.

Jo did a search and discovered Moorabbin did indeed have a small airport, which boasted a host of flying clubs. Surely she'd find young pilots like Jack, keen to build up their hours, who'd jump at the chance of flying to Shep if she offered to cover the cost.

To Jo's delight Moorabbin Airport was near Cheltenham station, just eleven stops, according to Metlink's online map, from Frankston. Well that answered the question of where she'd be heading after her 11.00 a.m. coordinates posting. A sudden beeping reminded her that only five minutes remained until *this* posting. Almost simultaneously, George spoke to the rearview mirror.

"We're here, Mrs. Wiseman. The Frankston traffic slowed us down a bit, but we made good time once we were through it."

Jo looked out of the window. It was a beautiful winter's morning. On her right the ocean sparkled under a clear blue sky. On her left the shops and cafes of the seaside town were opening their doors onto a new day. She grabbed her bag and put on the blonde wig.

"Well done, George. Right on time."

Ahead she spotted a cafe and said, "My meeting's at Cafe Jett, which is coming up. You can let me out here and then head to that parking area by the jetty. I'll join you in about ten minutes and we'll go straight onto Mornington and meet Andy for breakfast."

"Okay, Mrs. Wiseman." He briefly double-parked to let her jump out and then nosed the car back into the traffic.

Jo entered the cafe and headed for the restrooms, where she took some time to wash up, brush her teeth and make herself presentable. She was pleased to see the face in the mirror had regained its old confidence.

When the waitress delivered a frothy cappuccino to her table at one minute to eight, Jo sipped it in satisfaction. Soon the Hunter would be receiving another nasty shock. She'd love to be a fly on the wall when he discovered that far from having her cornered in Shepparton, he'd once again let her slip through his fingers. She wondered how many agents he'd mobilized to Shep on receiving her Seymour coordinates. They would not be thrilled to learn the lead had been false and that she was actually in Dromana. By the time she *did* get to Shep, this afternoon she hoped, if things went well, the agents would all be back down here.

The numbers on her watch changed to 8.00 a.m. and realizing she'd come through her first twenty-four hours with flying colors, Jo was unable to resist smiling and raising her cup in a mock salute.

In the two minutes that followed, she set a new alarm for 10.58 and finished her coffee. Then she paid at the register by the door and strolled out into the winter sunlight. Crossing the road, Jo spied the Lexus standing apart from the few other cars using the jetty parking. Her driver however, was nowhere in sight.

She ran to the car and tried the doors. Locked. In panic she scanned the area for George's solid build. At the end of the jetty a few fishermen sat idly behind their motionless, ocean-pointing rods. On the sand, seagulls preened then scattered at the approach of a gamboling Labrador pup trailed by its elderly owner, and in the nearby picnic area a couple of young mothers sat chatting while their preschoolers played on the climbing equipment. There was no sign of George.

Don't be silly, Jo told herself. He'd hardly abandon his car. He must have gone to stretch his legs or... she spied a public toilet block, to relieve himself.

Suddenly she felt horribly exposed. In the almost empty car park she was visible from every direction. She ran to the ocean side of the car and crouched, dragging off the blonde wig. The black one was in her bag, and she put it on. Where to change the rest of her clothes? The toilet block, on the other side of the picnic area, was the obvious place. She sprang towards it.

Drawing close, she spotted an opening with a female symbol and slipped inside. The dim interior had a dank, old concrete smell. A series of toilet cubicles lined one wall, with shower stalls opposite. Jo locked herself into a shower stall and dropped her bag onto the knee-high shelf. She rummaged through and found the track pants. The hoodie, she now remembered, was on the back seat of the Lexus, where she'd used it for a pillow. Well, beggars couldn't be choosers. Stripping off her jeans, she pulled on the track pants and beige shirt. It was horribly creased, but it covered the money belt and blended somewhat with the grey pants.

As she thrust the black shirt and jacket into the bag, Jo sneezed. The thin beige shirt provided no protection from the cold morning air. If George didn't return soon she'd freeze to death.

In the doorway she stood squinting towards the jetty parking area. The morning sun was in her eyes but she spotted George leaning against the front door of the car. Relief projected her forward but two steps out she realized something was wrong. Would George slouch in such an unprofessional way? The slanting rays were making her eyes water but the person by the car now also seemed too slender.

Jo pulled up, turned sharply, and ran to the beach wall, where a set of stone steps led to the sand below. Keeping close to the wall, she covered the distance back as quickly as her sinking feet allowed.

At the barnacle-encrusted piers, more stone steps led up to the car park. By standing on the bottom one, Jo could just see over the wall. The sight made her freeze. The man leaning against the car was most definitely *not*

George. He was younger, slimmer and had not a hair on his head. George, she could now see, was sitting in the car, talking to the man through the open window. As she watched, the leaning man straightened and began slowly and carefully scanning the surrounds. She dropped, her back pressed to the wall and her heart pounding.

Agents should *not* have had time to get here yet – it was only ten past eight. Maybe one of the agencies already had someone in the area, working on another case and they'd lucked-out. Was this guy by himself? What had George told him?

She considered taking off on foot, but a tiny seaside town like Dromana would be easy to contain. No, she had to get out of here quickly before reinforcements arrived. Jo returned to the bottom step and peered over the wall in time to see the agent swiftly crossing the road and turning left to traverse the shops and cafes.

Keeping low, she crept up the steps and then headed for the car in a crouching run. As she opened the back door, the driver jumped and twisted around.

"Mrs. Wiseman," he exclaimed, and then quickly, "I think we should leave straight away. And it might be prudent if you were to take another 'nap' while we drive."

These were not the words of someone who'd changed loyalties, and Jo gladly clambered in, closing the door and stretching out along the back seat. George pulled smoothly out of the car park and turned left onto the beach road, continuing towards the freeway turnoff. Jo meanwhile retrieved the hoodie and pulled it on, thankful for the additional warmth. Then she spoke into the silence.

"You weren't at the car when I arrived, George, so I went off to change."

"Sorry, Mrs. Wiseman. I thought I'd be back in time." He paused and added, "Soon after I returned to the car, a rather smarmy gentleman approached and showed me a photo of you on his cell phone. He said he was looking for a young blonde woman – a drug addict who had kidnapped a baby."

"George, I can't tell you what's going on, but I swear I'm neither a drug addict nor a kidnapper," she said quietly.

"If I thought you were, we wouldn't be having this conversation," he said. "The young man asked whom I was driving at the moment and I told him I'd just finished taking an elderly couple to their son's place in Dromana, and was now on a break before returning to base."

"You're the perfect chauffeur George!"

"Client satisfaction is our aim, Mrs. Wiseman."

As they hummed along the highway, Jo considered the incident. Had she slipped up somewhere? Perhaps the bulk of the agents weren't in Shepparton at all, but had followed her to Dromana. No, if that were the case they would have hit the cafe within minutes of her coordinates posting, *and* would have arrived in force. George's questioner had been operating alone.

A chilling thought occurred. Could it possibly have been the Hunter himself? Had she been too predictable? She'd made long trips west and north. There were few places east of Seymour to hide. Maybe he guessed she would turn back south. If so, he couldn't have been confident about that prediction. The most likely thing for a panicked eighteen-year-old to do would be to run home, and her postings had indicated she was doing just that.

To play it safe, he would *have* to have sent his agents to cover Shep, but maybe he hadn't gone with them. She'd been trying to put herself into his shoes. He was probably doing the same. If *she* could use Google to measure a three-hour trip south from Seymour, so could he. Maybe he'd headed down this way, anticipating her trick. Even if he'd gone beyond Dromana, or not as far, he'd have been near enough when her coordinates were sent, to get here within minutes. If that's what he'd done, this guy was scarily intuitive.

Jo suddenly realized there was a way to know for sure whether the questioner had been the Hunter – the photo he'd shown George. If it was this morning's photo, it *had* to be him. There hadn't been enough time for him to send that photo to the detective agencies and for them to forward it to their agents. And in any case, the Hunter wouldn't be so stupid as to regularly send updated photos to the two agencies. It was one thing to tell each that the other had a confirmed sighting of her, but providing fresh photos as well would be too suspicious. Operatives who'd gotten close enough to take clear photos, but who had somehow failed to catch her on every such occasion would be too incompetent for belief.

"George, the photo that man showed you, can you describe it?"

The driver considered. "You were sitting at a table, holding up a coffee cup and smiling at someone out-of-shot."

My 8.00 a.m. pose. That man *was* the Hunter. If I'd run straight across from the toilets, I would have jogged right into his arms! Where is he now? Still searching the shops of Dromana, or sitting quietly with a coffee, already predicting my next move?

A wave of dismay washed over Jo, her morning's high spirits crushed by the frightening evidence of her pursuer's ability. Don't get spooked, she told herself. Dad always said every experience teaches you something, so what have I learnt? Well, not to underestimate the Hunter for a start. And now at least I know better what he looks like. I've confirmed he's a male, and bald. George will have got an even closer look.

"George, can you describe the guy who showed you the photo?"

"An unpleasant young man," was the immediate reply. "With a false smile and an air of self-importance."

"Young?" said Jo. "How old would you say?"

"Early twenties, if that. He seemed to assume his charm would be sufficient for me to happily answer all questions. He implied he was working for the law but failed to provide any kind of identification."

More proof it was the Hunter. An agency employee would surely have introduced himself and shown ID, and maybe through such a display of legitimacy, have convinced George that I was a bad one. It seemed the Hunter had done her a service in conducting the questioning himself.

"Go on George."

"He was bald, but shaved not natural, with a shadow indicating he'd have dark hair if he grew it out. He was wearing a suit, but as he walked away, he pulled down on the jacket and I'd swear I saw part of a tattoo on the back of his neck."

"This is great George. Do you remember anything else?"

"Sorry Mrs. Wiseman, his face was ordinary, no distinguishing marks… but I'd say he was slightly shorter than me."

"Thank you George, I'll pass this on to Andy. He'll know what to do."

"Speaking of which, we're close to Mornington. Where will you be meeting Mr Wiseman?"

"At a cafe, but I've forgotten the address. I'll look it up as you drive."

Moving awkwardly from her horizontal position, Jo opened the laptop and accessed the online Yellow Pages. A large number of cafes were listed in Mornington, most of them in Main Street. Good, she thought. That means a lot of people. She picked one at random and said, "31 Main Street, George. The cafe's called Avocado Blue."

"I know Main Street, Mrs. Wiseman. We're not far from it now."

Jo checked her watch. 8.25. Unless they arrived in the next couple of minutes, she'd have to tell George to pull over. It would be trying his tolerance too far if Fitani suddenly appeared in the car.

"Mrs. Wiseman," George spoke cautiously, "I don't want to alarm you, but a silver Ford Falcon has followed us off the freeway into Mornington."

Jo drew a quick breath and tried to keep her voice calm. "Where is it now?"

"Three cars behind us."

"Okay, change of plan. Turn into the next busy street and let me out. Then drive around for a while. Park in a public place and do some shopping if you like or have something to eat. Take your time. I'll find my own way to Avocado Blue and you can meet me there at 9.15."

"Right Mrs. Wiseman. A street's coming up."

Jo pushed the laptop into her straw bag and braced herself as the car turned sharply. It slowed and she rested her fingers on the handle. As they came to a stop, she flipped open the door, leapt out between two parked cars, and threw the door closed. There was a fruit shop in front of her and Jo ran a good way into it before turning to view the street from the cover of a stand of oranges. The Lexus was already out of sight.

About ten seconds later the silver Falcon came gliding by. She made out its single driver, bald, before the car passed from view. The Hunter! Why had he decided to follow George? Another intuitive leap?

Jo went cold. The hoodie. If the Hunter had seen it in the back seat, he'd have known George was lying about having finished his assignment. He'd certainly have got one of his agencies to find out which limo company the Lexus belonged to and who had recently hired it. She'd learnt not to underestimate the Hunter. The married couple story wouldn't have fooled him once he'd heard the pickup had been from a hotel in Brighton last night.

So what was he planning now? He couldn't grab George for questioning without involving the police, which he'd no doubt prefer to avoid. Would he send agents after the Lexus? He wouldn't have many to send. Most would still be travelling down from Shepparton.

Then what would he do? Since his Prey wasn't in the Lexus, and the last broadcast had put her in Dromana, he'd probably use whatever agents he had down here to block the exits out of Dromana. Meanwhile, he'd follow the Lexus himself to make sure the driver really *was* returning to base and not about to double-back and pick up the Prey.

Damn! Jo bit her lip. She hadn't wanted to leave the limo this soon and she hated the idea of failing to meet George after all his loyalty. Nor did she want to get him into trouble over the loss of the laptop.

But George was a smart guy. He'd now be watching for a tail and he wouldn't lead the Hunter to her if he could help it. Not sure about the wisdom of her decision, Jo decided that she *would* meet George at Avocado Blue, at the very least to return the laptop and learn what had happened after he'd dropped her off. If he'd managed to throw the Hunter off his tail, she might even be able to risk going a little further with him.

Jo tore a plastic bag from the roll on a nearby stand and dropped in the orange she'd been clenching in a bruising grip. Adding a couple more, she made her way to the cash register.

As the young Asian checkout girl placed her bag on the scales, Jo asked, "Where's Main Street from here?"

The girl pointed. "Three down."

"Thanks." Jo handed over a note and received some coins in change. As she stepped from the shop a gorgeous display caught her eye. Joseph's famous coat had been made from the feathers of a peahen compared to *this* shimmering creation. The migraine-inducing blouse was accompanied by a pair of pantaloons, which, embroidered from top to bottom with the usual gold logo, provided a positively dull relief.

"Good morning my dear. How nail-biting *that* little escape just was!"

Jo answered calmly. "Yes, but at least I now know that the man who questioned my chauffeur is the Hunter."

Fitani grinned. "Naturally I can neither confirm nor deny it, but I'd be interested in hearing why you think so."

"A number of reasons, but the clincher was the photo," she said. "The odds were just too small that anyone other than the Hunter would have had my most up-to-date photo at the time he showed it to my driver.

"I see," said Fitani. "In any case, I'm glad *you're* still beating the odds."

"*Are* you?" Jo's tone was dry. "Perhaps you've wagered a few Personal Points on my progress?"

Fitani chuckled. "Our audience does love Prey with a sense of humor. However, you haven't yet *quite* achieved your next thousand points, so I can't answer the questions you've just asked. What I can and *will* do is finish answering your question about my world and my people. It's why I returned if you'll recall."

"I'm listening," said Jo, striding down the street.

The host kept up without effort.

CHAPTER 19

"I believe I was about to describe Play-Time. Play-Time is when the people of my world spread their wings and live life to the full."

Jo crossed the first street and then turned to Fitani. "Hard to imagine a bit of gym equipment and a few fairground rides providing so much satisfaction."

"Wha..." Fitani spluttered and then laughed. "Ah, you're teasing me. You've guessed Play-Time is much more than that. True, we have a variety of exercise Playrooms – a fit employee is a happy employee, but exercise and fairground rides, as you call them, form only a miniscule part of the options available to us.

"The majority of Playrooms are dedicated to particular activities, but there are also *blank* Playrooms, which can be rented from The Company and used for anything the renter cares to do. Blanks are expensive, so usually only a group, pooling their Personal Points can rent one – and then not for more than a day or two. However, if the group uses the blank Playroom for an activity that *brings in* Personal Points, extended renting becomes possible. I, in concert with some others, have been renting the same blank Playroom now for over three years!"

Fitani waited, obviously expecting some kind of congratulatory remark.

"I'm scared to think what activity you've devised that pays your exorbitant rent."

"What are you talking about?" He said impatiently. "You *know* what it is. We produce and broadcast *Play or Die.*"

Jo frowned. "You mean you've turned your blank Playroom into a television studio? But to do that you'd need expertise in a whole range of areas, *and* you'd require specialized equipment."

"Exactly," Danny agreed. "And where does one acquire expertise and equipment – the Playrooms!"

Jo had now passed the second street and could see the third coming up. This should be Main.

"So you learnt your hosting skills in a Playroom." She tried to make it a statement, but needn't have worried. Fitani, anxious to get his point across, had forgotten about not answering questions she hadn't earned.

"Of course I learnt them in a Playroom. Just as my camera operators and technical crew went to Playrooms to learn their skills."

"But using microwaves to view the past – that discovery would have involved complex science. It couldn't have been made in a Playroom."

"Where else? The research and development Playrooms are popular with our more intellectual employees. In fact, we have many Playrooms devoted to different branches of math and science."

"And the people who use those rooms…"

"Study, experiment and push forward the boundaries of our knowledge." finished Fitani.

Jo felt dazed. "For no reward."

"There are *many* rewards." Fitani began counting them off on his fingers. "The joy of tackling knotty problems with like-minded employees; the satisfaction and kudos of expanding human knowledge; the Personal Points awarded by The Company for significant discoveries or inroads; and for employees whose discoveries are used in some *practical* way, those Points can really begin to roll in.

Take interacting with the past via microwaves. The employees who discovered how to do this received a reward from The Company, but when I and some others, made practical use of the process to create *Play or Die*, the original discoverers continued to gain. Hundreds of thousands of viewers pay Personal Points to watch *Play or Die*. The Company takes eighty percent, but my team receives the rest. We in turn give a percentage to the originators of the process that made the game possible. Everyone wins!"

"The Company, with zero contribution, winning the biggest slice of all," said Jo, turning into Main Street.

"Without the Company none of this would be possible," growled Fitani. "We'd still be running around in the wilderness like savages."

"And now you have no wilderness to run in at all. Your movements are restricted to a few dozen silos, thanks to The Company."

Fitani responded angrily. "We need the clean ground for food production."

"So you say." Jo's voice was mild. "But you showed me a tremendous amount of land under cultivation. You seem to be producing more than the needs of a few hundred thousand people."

Fitani sneered. "What would you know about it?"

"Well, having been in the farming business all my life," said Jo, "I do have *some* understanding of crop yields."

"We don't just supply our *own* Safe Place," Fitani admitted. "We export a large percentage of our crops to Safe Places that specialize in meat, fruit or mineral production and they send a portion of their produce to us. It's more efficient for each Safe Place to devote their land to just one kind of production."

"Is it?" said Jo, spotting Avocado Blue and turning into it. "That approach certainly makes it hard for each Safe Place to know when they're producing enough, and can start devoting some of their land to leisure pursuits."

"You're making it sound as though The Company *wants* to keep us constrained. Nothing could be further from the truth. The Company's great aim is to enable everyone to roam the world again. That's why they employ us to clean the earth."

Jo spied an empty table at the rear of the cafe and checked her watch as she moved towards it. 8.45. She had half an hour to make decent inroads into a meal and was confident as her stomach quietly rumbled that this would be no problem. Taking a seat, she looked up at one of the passing waiters.

"With you in a minute," he called, disappearing through a door at the back and returning a few seconds later with a couple of menus. Jo waved them away and pointed to a laden plate on the next table.

"That's what I'd like. Andy will have a bowl of muesli and we'll both have orange juice and tea."

"No worries." The boy scribbled in his notepad and disappeared through the back door.

"No-man's land," Jo said to Fitani who had taken the seat opposite. "That area of cleaned earth between the fields and the radioactive land. How long did it take to create? And how do you plan to use it?"

The host frowned. "A lot of questions, for one who has none. I shall complete the question I returned to answer and you shall listen."

"I'll try," she said meekly.

"Now, I was telling you about the Playrooms. Our Playroom activities cover every need of a functioning society..."

As Fitani waffled on, the orange juice arrived and Jo drank thirstily. It was freshly squeezed and delicious. She drained her glass and swapped it for Fitani's full one, just ahead of the waiter returning with the tea.

The large pot was placed on the table between them, along with cups, a jug of milk, a strainer, and a container of sugar straws. Jo added milk to the cups while she waited for the tea to steep.

Fitani watched her. "Are you ready to hear how the Playrooms work?"

She stared at him. He actually *wants* to tell me, she realized. For all his complaints, he's proud of his people and their achievements.

"Go ahead," said Jo.

"I'll use a food Playroom to demonstrate," said Fitani. "The same principle applies to all. Now you *might* go into a food Playroom just to eat, in which case you'd enter the dining area, choose a meal, pay the Personal Points, eat and leave. On the other hand, you might go in to play!

"Instead of the dining area, you'd go to the Play-Wall and check out the activities listed. Beside each one is a Personal Point value, a time allocation, a skill-designation and a flashing "A" or "T" for "Available" or "Taken'. You can join any available Play-Activity you're skilled for.

"Skilled? You mean like having an accurate throw for hurling mashed potato in the food-fight game?" Jo said with a straight face.

Fitani glared. "With *Food-1* skills you can take on activities such as: cleaning, chopping ingredients, waiting tables, etc. An hour's scraping and stacking of dishes into the crockery cleaner for example, wins you two Personal Points."

Jo gave an incredulous huff. "Not what *I'd* describe as play."

She placed the strainer on her cup and lifted the teapot, rocking it gently before pouring out the golden liquid.

"Well," admitted Fitani, eyeing the stream, "that particular activity is not everyone's cup of tea, but *some* like it as a way of winning Personal Points and those who don't, choose something else. The higher skilled activities are more interesting and you can take them on after successfully completing training courses from instructional Playrooms.

"Those reaching the highest levels of expertise in any play activity can apply for "Creative Status'. This means they can submit their own ideas to The Company. To continue with the food example, an employee with a skill designation of *Food-10*, would be allowed to submit menu ideas and be supplied with appropriate ingredients. If the dishes proved popular, the employee would win bonus Points."

Jo frowned. "Surely there'd be activities so unpleasant no one would want to do them."

Fitani shook his head. "The Personal Point awards are constantly fine-tuned. If insufficient people are signing up for an activity, it means not enough Points have been allocated to it. Increase them and suddenly employees are clamoring to play."

Before Jo could comment, breakfast arrived, and it was all she had hoped for. On a thick, perfectly toasted slice of sourdough bread sat two plump poached eggs. Beside them lay rashers of bacon, a little hill of seared baby spinach, some miniature mushrooms, two halves of a fried tomato and a spoonful of rich chutney. Jo speared the eggs, spreading their soft yolks over the toast and adding a sprinkle of salt. Then she waded in.

Fitani seemed to be waiting for some kind of appreciative comment.

"It's a wonder employees ever want to leave the Playrooms," said Jo sardonically around a mouthful of toast.

He took her literally. "Employees *can* get caught up in a play activity," he said. "But our halo system solves that. Halos appear around the heads of any employees who are not in the cloaking room at least eight minutes before their work shift. The halo displays a countdown to remind the employee of the time remaining before work. If the countdown drops to five minutes, the halo changes to a black cloud. You're forced to stop your play then, because you can no longer see what you're doing."

Jo sipped her tea, reluctantly fascinated.

"Nearby employees are compelled to action. It's a crime not to assist if you see an employee wearing a black cloud. People guide the wearer down to the cloaking room. With luck they'll be able to don their protective suit and get to their work pick-up point on time."

"Seems a bit over the top," said Jo. "So *what* if they're a few minutes late."

"For each *second* an employee is late, there is a fine of thirty Personal Points – a day's salary, and the late seconds are added to the end of the work shift. It's rare for anyone to be as much as a minute late. Who would want to be fined 1,800 Personal Points and have to check into the prison silo for a tube and a play period? So you see, everyone's grateful to the halo system for ensuring we get to work on time."

Jo goggled. "Let me make sure I've got this straight. If you are one *minute* late for work, you have to make up that minute, you're fined over two months' salary and you have to spend twenty hours in jail."

"Exactly!" Fitani beamed like a teacher pleased with his student's performance. "But," he added seriously, "it's extremely rare for an employee to be as much as a *minute* late. In my Safe Place I think it's only happened once in the past ten years."

"How," declared Jo when she could finally get words out, "was such a law ever passed!"

Fitani seemed bemused at her reaction. "It's not so much a law as a contractual agreement. The Company must have an expectation that employees looked after as well as we are, will fulfill their side of the bargain when it comes to work. After all, we are provided with comfortable housing, well-equipped Playrooms and of course our salaries."

Jo speared a crust with her fork and ran it around her plate to mop up the last of the egg.

"Which you've told me are thirty Personal Points a day. But without knowing the cost of living I don't know if that's good."

"Unfortunately," said Fitani gruffly, "one of the evils from your time that clawed its way through to ours, is taxes. Half the Personal Points we earn are deducted for taxes and most of the rest goes in tube rental and Playroom access. Only a few Personal Points can be saved each week. Not that we need any more," he hastened to add. "Employees can live comfortably on this as long as they don't mind sticking with plain food, a restricted range of holographic clothing and basic, low cost entertainments."

"Sounds a bit depressing."

"Most prefer more than the basics," Fitani admitted. "Fortunately Play-Time gives us the opportunity to win extra Points and indulge in a few luxuries."

Jo rounded up the last of the spinach and chutney and spoke cautiously. "Danny, you must be aware from observing our society, that what your people call *play*, mine call *work*, and we earn a lot more than a few token dollars for our efforts."

Fitani replied tranquilly. "My dear, it's you who are confused by what is no more than a superficial resemblance."

Jo lifted an eyebrow. "Superficial."

The host leant back, smiling. "Would you agree that work is linked to survival?"

Reluctantly drawn in a direction of Fitani's choosing, Jo gave a nod. "I guess so."

"Okay, we have our definition. *Work is something one must do on a continual basis in order to survive.* Would you also agree that most people do not head off to work with joy in their hearts?"

Jo hesitated. "I suppose if they had the choice, most would choose not to work, but many in my world still enjoy their work."

"Perhaps," said Fitani. "But not nearly as many and not nearly to the degree that my people enjoy Play-Time. Even amongst those in your world who are lucky enough to find work in areas that interest them, most will ultimately tire of doing the same thing year after year. The compulsory factor alone in work eventually makes people grow to resent it, not to mention having to endure daily interactions with colleagues or supervisors one would not normally choose to socialize with.

"In Play-Time, nothing's mandatory. People do whatever they wish. There's even a room for just sitting around. That quickly gets boring. Humans want activity – just not the same activity over and over again, although it's true, some of our employees *do* regularly frequent the same Playrooms. Most however, prefer variety.

"If you engage in productive activities you win Personal Points. For non-productive activities, you *pay* Personal Points. Either way the choice is vast and it's amazing when you explore the Playrooms, how many productive activities you can discover, which are interesting, exciting, illuminating and satisfying."

"Along with many which aren't," said Jo.

"You don't have to do the ones that don't appeal. Others will find them interesting, or be happy to take them on for an hour or two to win some Personal Points. Can you see that when it comes to defining work and play, neither the type of activity nor the time one spends on it, is relevant to the definition? The only difference between the two is that play is optional and as varied as the player wishes. Work is mandatory and repetitive.

"Put that way," Jo said, "I guess your Play-Time *isn't* work, which is just as well, since your Work-Time sounds horrible."

"It is," Fitani admitted. "But at least it's short. In your world mandatory, repetitive work consumes eight to twelve hours of the day. Work-Time in my world consumes only four. In your world, those who can't find work must endure a miserable standard of living. In mine, everyone works except the very young and the very old, and everyone is decently fed and housed."

"If things are going so well in your society, I don't understand why you can't forgive and forget when it comes to the people of mine."

Fitani frowned. "You're the one forgetting that your world has deprived us of the most precious thing human beings can have – freedom to roam. We have no weekends or holidays as there's nowhere for us to go. Employees can only visit other Safe Places virtually. The few heavily shielded vehicles that make the dangerous journeys between Safe Places do so for the sole purpose of transporting goods.

"An employee's physical movement is restricted to the silos and the Edge. From that day in our childhood when we realize this, we live our lives with an aching desire to break free of our confines... with nowhere to go."

Jo put her knife and fork together on the empty plate and spoke cautiously. "You know, even from the little I've learnt about your world, I'm starting to doubt that. In fact I'm thinking you may well have reached a stage in your history where change *is* possible."

"What on earth can you mean by that?" said Fitani angrily.

She eyed the bowl of muesli opposite. There may be no opportunity for lunch. Swapping her plate for the cereal bowl, she poured creamy milk over the muesli. Fitani, waiting, grew progressively grimmer and redder.

Finally Jo spoke, choosing her words carefully. "Your people have lived with their situation for so long, it's easy to see how they could come to believe that in their own lifetimes at least, there was no way out. As much as you guys crave open spaces, you're comfortable with your lifestyle. When you're comfortable, you miss opportunities for change, or find it too scary to grab opportunities you see."

"So, we're disparaging my people now?" Fitani mocked.

"Not at all, I'm blown away by how well you've done in the survival stakes. But I'm looking at your situation with fresh eyes, and seeing things that apparently aren't obvious to you guys."

"So you will now give us the benefit of your great wisdom?" said Fitani.

Jo laughed. "I have no great wisdom. I haven't been around nearly long enough to earn my 'Sage Certificate'. But from where I'm standing there seems to be a clear path to achieving what you crave, so maybe it's time you were honest with yourselves and decided whether you truly *want* change. If the answer is yes, then the first step would be to take a fresh look at things."

"Huh," said Fitani. "A teaser without substance."

Jo dipped her spoon into the muesli. "If you choose to take it that way."

"I suppose now you've figured us out," he continued snidely, "you're no longer interested in learning about our Work-Time?"

"Oh but I am," said Jo. "I can't wait to learn how you clean the Earth. Please continue."

CHAPTER 20

"Very well," agreed Fitani, sulkily. "From twelve years of age until seventy, every employee works. Only certified illness allows you to miss Work-Time, which as you know, is a mere four hours. The work however is arduous – summer and winter, sometimes under lights in the dark depending on your shift, and employees return exhausted."

Jo munched, her eyes glued to Fitani.

"Work-Time is the only occasion we wear clothing, and no one ever gets used to the harsh heavy material of the protective suits. The science Playrooms have improved them over the years, but as lead must always be a component, everyone's worn out after working in the suits for four hours."

She tried to imagine four hours of manual labor in a lead-lined suit and shuddered.

"At the beginning of Work-Time, employees wait at the pick-up areas outside each silo and take the automated transport trucks over no-man's land to the black lands. Here they join the line."

"That line of people in white I saw on your holographic map?"

Fitani nodded. "Though our Safe Place was spared from direct hits during the Great Destruction, the land around us was charred and covered in radioactive fallout. Over the years, rainfall washed it into the soil and it currently goes down about a meter and a half. In some places, due to cracks in the Earth or the particular composition of the soil, the radioactivity goes deeper. Machines follow the workers, removing the top two meters of soil and transporting it back to no-man's land for cleaning.

"I don't understand how it *can* be cleaned," said Jo. "I thought it was impossible to neutralize radioactivity."

"Correct," agreed Fitani, "and we *don't* neutralize the radioactivity. We *extract* the radioactive elements from the soil and store them safely."

Jo looked at him skeptically.

"It's a simple process," he said. "Attrition machines break down the contaminated soil and clay to fine granules. Those granules are then fed in a controlled stream through the extraction machines."

"Whose technology, I suppose, is too difficult for me to understand," said Jo.

"No, the principle is quite straightforward. The extraction machines contain metal-binding chemical compounds mixed with pressurized, heated carbon dioxide.

"Under heat and pressure, carbon dioxide becomes liquid-like. It flows through the granules and the metal-binders pull the radioactive compounds into its stream. The stream is then shunted into a secure canister and depressurized to return it to a gaseous state, which causes the radioactive compounds to drop out.

"The process is called supercritical fluid extraction and has been around since before your time, when it was used for things like extracting asphalt from oil and decaffeinating coffee. In your time they'd begun experimenting with it to extract plutonium from soil, with some success. Naturally our methods are much more refined and our success rate is a hundred percent."

"So you *can* clean the Earth," said Jo in wonderment. "But I don't understand then why you need that line of people."

Her watch read 9.15, the time she'd arranged to meet George. Waving to a waiter across the room, she mimed signing a bill before turning to Fitani.

"I need to use the ladies room. If George arrives while I'm away, tell him to take a seat."

Before Fitani could object to being used in this way, she hurried over to the alcove with the restroom sign. When she returned, Jo saw with dismay that Fitani was still alone. If the Hunter's agents had picked George up, and he'd spilled the beans, she wasn't safe here, but she couldn't help feeling he would not lightly betray her. She would wait a little longer.

The bill had been delivered in her absence and Jo took out her wallet and withdrew an amount to cover the meal and a tip. Then she shifted slightly to keep an eye on the door and nodded to Fitani.

"You were about to explain about the human line."

"The purpose of the line is to discover areas where the contamination has gone deeper than two meters and to map the extent of its penetration. Employing two thousand hand-held probes is the most efficient way of doing this. The probes detect radioactivity to a depth of ten meters and send a data map of dangerous areas to the surgical excising machines, which later remove the contaminated sections in cores.

"New workers arriving at the line, go and stand behind anyone whose helmet is red. If there are no red helmets, they wait behind yellow ones.

Employees' helmets light up yellow two minutes before their shifts end, and red when their shifts are finished.

Jo was puzzled. "I don't understand why they need to wait behind anyone. Surely new workers could just move into a gap in the line."

Fitani's brow wrinkled. "There are no gaps. The shoulder pads of the suits contain flexible, telescopic rods – lightweight but strong. These automatically extend to connect with the rods of adjacent suits, holding each employee in the line at one-meter intervals. The flexibility allows for height differences and gives employees arm movement, but once you step into the line, you're locked into it until your helmet turns red and a signal from the helmet of a replacement worker standing behind you, breaks the link."

"A chain gang," gasped Jo in horror. "You allow yourselves to be treated like that? You guys need a union."

Fitani tilted his head in puzzlement. "We are in complete union in the line. It must be held in place during the probing to ensure that no millimeter of soil is missed. I agree it's not the most comfortable way of working, but there's no alternative."

"People must need toilet breaks!"

"There are no toilet facilities. We are only on the line for four hours. People relieve themselves before suiting up."

Jo exhaled in disbelief. "Even so, out of two thousand people, surely some will need to go. And what if a worker becomes ill or has a heart attack?"

"The suits we wear have similar arrangements to the space suits once worn by your astronauts. If anyone needs to "go" as you put it, they can go in the suit. As for illness, the suits, like the smart-mats in our tubes, monitor the health of the employees wearing them. Medical emergencies trigger a helmet to turn red and as soon as the employee is released by a replacement worker, he or she is helped to a transport truck and delivered to the hospital silo."

"You wouldn't get me joining that chain gang," said Jo. "I'd turn around and go home."

Fitani laughed. "How would you get home? Return trucks don't allow anyone with a white helmet through their doors, and the trip back is too far to walk in a lead-lined suit. In any case a lone employee wandering across no-man's land would stand out like a white flag. You'd immediately be picked up and returned to the Edge. After your shift you'd be taken to the prison silo. Dereliction of duty is a serious thing."

"Well then," said Jo stubbornly, "I wouldn't board a transport to the Edge in the first place. After I'd checked in at the pick-up area, I'd nip across into the fields and lie low until my shift was over."

Fitani snorted. "A criminal as well as a ridiculous act. The perimeter alarms would sound as soon as you set foot in a field and you'd be imprisoned for trespass in addition to dereliction of duty."

"Well, how bad would that be?" Jo argued. "Given the population is already confined, I don't see much deterrent in a prison silo."

"No? Wait till you try it," said the host severely.

"The tubes in the prison silo are unequipped save for a thin sleeping mat, which is not the smart-foam variety. There are no holographic environments or communication facilities, which means that during Tube-Time you lie for twelve hours, completely isolated in a concrete casket. Nor is prison Play-Time much better. Playrooms are small and bare, with only one occupant per room allowed. There are no activities other than walking around within its limited confines and perhaps jumping up and down. The two meals a day consist of nutritious but flavorless gruel. During Work-Time you go to the Edge as usual – the only reason to miss work is certified illness, before returning to the prison silo if you still have time to serve. Believe me," he said, "you do not want to do time in the prison silo."

"Okay, you've convinced me. I'd go stand in the line. Tell me what I'd have to do."

Jo glanced at her watch. Past 9.20 and still no sign of George.

"The work is not difficult, but it *is* tiring. Keeping their legs straight, all employees drop forward at the waist. A laser in their suit helmets outlines a red rectangle at their feet, a meter wide and half a meter ahead."

"But rectangles projected from helmets would move around as employees moved their heads," said Jo.

"Controls in the helmets ensure that regardless of head movement, each rectangle is projected onto a fixed area," explained Fitani. "Furthermore the positioning of each is synchronized exactly with rectangles projected by helmets on either side to ensure no millimeter of ground is missed."

"Okay," said Jo. "I'm bending over a red rectangle."

"You begin by pointing your probe at the top left corner. Probes throw a white square of light onto the area they are analyzing, which turns green after 20 seconds, signaling employees to move the ray along. The helmets maintain a green lighting of the probed areas so employees can see where they've been."

"Seems foolproof," admitted Jo, "except for the fact that there's no way I could bend over like that for four hours."

"Breaks are built-in. Every five minutes the power turns off and employees straighten and stretch for 20 seconds. When stretch time is over, the helmets emit a beep and the line bends to its work once more. When the rectangles are filled with green light, the line steps forward in unison to the front edge of the old rectangle. A new red rectangle is then projected and the process repeats. By this exacting and arduous method we undo the legacy of your era."

Jo shivered. "It sounds horrible."

"There are some silver linings though. Right now for example, we are at an exciting phase in our history. After thirty years, no-man's land has almost reached its celebration size of one hundred square kilometers and *Relocation Day* looms!

We'll build a line of new silos, two kilometers from the leading edge of no-man's land and raze the old ones. The ninety square kilometers of cleaned soil, now behind us, will be added to our production fields. Our new silos will incorporate many exciting technical innovations and improvements, making our lives even better than before.

Jo pushed a little pile of spilled salt around in front of her. "Danny, you've indicated that the people living in all the Safe Places are well fed and housed."

"Certainly. The Company cares for its employees," he said shortly. "And now, having finally answered the question I came back to complete, I will bid you adieu."

"But you *haven't* fully answered my question," said Jo.

Fitani reddened. "You asked to know all about my world, and I have described it in great detail, despite the time it took to do so."

"You've told me all about the lives of *ordinary* employees," Jo agreed, "but what of The Company's Directors and Secretaries and their families? Do they have their own special silo, or do they share the same tubes as the rest of the employees?"

Fitani looked horrified. "The Directors and Secretaries *run* the Safe Places. They must have an overview of both production and of employee activities, which cannot be done from the perspective of a silo."

"So, as I suspected, they have other accommodations. Why haven't you told me about these?"

A crimson tide washed over Fitani's face. "It is not for employees to discuss the inner workings of The Company."

"But you agreed to answer my question, and clearly you haven't fully done so," said Jo. "If you are unwilling or unable to complete your answer, you have broken your own rules. That means you must forfeit the game to me and nullify the Hunter immediately."

Fitani's jaw dropped. Then he closed it grimly. Jo waited.

"Directors, Secretaries and their families," he finally ground out, "live and work at the centers of the Safe Places. I hope that satisfies you."

"Thank you," said Jo. "It certainly solves the mystery of that great opaque blur on the map you showed me. But it seemed to cover hundreds of square kilometers. How can so few people need such an enormous area?"

"I have now answered your question with sufficient detail that no forfeiture is necessary," said Fitani angrily. "The game must go on."

"All right," said Jo. "Thank you again for your description." She looked into the middle distance and addressed the viewers. "I feel I understand you all much better now, so I hope you won't think I'm taking liberties if I ask you to discuss something among yourselves.

"If your Safe Place and all the others are feeding and housing everyone comfortably, what is the point of adding another ninety square kilometers to your production fields? Rather than waste that land on excess food production, why not use it to create a nature holiday reserve for employees? Overnight you could turn your dream of freedom into reality."

Fitani gasped and then sneered. "So, you were unable to resist dispensing some 'wisdom' after all." He disappeared without further comment.

Alone, Jo wondered if she'd gone too far. She'd obviously alienated the game show host, but what about his viewers? Had the comments she'd been dropping throughout her conversations with Fitani, sown any seeds of doubt about the 'goodness' of The Company? Had she primed the people of the future enough to want to take things into their own hands?

Jo checked her watch again. It was 9.30 am. She had to accept that her driver would not be coming. She stood, finding her legs unexpectedly wobbly, and turned to the doorway. A familiar shape filled it. George! Jo could not believe the depth of her relief as she strode to greet him.

"Mrs. Wiseman." He spoke quickly. "Can you follow me?"

"Right behind you George."

He turned before she'd even finished her answer and headed across the road.

CHAPTER 21

The luggage carousel at Melbourne's Tullamarine airport was attracting growing numbers. They milled to position themselves around its empty revolving belt and watched the hatch, willing the luggage to start flowing.

Richard Sayers smiled sympathetically as he passed. Travelling light meant he never had to endure that. He'd phoned ahead to his Melbourne contact and the car they'd arranged for him would contain a suitcase with toiletries and fresh clothing.

He stepped outside the building and waited barely a minute before a white Holden Commodore pulled into the curb. A slim brunette in tailored slacks and jacket climbed out and rounded the car with a smile.

As he watched her approach, Richard was struck by how much she'd changed in the last two years. At uni Marilyn had been the typical political science student – wearing old jeans with a variety of layers on top that she'd picked up from charity shops. Back then she'd despised 'the man', but now he realized her passion had probably been more a rebellion against her conservative middle-class parents. He wondered if she knew how close she'd gotten to falling back into their mold.

"Rick," she gave him a hug. "I've missed you."

Another complication. At university, Marilyn had seen herself as a free spirit. Sex had been for fun with no strings attached and the memory of that time had tricked Richard into doing the stupidest thing in the world – having a fling with a colleague. 'Uni-Marilyn' may have been a free spirit, but 'colleague-Marilyn' viewed their liaison as something more permanent.

He took the car keys she was holding and gave her a quick peck on the cheek. "I've got to head straight off. I've heard nothing from Bill Warrington for nearly a month."

She pouted. "What, not even time for a little… drink before you go?"

"Marilyn, this is serious. I'm worried."

He saw her stiffen and although she spoke calmly, he heard the anger in her voice. "Well then, why did you let it go so long?"

"I'll fill you in when I get back," he said, walking to the car. Marilyn had a readiness to criticize, which was far from endearing. Likewise, her need to constantly control her environment and the people in it made her good at her job but tiresome in social situations. His resolve to end the relationship strengthened, but he couldn't ignore the twinge of guilt. It was Marilyn who'd brought him into BEAM in the first place.

It had been in the last year of his economics degree, at a time when his rage over *The Incident* as he always thought of it, was never far from the surface. He'd joined a radical group and participated in a number of noisy anti-globalization demonstrations, which had felt good at the time, but after the police and the headlines, the news media had gone hunting fresh meat and the public had forgotten their message, if they'd ever understood it in the first place.

Just as Richard had thought everything completely futile, someone in the group had introduced him to Marilyn. He still remembered their first conversation. He'd been complaining what a waste of time their protesting had been and she'd cut him off.

"If you're really serious about doing something, you can."

"What? Another protest? The reporters are sick of our mob at the moment."

"I meant something actually useful. And long-term."

He'd been intrigued. "Such as?"

"Buy me dinner and I'll tell you."

She wouldn't say more in front of the others, but at dinner told him about BEAM – an organization that had recruited her the year before. She was working in their operations office part-time while she finished her degree.

"I've never heard of BEAM," he said.

"What about WASB?"

"The Worldwide Association of Small Businesses? Sure, my folks were members. Their advice and support for small businesses is good value."

"They also have a secret arm called BEAM – Businesses Exposing Antisocial Monopolies. It's funded through WASB membership fees.

Richard frowned. "Why a secret arm?"

"Because when you're trying to discover the illegal alliances and maneuverings of big business, it helps if they don't know you're investigating them."

"But WASB *helps* businesses."

"*Small* businesses. That's the whole point. The giants are spreading their tentacles around the globe. Rather than producing superior goods, they're using their wealth and questionable practices to swallow the little guys."

Richard nodded. "And every very time that happens they increase their own powerbases, and true competition and business diversity are lost. It's what we've been protesting about. Anti-monopoly laws are a joke."

Marilyn nodded. "They're only as good as the governments that enforce them and when the giants line politicians' pockets, they don't try very hard to find anti-trust violations. That's why BEAM was formed. Small businesses need to protect themselves."

"But what can BEAM do?" said Richard.

"Plenty. We have links with anti-globalization groups in every country, and through them and our own people, we watch the operations of the giants and continually expose their attempts to use unlawful means to annihilate small businesses."

Richard was curious. "How do you do that without exposing BEAM?"

She grinned. "The Internet. Drop enough evidence in enough places, and public outcry pressures law enforcement and governments to take action."

It made sense and on finishing his degree, Richard asked Marilyn to recommend him. When BEAM learnt of Richard's background, they welcomed him with open arms. On the surface, he became a sale's rep for an Australian farming machinery company, which was a front for BEAM's Aussie operations. In reality he was one of many agents working on BEAM's most ambitious project yet – Operation H Group.

Over the following two years Richard developed expertise in talking to farmers and learning to read people. The task of collecting evidence against the H Group and helping farming communities to resist them was satisfying. If only the job weren't so lonely. He was constantly on the move between trouble spots, and never able to shed his travelling salesman persona. It was no wonder he'd succumbed to the convenience of a fling with Marilyn.

As Richard accelerated onto the freeway, he sighed. Maybe it was time to think about moving on. He was only twenty-four, not too old to look for another job – one where he could tell people honestly what he did, and go home to the same place each night. But Operation H Group was too important to abandon. Before anything else, the H Group had to be stopped. After that, he thought, perhaps I'll call it a day.

BEAM's overseas branches had uncovered the H Group's hidden agenda some years earlier. The H Group was ostensibly a small investment company set up by some top international businessmen. Among them, these businessmen held large financial interests in many of the world's major supermarket chains and retail outlets. Through the H Group, they planned to acquire eventual control of primary production around the globe. It was a long-term project, but these men had vision, resources and patience, and their initial forays into the world's orchard communities, had to date been promisingly fruitful!

BEAM had learned from bitter experience to move carefully when it came to the H Group. It had taken years to link the rise in seemingly unconnected foreign acquisitions of local orchards back to this single group. The H Group's connections with the foreign buyers were buried in a highly tangled web, and those who wandered too close to discovery tended to meet with fatal accidents. Nevertheless, through the cautious persistence of their field agents, some brilliant investigation from their economic analysts, and just a few sheer lucky breaks, BEAM was now in the process of building a portfolio of incontrovertible evidence against the scions of industry involved in the H Group.

In a few years they expected to have such a watertight case against them that when released on the net, it would jolt people from complacency and popular outcry would force world governments to not just break up the H Group, but to co-operate in formulating extensive new anti-trust laws and processes to ensure such a situation could never re-occur.

Richard faced facts. He wouldn't be quitting this job anytime soon. For all its disadvantages, the work he was doing satisfied an emotional need. *The Incident*, never far from his consciousness, which had precipitated his joining BEAM, had set the course of his adult life.

CHAPTER 22

Jo kept an eye on George's retreating back as she dodged between cars, and finally made it across the road. She pelted to the laneway down which he'd disappeared and saw him at the far end, peering around the corner. At her panting approach he turned and she glimpsed a supermarket parking lot beyond.

"Wait here Mrs. Wiseman. I'll collect the car and drive past in one minute."

Before she could speak he was gone, moving swiftly between rows of compacts and SUVs, and Jo sagged against the alley wall, gulping air.
Less than a minute later the Lexus drew level with the alley and Jo leapt in, not requiring the warning to stay low. Smoothly George turned out of the car park and navigated through the shopping streets to the main highway.

"It's safe to sit up now, Mrs. Wiseman. We haven't been followed."

"Are you sure?" Jo's heart was still thumping.

"Pretty sure. I think I've outsmarted him. Where would you like to go from here?"

"Bayside Shopping Centre in Frankston. That's the end of my trip, but George, what happened?"

"I must apologize for arriving late…"

"Don't worry about that! Fill me in," Jo demanded.

"Well, after dropping you off, I did as you suggested and parked a few blocks down the street in full view. The silver Ford Falcon drove past and turned the corner, so I thought perhaps I'd been mistaken about it following me. I decided to stretch my legs and buy a paper. I was in the newsagency when I glimpsed a bald head passing the front window.

"Unfortunately by the time I rushed out the fellow was gone, so I couldn't confirm my suspicion. I went across the road to have a coffee while I read my paper, but I didn't take much in." He gave a laugh. "I was too busy peeking over the top of it every couple of minutes, hoping to spot our chrome-dome friend."

"And did you?" Jo held her breath.

"Not a sign. I decided I'd let my imagination get the better of me and returned to the car, but to play it safe I drove in a random pattern around the streets, keeping an eye out for the silver Falcon, and I'd swear that neither it nor any other car followed me.

I had about twenty minutes before I needed to be at your cafe, and I remembered Cassie had asked me to pick up a bottle of wine, so I drove into a liquor store car park. I bought the wine and was just about to leave when the Falcon entered the parking lot, and pulled into the back row."

"Bloody hell!" the words slipped from Jo's lips.

"Exactly. Although I'd seen no one following me, its turning up couldn't have been a coincidence. Then I realized there *was* a way I could have been followed unseen – if the car had been fitted with a tracking device."

George glanced at Jo in the rearview mirror as though expecting an objection, but she sat still and pale.

"I thought of it," he added quickly, "because of my cousin's wife's dog."

"Dog?"

"Mixie, a little Yorkshire terrier. She's a real escape artist, always running away but not smart enough to stay off busy roads. Con was going crazy trying to keep her contained. Finally he bought a dog tracker. It came in a box with two parts - a tiny GPS device that you clip to the dog's collar and a handheld unit. Now when Mixie wanders beyond a set range, the unit beeps and displays a map pinpointing her location. It's easy to buy these trackers, so anyone could attach something like that to a car."

Jo nodded. She wouldn't have been surprised if the Hunter had equipped himself with a pocketful of tracking devices, probably far more powerful than those used to locate dogs. He could easily have strolled back to the Lexis when George was buying his paper and attached one.

George continued. "I drove away from the liquor store as though everything was normal, but I couldn't risk going anywhere near your cafe. For a while I was stumped. I had to find a way of checking the car for a tracking device without being obvious and then I remembered."

"What?"

"During all the driving around I'd just done, I'd passed one of those do-it-yourself car wash places, so I went straight back there and gave the Lexus a thorough wash."

"And you found something?"

"Eventually. It was high up under the front fender. A small black box held magnetically in place. It took quite a yank to get it off."

"What did you do with it?"

"Slapped it under the rear bumper of the car at the station in front of mine while its owner was hooking back the vacuum hose. When he drove off I followed him just in case anyone was watching. That way my car's movements would correspond with the signal being sent by the tracker, and calm any concern that I might have found or dislodged it. Eventually I peeled off and parked in the supermarket car park. I loitered around in the alley for a while keeping an eye out for the Falcon but it didn't turn up, so I figured it was safe to come and get you."

"You're amazing, George," said Jo.

"I'd like to say it's all in a day's work," he replied. "But I can't really admit to having done that kind of day's work before."

"Well if you ever get tired of driving limos I'm sure ASIO would take you on as a secret agent."

George gave a bark, but quickly sobered. "I don't like the idea of abandoning you in Frankston, Mrs. Wiseman. That creepy young punk has me worried."

Not half as worried as he has me, thought Jo. The Hunter's out-thinking me at every turn. If George hadn't found his tracking device, Frankston would have been my last stop. Will the Hunter have discovered yet that his tracker is on the wrong car? He's bound to have, she thought grimly, and that will be his confirmation I'm still using the Lexus. He'll be telling his agents to look for it. I couldn't be in a worst place than this car!

"George," she said. "Is it possible we're being followed right now?"

"I've been watching the highway since we entered," he said. "No one seems to be following."

Jo looked out of the window. They were on the outskirts of Frankston.

"How long to Bayside Shopping Centre?"

"We're only a couple of minutes away. Or would you prefer me to take you to a police station?"

"I need to meet up with Andy," said Jo quickly. "He had to catch a taxi when you didn't arrive on time and he'll be waiting for me at the shopping center. We'll go to the police together."

"You should do that Mrs. Wiseman. Tell your husband I strongly believe this warrants a police report. I don't want to scare you but I have a nasty feeling that the kind of stalking Baldy's up to is not the harmless variety."

"I agree."

Jo jammed her bits and pieces into the straw bag and eyed the laptop ruefully.

"George, would it be possible for me to rent the laptop for a few days?"

In the rearview mirror she saw him draw breath and hesitate.

"I'd be happy to leave a large enough deposit to cover the entire replacement cost. Would $2000 do it?"

"Mrs. Wiseman, for that amount you could buy a new laptop."

"Yes, but I only need this one for a few days, so I'll expect to get most of my deposit back when I return it, and it's convenient to have the Internet dongle," she added.

The dongle was what she really wanted. She couldn't buy one of her own because of the law requiring ID for purchasing wireless communication devices, but this one was registered in the limo company's name.

"I guess it'll be okay," he said, smiling into the rearview mirror. "The company would probably be satisfied with a hiring fee of $100 a day. We'll refund the balance of your deposit on return of the equipment in good order."

"Great."

George negotiated a turn and pulled into a vacant spot in the shopping center parking. "I'll get the laptop's power cable."

As he walked around to the boot, Jo pulled an entire wad of notes from one of the untouched pockets in her money belt. Quickly she peeled nine off and pushed them into her wallet.

George returned with the power cable and Jo counted twenty hundred-dollar bills into his hand, then added another.

"The extra hundred is for you George. You've been a truly excellent chauffeur."

"Thanks Mrs. Wiseman, but my gratuity was included in your initial payment."

"Well however much that was, it wasn't enough," said Jo.

While George wrote a receipt for her deposit, she climbed out of the car and walked around to his window. The straw bag was now bulging with far more weight than it had been designed to carry. She urgently needed a new one.

Jo pocketed the receipt and extended her hand. "Thank you again, George."

The chauffeur shook it firmly. "All the best, Mrs. Wiseman."

As Jo walked through the doors of Bayside Shopping Centre she noted it was close to ten. She had an hour to remake herself.

CHAPTER 23

From the studio Playroom, Angela Karpin watched the Prey enter the shopping center. Jo had made a mistake getting back into the Lexus at Mornington, but luck had been with her. The Hunter, confident his tracker would enable him to keep tabs on the Lexus, had stationed his few agents around Dromana, blocking escape routes. When he'd discovered the trick, he'd sent instructions for them to locate the limo, but Jo had reached the shopping center before they found it.

Now fresh agents heading to Mornington from Shepparton had spotted the Lexus travelling towards Melbourne. When they stopped it and found only the driver, Angela figured they'd backtrack to possible places he might have dropped Jo. The Prey probably imagined she had a safe hour before the 11.00 a.m. posting, but she might well be in for a shock.

Angela looked down to find her hands clenched, and realized with surprise it was not through excitement of the chase, so much as fear for Jo. Selfish Ancestors deserve no pity, Angela reminded herself. But if she's so selfish, why does she care about us?

The chase was heating up and with all the agents involved, the technicians and programmers were working frantically. They'll probably need my help soon, Angela thought, and then did something she'd never done during such a frenzied part of the game. She left the Playroom.

Taking the elevator to the sub-ground floor she set off through the connecting passageway to the children's silo. I just need to clear my head, she thought. A visit to Ben and Sandra should do it. But as she walked, a phrase kept playing thought her mind. *Ninety square kilometers.* What they could do with that land! Could Jo be right? Were the Safe Places now all producing enough? The Company said no, not quite. Just a few weeks ago they'd issued a notice that on *this* Relocation Day there would be no spare land, although by the next one there *would* be, guaranteed.

How long had they been saying that? In the last hundred years there had been three Relocation Days. According to her parents, The Company had also promised spare land before theirs and her grandparents' Relocation Days, only to regretfully recant at the last minute, saying it wasn't quite possible yet.

How could there still be insufficient food and resources when none of the other Safe Places were complaining of a lack? Ben was turning five this year and Angela had imagined taking him outside on his birthday. She hadn't expected a great deal – just a tiny part of their ninety square kilometers made into a park with trees and grass for the children to run on, but apparently even that had been too much to ask. And here was Jo, telling them to use the lot!

Having always regarded herself as a good employee, Angela was amazed at the rebellious things she was thinking. Why *did* The Company never release figures on the production yields of the Safe Places? What kind of work were the Directors and Secretaries actually doing within the blurred area that was for Sacred Company Business? Why had employees been taught from birth that all Ancestors were despicable? Jo wasn't despicable, Angela finally admitted to herself. How many Ancestors were like Jo?

She pulled up short. Employee knowledge of the past had always been restricted to the little The Company had told them, but with the Microwave Time Viewing technology, the means to gather their own information was at hand. Did she dare? She thought of the opportunity her children had just missed. They'd be in their thirties by the next Relocation Day. Would that one also be a bust? Would their children miss out too?

If The Company's being completely honest with us, she decided, they shouldn't object to my accessing records from the past. Such records would only confirm what they've told us.

Angela checked a virtual map and then ran through the underground passage to silo twenty-seven. It had a programming Playroom. She took the elevator up, found an empty terminal and typed in a routine to mask her address. Then she set about hacking into the *Fun 'n' Games* pipeline to Jo's era. It wasn't hard. She knew that pipeline inside out, and in a matter of minutes had accessed and downloaded copies of historical data digitally stored in the libraries of Jo's world. Her programming team, Angela noted with pride, had already discovered the hack and were working to trace it. She pulled out. She had what she needed.

Working fast, Angela sent the zettabytes of information through a translation program and finally into the info stream accessed by all employees. Only then did she wonder what the penalty might be if The Company was displeased. Fitani, in charge of the equipment, would face the blame.

She hoped the information would be worth it.

CHAPTER 24

Jo walked past the umpteenth window of uninspiring mannequins. Apart from out-of-the-question eveningwear, none of the outfits she'd seen were much different from those the Hunter and his agents already knew. She needed a disguise! She could feel her breathing becoming rapid and clutched the back of a nearby bench seat. Calm down, she told herself. There's stuff you need to get rid of. Do that now.

Sitting, she dragged out the jeans, black shirt and jacket, and transferred the money from their pockets to her wallet. Should she just fold the clothing and walk away? Someone might be grateful for a new outfit.

Jo, you're losing it, she told herself angrily. You can't leave evidence for the Hunter you've been here! The shock of what she'd nearly done made her jump up, grabbing everything. She dumped the clothes into a bin and checked her watch. Barely forty-five minutes to find something new to wear and get away.

Her heart began to pound. It was going to be impossible to change her look and now the plan she'd devised in the safety of the Lexus, seemed pathetic. On Google maps the station had looked close, but half a kilometer from the shopping center could take ten minutes after the 11.00 a.m. posting and then she'd have to wait for the train to arrive. The Hunter's agents would be swarming to the station. She'd set herself a trap, not an escape route! Maybe she should catch one of the buses servicing the shopping center. But she had no idea which ones travelled near Moorabbin airport.

As Jo staggered through the shopping center, her head spinning with the needs of clothing and transport, she almost missed the solution. On her left, brashly flaunting its colorful wares was a bicycle shop. That was it! She could buy a bike, kit herself out in Lycra and helmet, and be indistinguishable from the dozens of cyclists weaving through traffic and giving motorists ulcers.

She'd get to Frankston station quickly on a bike and could take it with her on the train. Then when she got to Cheltenham station, she'd be able to cycle to the airport.

Almost floating, Jo entered the shop. A lanky guy in his twenties lurched across to intercept her.

"Can I help you? I'm Andrew."

Jo flashed him a warm smile. "Hi Andrew, I'm after a bicycle and cycling gear."

He looked her up and down knowingly. "First time rider?"

"I had a bike when I was a kid."

He gave a condescending nod. "We're getting a lot of customers like you. People who decide cycling would be a great way to get some exercise and save on petrol costs, but who aren't so hard-core they're prepared to ride in bad weather or do really long distances. Have you considered a folding bike?"

"A what?" Jo was beginning to regret her earlier smile. Did he think she had all the time in the world?

"A folder is ideal for urban travel. Ride to work, then fold it up and stow it in a cupboard. It fits easily in a car boot, so you can take it with you on holidays."

His words penetrated. Jo had pictured having to abandon her bicycle at Moorabbin Airport when she flew to Shepparton, but this sounded much better. A folding bike would fit on the plane, which meant she'd have transport when she got to Shep and could get away quickly after coordinates postings.

"Let's have a look at them."

Andrew led her to a corner of strange specimens. Their wheels were tiny and some had rearing frames like giraffe necks. Jo sighed. She needed to merge with the cyclists and those bikes were head-turners.

"We do have *one* folder that looks normal," said Andrew. "It's more expensive, but beautifully built."

He reached in and pulled out an attractive bicycle. "This is the Montague SwissBike TX Commuter. It has a pivot joint rather than hinges, which makes it stronger, more stable and comfortable. Let me show you how it folds."

Andrew demonstrated and Jo had a try.

"The folding seems easy enough," she said. But I'm a bit worried about the carrying."

Andrew pulled a vinyl bag from one of the shelves. "This is our store's own bike carry bag. See the two wheels in the base? As long as you're on a fairly smooth surface, you can pull it along rather than carry."

Jo nodded. "You've sold me. I'll take the bike and the wheeled carry bag."

"Are you planning to cycle after sunset? If so the law requires you to fit front and rear lights. You'd also be wise to attach a water bottle cage and pump, and if you intend to carry anything, you'll need a rear rack and a pannier."

He pointed to a set of pannier bags pinned out in display on a wall. "That's my favorite. It has Velcro straps to attach to the bike rack and when you take it off, the bags fold into a backpack, so it's a breeze to carry your gear when you're walking."

"Won't all that stuff impede the folding of the bike?"

"Only the pannier, which is why you should get one that's easy to remove and carry."

Jo felt herself tensing. This was all taking too long. She spoke quickly. "Okay, I'll buy that pannier and the other items you mentioned. Can you fit them while I try on some cycling gear?"

She left the bemused but happy salesman and headed over to the racks of clothing, where she grabbed cycling pants, a T-shirt and a lightweight yellow rain resistant jacket.

In the changing cubicle Jo dropped the clothing onto the ledge and pulled out her wallet. It had nearly fourteen hundred dollars. From her money belt she added a further six hundred. The padding around the belt was now quite irregular, with some pockets still stuffed and others empty or nearly depleted. Rapidly she redistributed the notes and clipped the belt back on. It was lighter and more comfortable, but this she calculated with a sinking feeling, was because she'd spent nearly half of her twenty thousand.

And I'm not even through day two, she thought grimly. I hope this purchase will be worth it. Her watch read 10.40 a.m. No time to try things on. Gathering bag and cycling gear, she stepped from the cubicle and saw that Andrew had already fitted the rear rack, and was in the process of attaching the lights. The pump and water bottle cage lay on the floor beside him.

"Can I pay for all this now and come back for the bike in fifteen minutes?" she asked.

Andrew stood up and dusted himself off. "Sure, that'll give me enough time to finish."

He led the way to the counter, scanned and bagged the clothing and began adding in the other items on the computer.

"Did you get a helmet?" he asked.

"Oh, I forgot."

"I'd also recommend riding glasses," he said, waving towards some racks. "Don't want to risk eye injuries."

Jo raced across and grabbed a silver and black helmet. Glasses were a good idea. They'd help hide her face. She pulled a yellow-tinted pair from a nearby rack.

Andrew added them in and announced a grand total of $1,879.

"I'll take the gear with me," she said, counting out the cash.

"No problem. Your bike will be ready in fifteen minutes."

Jo picked up the plastic bag containing her new clothes, tucked the straw bag under one arm and the pannier and bike carry case under the other and left, feeling like a packhorse.

Around the end of the next corridor she found a public restroom and locked herself in a cubicle. Now moving as fast as the small space allowed, she stripped off her tracksuit and pulled on the Lycra leggings, cycling shirt and thin yellow jacket. Then she re-donned the track pants and hoodie to cover it all.

Maybe I should stay here for the broadcast, Jo thought. No, I still need to pick up my bike. I don't want them coming into the shopping center looking for me. Better to make them think I've caught a bus out.

Jo left the blonde wig in the straw bag and transferred everything else to the pannier bags. Then she edged out of the cubicle. At the basin she washed her hands, folded the pannier into a backpack and slipped it on. Five to eleven – time to go. Large exit doors opened at the end of a corridor and Jo strode towards them. Outside, some of the shoppers were crossing to the car park, while others strolled with plastic bags to various sheltered bus stops. Jo picked a bus stop with no people waiting and pushed her backpack well under the seat until it touched the wall behind. Then sitting with her legs demurely together to hide the backpack from view, she folded her hands over the straw bag on her lap.

When her watch alarm sounded its two-minute warning, she pulled off the black wig and dropped it into the straw bag before reluctantly putting on the blonde. The agents would all be on the roads searching for the Lexus, wouldn't they? But what if they'd already found the Lexus and discovered she'd left it? This was a place they might well predict she'd come.

Jo was already regretting her decision to sit in such an open spot. She pushed herself back in the seat, willing the seconds to pass. Finally eleven o'clock appeared on her dial. Now she had to wait for a safety margin. She set a new alarm for three minutes to two, dismayed this action had used up less than thirty seconds. At 11.01, unable to hold still any longer, she raised a hand to pull off the blonde wig.

That was when she saw the man coming from the car park. He was staring intently at her and dragging something from his pocket as he came. Jo lowered her hand and reached under the seat to yank out the backpack. Then she turned and ran back into the building, straw bag and backpack clutched to her chest. A yell from behind gave her legs an added spurt she didn't know was in them and at the end of the corridor she rounded the corner and flew into the ladies' room.

In the cubicle Jo cursed under her breath as her hands shook and fumbled. Blonde wig, track pants and hoodie were shoved into one of the pannier bags. Black wig and riding glasses went on. She'd been out of the agent's sight when she'd ducked into the ladies' room. Would he have run past and now be checking shops and other corridors, or would he have guessed she'd come in here and be waiting outside? There was only one way to find out.

Jo hung the empty straw bag over the hook on the back of the door, grabbed the backpack and stepped into the washroom. Her hopes lifted a little when she saw her image – the generic cyclist. She drew a deep breath and pulled the zipped yellow jacket further down over the money belt. If the Hunter's man *was* waiting outside, she had to hope he was expecting a blonde in a grey tracksuit to emerge. Jo shouldered the backpack and walked casually out into the corridor and down to the bicycle shop. No one stopped her, and as she entered the shop, Andrew approached, wheeling her bike.

She handed him the pannier and he strapped it onto the rack and helped her adjust the seat height and steering. As he passed Jo the helmet, she asked him the best way to the station.

He pointed. "Take the exit near the Gloria Susan cafe, turn left and keep going till you reach Ross Smith Avenue, then turn left again. The road goes straight to the station."

Jo put the helmet on and wheeled the bike from the shopping center. Still no one stopped her. At the road she mounted and cycled a little unsteadily to the intersection. She turned left and continued down the avenue, gaining speed and confidence. Both dipped sharply when she saw the traffic jam ahead.

A double-parked car was blocking the left lane. Vehicles queued up behind were being forced to wait for breaks in the oncoming traffic before they could pull out and go around it. There was a fair bit of horn tooting and as Jo got closer, she could see why. The driver of the blocking car was sitting at the wheel, making no attempt to move. Instead he was leaning over conversing with a couple of beefy types in the car he'd drawn up beside. It wasn't the blatantly inconsiderate behavior that got Jo's pulse racing, but the fact his vehicle was a silver Ford Falcon and his head was hairless.

She slowed in fright and at a loud ringing behind her, nearly wobbled over. A cyclist sailed past, bent over his handlebars, tight muscles moving under his Lycra shorts. He seemed unfazed by the problem ahead and on impulse Jo stood on her pedals and cycled hard to catch up with him. As they closed in on the blockage, the cyclist coasted past the line of queuing cars and followed the red Fiat at their head, which was pulling out around the Falcon.

Jo followed the cyclist and the three of them just made it back into the left lane before a group of cars bearing towards them swept past. The Fiat sped off and the cyclist also accelerated, leaving Jo trailing, but still putting a good distance behind her. Her cycling disguise had enabled her to pass right by the Hunter and his henchmen. She was going to make it!

The street ended in a roundabout and Jo stopped to get her bearings. She could see the station's entrance on her right, a little way down. Remounting, she noticed across the road, just before the roundabout, two cars were slowing and parking, one behind the other. Two men leapt from the first, and a man and a woman emerged from the second. The four quickly consulted and then hastened along the footpath toward the station's entrance.

She was too late. The Hunter's agents were here. Jo turned left, riding away from the entrance with blood pounding in her ears, but the hurrying agents on the opposite footpath were intent on reaching the station and never glanced her way.

At the next street Jo turned left again, cycling up towards Nepean Highway.

CHAPTER 25

Deep within the blurred area of Fitani's Safe Place, Secretary Melvin Briggs woke to a new day. A ray of sunlight, having found a gap in the curtains, was bringing out highlights in his wife's hair as she lay beside him in their king-sized bed. She was so much more peaceful, asleep. Not that he could fault Elizabeth's energy. As she always said, just because the Briggs family had been in charge of employee morale for five generations, didn't mean they should neglect to maintain their standing with the other Secretaries. For Elizabeth that meant keeping up a constant round of social engagements and networking.

Melvin sighed. He'd rather boil in oil than attend those dreadful parties. Usually he managed to get out of them with the work excuse – he hoped his wife never learnt how little work he really did. Unfortunately today's event was one he'd been unable to wriggle out of – a luncheon at Howard and Patricia Smythe's Estate. Howard was a Secretary in a neighboring Safe Place, just a thousand kilometers away. By fast tube, the trip would take less than two hours.

Elizabeth woke, stretched, and reached for the remote on the bedside console. She pressed a button and the bots went to work. One rolled in with a tray bearing cups and a coffee pot. Another pulled the curtains wide and exited to run the bath. A third inquired what Sir and Madam would like for breakfast. The day had begun.

Later that afternoon, as they lounged around the Smythe's sparkling pool, Melvin decided that perhaps some social engagements weren't so bad after all. He snaffled a fresh martini from the tray of a passing mini-bot and was nodding in the pretense of paying attention to the conversation, when one word penetrated – employees.

It had come from Carla, Howard's daughter, and Melvin sat up, sloshing his drink. Employee morale was *his* domain. What was Carla saying?

"Do you watch *Play or Die*?" she was speaking to Elizabeth. "I find some of their shows quite entertaining."

Melvin knew Elizabeth under her calm demeanor, would be flustered. She had no interest in employee entertainment. Her social calendar took up most of her time. But her response was smooth.

"I haven't caught up with the latest," she said. "Should I take a look?"

"Absolutely," said Carla. "The current Hunt is fascinating. The girl they've selected as Prey is different from the others. She's actually interested in the silo dwellers and how they live. *And* she's been criticizing The Company."

Carla's parents glanced at Briggs in mild alarm.

"Disconcerting," he admitted, "but the Hunter's probably caught her by now. Prey never last long in these games."

"She's not dead yet." Carla was tuning in on her portable viewer. "And her strategies so far have been sound. I wouldn't be surprised if she lasted the whole distance."

Carla's mother turned anxiously to Melvin. "Your people should be looking into this. Morale in the silos is *your* family's responsibility."

He responded automatically. "Not to worry Patricia, the employees love their Company. Criticism from an Ancestor will backfire, making them madder at her."

"I don't know about that." Carla fanned the flames. "Jo's been skillful, which people admire, and her interest in their lives has to count in her favor. Did you know she suggested that on Relocation Day they use all the reclaimed land to make themselves a holiday reserve?"

"What!" Her father choked. "Melvin, this is too much."

Melvin prickled. "Well, Howard, if you'll recall, I've been sending memos to Secretaries at all the Safe Places for some time now advocating setting aside a little land for the employees. Tension in the silos has risen steeply in the last decade and the usual entertainments haven't been doing enough to lower it."

Howard exploded. "Well letting them wander outside can never be the answer! I'd get hell from my Director if I dared bring him such a proposal, which I most certainly will *not*. His family is already planning a new pleasure garden complex with the forty square kilometers they'll be receiving on *our* employees' Relocation Day, and no doubt the CEO's family is likewise looking forward to expanding their grounds on yours. And what about our Secretarial allocations? Everyone gets to expand every thirty years and we *need* to. Our families are all growing. Do you know anyone willing to give up their allocation? Would *you*?"

Briggs kept his tone mild. "It's not a matter of giving it up. If everyone donated just one percent of their allocation, each Safe Place could set up a nice park for the employees to enjoy some outdoor time. That would keep them happy until the next Relocation, when we could add a bit more."

Elizabeth chimed in loyally, "One percent doesn't seem too much to ask, for a little peace of mind."

"Howard is correct," Patricia said coldly. "Executive families need their entire allocations and no one should be expected to give up anything. Allowing the employees out of their silos would be a disaster. Do you think they'd be content with a small park? One taste of the open and they'll be wanting more and more."

The afternoon soured somewhat after this, and the Briggs' departed early. In the tube on the way home, Elizabeth reopened the issue.

"You know, much as I hate to admit it, Patricia may have a point. Wouldn't it be risky giving the silo dwellers a taste of the open?"

"Yes it would," Melvin agreed. "But it would be riskier *not* to. It's been a long time since the silo dwellers were the savage survivors we scooped up and dumped on the fringes of the Safe Places, yet to this day the Families insist on viewing them as little more than amusing pets – this despite the fact that almost all our present comforts are a result of employee science and technology."

Elizabeth frowned. "That can't be right."

"Where do you suppose the mole machines that drill and shield the vacuum tubes we're travelling in came from? How did our production become so efficient that despite the rising populations of the Safe Places, only a small fraction of the ninety square kilometers we receive on Relocation Days is needed for food crops? Where do you think we get the smart machines that run our industries and maintain our households, allowing us to live in immaculate luxury while barely lifting a finger? It's all from innovations developed by the employees."

Elizabeth protested. "No, surely it's the *Families* we have to thank for our current standard of living."

"So we like to kid ourselves, but overseeing the transportation of equipment from the silos to our holdings, and then organizing its deployment for our own use, is the limit of what the Families have been willing or able to do, for many years now, and I'm talking *Secretarial* families. God help us if *Directors'* families ever decided to lay down their opium pipes and lend a hand!"

"Now Melvin," Elizabeth pursed her lips. "That's unkind and grossly exaggerated."

"Is it? My God Elizabeth, without the employees *we'd* be the savages. Look at the power we use to run our highly automated society. Do you know where it comes from – the fusion power silos. Each Safe Place has one. *Fusion* power. The people who lived before The Great Destruction only dreamed about it, and our employees developed it a hundred years ago."

"Well if our employees are so clever," she said tartly, "why do they stay meekly in their silos, when according to you, they so very much want to get out?"

"Because they still believe the myth – and by extension, the lies."

"What myth? What lies?"

"The myth: that the Almighty Company exists to serve, and so has their best interests at heart. The lies: that the land they clean and hand over every thirty years is used solely to sustain the population; that the hostile areas separating Safe Places prevent recreational travel between them; and that handheld probes are still the most effective method of detecting underground radioactivity, making land reclamation too slow to be used for anything other than food production."

Elizabeth pouted. "Well, what are a few little white lies? We *have* looked after them – very well!"

"We've looked after our own interests by keeping the employees productive, contained, and accepting of their lot. That can only go on for so long. Before Fitani came up with *Play or Die*, there'd been many signs pointing to a general rise in discontent and restlessness..."

"But now things are back to normal, right? So let's say, "Thank you Mr. Fitani," and give him a Personal Point bonus. You are *such* a worrywart Melvin! I think I shall call Patricia when we get home and tell her I believe she's right about keeping the employees in their silos."

"And what of the girl in the current game, who's giving the employees ideas about moving out into the open?"

"Well as you said yourself, she'll probably be dead soon, but if she's not, it's your job to ensure she stops saying things that upset our employees."

Elizabeth refused to discuss the matter further and donned her virtual headset. Melvin put his on also, but not to access the entertainment channels. Using his high-level Secretarial password, he invisibly eavesdropped on a number of virtual employee discussion rooms. What he saw and overheard was so disturbing that on arriving home, he hurried to his office and accessed the game.

Quickly he skimmed through what had been broadcast so far, slowing to normal speed during Jo's conversations with Fitani. Each time she made a disparaging comment or innuendo about The Company, Melvin flinched, and at the part where she suggested turning the ninety square kilometers of reclaimed land into an employee holiday reserve, he groaned aloud, knowing strong measures were called for.

He crossed to his 'Secretarial Chair', with the framed picture of the CEO behind it, and sitting, initiated contact with Fitani. The game show host was suitably awe-struck when Melvin informed him that he was passing on a message, which had come straight from the lips of the CEO himself.

141

"Praise The Company!" Fitani gasped. He then quickly added for good measure, "And praise the CEO!"

Imagining what that old letch was probably up to right then, Melvin had privately thought he was hardly deserving of praise – or perhaps he was! In any case, he reminded himself, now was not the time for levity.

"The CEO," he told Fitani sternly, "is not pleased."

The sight of game show host visibly blanching was reassuring. At least *some* employees were still suitably in awe of The Company.

"Your Prey has been making untrue and disturbing comments about The Company, causing confusion and unhappiness among the employees."

Fitani gulped uncomfortably, but did not contradict him.

"In his wisdom, the CEO has made the following ruling:

"*No Ancestors participating in* Play or Die *may ask questions about our society, and you may not engage them in any conversation about us.*

"Is that clear?"

"Yes, very clear, Secretary Briggs." Fitani's answer came with a quaver.

"Good. The CEO did consider withdrawing your licence to run *Play or Die*, and will certainly do so if his ruling is not followed."

Fitani was still giving assurances when Melvin broke the connection, hoping this would be enough to stop the rot. He would have preferred to cancel the game outright but feared such a move would do more harm than good.

CHAPTER 26

Jo made a right turn into Nepean Highway, and kept her head down as she cycled along in the bike lane. The Hunter's agents were everywhere! How had they got here so quickly? Obviously he'd once again out-thought her. Fitani was right – it was only a matter of time before she was caught. The biting air was stinging her face and making her nose run. She was an idiot for even trying. She should get off her bike right now and just surrender. But Jo's legs seemed to have a mind of their own and continued moving up and down.

She sniffed. The Hunter hadn't completely out-smarted her. She'd managed to slip out from under his nose with this brilliant disguise. If she kept on cycling she could still get to Moorabbin airport. Jo blinked away tears and sniffed again. Her watch showed 11.22 a.m. How long would it take her to cycle to the airport from here? She'd have to stop somewhere and check the map but not yet, with the Hunter's agents breathing down her neck.

A car tooted as it went past. Oh shit, she thought, but the car sailed on without stopping. A few seconds later, there was another toot. Her skin crawled. What was going on?

"Great strategy, Jo!"

Her head jerked around to see Fitani propped on the bike behind her. His billowing maroon smock fluttered with life-like canaries. She swerved, narrowly missing a parked car, but managed to pull off into what seemed to be a small reserve. A footbridge over a creek led to an area out of sight. Jo dismounted and crossed. She came out into a small park of eucalyptus trees and laying the bike down, sat.

As Fitani dropped beside her, crossing legs encased in bright tartan pants, the canaries on his shirt actually fluttered up a few millimeters before settling again.

Jo opened her mouth to give him an earful, but hesitated. Fitani's usual smug expression seemed closer to a nervous smirk and was she imagining it, or were his eyes showing signs of strain?

"Before you ask your three questions," he announced with forced bravado, "I have to inform you of some rule changes."

Jo stared. What was going on here? Fitani was obviously uncomfortable about this.

"In its infinite wisdom," he cleared his throat, and patted the logo on his breast pocket, "The Company has decided that the scope of questioning by Prey, shall henceforth be restricted."

Jo lifted her eyebrows. "I was under the impression it was your studio and occasionally the viewers themselves who made the rules."

Fitani flushed. "That *has* been the case," he admitted. "But we have just received a rare honor – an edict from the CEO himself regarding *Play or Die*: - *No Prey may ask questions about our world or our people*."

"Interesting," Jo's voice dripped sarcasm. "I wonder why."

"There is to be no discussion!"

As Fitani's voice rose to a squeak, Jo felt a surge of elation. The CEO had seen fit to buy into the game, so her words must be having an affect. Had the employees started asking awkward questions? If they'd finally decided they were ready to run their own lives, they might even change their minds about ending hers.

Stirring the pot, she taunted, "A Company that fears the words spoken by one girl from the past doesn't sound very powerful."

"Enough!" Fitani looked shocked. "The Company can close down the *Fun 'n' Games* Playroom any time it likes. Noncompliance with the new rule risks *Play or Die* being cancelled altogether."

"Fine by me," cried Jo in delight. "*Let* it be cancelled."

"It may not serve you as well as you think. All communication between your world and mine would instantly be severed. The Hunter wouldn't know the game was over, and not receiving your coordinates would be no guarantee it would cease its attempts to kill you. Furthermore it might fail to abide by the five-day limit. That's one of the reasons we send assassins after Hunters who fail. Some become so obsessed with the hunt they refuse to stop after their time has elapsed."

"Oh," Jo sobered quickly. "In that case I will abide by The Company's ruling and ask no further questions about your society. In fact on this occasion, I will ask no questions at all. Instead I'll invoke my right to one count of technical assistance."

Danny seemed to relax and some of his old jauntiness returned. "Excellent! What assistance do you require?"

"I need to get into my house in Shepparton but I suspect the Hunter will have it alarmed or booby-trapped. I would like to be undetectable to any electronic surveillance, alarms or traps."

"That we can do. You will be safe from all such technology within a hundred-metre radius of your house. Good luck."

Fitani vanished and Jo pulled the laptop from a pannier bag. She discovered the footbridge she'd crossed was part of a closed off street called Allawah Ave. To get to the airport, she would have to return to the Highway and follow it to Mordialloc. There she'd turn off into McDonald Street, and minor roads would take her to the back of the airport. The whole distance was thirty minutes by car – an hour or more by bike.

Jo looked at her watch. 11.30. She'd better get going! She stood and wheeled her bicycle back across the bridge to Nepean Highway, then mounted and began cycling fast.

How long would the flight take, she wondered. Say she got to the airport some time before 1.00. She'd have to look for a young pilot willing to fly to Shepparton, and if she was lucky enough to find someone, there was still the hiring of the plane to do. She could end up being in the air for her 2.00 p.m. posting and that would be a disaster. The Hunter would be waiting for her at Shepparton airport when she landed.

A better approach would be to go to the airport and ask around, hoping to find someone willing to fly to Shep as soon *after* two as possible. She could then place herself away from the airport for her 2.00 p.m. posting and return straight afterwards to jump on the plane.

Jo sighed. The more she thought about it, the less likely it seemed that *any* plan based on hitching a ride on a plane would succeed, but having taken this path, she wasn't turning back without at least trying. Don't think about it any more, she told herself. Concentrate on the cycling.

The road was good and the seaside towns slipped by. When Mordialloc appeared, Jo was delighted to see she'd made it in forty minutes. She spotted the sign to McDonald Street and followed the roundabout onto it. Halfway down was a sports reserve and she pulled over to have a rest and check the route. Pretty straightforward. She memorized the three turns and put away the laptop.

Within ten minutes Jo was cycling up the final street – Bundora Parade, and looking around with interest. Extensive grassy vacant lots gave a country feel. Dotted among them small offices and shabby buildings catered to the amateur flying industry. Some were repair shops. Others had signs in front advertising helicopter rides or flying lessons.

The road ended with a larger building displayed the name of a flying club. Coasting into the tiny parking square beside it, Jo felt a knot of anticipation. She dismounted and leaned the bike against one of the surrounding trees, noticing the silence. The place was empty. Should she risk leaving the bike unattended? No, better to get in some folding practice.

The folding turned out to be the easy part. She broke into a sweat trying to zip the bike into the carry case, but eventually triumphing, tucked her helmet under one arm and shouldered the pannier pack. With her free hand she dragged the case on its tiny wheels towards the single door.

The comfortable room she entered was a definite improvement on the building's plain exterior. A pleasant lounge area contained seats and a low table with magazines. Across the modern front desk a stiff, rather self-important young man in a spiffy pilot's shirt was talking to a thin Asian guy who looked like a student. Apart from the three of them, the room was empty. There were certainly no eager young pilots strolling around asking who wanted to go flying to help them build their hours.

Flushed and nervous, Jo watched the student pass over his debit card to pay for a lesson, and wondered what on earth she was going to say when her turn came. From a darkened doorway behind the desk, a slightly chubby guy emerged. He had a rounded baby face that probably made him look younger than he actually was. His pilot's shirt was less crisp than his colleague's and his body language more relaxed. Spotting Jo he walked over.

"Can I help you?"

"I hope so." Jo smiled brightly. "I need to travel to Shepparton fairly quickly and wondered what my chances were of getting a flight."

By now the student had departed and the first pilot was walking over to butt in on the conversation.

"I don't know how quick it would be," he said. "We'd have to phone around to see if anyone was available. When were you wanting to go?"

"I was hoping soon after two."

The pilots glanced at the wall clock, which displayed 12.31, and exchanged dubious looks.

"The flight to Shepparton's not long," said the baby-faced one. "Only about forty-five minutes, but a 2.00 p.m. departure is pushing it. We might be able to find a pilot who'd be available towards the end of the day or early tomorrow."

"You do realize it's an expensive way to go, don't you?" warned the first sternly. "You're looking at fourteen hundred dollars or so to charter a plane with a pilot."

Jo gasped. "I was hoping maybe I could hitch a ride with someone who was going that way, and just contribute towards the fuel and plane hire cost."

The first pilot frowned. "Who said you could do that?"

Jo faltered. "A friend of mine some years back was a pilot, and he was always looking for people to help out with the costs of building up his flying hours."

The man's frown deepened and Babyface broke in apologetically.

"That doesn't happen any more. The pilot would have to know you. There have been too many cases of people hijacking small planes and especially helicopters, which are highly maneuverable and can land anywhere, to carry out criminal acts like breaking mates out of prison or pulling robberies."

"Even to book a charter flight," the first came back, "you need to provide a fair amount of identification. Someone who just bowled up with a wad of cash, 'no questions asked', would have us phoning the police in a heartbeat."

Jo flashed a sickly grin. "Well, I sure can't afford a fourteen hundred dollar charter flight, so I guess I'll have to get to Shepparton some other way."

"What's in your funny shaped bag?" said the first pilot suddenly, a suspicious note in his voice.

Jo tried to sound happily innocent. "This is my bicycle bag. Isn't it great? My bike folds up and I can take it anywhere."

She unzipped a small section, revealing part of the wheel and said, "Since I won't be hopping on a plane, I guess I'll be unfolding it again and going on my way."

Babyface came around the counter eagerly. "A folding bike – what a great idea! Can I see what it looks like unfolded?"

"Sure. You can give me a hand if you like."

Jo dragged the bike bag to the door, followed by the pilot. In the still deserted car park they extracted the bike and restored it to riding state. The young man beamed. "This is *such* a cool bike."

"Yes, I haven't had it long, but I'm happy with it so far. I'm Judy, by the way." Jo extended her hand, smiling.

"Jeff." He shook it with a grin.

Jo gave a laugh. "Your mate back there was starting to make me feel like a terrorist," she said.

"He's pretty down the line when it comes to regs," admitted Jeff. "What's your hurry in getting to Shepparton?"

"A party." Jo wondered how *that* had popped out of her mouth and realized she'd need to embellish. "Kind of an impromptu half-year reunion of my graduating class. I've no idea why they made it on a Tuesday night." She laughed. "Must have been the brainchild of a happy-hour group.

"I'd decided to give it a miss – without a car, a midweek trip to Shepparton's a bit of a drag, but this morning I woke up regretting that decision. I organized a couple of days off work and got my gear together and then realized I wasn't going to make the train. That's when I remembered Jack Hudson, my pilot friend. He was the one who told me about hitching a lift with a pilot, so I hopped on my bike and came over to see if anyone was flying that way… Pretty silly, I suppose."

"Well, maybe not." Jeff's pudgy face split into a grin. "When I came into the office before, I'd just been out at the hangar with my sister and her boyfriend. They're flying to Echuca as soon as Vicky finishes doing the plane checks."

He glanced across to the hangar sheds. "If they haven't left yet, and you can pay, say three hundred and fifty towards costs, they'll probably be happy to drop you off in Shepparton."

Jo gaped. "That would be fantastic!"

"I'll nip across and see if I can catch them. Pack up your bike and follow me through that gate. Don't forget to relock it." He ran towards a padlocked gate, dragging a bunch of keys from his pocket.

Praying that Jeff's sister had not yet departed, Jo folded the bike and began repacking it into the carry case. Haste made her fumble and curse but finally the bag was zipped and she hauled it through the opening in the cyclone wire fence. Closing the gate behind her, she clicked the padlock and turned towards the hangar sheds.

Jeff was nowhere in sight and she wondered which shed he'd gone to. Well, it had to be one of them. Lifting the cycle bag, she crossed the grassy strip to the asphalt and thankfully set it down on its wheels. Then she straightened her backpack and began walking towards the nearest shed.

A familiar round head popped out from the second hangar down and a hand waved. Jeff came jogging towards Jo with a smile on his face.

"They're still here. Vicky's finished her checks and they're ready to go."

He grabbed the bike case and led Jo over to the hangar, where the tiny single engine Piper stood with two people beside it.

Jeff's sister was short, with his same rounded face, but curlier hair. Her boyfriend towered above her and Jo suspected he'd be pleased to break the trip and stretch his legs at Shepparton.

"Hi, Judy." The girl smiled at her. "You just caught us. I'm Vicky and this is Adam. Space is a bit tight I'm afraid. We've had to rearrange the luggage in the back."

Jo grinned. "No problem, if we can fit mine as well."

Adam picked up Jo's bicycle case as though it were a giant marshmallow and climbing the wing, gently maneuvered it through the door. He strapped it down securely with the other luggage, which was arranged on and under the left back seat. The pannier pack and helmet quickly followed, leaving just enough room for Jo to squash into the adjacent seat.

Jo turned to Adam and Vicky before climbing the wing.

"Thanks so much for this. I really appreciate it."

"Well, we're happy to have the contribution towards our costs, so everyone wins," said Vicky.

Jeff gave a wave. "I'd better be getting back to the club before Dylan blows a fuse. I'm supposed to be relieving him at the desk."

Jo climbed into the back and Vicky and Adam took the front seats. Vicky started the engine and taxied out towards the runway, speaking into a two-way radio all the while. Adam twisted around.

"Have you flown in a small plane before?" he called over the engine noise.

"Yes, but I'd forgotten just how small they are," said Jo, fastening her seatbelt.

"Not really designed for people my height," he agreed.

The plane stopped short of the runway and Vicky turned her head.

"I've just called the tower for clearance to take off," she said loudly. "We should be away in a minute or two."

Jo nodded and settled back checking her watch while a garbled voice through the radio directed Vicky to the appropriate runway. It was 12.45 p.m. A forty-five minute flight meant they'd arrive in Shepparton at 1.30. From the airport the farm was fifteen-minutes by car – too far to cycle to in time, but taxis were safe while the Hunter had no idea she was in Shep. That left barely fifteen minutes to get into her house, grab Dad's paperwork and get out. Cutting it fine, but not impossible. The question was where would she go after that? Jo sighed. She didn't want to put any of her Shep friends at risk, but she needed a safe place to hole up and go through the papers.

Distracted by these thoughts, she suddenly became aware they were accelerating down the runway with a great deal of noise and shuddering. Just when it seemed the tarmac was ending, the nose lifted and they soared into the blue sky of the cloudless winter day. Below them houses and roads followed the curve of the bay and white sails dotted the wrinkled sea. Sunlight streamed into the little plane, filling it with bright warmth. Adam looked around to check on her and she gave him a thumbs-up. It was too noisy for conversation and for the moment Jo was content to watch the main highway as they followed it from above, barely aware of her drooping eyelids.

CHAPTER 27

At the red light, Richard stretched and rotated his neck. The drive to Shepparton had been uneventful, but after two and a half hours, he was ready for a coffee. He'd check into his motel before going on to the Warrington Farm.

Bev was at the reception desk and her face lit up when she saw him in the doorway. "Richard, it's been a while. How many nights shall I put you down for?"

The 'Welcome Inn' was a small family-owned motel on the outskirts of Shepparton. Bev and her husband had ties with the farming community and operated their business with the reluctant assistance of their two sons, who kept threatening to depart, but who so far had been unable to find anything better.

"Just doing a spare parts round this time, Bev. I'll probably only be here a day or two, so put me down for one night and I'll let you know if I need to extend."

Richard made a point of staying at the Welcome Inn whenever he came to Shepparton. It lent legitimacy to his farming machinery salesman persona and kept him up with the local news.

"Any exciting events in my absence?"

Bev tilted her head, considering. "Well, Popsie's just had a litter of four kittens, which are so cute. It'll be heart wrenching when the time comes to give them away. We might keep one to help Popsie with the mousing. Not that we have a mouse problem," she hastened to add. "But with this drought on, the field mice may well start heading into town."

Richard signed the register and Bev handed back his company credit card.

"Have you heard how the new bloke's getting on at the Davies' place?" he asked.

"Jack Murray? Seems to be doing okay. Are you looking to sell him some equipment?"

Richard winked. "Always on the lookout for new customers, Bev."

Her smile faded. "Well, you may have a new customer up at the Warrington farm soon. I imagine Jo will be selling."

"What do you mean *Jo*? Has something happened to Bill?"

"Oh, you hadn't heard? There was a terrible accident, nearly a month ago now. Bill was killed."

"Killed! What happened?"

"He was crushed under some machinery. They had a coroner's inquest and all."

"My God, Bev, I had no idea. I've been interstate for the last month."

"Such an awful thing. From what I gather, a part of his tree shaker worked loose and came down on him while he was standing under it... you didn't *sell* that to him did you?"

Richard answered vaguely, still stunned by the news. "No, the big tree shakers come from overseas. I can hardly believe this has happened. I must go and give my condolences to Jo."

"I don't think Jo's around at the moment. Stuart drove past the place yesterday and said it seemed to be all locked up."

Richard fumbled the room key into his pocket. How could this have happened? Bill Warrington was well aware of the danger of displaying knowledge about the H Group, and would surely never have done so, but this unlikely death couldn't have been an accident.

Numbly he returned to his car and sat for a moment in a state of shock. I have to go out to the farm, he thought, unwilling to communicate the news to his superiors just yet. Maybe there'll be a clue, or at least I can speak to Jo about it. He started the engine.

The first thing he noticed was the padlock on the gate. Never in all Richard's visits to the Warrington's had the front gates been closed, let alone padlocked. He pulled off a short way down the road and walked back.

The farmhouse was typical of its kind, set in a field of clumpy grass and straggly gum trees. Nearby, the huge packing and cold-storage shed was shut up tightly with some empty crates stacked in front. Beside it, the doors of a smaller toolshed were also closed, and the surrounding fields, filled with rows of stark bare-limbed apple trees, added to the sense of desolation.

A cold wind whistled around Richard's head as he grabbed the top bar, vaulted the gate and jogged up the track to the farmhouse. Silence greeted his knocking, and a walk around the house confirmed that all blinds were down and doors were locked. Richard returned to the front verandah and sat in an old cane chair pondering his next move.

He needed to locate Jo. She might have gone to stay with relatives or could be in Melbourne dealing with business relating to the will. Either way,

BEAM should be able to track her down. It was vital to find out how much she knew. If the H Group *was* involved in her father's death, Jo could also be in danger. Guilt and fear for Jo swept over him. Could this be *his* fault? Had he slipped up somewhere?

A heavy hand fell on Richard's shoulder, electrifying him. He twisted and tried to rise but the hand was an extension of a thick meaty arm, which in turn was attached to a huge body that was leaning, easily exerting enough pressure to keep him in place.

"What the hell!" he yelled, as a second giant moved into view. There were no other cars parked out the front, so these goons must have come from around the back, and big as they were, they'd done it without a sound.

"This is private property," growled the thug holding him down.

"It's the *Warrington* property," said Richard angrily. "I've come to pay my condolences to Jo Warrington on the death of her father. Please remove your hand!"

The hand lifted and as Richard stood, the two men positioned themselves on either side of him.

"Anyone can see no one's home," stated the second thug menacingly. "You would have had to climb that gate to get in."

Richard was recovering from his initial shock. "And who are you?" he demanded.

"Security."

"Well if Jo's employed security, she must plan to be away for a while. What's the name of your company? I need to contact them about getting in touch with her."

"It's not our job to put you in touch with anyone. Leave now or we'll assist you on your way."

The second made a menacing move and Richard locked eyes with him for a second. "Thanks for your help."

He walked down the verandah steps and out towards the gate, feeling their stony gazes drilling between his shoulder blades all the way. As he leapt the gate and strode towards the car, thumbing the lock release on his key, Richard could still feel them watching. He climbed in and driving off, glanced back. Their Easter Island stance on the porch remained unchanged.

It was eleven forty. He'd return to the motel and send in his report, which would include a request that BEAM track Jo down and investigate the unlikely "home security" she'd supposedly set up. Having done that, he'd grab some lunch and head back to the farm, less obviously this time, to see if he could find just what it was out there that required the protection of two hefty guards.

CHAPTER 28

Bladder pressure finally woke Jo. Damn, she thought, realizing her last toilet stop had been at the cafe that morning. From her window she could see the main highway below, running through farmlands. Adam and Vicky had their heads together in conversation, which failed to carry back over the engine noise. A check of her watch sat Jo up in fright, fully awake. 1.40 p.m. They should have landed at Shepparton ten minutes ago.

Feeling sick, she leaned forward and tapped Adam on the shoulder. Had Vicky forgotten about the Shepparton stop? Were they halfway to Echuca?

Adam turned with a smile. "Awake at last. We're running a bit late. Soon after we left Moorabbin, a northerly sprang up. We've been flying into it the whole time and it's slowed us down. We've only just reached Shepparton."

Sure enough, two runways came into view and Vicky began a static-masked conversation over the radio. Jo wanly returned Adam's smile, knowing that the process of landing, finding a phone and waiting for a taxi, would use up too much time. Her plan, to get into her house grab her father's papers, and be out before two was no longer viable. All she could do now was decide where to be for her 2.00 p.m. posting. As the plane circled to position itself above the runway, Jo considered her options.

One: Get close to the house and race in straight after the posting. Downside – if the Hunter had men nearby, they could intercept her before she even got to the door.

Two: Distance herself from the house, hoping to draw any agents away from it and then somehow work her way back. Downside – if the Hunter had enough people in Shepparton he could leave some to guard the house while sending others to surround her coordinates. She shook her head. That was crazy. No way would the Hunter have more than one or two agents in Shepparton right now. He had every reason to believe she was currently in the Frankston area. That's where his people would be. If he were to suddenly receive her coordinates in Shepparton, he'd contact the agents staking out her house and tell them to head for her location, confident that if she somehow made it home, the alarm systems he'd set up would warn him.

So she had to get close, but not too close – far enough to lure any agents away from the house, but near enough to get in before they returned.

Jo twisted uncomfortably, her ever-tightening bladder finally overriding all other thoughts.

Vicky began her descent, and Jo quickly transferred three notes from her money belt to her jacket pocket. As the wheels touched the tarmac, she clenched sphincter and teeth against a series of bumps, only letting out her breath when they turned off the runway and taxied smoothly towards the hangars. In an open area, Vicky turned the plane around and shut off the engine, bringing sudden quiet. She turned to Jo.

"Well, here we are, later than planned, but still a lot faster than the train. We'll all need to get out so Adam can unstrap your things."

Vicky unbuckled her belt and pushing open the door, climbed onto the wing. She jumped down and Jo followed awkwardly. Adam climbed back to retrieve her luggage.

"Will you be staying for a while?" Jo asked Vicky as they waited.

"No, this stop wasn't on my flight plan and the northerly slowed us up. It's finally turned west, so we'll make better progress for the rest of the trip, but I'm not liking the look of those clouds."

She pointed to a distant glowering bank. "The forecast predicted storms for late this afternoon, but it looks like they might arrive early and I want to get to Echuca before they do."

Adam handed the pannier pack down to Jo and she opened one of the bags and retrieved her wallet. From it she took a fifty-dollar note and added the three hundreds from her pocket. She passed them to Vicky.

"Thanks again for the lift."

Vicky put the money into her own pocket and grinned. "No worries, hope the reunion's worth it."

Jo almost said, "Reunion?" but was saved from this gaffe by Adam calling for help to guide the bike case down.

"All set?" Adam jumped down to join them.

"Yes, and thanks for your help with the luggage. Have a great time in Echuca."

"That's highly likely now we're flush with funds," said Vicky.

Jo shouldered her pack and gave a parting wave. She wheeled her bike bag towards the glass doors of a building set a little back from the runway. It displayed the name of a flying club and with her bladder dictating her actions, she stepped inside, hoping to find the toilets before someone questioned her.

Her luck held. The place was empty and spotting the ladies room, Jo pushed in, leaving her bike bag in the little wash area while she entered a cubicle.

Back at the washbasin Jo again checked her watch, 1.44 p.m. and decided now would be a good time to get into her "photography gear". She pulled the track pants on over her leggings and removing the cycling jacket, donned the hoodie. Then she put the jacket back on and zipped it.

As she left the restroom, Jo braced for a challenge, but the place was still empty and she slipped quietly out of the door. At the side of the building she set up her bike and fastened the pannier to the rack. With more than ten minutes before the Hunter received her coordinates, she'd be able to get a good way to her house.

An exit gate led to the Goulburn Valley Highway and Jo turned left towards River Road, pedaling hard. The strong westerly was fast bringing rain clouds but Jo was glad of its direction. On River Road, it was at her back, pushing her along. The area she was cycling through, south of the main Shepparton township was still mainly bushland and farms, and nothing slowed her progress. When her watch alarm went off at three minutes to two, Jo estimated she was five kilometers from home by the main roads, but a cross-country shortcut she knew of would cut the trip to little more than a kilometer.

She stopped and wheeled her bike into the shallow depression by the side of the road. Removing the cycling jacket, helmet, black wig and glasses, she tucked them under the bike. In a pannier bag, Jo found the blonde wig and fitted it on as she jogged down the road to a large gum tree. She sat beneath it and checked her watch. 1.59 p.m.

Jo reset the alarm for three minutes to five and waited, her thoughts racing. Would an agent be camped in her house? Probably not, she decided. Her neighbors would ask questions if they noticed a stranger living at her place. More likely the Hunter had agents stationed nearby, ready to respond to alarms set up around the house. Hopefully, when he received her coordinates at this location, he'd send those agents out along this road, which would give her the opportunity to sneak into the house, undetectable to any alarms, if Fitani had done his bit.

It seemed like a plan, and at two minutes past two, Jo leapt up and tore back. She stripped off the track pants and wig and shoved them into a pannier bag, then re-donned the items she'd left under the bike. Now she cycled flat-out until the dirt sidetrack she'd been looking for appeared on her right. As she turned onto it Jo felt a surge of optimism. This track, used only by local kids and a few farmers, not only cut nearly four kilometers from her trip, but kept her off the main roads, away from any agents.

The afternoon had darkened and the strong west wind now hit her from the side. It cut through her clothing as she hunched over the handlebars. Rain would be coming sooner rather than later, but Jo realized that with luck she'd be sheltered from it, snug in her own house. She put on a burst of speed, bumping over the stony track. A couple of barking farm dogs ran out, but after following for a short distance, returned to their properties, and in good time she made it to the outermost orchard.

Laying down the bike, she wiggled it under the barbed wire fence, and then, pushing down on the lower strand, climbed gingerly through herself. As she cycled between rows of trees, Jo was thankful winter meant not having to dodge fallen apples. She worked her way through the orchards, negotiating two more fences before coming within sight of the farmhouse.

From the side, the place looked peaceful. Jo delved into a pannier bag and pulled out her wallet. The key was in an inner pouch. Slipping it into her jacket pocket, she considered leaving the bike among the trees, but decided against it. The Hunter's agents might well sweep the surrounding orchards. Safer to keep the bicycle with her and better for fast getaways. Jo pushed it under the last fence, scrambled through herself and then lay flat, watching for movement from the house or surrounds.

The only sound was the whistling wind. She drew a deep breath and pedaled across the lumpy field. As she circled to the front, Jo was shocked to see the closed, padlocked gate. Did that mean the Hunter had left a man inside after all? Her heart was racing as she lifted the bike up the two porch steps and put her ear to the door. Dead silence. She had to risk going in. Staying in full view a second longer was madness. She turned the key, wheeled her bike through and closed the door quietly behind her. Inside she stood and listened. The howling of the wind outside emphasized the silence within.

Jo let out her breath, aware of the gloom. *She* hadn't pulled down all the blinds but someone had, and now she neither dared raise them nor turn on a light. She pushed the bicycle down the dim hallway and into the spare junk room, propping it against a wall. An old art easel nearby gave her an idea and Jo leant it against the front wheel before throwing a paint-spattered smock over the pannier. Did the bike look sufficiently part of the junk in this room? Yes. Now what about herself? If the Hunter or his agents decided to check the house, she needed a place to hide.

Walking from room to room, Jo inspected and rejected various nooks and wardrobes, becoming increasingly anxious. Nothing was suitable. Then she opened the door of the linen cupboard in the hall. Instantly the memory of her childhood hidey-hole flashed to mind and looking up she spied its entrance – a manhole into the roof space. Who knew why the builders had placed it in this cupboard, but her delight as a child had known no bounds when she'd realized she could climb up the open shelving, push the cover aside and scramble into the scary but secret recess under the tiles. It had turned out to be nowhere near as dark as she'd imagined, mainly because of the skylight above the bathroom, and she'd created a retreat near that light source, laying short planks and flat pieces of wood across the ceiling beams to make moving about easier.

She'd also discovered that sounds from the house rose clearly up to her, but the initial thrill of finding she could listen in on the conversations of those below, had been dampened when it turned out that sound carried just as easily in the other direction. Her parents had heard her moving above them and once her hidey-hole had ceased being a secret, she'd lost interest in the place. Now it again presented possibilities.

Jo climbed the shelves and pushed the manhole cover up and across the beams. Cautiously she raised herself into the cavity and waited for her eyes to adjust to the gloom from the minimal light bleeding between the tiles. A small distance away, more light escaped from around the skylight over the bathroom, revealing the resting platform Jo had created as a child.

This hidey-hole would work as long as she remembered to keep perfectly still. Jo left the hole open and climbed down, closing the cupboard door. Her retreat was ready if she needed it.

It was nearly 2.30 p.m. With two and a half hours until the next broadcast, her own house was the safest place she could be. Invisible to electronic alarms and surveillance, thanks to Fitani, and hidden from outside view with all the blinds down, she was in the perfect hideout. Jo made for the kitchen. She had time to refuel before checking Dad's papers.

Thirstily she gulped down two tumblers of water and then washed, dried and replaced the glass. From the fridge she grabbed a block of cheese and a soft tomato. Taking two slices of bread from the freezer, Jo zapped them in the microwave and made a quick sandwich. Again she cleared away all traces of her activity before carrying the sandwich on a plate through to the office.

The 'office' was a little study where she did the books, and where paperwork relating to the farm was filed. Taking a bite of her sandwich, Jo turned the key in the filing cabinet. She pulled open the top drawer and cast her eye over the tabs. 'Correspondence' was the most likely one and she lifted out the file and flipped it open on the desk.

The first few papers were copies of her own correspondence with a funeral director and Dad's solicitor. She blinked as her eyes blurred. Oh, Dad, she thought. I'm going to find the people who did this to you and they're going to pay. She turned the papers over and reached for the next. This was a copy of the minutes of the meeting in which her father and the other apple growers had voted unanimously to refuse to go below a set price when selling their next lot of apples held in cold storage, to the supermarket chains. This too she turned over.

As Jo picked up the next letter, she squinted. The room had grown much darker and she walked across to the window to use what light was seeping through the side of the blind. Not enough. She pushed the blind slightly to let in more. A crash of hailstones made her jump. The storm had arrived in fury.

As hail gave way to pounding rain, Jo shivered, glad not to have been caught in it, but frustrated by the lack of light. She pulled a penlight from a drawer and crawled under the desk to mask its glow. Clicking it on, she directed its narrow beam over the letter in her hand. This appeared to be an unsympathetic reply from the supermarket chain they dealt with, to a letter her father had written describing the apple growers' need for a greater margin than the supermarket was offering. As her light beam reached the end of the letter, Jo gasped. The signatory was Simon Brooks! Before she had time to check his title, a voice said speculatively, "Just what might *you* be doing, I wonder?"

Jo lifted the penlight. A pair of damp jeans ending in sneakers boxed her in. Reflexively she hurled the torch away, seeing the legs twist slightly to follow its path. Jo grabbed both ankles and pulled with all her might. The agent went crashing to the floor and she squirmed out and ran for the door. But now *her* ankle was grabbed, and she in turn hit the floor, cursing in her mind the storm that had masked his entry. Before she could rise he was on her, twisting an arm behind her back and pulling her painfully to her feet.

"Let me go. This is my house!" cried Jo, hoping to convince the agent she was *not* Kylie Marshall, drug addict and kidnapper.

"Jo?" One hand released its grip to turn on the light.

Jo's black wig had come askew in the struggle and she now felt it being lifted off her head.

"Yes, I'm Jo Warrington!"

She staggered at her sudden release and turned to face her attacker.

"Richard?" Surely he hadn't come by in the rain to sell farming equipment? "What are you doing here?"

"Jo, I'm so sorry." His hazel eyes looked contrite. "I thought you were an intruder."

"You thought *I* was an intruder!"

"Er, yes." He looked uncomfortable. "I was told you were away, and something strange seemed to be happening around this house, so I thought I'd check it out. When I saw you under the desk with a penlight..." he faded off.

"Oh, my God," cried Jo, remembering. "You'll have tripped the alarms. Agents could be here any second!"

"Well I trust you'll vouch for me. I didn't mean any harm."

"No, it's *me* they're after. You can't tell them I was here."

"What?"

"No time to explain." Jo flipped off the light. "Get out of here while you can!"

She ran into the hall and slipped into the linen cupboard, closing herself in just as the front and back doors crashed open. Amid sounds of yelling and commotion, Jo climbed into the roof cavity and replaced the cover, stretching out along one of the planks and trying to control her breathing. Eventually both it and the uproar below calmed, and Jo was able to make out two voices.

"How the hell did he get past you?"

"Thought I'd dropped the bastard, but he slithered between my legs and kicked me in the calf muscle. Man that hurts!"

"Should we go after him?"

"No, he'll be away by now and he's not the one we're after."

"It *was* the bloke from this morning, wasn't it?"

"Think so. What's *his* interest I wonder?"

"He's no casual thief or he wouldn't risk returning to a place he knew was patrolled. Marshall's boyfriend?"

"If so he must have arranged to meet her here. It seems our client may have been right about Marshall coming to this house."

"Shit, if she's not here already. Lock the doors and search the place!"

Jo froze as footsteps moved around below and thuds and bangs accompanied the search. The cupboard door beneath her creaked open and she held her breath.

"I found something!"

The door closed and footsteps moved down the hallway.

"What?"

"A half eaten sandwich and an open file of papers. Seems the boyfriend was going through some correspondence when we disturbed him."

"Why would he be doing tha… what's this?"

"Looks like a wig."

"Definitely a wig. He could have brought it along for his girlfriend. That would confirm they're in the kidnapping together. We need to make a report."

"Should one of us stay here?"

"No, the client's instructions were not to stay in the house. We'll reset the alarms and lock the doors. If anyone comes in we'll know about it."

"What *I'd* like to know is how our client guessed that Kylie Marshall might come *here*. What's her connection with the Warrington woman who owns the place?"

"Maybe they were school chums. Maybe she knew the owner was abroad and the house would be empty."

"A lot of maybes. I think *maybe* our client is not giving us the full picture."

"Well he's the one paying the money. If it takes longer to catch her because he's not telling us everything, he's the one who loses."

A grumble. "The longer we're on this case, the less I like it. I don't care how rich the client is. The boss shouldn't be letting him dictate our moves like this. One minute he's got all our agents, plus the opposition swarming around Shepparton, the next he's sending them south. Now apparently they're all coming back again."

"Well he needs more than the two of us to round up Marshall. She's a slippery bitch. Do you think she really *was* on that road we were sent to just now?"

"I don't know, but if we hadn't been away searching for her when the alarms went off, we'd have got back here sooner and maybe caught her with the boyfriend."

"No, I don't think she's made it here yet. I think the boyfriend was waiting for her. He still had the wig remember."

Footsteps retreated and a door was slammed, leaving the house in silence. Jo noticed the storm had also passed, and apart from an occasional drip, all was still. She found she was shaking and it wasn't just from the cold. If the agent who'd opened her cupboard door hadn't been distracted by his colleague, he could have looked up and seen the outline of the manhole.

It had been too close for comfort. She'd planned to stay here until almost five, but confirmation that a swarm of agents was on the way, including no doubt the Hunter himself, now made her refuge feel like a trap. The longer she waited, the harder it would be to get out of here.

Jo felt for the handles of the cover and lifted it off. Then she eased herself through the hole and climbed stiffly to the floor. With the passing of the storm, the house had lightened a little and Jo tiptoed back to the office. Under the desk where she'd dropped it, was the Supermarket chain's letter with Simon Brookes' signature, and seeing his title, her eyes widened. He was Director of Operations for the Northern Victorian Region. This couldn't be. Such a person would be a pillar of society, not someone who employed hit men! What could possess him to do such a thing – surely not the dispute with apple growers over buying prices? That would be insane, for in the end, regardless of the amount both parties agreed upon, it wouldn't affect his *own* pocket.

Numbly Jo folded the letter and slipped it into her jacket. She needed time to think about this but not here. Her watch now read 3.09 p.m. She crept to the junk room, uncovered the bicycle and wheeled it to the front door, where she hesitated. It would be wise to grab a few provisions. Leaving the bike in the hall, she headed for the kitchen.

There was not a great deal in the fridge – she'd cleared out most of the fresh food before leaving for Melbourne on Sunday. Some apples, bread and cheese would have to do. Jo cut a chunk off the cheese block and as she washed the knife, realized the thought of arming herself hadn't occurred until now. Would a knife help or hinder? She had no fighting skills and in close combat a knife might easily be wrenched away and used against her. Furthermore a large one would be awkward to carry and conceal.

In the end Jo took a sharp paring knife from the drawer and a cork from the cork jar. She pushed the knife tip into the cork and reaching behind her, worked the weapon into the back pocket of her money belt. Not too uncomfortable, and it was close to hand if she needed it.

Bagging the cheese, bread and two apples, she took a small plastic bottle of mineral water from the fridge and returned to the bike. Jo inserted the bottle into the cage the salesman had fitted to the frame, and thrust the food bag into the closest pannier. The only thing left to decide was which way to go.

In an hour or less, agents would be cordoning off Shepparton, so riding into town felt like a bad idea but what were the alternatives? Heading out into the countryside was little better. There'd be fewer places to hide and when darkness hit she'd be vulnerable. A well-populated area was her best bet and given that she also wanted to follow up on Simon Brooks, she should try getting back to Melbourne, although that was easier said than done. The distance was too far to cycle, and now the Hunter knew she was in Shepparton, catching a bus was out of the question. There was always hitchhiking, and the more she thought about it the more appealing the idea became. At three-fifteen in the afternoon most drivers should be safe. Maybe even a woman would stop.

Her best chance of getting a lift would be on the main highway. The two Shepparton agents would be writing up their report and watching the house alarms from wherever they were holed up, so they were out of the way, and the other agents were yet to arrive, which made it safe to take her chances on the highway for a while.

The decision made, Jo ran a hand over her cropped hair and fitted the helmet. In a way it was liberating to be wig-free, but thoughts of the Hunter discovering her short cut, made her stomach churn.

Easing open the front door, she peered out. No sign of any agents. Jo pushed the bike through and shut the door gently behind her. At the bottom of the steps she tried to mount but the ground was waterlogged. Wheeling her bicycle, she headed for the orchard through the wet grass.

CHAPTER 29

The guards failed to follow when Richard hit the porch running, which surprised him until he remembered Jo had said *she* was their target. Before disappearing down the corridor, she'd ordered him out so decisively that he'd responded to the authority in her tone and fought his way free. Now, as he crouched behind an apple tree in the adjacent field, his conscience was screaming. He should have stayed to help her.

All three were now in the house and who knew what was happening. Had Jo hidden herself in time, or were those thugs standing over her dead body? How the hell had this mess happened? He'd never known the H Group to act so recklessly. Perhaps they could get away with a farmer's 'accidental' death, but a vicious attack on his daughter just three weeks later? It didn't make sense.

And what had Jo been reading under that desk with her flashlight? Had Bill done some investigating on his own and come up with something so damning the H Group felt the need for these drastic steps? It all seemed too improbable. Bill was highly concerned about his daughter's safety and wouldn't have done anything to jeopardize that.

The two gorillas appeared on the porch. They scanned the surrounding area and conferred together before walking off towards the packing and cold storage shed. At the shed they again stopped to look around and then moved out of sight.

Richard ached to sneak back to the house, but doing so would trip the alarms, causing more harm than good if Jo was just emerging from her hiding place. Better to wait. If Jo was okay she'd come out eventually and then he'd be able to help her. At least he was still in a position to do so.

He gingerly massaged his throbbing jaw, thanking his lucky stars he'd turned his head in time to receive only a glancing blow instead of the intended king hit. The goon who'd thrown the punch believed he'd knocked him out cold and had been unprepared for the slam of Richard's heel into his calf muscle, which had enabled him to escape.

Fifteen minutes passed and Richard grunted and changed position to ease a cramp. Still no sign of movement. He was starting to reassess his options when he saw her on the porch. She wheeled a bike down the steps and began crossing the paddock, heading towards a point in the fence about thirty meters from where he was.

Quietly Richard stood and worked his way through the trees in that direction. Jo, struggling through the wet grass, arrived only seconds before him. As she wiggled her bike under the fence, he whispered, "Jo, it's me, Richard."

The helmeted head jerked up at his voice and she froze, white-faced.

"It's okay," he said, stepping out from behind a tree, "I waited for you."

"Richard, I…"

"Let's get you under cover," he interrupted, moving to stand on the bottom wire of the fence and lifting the one above it.

Jo scrambled through and Richard took her hand.

"My car's nearby. We're going straight to the police."

"No!" She withdrew her hand sharply. He must have presented a gob-smacked expression, because she hurried into a garbled explanation.

"There's been a mix-up with the police. They think I'm someone else and they'll hold me for too long before I can get it sorted out. I'll be trapped in a cell where he can get to me!"

She seemed on the verge of hysteria and he adopted a soothing tone.

"All right, no police. Come back to my motel. We'll sit down with a hot drink and you can tell me about it."

Jo hesitated and then nodded. "Okay."

As they walked between the rows of trees together, neither spoke. Jo seemed exhausted, staggering occasionally, but Richard had the bike and was unable to give her a hand. He suspected she would not have welcomed it anyway.

He led her to where he'd parked the Commodore on a track on the other side of the fence.

"Here we are, though I'm not sure whether your bicycle will fit into the boot," he said.

"It will, I'll show you."

Jo pulled at some Velcro straps and lifted the pannier bags off the bike rack. With quick movements she folded the bike and when she pulled a plastic cover from one of the panniers, Richard helped her to zip the bicycle inside. He lifted the package over the fence and then created a gap for Jo to crawl through. On the other side, she did the same for him.

As he took the keys from his pocket and flipped the boot, Richard noticed that rather than going to the front passenger side, Jo had opened the back door.

"Do you mind if I stretch out in the back?" she said. "I'm a bit tired."

She looks wrung out, he thought. Well who wouldn't be after escaping the clutches of those two bouncers?

"No problem, it's about twenty-minutes to the motel. You take a nap."

He watched her climb in, remove her helmet and lie down in a huddled position. Her thin cycling gear was hardly suited to this cold winter's day. He needed to get her warmed up quickly or he'd soon have a sick young woman on his hands. He slid into the driver's seat and started the engine, turning the heater to full before heading down the short track to the road.

During the trip back, Richard began planning. If the H Group was after Jo, the time for collecting data on them had come to an end. The best way to protect her was to publicly expose their activities and techniques, which included murder and attempted murder. This all hinged on Jo being able to provide information that proved the H Group was responsible for her father's death. She must *have* that information, even if she didn't fully realize it – otherwise why would they be after her? Meanwhile, until the key players in the H Group had been neutralized, Jo had to be kept safe, which meant not letting Bev or any of the motel staff know she was with him.

He'd sneak her into his room and contact BEAM. They'd arrange a safe house and send in experts to talk to her. Once she'd given them the proof they needed, the great exposé could begin!

Richard gripped the steering wheel. He'd been working towards this for a long time and hadn't expected the reward to come so soon. Then he remembered Bill had paid the ultimate price for this reward, and that *he'd* been the one who'd persuaded the farmer to join the fight, assuring him there'd be no danger if he 'played by the rules'.

Bill, he was certain, *would* have played by the rules. He was too concerned about his daughter's safety to have done anything to draw the attention of the H Group, and yet somehow their attention had been drawn. Again Richard wondered whether he or someone at BEAM had slipped up. He couldn't see how, but if it *was* his fault, Jo would never forgive him. Jo... she *had* to have some answers, and he wondered what they could possibly be.

He swung into the parking space outside his motel and turned off the engine. Jo was sleeping, her slender legs curled up on the back seat. He wondered why she'd cut her hair short. The longer style had suited her much better. He reached down to touch the flyaway tips and stopped, suddenly realizing the irony of the situation. Now when he could finally tell Jo who he really was, he could still do nothing to show her how he felt. She was completely vulnerable. Her father had just died – the second parent in two years, and the H Group was sending its thugs after her. What she needed from him right now was support, not seduction.

...

The thump of the closing door woke Jo and for a moment she was in utter confusion. Had George pulled into a service station? No, this wasn't the Lexus. She was in Richard's car. The physical and emotional toll of the past two days, followed by the prospect of a safe, warm shelter with Richard, had broken the tight control she'd been keeping and she'd put herself into his hands. Since he had no idea of the stakes, it could only lead to disaster.

Jo sat up quickly and spotted him opening the door of a motel room. He turned and seeing her, looked rapidly around the parking area before beckoning urgently. She leapt from the car and dashed into the room. Richard followed, closing the door. Then he drew the curtains and flipped on the lights.

As she stood in the middle of the room watching these actions, Jo wondered helplessly what she was going tell him, but for the moment he seemed wrapped up in his own rituals.

"I think a hot drink to start with," he announced jovially, turning up the room heating. He grabbed the kettle from the side bench and filled it with water. "Tea, coffee or hot chocolate?" He fanned out sachets of the instant versions provided by the motel.

"Er, chocolate sounds good," said Jo sitting on the bed.

Though now he seemed content to run around waiting upon her, she knew the questions must inevitably come. A glance at her watch showed it was just after four – plenty of time to spin a story and hopefully persuade him to give her a lift to Melbourne, but as she watched him bustling about setting out cups and saucers with packets of complimentary crackers, warning bells started.

Why *was* he so eager to please? It wasn't as though they were close. True, she enjoyed his visits to the farm, and had even indulged in a few private fantasies about him – who wouldn't with such a hot salesman, but it was her father he came to see. Towards her he'd only ever been casually friendly. Now this afternoon, he'd seen her acting like a madwoman *and* it looked like he'd copped a beating from the Hunter's agents. On top of that she'd refused to let him go to the police, even giving him reason to believe the police might be after *her*. Most guys would be heading for the hills by now. Yet here he was, cheerfully making afternoon tea as if they were on a date.

She grew cold, remembering something else. Richard had broken into her house this afternoon. Had he been co-opted by the Hunter? Maybe this nice-guy act was a ploy to lull her into a sense of security until his boss arrived. If that were the case she had to get out of here, but her bike and gear were in the boot of his car.

CHAPTER 30

As he brought Jo the steaming drink, Richard was dismayed to see she looked more pinched than ever, despite the room now being quite warm. She seemed to actually flinch when he placed the saucer on the bed beside her and he retreated quickly to give her space.

"So," he spoke quietly, taking up his own coffee and sinking into a nearby chair. "I believe you have a story to tell me."

"I think," she replied, sitting stiffly on the bed, "that I'd like to hear *your* story first, starting with why you broke into my house this afternoon."

Richard was caught off guard. Not so defenseless after all! He belatedly recalled the authority with which she had ordered him from her house earlier that day and wondered how he'd been lulled into imagining she was unable to look after herself.

He cleared his throat. "Well, as I told you, something seemed wrong. I'd come around earlier to pay my condolences – I was *so* sorry to hear about your father's death. He was a good man…"

Jo said nothing, forcing him to continue.

"When I arrived, I found the front gate padlocked, something I'd never encountered before, and the house was patrolled by two guards who said they were security but wouldn't give the name of the company they worked for."

She nodded. "Strange, yes, but not strange enough for most people to return later and break in."

Richard took a deep breath. He'd obviously lost her trust and if he didn't come clean right now he might never win it back. "Jo, I'm not exactly who you think I am," he confessed, and was shocked to see her body tense and fear jump into her eyes.

"It's okay, I'm one of the good guys," he said quickly, hoping it was true and that her father's death could not be laid at his door. "My farm machinery

166

company is actually a front for a secret organization. We fight giant corporations trying to trample small business."

He watched Jo's fear become confusion and quickly continued. "Your father agreed that the trend of allowing control of the world's resources to fall into an ever dwindling number of hands, was not desirable, and he joined our fight."

Jo blinked and shook her head. "What?"

He gave her a self-conscious grin. "You could say I'm a secret agent, but not for the government. My salary comes from the fees and donations of many thousands of small businesses around the world. I'm employed by BEAM - *Businesses Exposing Antisocial Monopolies*. We keep tabs on the giants and help the little guys wherever we can."

"And you're saying my father was working for you?"

"*With* us. Some years ago we uncovered an alarming trend of orchards worldwide being bought up by foreign interests. Investigation revealed that a single group, the H Group, was behind all the purchases, their goal being to acquire every commercial orchard. We have reason to believe that orchards are just their starting point in a long-term aim to control the world's primary production.

Jo gave a hoot disbelief. "That's a plot from *Get Smart*." She began laughing.

Richard heard a note of hysteria in it and guessed he'd opened a valve on some pent-up stress. He sipped his coffee and waited. When she finally stopped herself with a gulp of hot chocolate, he continued.

"Your father was also skeptical until we showed him the data we'd collected, along with evidence that the Shepparton apple growers are on the H group's list."

She frowned. "Dad never said anything to me about this, which leaves just your word."

"There's plenty of data I could show you but it takes time to go through. Meanwhile you have some evidence in your own recent experiences. Who do you think it is, who's been after you?"

For a moment Jo stared at him open-mouthed. "Well it certainly isn't the H Group," she cried, her laughter returning.

He needed to shock her out of it. "What if I told you I believe your father's death to be no accident?"

She sobered quickly, but surprised him again. "That I already know, but your H Group had nothing to do with it. Unless Simon Brooks is a member."

"Simon Brooks?"

"The man who ordered the hit on my father. *Is* he an H Group member?"

"The name's not familiar. He may be linked to them in some way but... how do you know he ordered the hit?"

"I not only know he ordered it, I also know the hit man was Morris Blatman."

"Is he the one who's after you now?"

"Funnily enough, no," said Jo with a gurgle. "The guy coming after me isn't a professional hit man. He's a sociopath in his early twenties. He's bald – shaved not natural, with a tattoo of some kind at the base of his neck. If he succeeds in killing me he'll win a great deal of money. Oh, and he's also employed two top detective agencies to help catch me, though they don't know he's planning murder."

Richard stared at Jo in horror. The experience of her father's death along with having her own life threatened, had apparently unhinged her. BEAM would have to bring in professionals to help her before she could provide them with any useful information, but first he needed to win her trust.

"Jo, regardless of who is after you, BEAM can offer you a safe house until the bad guys are stopped."

"Richard," she said seriously, "if you were really able to do that, I'd jump at the chance, but unfortunately no place is safe for me beyond three hours."

"Why would that be?" he said cautiously, feeling his way.

Jo sighed. "I can see you don't believe what little I've told you, so you'd never believe the full story."

"I'm willing to listen. I'd like you to feel you can trust me."

She looked at her watch and in reflex he glanced at his. 4.28.

"The time for talk has passed," she said. "But if you want me to trust you, are you prepared to trust *me* and follow my lead for a while?"

Richard swallowed. He didn't like the way this was going, but Jo was his only hope of collaring the H Group immediately instead of having to spend who knew how many more years secretly resisting them and building up evidence.

"I'll go along," he agreed. "Within reason."

She nodded. "Okay. You can start by bringing my things in from the car."

Richard rose, dragging the keys from his pocket. When he returned to the motel room with Jo's gear, she pounced on the pannier pack and took it into the bathroom, closing the door. For a while he listened to sounds of movement and then the door opened and a new Jo stepped out, or actually, he corrected himself, the old Jo. She was dressed in grey track pants and a hoodie, and long blond hair hung smoothly to her shoulders. She smiled, triggering a stirring in his groin.

"We need to go for a little drive," she said.

"Where to?"

"Let's head towards Benalla. With luck he'll think I'm on route to Wangaratta and places north."

"He?"

"The Hunter."

Richard refrained from comment. If she chose to personify the H Group's forces in the form of a young skinhead punk, he could live with that fantasy.

"Will we be returning? I only want to know so I can checkout if not."

"Oh yes, it's just a short trip."

Richard opened the door, looked out and thumbed the lock release on his car key.

"All clear. You go first and I'll close up."

Jo slipped past him and once more dived into the back of the car. At least, he thought, as he closed the door, her paranoia can't hurt in avoiding the H Group. He slid behind the wheel and started the engine.

"Head east on the Midland Highway," called Jo from her supine position, "and keep driving. I'll tell you when to stop."

Richard followed her instructions, wondering if humoring her had been the right move. He could see she was once again dozing on the back seat, and after twenty minutes had passed, he decided to try to wake her with a question, but was beaten to it by a high-pitched beeping sound.

Jo sat up, silencing a wristwatch alarm. "Okay, do a U-turn, then pull over by the side of the road."

Richard complied and Jo opened the door.

"I'm just going a short way down the road," she said. "Wait right here. I'll be back in four minutes and we can return to the motel."

In his rearview mirror Richard watched her jog about twenty meters down the road, and then stand on the edge looking at her watch. After a couple of minutes she adopted a hitchhiking stance, which she held, although no cars were in view. Finally she dropped her arm and stood looking at her watch again.

What on earth would he say in his report to BEAM? He had to let them know he'd found her, but beyond that he was no longer sure what was going on. He had assumed the big bruisers at her house were H Group goons, but now he wasn't so sure. If Jo had lost her marbles to *this* degree, she could have attracted undesirable elements all by herself. And was there a genuine reason for her being so wary of the police?

His thoughts were interrupted by her return. She scrambled in and lay down, grinning up at him. "To the motel, Jeeves, and don't spare the horses."

As he looked at her with raised eyebrows, she became serious. "Richard, I *do* appreciate your help and I promise to give you the full story when we get back, even though I know you'll think I'm a candidate for the loony bin, if you're not convinced of that already."

He nodded solemnly. "Okay," he said, and then winked. "Guess I'd better get these horses moving."

They reached the motel twenty minutes later and as they walked into the room, Jo turned to Richard. "I'm dying to get cleaned up. Could you buy us some burgers while I'm showering? Then we can eat while I tell you my story."

Richard hesitated, strongly suspecting if he left to buy burgers she wouldn't be there on his return. Refusing to go, however, would be a sign he didn't trust her, which in turn would give her reason not to trust him.

"What would you like?"

"Chicken burgers are fine and fries are always good."

"Okay, I'll be back soon."

Richard left, but instead of getting into his car, walked around the back of the units until he reached to the bathroom window of his own. It was venting steam and he could hear the sound of water running. She seemed to be doing what she'd said, which was a good sign.

Quickly he circled to the car and drove to the nearest burger outlet where he ordered several different kinds, along with fries and soft drinks. Half an hour had passed by the time he got back to the motel, and turning the key in the lock, he held his breath.

Jo was inside wearing the track pants and hoodie, with her hair again short. She was rinsing out the coffee cups and her cycling shirt and jacket were draped over a chair near the heater. At the sight of his large paper bag, she grinned.

"Great, I'm starving."

Richard unloaded the bag onto the breakfast table and Jo immediately grabbed a chicken burger and began unwrapping it. He reached for some fries and munched on them as he watched Jo sink her teeth in. For a while she ate with singular focus, pausing only to crack open a can of Sprite and swig from it. Finally she picked up one of the napkins and wiped her mouth.

He noticed a blush rise to her cheeks as she looked up at him. Or was it just the warmth of the room?

"Guess it's time I told my story."

"I'm ready when you are."

She started badly. "It's 6.15. I can talk for an hour and three quarters before I have to move again. That's because every three hours my coordinates and photo are sent to the Hunter."

Richard felt a wave of disappointment. Jo had seemed so normal and vibrant when he'd returned with the food, he'd almost forgotten her behaviour on the highway. Now her paranoid declaration brought it all back. She seemed to be waiting for a comment, so he obliged, saying mildly, "You'll have to explain."

She nodded and pulled some fries from the paper bag. "Thanks for being prepared to listen. I know how that must have sounded. I'll start at the beginning.

"It began on Monday morning at eight a.m.... God that seems like forever ago but it hasn't even been forty-eight hours yet. I was in Melbourne on my way to an interview for a Uni course. I was stopped on the street by what I thought was a weirdo, but who turned out to be a holographic projection of a game show host from the future. This hologram, Danny Fitani by name, said I'd been selected to play a game in which a Hunter from my time but chosen by them, would have five days to kill me."

Richard said nothing. What *could* he say without revealing his conviction that she'd lost it?

Jo chewed and swallowed a fry before continuing. "You might ask why people from the future would devise such a nasty game – I did. Well it turns out they don't like us much. This era's failure to control its population growth will ultimately result in nuclear warfare, which will wipe out nearly all life on the planet. Those left will struggle to survive until The Company – a group that hid underground during the worst of it, emerges. The Company will co-opt the survivors into a workforce to clean the radioactive land and produce food. It will take hundreds of years, but eventually the people will end up in pretty good shape, except for one big downside. They have to live their lives in silos."

Richard choked on his burger. "Silos?"

"You got it. Their clean land is used for food production, so except for Company Executives, everyone lives, eats and sleeps in silos. They only ever leave them for four hours each day when they go out to work on the radioactive fringe, cleaning the earth."

Jo took another swig from the can of Sprite, but Richard still had no words.

"Anyway, something to do with microwave photons enables the people of the future to connect electronically with us through time. They can view us on their virtual TV sets, send holographic projections of themselves to our era, and even control *our* electronic devices."

"How nice for them," he managed.

She looked at him. "It enables Fitani and his friends to run this game. Through *Play or Die*, the people of his time can vicariously enjoy our open spaces while getting revenge on individuals from our 'evil' era."

"Er, I guess you tried reasoning with this man from the future?"

"Reasoned, ranted, pleaded. He was un-swayed. The game runs for five days. If the Hunter hasn't killed me by then I go free."

"You seem to be taking this rather matter-of-factly."

"Raging against fate gets you nowhere. I learnt that lesson when mum died. In any case, I haven't had much time to feel sorry for myself. The Hunter's been on my trail since Fitani told me I was Prey. I've already had more close calls than I like to think about."

Richard decided to play along. If he could show her the holes in this fantasy, it might help bring her to back to reality.

"So they send the Hunter your coordinates and photo every three hours? That hardly seems fair."

"Oh, they pride themselves on being fair. To balance that, I get to build up game points when I impress the viewers with smart moves. For every thousand points I receive, Fitani appears and I can ask him three questions. The Hunter and I were also allowed a single technological request. His was to set up a false ID for me in the national police database. In that database my photo and fingerprints identify me as Kylie Marshall, a drug addict with priors for theft and assault, who is wanted for kidnapping her baby son after the court awarded custody to the father."

"This Hunter seems smart." He mentally kicked himself. Really showing Jo the holes in her fantasy, he thought.

"You think *that's* smart? With my false ID in place, the Hunter approached two detective agencies as the representative of a billionaire whose grandchild Kylie had kidnapped, offering a big bonus to the agency that found Kylie first."

"Why two agencies?"

"So when the Hunter receives my coordinates, he can pass them on without creating suspicion, by telling each the other had located me there."

He raised his eyebrows but managed to refrain from comment this time.

Jo stood and carried the remnants of the meal to the bin. She filled the kettle.

"Coffee?"

Her matter-of-fact actions clashed with the crazy story she'd just told him.

"Thanks, milk and one sugar."

"How am I doing so far? Getting ready to call the men in white coats?"

"You tell an insane story very sanely," he said. "But do you have evidence to prove any of it?"

Jo gave a short laugh. "The best evidence would be for you to meet Fitani, but I never know when he'll show up. Since his last appearance I've hitched a ride on a small plane to Shepparton; snuck into my guarded house and successfully hidden from the Hunter's agents in the roof space; sent the Hunter a false indication I'm on my way north; and now I'm holed up safely for the moment, in this motel. All that should have earned me a few points. If you stick around, Fitani's bound to show soon. In the meantime…"

Her face suddenly became animated and she held up her hands. "Take a photo of me and my fingertips. Send them to BEAM to check against the national police database. *You* know I'm Jo Warrington, but the database will say I'm Kylie Marshall."

Richard took out his iPhone and snapped photos, forwarding them with a note to BEAM. While he did so, Jo made the coffees.

"I've just thought of some *more* evidence," she said, bringing their cups to the table. "Those men at my house – they were detective agency operatives."

He frowned. "Maybe. And maybe they were from the H Group."

"Well what about the fact that I was able to get into my place without triggering any alarms? That was *my* technological request – to be invisible to electronic surveillance the Hunter had set up around the house."

Richard looked at her speculatively. "It seems you were. The guards only showed up each time *I* went to the house. But there's something I don't get. If you anticipated the Hunter would stakeout your house, why go back at all?"

"To investigate my father's murder. You wanted to know how I knew about Simon Brooks? I knew because I'd asked Fitani. With their equipment they can view any event in our era and he told me Simon Brooks had paid Morris Blatman to make the hit.

"I figured if Simon Brooks ordered the hit, he must have known my father and had a reason. So I went back to the house to check through Dad's correspondence for any reference to him."

"That was incredibly reckless."

Jo shrugged. "According to Fitani, my chances of surviving five days of the hunt are minimal. I figured since I was probably going to die anyway, I'd try to track down my father's murderer before it happened and hopefully leave enough proof to have him convicted."

Richard blinked. Jo was either amazingly gutsy or even crazier than he'd thought. "Did you find anything?"

"Yes, but it doesn't make sense. Simon Brooks works for the supermarket chain we sell to. He's Director of Operations for the Northern Victorian Region. People like that don't go about employing hit men."

Richard's phone chimed and he read its text message in disbelief. Jo's photo and fingerprints were listed on the police database as Kylie Marshall's! His head spun. Since finding her this afternoon he'd oscillated between admiration for her quick thinking and courage, and fear she was raving mad. Now he held corroboration of at least one part of her story. Could there be more evidence?

"Jo, you don't by chance know the names of the detective agencies the Hunter employed?"

"I do. It was one of the questions I asked Fitani." Jo dived for the pannier bags, searching in first one and then the other before holding a notebook aloft. She flipped through its pages and announced, "They are *Eagle Investigations* and *SIS – Secure Investigative Services*. If BEAM can confirm they're both after Kylie Marshall, you'd have another piece of evidence, yes?"

Richard replied cautiously, "Detective agencies keep their assignments and clients confidential. It won't be easy to discover if they're going after Kylie Marshall, but I can certainly get BEAM to make inquiries."

"What about Simon Brooks and Morris Blatman?" cried Jo. "If BEAM can find evidence they're responsible for my father's murder, it's *more* proof!

Fitani gave me those names. There's no other way I could have known about them."

Richard made up his mind. Discovering the truth about Bill Warrington's death was his top priority. If he could prove it was an H Group hit, BEAM would be able to take immediate steps to bring them down. Right now his only two leads were the names Jo had provided, and since at least one of them had turned out to be a real person, he intended getting BEAM to investigate.

The problem was that he could hardly tell his bosses he'd received the information from a girl who claimed she'd obtained it by communicating with people from the future. That ruled out taking her to a safe house. If BEAM came to suspect she was off her rocker, they'd drop that avenue of investigation and he wanted all their resources focused on it.

On the other hand there was no doubt Jo was in danger, whether from the H Group or her mysterious Hunter. One way or another she needed his help until this thing was resolved. He turned to her.

"Jo, I can hardly believe I'm saying this, but I'm starting to think there may be something to your story. I'm going to set BEAM onto investigating Brooks and Blatman, and also to see if they can find out whether those detective agencies are after Kylie Marshall. In the meantime, in order to help keep you safe, I'm prepared to offer my services."

CHAPTER 31

He watched the cup in Jo's hand tremble. She put it clatteringly on the saucer and stood, tears spilling down her cheeks. She must have been steeling herself so much for his rejection that when it hadn't come, her defenses had crumbled. He moved towards her and suddenly she was in his arms, holding him as tightly as he was holding her.

"Ah, how the audience loves a bit of schmaltz!" pronounced a gleeful voice. "That little clinch added just enough points to pop you over the thousand."

Richard jerked at the sound and twisted towards it, putting Jo behind him. As he tried to take in the bizarre sight, he heard Jo's voice saying sarcastically, "Nice costume Danny. I see you're still into the animal theme."

The thing preening before him, Richard now saw, was a thin man. His entire body was sheathed in what appeared to be tree bark but couldn't have been, as it was completely flexible, adjusting to every muscle twitch as he spread his arms and pirouetted. Thin branches sprouted from those arms, ending in clusters of eucalyptus leaves. The red hair, standing up in stiff strands from his green head, was likewise topped with leaves. More horrifying than this though, was the animal life traversing the tree-body.

Colonies of ants moved up the trunk and apparently into knots and under loose pieces of bark. In a forked branch near his shoulder, a koala with a baby on her back sat contentedly chewing leaves, and at his forehead a small spider hung at the end of a silvery thread that descended from a web glittering between the vertical strands of his hair. The web was the only unnatural element, having been spun in the design of a logo.

"That must have cost you a pretty Personal Point," Jo's voice continued.

The tree-thing spoke loftily. "What are a few thousand Personal Points, when it comes to showing one's support for our great Company?"

"Hmm," Jo's tone became speculative. "Since when did The Company need a show of support?"

"No talk of The Company! I am here only to answer your three questions."

Richard strode forward, and with his entire weight threw a punch at the green face, regretting only that the koala and her baby might be injured in the tree-creature's fall.

Inexplicably he found himself sprawled facedown on the bed behind the tree-man, who had stepped towards Jo and was continuing to talk to her as though nothing had happened. Leaping up Richard aimed a karate chop at the trunk-neck, and tottered as his hand sliced through an apparently solid body without resistance.

"Richard," Jo's voice penetrated his shock. "This is Danny Fitani, or his hologram at least. He's the one I told you about – the host of *Play or Die*."

Richard moved to join Jo, passing ghost-like through several branches before turning to scowl at Fitani. The host gave him a desultory wave and turned back to Jo.

"So, what is your first question?"

"All in good time Danny."

Jo put her hand on Richard's arm, which helped bring him out of his daze. "He takes a bit of getting used to," she said quietly. "But Fitani's not the one we have to worry about. He can actually give us valuable information if we ask the right questions."

She turned back to speak to the host, but Richard beat her to it. "You green prick! What the hell gives you the right to inflict this vicious game on an innocent young woman?"

Fitani flicked him a dismissive glance and grinned at Jo. "Just as well *he's* not the one I have to answer, or you would have wasted a good question."

"Indeed," Jo said calmly. "But since he's now helping me, we'll be discussing together which questions I'll be asking, so I suggest you wait over there while we do so."

She pointed to a corner of the room, but Fitani frowned and stayed where he was. Jo ignored him and seated herself at the breakfast table, gesturing to Richard to take the chair opposite.

"Any ideas?" she said as he sat.

Richard found himself speechless, but Fitani's derisive chuckle did wonders to focus his mind. He turned his back on the game show host and spoke to Jo.

"Could you ask him how to avoid being killed by the Hunter?"

"That's a bit general. He's likely to respond with something like – *Stay out of its clutches*. Better to be as specific as possible."

"Well, how about asking where the closest agent is?"

"Yes, that's a good one."

"In fact," said Richard, getting into his stride, "why not ask where the nearest *six* agents are."

Jo glanced at Fitani and Richard followed her gaze, catching a smirk on the green face.

"Risky," she said. "He might regard that as six separate questions and after telling me the location of three of them, disappear on us."

"Save that for last then. Should we ask about the *Hunter's* location? Or is he likely to be with his agents?"

"When it comes to the Hunter, I've learnt not to assume anything," she said, and turned to the tree-man. "Okay Danny, question number one – where is the Hunter right now?"

Fitani tilted his head, appearing to consider for a second before replying. "Your Hunter is sitting inside a building at the Shepparton airport."

Richard raised his eyebrows. "Why the airport I wonder?"

Jo's eyes narrowed. "I think I can guess. He likes to keep a step ahead of the game. In a little over forty minutes he'll receive my new coordinates. By now he's probably positioned the majority of his agents around Shepparton. Some he would have sent on to Wangaratta and Albury-Wodonga in case I really *was* headed that way, but he's learnt I have a few tricks of my own.

"I'm guessing he's chartered a helicopter with a local pilot. If they lift off and hover over Shepparton just before 8.00, the Hunter can be onto my position within a minute of receiving it. With a powerful searchlight he can keep me covered until the ground troops pick me up. Then he can just set the chopper down in a nearby field."

"But having caught you for the Hunter, wouldn't the agents be expecting to hand you over to the police?"

"They would," said Jo. "But all the Hunter has to do is offer to *fly* me to the Melbourne police, pointing out it's quicker than going by car. Then when he's got me in the helicopter…" she looked at Richard.

"What a neat way of both catching and killing me. During the flight he injects me with something nasty, simulates a struggle for the benefit of the pilot, and my subsequent dive from the chopper is put down to the escape attempt of a frenzied drug addict, high on some hallucinogen."

Richard regarded Jo with amazement but he couldn't fault her reasoning except in one area.

"This would all be highly expensive to organize. How could a young twenty-something punk have that kind of cash?"

"In the rules of the game, Hunters can elect to take a one million dollar cash advance on their potential fifty million dollar prize-pot."

He turned to Fitani in disbelief. "You pay a million dollars to fund a murderer and fifty million if he succeeds? That's obscene!"

Fitani looked through him as if he hadn't spoken and Richard felt his face grow hot with anger.

Jo's hand on his once more steadied him. "We'll need to move soon."

Something shifted inside him and Richard felt the last of his resistance drop away, finally accepting that the Hunter and the game were real.

He spoke decisively. "Right. The best approach would be to do what we did before. Get twenty minutes away from here for the broadcast and then return. At 8.00 p.m. there'll still be plenty of vehicles on the roads. Even if the Hunter guessed you were in a car, he'd be hard put to figure out which one.

"The broadcast point should be as far away as possible from agency operatives, so my suggestion for your next question is to ask which road twenty minutes from here is farthest from the nearest agent.

Jo's eyes glowed. "Excellent!" She turned to Fitani.

His tone was sulky. "They're supposed to be *your* questions, not his."

Jo gave a little laugh. "Danny," she said sweetly, "I recall quite clearly you telling me I was allowed to use help, and I know your sense of fair play would never let you go back on your word."

Fitani shrugged and the koala repositioned itself in his tree fork. "Go ahead."

"What's the name of a road twenty minutes from here by car, which is the farthest from any of the Hunter's agents?"

Fitani adopted his usual head tilt for a second. "That would be Huggard Drive."

"Do you know it?" Richard asked Jo.

"Never heard of it. I'll need to check the map."

"Then let's check it now." Richard glanced at his watch. "We have to leave in fifteen minutes and I'd like to send in my report before we go."

"No problem, you get started on your report and I'll check the route on *my* laptop."

An imperious throat clearing from Fitani was ignored by Jo, but made Richard ask, "What about the last question?"

"No rush. Danny will stick to me like glue until I've asked it."

"We won't have room in the car for that *tree-thing*!"

"He's a hologram remember. He takes up no room at all."

"Oh, yeah." Richard felt chagrined, but Jo smiled sympathetically. "Don't worry, *I* took a while to get used to it."

As the two of them set up their laptops on the breakfast table, Fitani began an annoying refrain. "I haven't got all day you know. Some of us have better things to do than watch people type their memoirs. You're boring the viewers. They want to know what your final question is."

Richard followed Jo's lead in ignoring Fitani, but found his whining litany a distraction. He decided to tell BEAM he'd located Jo and that she had allowed him to go through her father's correspondence, where he'd found a possible link to his murder through Simon Brooks and... Fitani's drone was destroying his concentration.

"Jo, what was Blatman's first name?"

"Morris." Her head shot up. "I know what my last question is. Danny, where does the Morris Blatman who sabotaged my father's tree shaker, currently live?"

"Jo!" Richard couldn't hide his dismay. "Your life's at stake. You should have used that last question to help you avoid the Hunter."

"I couldn't agree more," said Fitani. "She *does* love to waste her questions. But since she's asked, I must reply."

Danny provided a Melbourne address, which Richard added to his report.

"Blatman's a professional hit man," Jo told Richard earnestly. "We don't even know if that's his real name or an alias he used when Brooks hired him. BEAM would never find him without more information. Now they've got his address. You should tell them to go straight there. Who knows how long he'll stay put."

"Don't worry Jo. We'll get surveillance on him immediately. We'll also investigate Brooks' background to see if we can find a motive for murder."

"Thank you." She scanned the room and grinned. "Fitani's gone – and I didn't even notice his departure. It feels good."

She checked her watch. "Eight minutes before we need to leave. I've found Huggard Drive. It's a dead-end street north of Mooroopna. I've got the route on my laptop, and now I need to get my wig."

Richard nodded, finishing off his report. To his top-priority posting regarding Brooks and Blatman he added a side request that an attempt be made to discover whether *Eagle Investigations* and *SIS* were currently hunting Kylie Marshall. He knew this would raise a few eyebrows coming on the heels of his having sent in her photo and fingerprints, and that he'd soon have questions to answer, but he'd cross that bridge when he came to it. He ran the report through an encryption program and was emailing it as Jo emerged from the bathroom. She'd combed out the long wig, and the sight of her even in track pants and hoodie, took his breath away.

"Ready?" she asked.

"Ready."

Jo grabbed her computer and they headed for the door. Again she curled herself on the backseat, calling out directions in the glow of her laptop. They reached Huggard Drive a little under twenty minutes later and as Richard drove down it, he noted the trees and open grassland on his right. On the left side, warehouses and some light industry ensured that this road in the middle of nowhere had electricity poles and street lighting. He swept around the turning circle at its end and drove back a short way before pulling over.

The two stepped out and Richard realized this cul de sac was a good spot – just seconds from the fast and straight Echuca-Mooroopna Road, which though it had minimal traffic at this time of night, was only five minutes from the busy Midland Highway.

A sudden sharp beeping made him jump. Jo turned off her alarm and handed him the laptop. "I'll jog down to the end for the broadcast. If the Hunter *is* in a chopper, he could be onto us quickly, so we'll need to move fast afterwards."

"He'll have agents stationed along the main roads," Richard reminded her. "Perhaps you should ride in the boot for this trip, in case I'm stopped."

He watched as Jo cast a dubious eye over the boot. Though obviously not keen on the idea, she nodded before jogging off towards the end of the road.

...

Jo stood under a streetlight with a cyclone wire fence at her back, wondering if she'd been right about the Hunter using a helicopter. If so would she be able to hear it from here? They'd taken twenty minutes to get to Mooroopna by car on roads that looped around a forest reserve, but as the crow flew, Shep was probably only five or six kilometers from here. How far did sound carry?

The numbers on her watch changed to 8.00 p.m. and it took a huge effort to remain where she was, straining her ears as she set the next alarm for two minutes to eleven. Thirty seconds later, straining was no longer required. She could definitely hear a faint throbbing sound.

As she raced back, Jo found herself thinking her watch must be pretty close to spot-on correct and that she wouldn't need to wait as long as two minutes after the hour in future.

Richard was standing by the open boot when she reached the car. He helped her in and clicked the lid shut. Jo closed her eyes, trying to pretend she was simply lying on the back seat as usual, but cushioning was noticeably absent. As they sped along, she felt every bump, at times even having to press hands and feet against the molding to stop from being thrown about. She hadn't remembered this many turns on the way. Just as she'd decided that battling the movement at least helped to keep her mind off being closed in, all motion ceased. The engine died, replaced by the raucous clamor of a helicopter. Something was terribly wrong.

A loud screeching of tires sent a shiver down her spine. It was followed by the rocking whump of the car door slamming and Jo tensed, ready to leap out when Richard released her, but the lid remained closed. Where was he? Surely he wouldn't abandon her? Jo lay staring into the dark, trying to convince herself that the sensation of increasing suffocation was all in her mind.

CHAPTER 32

Richard had also heard the faint chopping sound as Jo came running to the car. He allowed himself no more than a twinge of anxiety about shutting her into the boot, before jumping behind the wheel and gunning the engine. When he turned left into Echuca-Mooroopna Road and found it empty, his foot snapped to the floor. If he wasn't off this road when the helicopter arrived... well, a single set of headlights travelling from the scene would be all too obvious from above.

Quickly paddocks gave way to houses and alongside the housing, a service lane appeared, separated from the main road by a wide strip of mature eucalyptus trees. Richard veered into the service lane, glad of the trees' spreading shelter, and slowed, looking for McFarlane Road. He'd studied the map while Jo had been waiting for the broadcast, and decided that rather than risk entering the Midland Highway from the Echuca-Mooroopna Road – a likely intersection for agents, he would wind through the suburban streets of Mooroopna and join the highway further down.

He could now hear the helicopter clearly and on impulse stopped the car to look back. Over the area of Huggard Drive, a searchlight was circling. Richard heaved a sigh, thankful he'd made it off the main road before being spotted, and felt another surge of relief as McFarlane Road came up on his left. Turning into it, he noticed a car travelling fast on the main road towards the searchlight and wondered if it contained agents hurrying to rendezvous with their boss.

On McFarlane, anxious to bury himself among the streets, Richard looked for a right turn and spied McKean Street. A pair of headlights swung into McFarlane a hundred meters behind him and bore down fast. Adrenaline kicked his foot to the floor and he shrieked into McKean, roaring down it for an interminable distance as he searched for a turnoff. Before he found one,

181

the headlights turned into McKean and accelerated towards him. A road came up on his left and Richard swung in. It was a short street ending in a T-intersection and as he turned right at the T, the headlights swept into the street he'd just left.

Richard floored the accelerator and suddenly realized he couldn't hear his own engine over the din of the approaching helicopter. His heart sank. He couldn't outrun both. He swerved into a street on the right and was considering stopping and trying to bluff his way out of it when he spotted an open driveway with an empty carport. Using the emergency brake, he spun the car into a sharp turn, ending under the carport. Then he killed lights and engine, and ducked down. Seconds later a screech announced the arrival of the following vehicle, and he let it roar down the street before leaping out, slamming the door and rolling underneath his car. He lay panting as though he'd run this race on his own feet and wondered how far his pursuer had gone. The racket from the helicopter made it impossible to tell, but he knew the car would return as soon as the agents realized he wasn't ahead of them. Richard worried for Jo, lying in the boot, but there was no way to reassure her.

· · ·

So far, Jo had kept a tight rein on her fears, but now it was stretching thin. She'd never been claustrophobic, but then she'd never been locked in a car boot before. The rational part of her mind told her that if Richard had left her there, it was because that was the safest option, and when the danger had passed he'd come back for her. But from the depths of her psyche a little bubble of primitive terror began rising and the more Jo tried to suppress it, the more persistently it pushed upwards.

She tried stern reasoning. You've been in the boot less than ten minutes, Jo. Think of Fitani's people locked in their tubes for twelve hours. They love it!

"On their soft mats with fresh breezes wafting around them," said another part of her mind. "Modern cars have thick seals. How much fresh air do you think you're getting in this boot?"

She sucked in a sobbing gasp. Was the air beginning to feel thick? Stop it, Jo, she thought. The more you panic, the more oxygen you use. Relax and slow down your breathing. But something was digging into her hip, making it hard to relax. She squirmed and her fingers found the outline of a rounded corner, which moved when pushed. The laptop! Richard must have dropped it into the boot. With more rolling and squirming, she managed to push it out and lift it onto her chest. The Internet dongle was still in its side and the realization that she had a connection with the outside world brought back her sanity. Jo closed her eyes, hugging the laptop like a teddy bear and feeling tears of relief roll down her face.

· · ·

On his stomach, Richard lifted his head to scan what he could of the world from under the car. The searchlight, shining from the helicopter above, lit up the pavement like day and as he watched, a set of car wheels came to a halt by the curb. He saw the bottom section of the door open and trousered legs emerge, standing until they were joined by a second set. Both sets began walking up the driveway towards him.

They were shouting to each other over the noise of the helicopter and when their shoes stopped half a meter from his face, Richard heard,

"… boss says no ones'… bushes… all clear around the area."

"… car hood… warm. White Commodore… boyfriend for sure. Must be inside… house."

"Tell the chopper… going in."

As Richard lay waiting for the agents to move, he grimly tallied his mistakes.

One – not changing the rental car. On the porch this morning the agents had been too far away to see his number plate, but they'd have noted his car's make and color, and catching him in the house a second time, would certainly have passed it on. Why hadn't he gone straight to the Shepparton rental outlet after dropping Jo at the motel, and changed the car? Because, he remembered, Jo had seemed poised to take off the minute his back was turned.

With everything going on, that mistake was perhaps forgivable. Not so, mistake number two – leaving his headlights on as he drove down the service lane. Could he have called any louder to the agents travelling towards Huggard Drive? Of course they'd aborted their trip to check him out.

Jo had managed to keep safe the whole the time she'd been alone, and the moment she'd put her trust in him, he'd handed her to the Hunter on a plate. Well, not quite yet, and not if he could help it.

Squirming, Richard withdrew the knife he'd strapped around his shin before heading out to break into Jo's house. The helicopter was moving away and as its noise lessened, the agents' voices became more audible.

"… take the back, I'll take the front."

"…boss going?"

"… wider perimeter. He'll land if we catch her."

The feet departed. Richard squirmed to the edge and sticking his head out, saw a shape at the front door and heard a bell chime. The darkness, which had fallen as the helicopter moved away, was broken by a flood of porch light. Behind the screen door a woman's voice rose querulously. The agent held up an open wallet. His voice was firm. Protests continued from the other side, but eventually the man prevailed and the door was opened.

As soon as he disappeared into the house, Richard rolled out from under the car and sprinted down the driveway to the vehicle parked at the curb.

Crouching by the back wheel, he thrust his knife viciously into the sidewall, and then moved forward, doing the same to the front. They wouldn't go far on two flat tires.

Now he ran back to his own car, grateful the helicopter, even somewhat removed, was still making enough racket to mask the noise of his engine starting. Leaving his lights off, he reversed into the street, and accelerated to the end, turning south, away from the circling spotlight. He figured he had only minutes before the men in the house, or new agents arriving, discovered the white Commodore was missing and informed the Hunter.

I can't drive to Shepparton, he thought. As soon as the Hunter learns I've gone, he'll sweep the Midland Highway with his helicopter, and send agents to cover the side roads. This car's a beacon. I have to get it out of sight.

Vaguely he recalled passing some kind of parkland near the end of the chase, and turned left at the next crossroad. Bingo – trees loomed at the bottom of the street. On reaching them, he discovered the 'parkland' was in fact a golf course behind a high chainmesh fence. A road ran alongside the fence and he turned onto it, hoping to find an opening. Eventually the road became a lane, running between the golf course and a construction site in which old buildings were being converted to something modern.

Richard entered the lane, but halfway down found it closed off by the building project. That's what happened when you drove without lights – such things weren't obvious until you got close. Quickly he flicked the headlights to double-check there was no way forward, and in doing so, glimpsed something from the corner of his eye. Another flick confirmed it - an open gate in the golf course fence gave access to a dirt maintenance track. Richard turned onto the track, driving slowly. It wound through a perimeter planted with native trees and he saw with joy that one of them was a large spreading grevillea bush. He spun the wheel, and leaving the track, drove under the heavy weeping branches. Limbs and twigs scraped across the roof and windows as he rolled close to the trunk.

...

When Jo heard the helicopter's roar fade, and felt the car start up and begin moving, she breathed more easily. Richard had returned and they were on their way – far more sedately this time, which she took as a good sign until a nasty thought occurred. What if the driver wasn't Richard? What if an agent was delivering her to the Hunter? No, she corrected herself. An agent would have opened the boot to confirm she was there. It *had* to be Richard driving, which meant she'd soon be out of this freezing, suffocating metal box and back in the warmth and safety of the motel room. Jo was just tasting the thought when the car rocked with a wild scraping and scratching on all sides. She braced herself, thinking they'd gone over an embankment, and then everything was still.

As she lay wide-eyed, the release catch popped and she pushed cautiously against the lid. Something was obstructing it and Jo was just beginning to tentatively apply some gentle force when more loud scratching shocked her into heaving up against the boot lid. It opened halfway and something swept inward, hitting her in the face. She screamed and heard Richard's voice amid frantic rustling.

"It's okay! We're in a bush. I'm trying to get to you."

Jo reached out a shaky hand and confirmed her assailant was indeed a branch of spiky leaves. She sighed weakly.

"Are you alright?" A dark shape was holding up the boot lid with one hand and trying to pull the branch clear with the other.

"Richard? Yes, I'm okay."

As he held the branch back, she struggled onto her belly and dragged herself forward, slithering over the lip and ending in a heap on the soft earth at his feet.

"Jo!" He dropped to a crouch and reached for her. She clung to him in the dark, choking back a sob, and he began to stroke her hair, but gave an exclamation when the wig came off. They both laughed and Jo's fingers found his and gently extracted the wig.

She tucked it through her money belt. "What happened? Did we go off the road?"

"I had to drive under a bush. They're looking for this car."

"So we're on foot?"

"Afraid so."

Jo shivered. She could still hear the helicopter.

"Do you know where we are?"

"I have a general idea, but I'd like to confirm it with the map."

"The laptop's in the boot," she said dryly. "Your turn to dive in."

Richard reached in and felt around until his hand brushed the computer. He pulled it out, careful not to dislodge the broadband dongle, and handed it to Jo. Then he stood and began a tussle with the tree branch in an effort to close the boot.

Jo crawled gingerly through the prickly leaves and stood up with relief when she finally broke through. It was pitch dark and she opened the laptop for some light. Richard joined her and studied the cached map on the screen. After scrolling and zooming, he pointed. "We're here. See this unnamed track off Park Street going through the golf course?"

Jo drew a breath. "That rectangle beside the golf course – it says Mooroopna Hospital. There must be cars in the parking area. Do you know how to hot-wire a car?"

Richard spoke regretfully. "Sorry to throw a dampener, but the label's out of date. The hospital's being converted to something else. Guess they figured they didn't need one with Shepparton so close. And you can forget about hotwiring a car, unless we find a model older than thirty years, which is how long they've been making them with steering locks."

"Oh," said Jo. "What do we do then?"

"Get out of here as quickly as possible. We're a minute's walk from the Midland Highway. Hitchhiking is fastest."

"But won't agents be stationed along the road?"

"I'm banking on the Hunter having called his agents over to the area where I last stopped. If he has, the road will be clear for a while, but we'll need to hurry. As soon as he learns we're no longer contained, they'll be swarming back."

Richard closed the laptop and tucked it under one arm. He reached for Jo's hand with the other, and as quickly as the darkness allowed, led her back to the construction site. From there a walking path took them to the highway. He drew her to the edge of the road and she followed reluctantly, pulling her hood up.

"I hate being in this outfit but at least the hoodie will keep my short cut hidden."

Richard's strained smile failed to reassure her. "Don't worry, we'll soon be out of here." He held out his thumb.

After three cars zoomed past, Jo stopped paying attention to the road and began looking for a hiding place to run to if the helicopter swooped in.

Suddenly Richard was tugging her hand. "Come on!"

An old green Ford Fairlane had pulled up ahead of them and was waiting, idling roughly. A young Sudanese couple occupied the front seats and in the back, two children around five and seven years of age grinned up at them as they opened the door.

"Move over kids," ordered their father.

Richard nodded to him. "Thanks, we appreciate the lift."

"Look!" The older girl was pointing. "A light from the sky. I want to see it!"

"We'll sit in the middle," Jo said quickly. "You can have the window seat."

With a grin, the girl scrambled out and Jo and Richard slid into the middle of the back seat.

"Come on, Nansi." An exasperated note tinged her mother's voice. "We have to get home."

The girl jumped in beside Jo and wound down the window to watch the approach of the helicopter's searchlight. The car resumed its journey along the highway and Nansi cried out in pleasure as the searchlight moved across to them, enveloping the car and lighting up the surrounds for a while as they travelled. She leaned out of the open window and waved up to it.

Her father, muttering behind the wheel, was less impressed. "Why is that helicopter following us? I thought we'd left all that behind in Melbourne."

At that moment, a white car travelling in the opposite direction whizzed past and the searchlight moved off them to follow it. Nansi twisted around, watching its path down the road through the back window, until they rounded a bend and it was no longer visible.

"It's so nice of you to give us a lift." Jo wanted to distract the father from speculating about whom the helicopter might have been searching for. "Our car broke down and we've been walking for ages. We thought we'd have to walk all the way back to Shepparton."

"Do you not have a phone?" inquired the wife.

"We do," Richard jumped in. "But our so-called friends were all too busy to come and pick us up. Wait until *they* get stuck one night. Then it won't seem such a joke to them."

"Poota!" The younger girl, sitting next to Richard, was pointing to the laptop.

"Yes, we didn't want to leave our computer in the car. Would you like to have a look?"

"*I* want to see it," demanded Nansi, leaning across Jo.

Richard flipped open the lid, and googled "kids games'. He randomly clicked one of the links that appeared, choosing a game called Treasure Hunt. As the girls watched avidly, he began steering the treasure hunter through a maze using the arrow keys.

"Go that way," instructed Nansi. "I see a key under the bush!"

The younger child was content to let Nansi navigate, and soon all four were involved in the game. Nansi successfully steered Richard around a crocodile-infested swamp, up a vine to avoid the zombies and finally into an underground cave where they found the ruby, which was level one's treasure.

Jo noticed they had crossed the river into Shepparton and were signaling to turn north on the Goulburn Valley Highway. Their motel was south and she glanced at Richard, but he shook his head. She assumed that like her, he'd observed the unusual number of cars parked beside the closed shops around this main intersection.

"Where would you like to get out?" asked their driver.

"A little further along if that's okay."

Richard gently resisted Nansi's urgings to progress to level two, and closed the laptop. The car continued to Nixon Street and turned right.

"Anywhere along here would be great," said Richard. They pulled over and Nansi leapt out. Jo followed and turned back to wave to the parents as Richard emerged. "Thanks again. You saved us a long walk."

Nansi's mother spoke to them over the back seat.

"You go home and rest now," she said. "And maybe get yourselves some new friends."

187

CHAPTER 33

Jo looked at her watch. "It's 9.15, we'd better get moving. I'd say we're about three kilometers from the motel. At least it's good to finally be back where I know the streets."

She turned south and Richard fell in beside her. They were in Corio, a wide street with a center planting of tall trees. Light industrial buildings, closed for the night, lined both sides. As they walked, Richard filled Jo in on the car chase, and she pulled up to stare at him in horror.

"If you hadn't spotted that empty carport..."

He spoke reassuringly. "But I did, and we live to fight another day." He paused. "I do feel bad for the woman in the house though. The agents were convinced we were hiding there and no doubt scared her witless storming around trying to find us and probably accusing her of harboring fugitives."

Jo grabbed his arm and spoke urgently. "Richard, that woman will survive. I wish I could be so confident about us. We have only an hour and a half until the next posting. Our transport is gone and the Hunter has us surrounded."

"I may be able to do something about transport." He pulled a phone from his pocket and tapped the screen before lifting it to his ear.

"Marilyn, hi... No I'm not back in Melbourne yet. I'm actually stuck in Shepparton without a car... Yes I know, long story, which I'll tell you over a drink. Right now though I was wondering if there was anything you could arrange... actually I was thinking of tonight... yes I know what the time is... yes I know I'm in a country town, but you have such a talent for... Okay, I guess there are limits. Don't suppose I could prevail on you to come up in your own car? ... It's not *that* far. What if I met you part way? Nagambie's less than an hour and a half from Melbourne at this time of night... It's a *nice* place. I was there for BEAM once... I'm not joking, it has lakes – in fact I stayed at a place right on the lake... No, very reasonably priced, BEAM got its money's worth… The Lake Retreat, I think…No, book the room in *your* name, I'll explain that too…So I'll meet you some time after eleven? You're a gem Marilyn. I owe you big time."

Jo caught Richard's eye as he put his phone away.

"Girlfriend?"

"Just a colleague," he lied.

"A colleague whose number's at the top of your speed dial and who's prepared to drop everything late on a week night and drive an hour and a half out of Melbourne to meet you?"

"What do *you* care?" he snapped. "I've organized a place to go after the next posting and a car when we get there."

She recoiled. What an idiot she'd been to think Richard was interested in her. She'd made a fool of herself clinging to him, and now he was regretting his decision to help. But if he didn't care about her, why was he running all these risks? Was it pity? No, she realized. Guilt. He'd got her father involved with the H Group, and now her father was dead. Richard was helping her because he felt responsible. That was the only reason.

A stone in her stomach weighed her down as she walked. Well if Richard *was* responsible for her father's death, she would go ahead and take his help, without qualms. The new resolve failed to reduce her leaden sense of loss.

Pull yourself together, Jo, she thought. Only two things matter right now – avoiding the Hunter and bringing down Dad's murderers. *Why* Richard's helping, isn't important, only that he *is*, and you can't afford to alienate an ally. She faced him squarely. "Sorry, didn't mean to pry." He had the grace to look contrite.

"We'll be in a shopping area soon," Jo continued, coolly. "The next main crossroad is High Street, which is actually the Midland Highway."

Richard could see it ahead. The shop and street lighting were much better down there. It was a main intersection – a place the Hunter might well have left agents, unless he'd drawn them all over to Maroopna by now.

Jo was waiting stiffly for his response and he felt ashamed at having snapped at her. His problem with Marilyn was hardly her fault, and tonight she'd been through hell in the boot of that car, for which she'd uttered not a word of complaint. He found himself deferring to her. "How do you want to play this?"

Still sick at the thought of Richard's girlfriend, and the fact that she'd misread him so badly, Jo wanted nothing more than for the walk to end. "We have to cross the highway at some point," she said. "And a long detour will take time. Why don't we just act like ordinary people out on a stroll, and go straight across."

Richard was startled. It wasn't like Jo to take this kind of risk, but having asked for her opinion, he wasn't prepared to shoot it down.

"Do you know any languages?" he said.

"I did some French at school." Jo was puzzled.

"Then let's speak French as we walk through that area. It might help to put off any agents nearby."

"And if it doesn't?"

Richard considered. "If we're stopped, I'll try to keep any agents occupied while you run. Get to the motel any way you can. Here…" he pulled a key from his pocket. "Wait in my room when you get there. Don't answer the door unless you hear my voice."

"What if you arrive before me?"

"I have things to do."

Jo took the key, but didn't move. "Tell me what you're thinking, Richard."

"I have an idea for organizing transport to get us out of Shepparton."

"You're not going to steal a car are you?"

"This from the person who wanted me to do *just that* only a short while ago."

"That was different. We were in a tight spot. Now we have a little more time to think through our options."

"It's okay Jo, I wasn't planning a heist. Bev's sons do the nightshift on the desk and they're always on the lookout for an easy buck. I can probably talk whoever's on tonight into letting me borrow the motel's van for a few hours."

Her matter-of-fact comeback made him blink. "So you'll need a bribe. How *much* do you think?"

"I'm hoping a hundred will do it," he admitted. "I don't carry large amounts of cash on me."

"Luckily I do." She fumbled under the hoodie and drew out two notes. "Here's two hundred."

Open-mouthed, Richard reached out. Jo pushed the notes into his hand, turned, and pulling her hood forward, continued down the street. Pocketing the money, Richard sprang to catch up, wondering if he'd ever get used to Jo's surprises.

As they began crossing with the lights, a tall man in an overcoat approached from the other side. Richard took Jo's hand and asked in his best carefree French accent, "Que fait-tu demain, Cheri?"

What am I doing tomorrow?" thought Jo. How do you say, running from the Hunter, in French? She strained for a quick response and a phrase from the conversational French CD came to her lips. "Je dois aller à la bibliotèque." I have to go to the library.

The tall man had drawn level as Richard asked, "Ah, pourquoi?"

Fortunately the CD had included a reason, so she responded with, "Je dois revenir quelques livres pour ma mère." I have to return some books for my mother.

The man passed by and they reached the other side, where a group of teenagers studied the menu in the window of a Chinese take-away and a middle-aged couple - both of solid build, walked slowly to the lights. Jo and Richard continued down Corio Street, but the middle-aged couple now turned and began to follow them.

"Ah, Cheri," said Richard, loudly. "J'ai oublié mes lunettes. Cours vite les chercher." He gave her a little push and Jo took off. Would the couple be fooled into thinking she was actually running to get his glasses?

As soon as Jo was clear, Richard turned, deliberately colliding with the couple, who had begun running towards him.

"Ah, excusez-moi."

The woman moved to dodge around him and he stepped to block her. For a few seconds they engaged in a to-and-fro dance in which the woman tried to step out of his way, and Richard pretended to be trying to move out of hers. "Si désolé," he said.

The man grabbed Richard's arm and the woman dodged past, speeding down the path in the direction Jo had gone. Maintaining his grip, the man spoke angrily. "What's your name?"

Richard changed to heavily accented broken English. "Ah, excuse me. My English is not good. Please, mon bras... let go."

The man released him, but stood close as he pulled out his wallet. He held up a photo ID card, which said he was a licensed private detective with Eagle Investigations.

Shrugging and smiling, Richard pretended ignorance with a French accent. "I am sorry. I do not understand."

"I have reason to believe," the man said clearly, "that you are aiding and abetting a fugitive. I am putting you under citizen's arrest."

He took a phone from his pocket and Richard instinctively swept it from his hand. The man recovered quickly, grabbing Richard's wrist and spinning him around to push his arm up behind his back.

The laptop skidded across the pavement and all the anger and frustration Richard had been unaware of suppressing, burst forth as energy. He rocked backwards, tipped the agent off balance and spun to break his hold. Then he threw a punch, rejoicing in the physical release. This man was his!

The fight was not easy. His opponent, though older, was tough and experienced. The two men fought silently and intently before Richard's youth and stamina won out. A feint and a trip sent the agent flying, and Richard heard a crack as his skull hit the pavement.

He stared at the unconscious man in shock. What had he done? The agent's phone was lying in the gutter and Richard picked it up and dialed emergency. He gave the operator the address and told her to send an ambulance for a man with a head injury. As she began asking for details of the man's condition, Richard looked up and saw the teenagers who'd been outside the Chinese restaurant, gawking at him from the corner. He severed the connection and dropped the agent's phone into his pocket. Then scooping up the laptop, he walked away quickly. Had those kids seen his face well enough to provide a good description? He didn't think so but with any luck they'd heard him speaking French and the police would be looking for a foreigner.

Richard weaved through side streets searching for Jo, but saw neither her nor the female agent. He became aware that his hand was aching, and realized he'd been gripping the laptop fiercely. Had Jo managed to lose the agent or was the woman now holding her for the Hunter?

Non-appearance of the chopper was a bad sign. If Jo had escaped, the agent would surely have called for the chopper's help with its searchlight, but if the woman had secured Jo somewhere in the heart of Shepparton where helicopters couldn't land, she'd have told the Hunter to drop his chopper off at the airport and come by car.

Richard pulled the male agent's phone from his pocket. No missed calls or messages. The woman hadn't tried to communicate with her partner. He dared to hope this was good news, but waiting for a possible message wasn't worth the risk of keeping the phone. He turned it off and ground it under his heel before dropping it down a storm water drain.

All he could do now was return to the motel. If Jo wasn't there, he'd borrow the motel's van as planned, and go looking for her. As he hurried back, Richard grimly considered what plans the Hunter would be making in regard to him. He'd hardly care to leave witnesses, so had probably already added Richard to his hit list. At some stage during the car chase the agents would have radioed the Commodore's number plate to the Hunter, and at opening of business hours tomorrow they'd learn the car had been hired for Richard Sayers, agricultural machinery salesman.

Logically, agency operatives would then contact Richard's farming machinery front company and inform them their salesman was aiding a fugitive kidnapper. The agents would ask for cooperation in apprehending him and the company would stall, saying he was in a country region and out of mobile phone range … Bloody hell, his phone! Richard pulled it out and shut it down. Another near disaster averted.

The farming machinery company would contact BEAM with the information that a detective agency had accused Richard of aiding a fugitive, and his real bosses would wonder what was going on. If he couldn't come up with a plausible story for them, they might think he'd lost his judgment in some unsavory emotional entanglement, and close down his Brooks and Blatman investigation.

Life wasn't getting any easier.

CHAPTER 34

Secretary Melvin Briggs stepped out onto the veranda of his country house and noted his son was already ensconced in a comfortable chair. Cedric was slurping a bourbon as he took in the view of trees and rolling pastures through half-lowered lids. At the slam of the screen door he looked around, but didn't bother to rise.

"Father, what's all this about? You've called me away from preparations for the most important event of the season. I know *you* don't care to keep up with such things, but I…"

Melvin cut in. "You think I would have summoned you here without a reason? Try to forget your social engagements for the moment. You have responsibilities and it's time you faced up to them."

Cedric went white, but before he could speak, Melvin continued. "You're my oldest child and will one day inherit the position of Secretary to the Secretary of the CEO. Meanwhile, as my 2-IC, you should be proving yourself worthy of leadership. Are you actually checking, for example, that your six brothers and sisters and eight cousins on the Morale Executive are doing their jobs of monitoring the world's silos? When was the last time you yourself used the passcode that makes surveillance invisible, to eavesdrop on employee Playrooms and discussion areas?"

His son exploded. "What nonsense is this, father? You call me out here on the eve of the new season hunt to talk about spying on the employees? The employees have been self-managed for years. They live their lives and we live ours."

"In other words," choked Melvin, "you don't even remember the last time you did your job."

Cedric waved away his father's words. "Everything's running smoothly. My siblings and cousins are quite capable of doing their parts and don't need me breathing down their necks. They have plenty of staff to monitor the silos in Safe Places around the world and my own staff monitors the silos here. I'd know if there were any problems."

"Would you indeed?" said Melvin. What guidance have you given your people Cedric? What have you told them to look out for? How long has it been since you've studied the psychology notes passed onto us by our great ancestor, Cedric Briggs, for whom you're named?"

"Father, employee morale is fine. You don't need to worry."

"No? That's what The Company thought after The Great Arising, hundreds of years ago, when they assumed the provision of safe, comfortable housing would suffice. It didn't, and the employees were on the brink of revolt by the time Cedric Briggs was given the job of calming them down. His success is why our family now has the role of Employee Morale. I don't suppose you remember what he actually did."

Cedric stiffened. "There's no need for sarcasm, father. The problem and the solution were obvious. Humans have a genetic need for activity, which wasn't being met.

Melvin nodded, relieved the child who would eventually replace him, at least had some grasp of the situation.

His son continued. "When automation gradually replaced the manual labor of the early years, the employees grew frustrated at being increasingly confined to the silos while Company Executives roamed freely on prime land at the centers of the Safe Places. My great, great, etc. grandfather, Cedric Briggs, realized that flaunting one's advantage was unwise and insisted all Safe Places wall their Executive estates. He also pushed through a ruling that only automated machinery could tend the vast production fields radiating out from the estates. As the fields extended, the silo dwellers literally lost sight of the Executives, but they still needed to be kept occupied. Shall I go on?"

"By all means," said Melvin.

"My forebear came up with the idea of adding Playrooms to the silos, along with the carrot of Personal Points, as an incentive for employees to channel their free time into useful pursuits. It was a stroke of genius. In the Playrooms, employees have pushed forward progress, while keeping themselves occupied and happy."

"Not *completely* happy," Melvin corrected. "Which is why the role of Employee Morale still exists. Tell me, Cedric, does your staff have the figures for employee suicides at their fingertips? Can they tell you to what degree depression amongst the silo dwellers has risen in the last two decades, or how many more drugs the tube smart mats are needing to administer? Can they describe trends in rage-related incidents, child abandonment and general neurotic behavior?

"These are all *recordable* indicators of employee unhappiness but there are also minor signs to watch for – a general rise in disgruntled conversations, an increasing tendency to criticize or question Company decisions…"

Cedric broke in. "Not much we can do about *that*."

"Really?" said Melvin. "Do you not remember Cedric's notes explaining the need for frustrations to be focused and released? If they're not, employees will vent their anger on The Company."

His son had the grace to blush. "Of course I remember. Cedric devised a brilliant focus for employee frustrations – the Ancestors."

Melvin nodded. "And he released those frustrations through events like the Four Seasons Raging Festivals – wild bacchanals, which end in the burning in effigy of the Ancestors who destroyed Earth.

"Don't forget the reading primers," said Cedric, anxious to redeem himself. "A whole range of stories for the young about the stupidity and selfishness of the Ancestors."

"Indeed. They were the precursors to the indoctrination games the children currently play. Thanks to the groundwork Cedric laid, today's employees view The Company and the Ancestors as extreme ends on the spectrum of good and evil. Their worst insult is to call someone an Ancestor, and you've heard their sayings: Selfish as an Ancestor, Dumb as an Ancestor, and Numerous as an Ancestor's Offspring."

Cedric tried to stifle a yawn. "So the job's finished."

"The job is *not* finished." Melvin spoke with quiet force. "You mentioned the human need for activity. It runs deeper than that. As a species, we seem to have a genetic imperative to roam free. Your forebear somewhat countered this urge by making the outdoor work shift as unpalatable as possible, but the need for open spaces remains at the root of their frustrations. Therefore, to keep the employees as happy as possible we must constantly observe and where necessary, tweak the doings in the silos. Done much tweaking lately?"

Cedric frowned. "As I said before, everything's fine and to quote an old saying, *If it ain't broke, don't fix it.*"

"Without maintenance, even the best machinery will eventually break," said Melvin. "And by the time it does, it may no longer be fixable. You should be maintaining the machinery your forebear put in place."

"Which is what you've been doing?" his son said with a sneer.

"I *have*," said Melvin grimly. "Here's an example. Thirty years ago, I took over my father's role as Secretary to the Secretary of the CEO, but prior to that I was expected to prove my fitness to follow in his footsteps." He glanced at Cedric, who sat stony-faced. "I spent weeks observing employee behavior, and finally I selected Danny Fitani."

"The game show host? He must have been a baby back then."

"He'd just turned four and had been living in the children's silo for two years. No father had ever come calling, and his mother's visits had already dropped off to a point where he rarely saw her. On the few occasions she did come by, he tried hard to win her approval. She fancied herself as a singer and actor and spent most of her play-times in various performance Playrooms.

"As is the custom with silo-children, Danny had accompanied her everywhere until the age of two, and had watched her starring on stage. When he moved to the children's silo, he began creating his own shows. He would make up little dances for her and sing songs, and if she liked them, she would stay longer and sing some of her own songs to him and the other children. But eventually her self-centeredness won out and her visits to Danny stopped.

Cedric harrumphed. "What scum those silo dwellers are."

"That comment tells me how little you've observed them," said Melvin. "The majority of employees are loving parents, who spend as much time as they can with their children, and given the tube, work and play cycles, that's not easy. I think you'll find every society, including our own, has parents who neglect their children. When this happens in the silos, it's an opportunity for us.

"Danny Fitani was a child in desperate need of love. Though his mother no longer visited, he continued to put on concerts for the other children. They now became the ones from whom he sought approval, and as he grew older, he showed great skill in organizing groups of children to perform their own shows. I could see he was destined to be a great entertainer – far more effective than his mother at bringing joy to the employees, and I supported him all the way."

Cedric looked puzzled. "Why? How?"

"How?" said Melvin. "I began contacting Danny during his tube time using an avatar I called Mother Company. The image of the woman I chose for the avatar was attractive and more importantly, available at his call. I got into the habit of watching his shows and contacting him afterwards as Mother Company, to tell him how wonderful his performances were and how proud and pleased The Company was at the way he made others happy.

"As he grew older, he came to realize the Mother Company avatar was just a representation and that it was The Company itself, which had been supporting him and nurturing his talent. He now loves The Company as much as he would have loved his real mother. His belief that The Company loves and knows what is best for its employees comes through in his shows."

Melvin paused. "Do you really need me to tell you *why* I supported him?"

"Yes," Cedric defended his question. "It sounds as though Fitani would have gone on to be what he is today, regardless of any intervention by us."

"It's possible. However, I suggest you take a look at the statistics on abandoned children to learn how they usually fare in later life. You'll see that without our intervention it's far more likely Fitani would have grown into an unhappy adult with low self-esteem who eventually came to blame The Company for his mother's rejection. He may still have put on shows, but their subject matter and flavor would hardly have been the kind of thing we'd want our employees watching."

Cedric shifted uncomfortably. "What kind of thing *do* we want our employees watching? Fitani's current show, *Play or Die*, is pretty violent."

Melvin sighed. "You *so* need to brush up on your psychology."

"I get that nice shows don't necessarily make people happy," said Cedric. "But what makes *Play or Die* suitable?"

"Remember the statistics I spoke of?" said Melvin. Data over the past two decades show increasing indicators of unhappiness among the silo dwellers in all the Safe Places. Three years ago I was a nervous wreck, wondering what to do about it.

"That was when Fitani approached Mother Company for permission to use the new Microwave Time Viewing technology to produce nature programs. He wanted to show people the world as it had been before The Great Destruction, and I thought it would be a good way of reducing employee stress."

"Makes sense," said Cedric. "What could be more calming than viewing a beautiful and intact Earth?"

Melvin smiled grimly. "Early results were indeed promising. Fitani's team put together spectacular shows in which employees were able to vicariously join mountain climbing parties, travel through glorious rainforests, and hike beautiful trails to lakes and waterfalls. Stress levels in all the silos dropped. But then they began rising again, faster than ever before."

Melvin locked gazes with Cedric. "Care to guess why?"

His son's eyes narrowed and then suddenly widened. "People always want what they can't have."

"Exactly," said Melvin. "And worse still, the nature shows became a catalyst, congealing all the unresolved frustration that had been building within the population. I needed to find an outlet for that frustration fast, before it turned against The Company.

Now can you see how my grooming of Fitani paid off? In the hands of a willing artist, that ball of frustration could be turned against the Ancestors, and released in a great catharsis!"

Cedric's voice held a note of admiration. "Good one Pop."

"I contacted Fitani as myself – Secretary to the Secretary of the CEO, and explained that I felt his nature shows were becoming rather tame and lackluster." Melvin chuckled. "He was naturally appalled by such criticism. I then hammered the point further, reminding him of the exciting game shows his team produced before they had the Microwave Time Viewing technology. I asked him what had become of the thrills and chills he'd once given his audiences and then I said, "How can you be content to let viewers see the Ancestors wallowing in Earth's beautiful environment, while they bring it ever closer to destruction?" Finally I threw in some good old mother-love emotional blackmail. "The Company has entrusted *you* with this new technology," I said. "It's therefore up to *you* to find a way of making those Ancestors pay for their evil ways."

"That was sufficient. Fitani went off and consulted with the inventors of the technology. He got them to make certain modifications and a month later his team brought *Play or Die* to the people. I'm sure even the great Cedric himself would have approved. *Play or Die* focuses employee frustration upon an actual live Ancestor. It uses the Hunt to build tension, and then provides a huge emotional release through the kill.

"Stress levels in the silos drop steeply after each game and months go by before they're back to a level sufficient to require a new one. Fitani produces three games per year and fills the intervening time with replays and panel discussions analyzing strategies used by Hunters and Prey. *Play or Die* has given us the best control we've ever had over employee morale."

"So where did you mess up?"

Melvin's eyes sparked with anger, but Cedric held his ground. "Something's gone wrong. Isn't that why you called me here?"

"You are correct," said Melvin. "Our problem is the Prey in the current game. She's been asking Fitani about the lives of the silo dwellers and pretending to sympathize with them in order to stir up resentment against The Company. Recently she suggested they keep their ninety square kilometers of cleaned land and turn it into a recreation reserve for employees."

"What? That's intolerable," said Cedric. "We need to act immediately."

"Any thoughts on how?"

His son's chin lifted. "Simple, we give Fitani a choice. Either kill her off immediately with a professional assassin or stop broadcasting the game."

Melvin sighed. "You are failing to consider employee-response. The situation is delicate. Already Jo's words have triggered much questioning of Company policy and motivation. Terminating the game prematurely would give credence to what she's been saying. It would also prevent the safe release of employee frustration and anger that has built up over the last few months. Their fury would turn against The Company and the result could be catastrophic."

"There must be something we can do."

"I've already taken an initial step," Melvin informed him. "I've ordered Fitani to introduce a new rule forbidding any discussion or questions about our society or people. That will stop Jo from making further inflammatory remarks and will also prevent this kind of situation from happening in future games. With luck, that girl will be eliminated shortly and the crisis will come to an end."

He looked at Cedric's expectant face. "But luck may not be on our side, so your job now is vital. Contact the rest of the Morale Executive immediately.

Everyone must be onto this. We need to monitor employee discussion rooms and tube chatter in every Safe Place on Earth. It's vital we track their mood. If dissatisfaction with The Company continues to escalate and Jo continues to survive, we have to be ready with a new strategy.

So while you and your siblings monitor the silo dwellers, wrack your brains for a way to eliminate Jo *without* turning the employees against The Company.

CHAPTER 35

As Richard turned to block the agents, Jo leapt forward. He wouldn't hold them back for long – she had to get out of sight. Dashing into an opening on her right, she found herself in a laneway lined with high brick walls. Halfway down, a metal staircase climbed the side of a building to a flat rooftop. Going up could trap her on the roof but was the alternative any better? In the dim light she strained to see beyond the staircase. It looked as though the laneway came to a dead end.

Take the stairs, she thought. Her legs disobeyed and ran past, hoping for a cross alley. Bad move. No cross alley, just a smooth, wooden fence, too high to climb. Jo turned. Was there time to make it back to the stairs? The female agent entered the laneway. A head taller than Jo, the woman had a muscular build and was dressed for action in a loose slack-suit and low-heeled shoes.

She strode down the alley calling, "You've had a good run, Kylie, but it's over. Come quietly and you won't be hurt."

Jo looked around. Trapped! Once this woman had her, she was as good as dead unless... an injured captive might make the agent less vigilant.

Jo turned and leapt high for the top of the fence. Her fingertips brushed centimeters short of the edge and she made herself fall awkwardly, crumpling and screaming as she hit the ground. A hand gripped her arm and began pulling her up.

She screamed again. "Ahhh, my ankle!" It wasn't hard to squeeze out tears, and sobbing she cried, "Let me go. Ow, my ankle."

The fingers tightened. "You'll get first-aid at the police station. Come on."

"I can't walk," said Jo, standing on one foot. Gingerly she touched the other to the ground and gasping, pulled it up again.

The woman sighed and adjusted her grip to lift Jo's arm across her shoulders. "Lean on me," she commanded.

Jo put her weight on the agent and hopped along with her 'bad' leg held out to the side. "Where are taking me?" she asked.

"We're going back to my partner. He's holding your boyfriend. Then we'll call Mr. Andrews, our client. Once he's verified we've got you, the next stop will be the police station. Where's the baby?"

"There *is* no baby," said Jo. "I'm not Kylie Marshall. I'm Jo Warrington. I've been set up."

The woman gave a short laugh. "You can tell your story to the police."

As they neared the entrance to the laneway, Jo made her move. Stepping onto her 'bad' leg, she thrust the good one in front of the agent. The woman stumbled, throwing out her hands and Jo assisted her fall with a hard shove between the shoulder blades before sprinting south in the direction of the motel.

Knowing she'd only bought seconds and desperate to lose herself in the streets, she turned right at the next intersection – Rowe Street. Another mistake. Its sides were lined with high-walled locked warehouses, stretching for half a kilometer. Her only option was to run the whole length.

As she tried to force more speed into her protesting legs, Jo glimpsed something on the other side and drawing level, found renewed hope. An alleyway, and not a dead end this time – she could see the twinkle of lights from the next street. Tearing across to the entrance, Jo glanced back in time to see the agent turn into Rowe Street and head straight for her. This woman wasn't just big, she was fast.

I'm not going to make it, she thought. Still her legs churned frantically and her feet splashed through an unseen puddle left by the afternoon storm. A voice in her head began chanting. She's faster, but you're younger. Keep going a bit longer and you'll wear her out.

The alley opened into Vaughan, a shopping street divided by center angle parking. Opposite the supermarket the parking strip was filled with cars. Jo pelted down the pavement. Should she go into the supermarket? No, she'd hide between the cars.

A pedestrian crossing led to where the head of the parking strip was delineated from the road by low concrete edging. The first two car spaces were empty and Jo charged for them, leaping over the edging. As she landed, her feet flew out from under and she fell flat, sliding until a sickening thump halted her progress.

For a moment Jo lay dazed beside a solid SUV, but the need to keep moving rolled her onto her stomach. She pushed against the ground and her hands shot out, leaving her facedown on the asphalt. Now she smelt it – oil. A car recently parked here must have been leaking copious amounts of it. Combined with rainwater in the shallow depression, it had turned the whole area into a dangerous slick. She looked back. The agent was running in her direction along the footpath, but hadn't yet seen her lying on the ground in the center-parking strip.

Jo wriggled under the SUV, assisted by her greasy clothing. Coming out on the other side she sat and tested her feet on the ground. Her well-oiled shoes continued to skid but she rubbed them back and forth against the asphalt until some grip returned to the soles, and then rose to peek over the car.

Standing in the glow of the shopping center lights, the agent was looking left and right. As Jo watched, she reached into a pocket and took out what had to be a phone. Oh no, if she calls the Hunter with his helicopter, I'm gone! Standing, she thumped the hood of the SUV. The agent twisted at the sound, and their eyes locked.

"Leave me alone," Jo screamed. "Stop chasing me."

The woman immediately ran to the crossing and followed the path Jo had taken. Like her, she leapt the concrete lip and hit the oiled parking space. A spectacular skid slammed her into the SUV and the phone flew from her hand, landing on the road. Jo circled and scooped it up while the agent floundered in the oil slick. Then she sped down Vaughan Street with the woman's curses ringing in her ears.

At the next intersection, Jo turned south into Maude. This wide street stretched on forever and panting, she staggered along, hoping for a turnoff before she collapsed. Only when Ashenden came up on her left did she dare to look back. The streetlamps showed an empty expanse. Jo gulped in relief and turned into the side street. A little way down an empty allotment was being used for opportunistic parking. She staggered to the back of the lot and crouched behind a sedan, sucking lungfuls of air as she waited for her heartbeat to slow.

That had been too close. Jo felt around in the gravel for a large stone. Then she put the agent's phone on the ground and smashed it. For good measure she jammed the wreck under the car's front tire. How long before the woman found another phone and called the Hunter? It could take a while, Jo thought. Public phone booths were usually vandalized, and if she tried the supermarket, she'd have to persuade the management to let her use theirs. Would she know the Hunter's number by heart? Not likely. She'd have to call her agency and get them to pass a message to the Hunter.

Jo figured she had ten minutes at least before the helicopter arrived, turning night into day. The motel was closer than that if she used footpaths, but with agents patrolling the roads she didn't want to risk it. She'd have to go over fences and through backyards. Luckily the evening was cold. People would be indoors but what about their dogs? She hoped they'd be inside too, sitting with their owners, watching TV.

...

Richard groaned. His motel unit was dark. He called softly anyway, but there was no response. Okay, he thought. Don't waste time. Get the van and get going. Seeing Mikey sitting behind the reception desk, he relaxed a little. Of the two brothers, Mikey was the one who complained loudest and longest about his lack of funds. He'd need little convincing.

Five minutes later Richard emerged with the keys to the van in his pocket and a spare room key in his hand. Quickly he packed his and Jo's belongings and loaded them into the back of the van. At the last minute he grabbed a blanket from the cupboard and threw that in too. The night was freezing and if he did manage to find Jo, he had no idea what state she'd be in.

Richard drove out through the gates and began a slow circle of the block, straining for a sign of Jo. He tried to suppress the vision of her locked up somewhere with an agent standing guard while they waited for the Hunter. If he harms her, Richard vowed, he'll learn what it's like to be hunted down.

There! Was that Jo up ahead? No, just a kid in a tracksuit. Gradually he became aware of something disturbing his concentration, a familiar noise – the helicopter. He stopped and tasted bile. The noise became a painful clamor and a spotlight swept over the van, flooding it and the surrounds with brightness.

Richard stopped and turned off his lights. He got out, and shading his eyes, peered up at the chopper, hoping by this action to look like an innocent bystander. It seemed to work. The spotlight moved on and when darkness returned, Richard climbed back behind the wheel. His hands were trembling, though he realized the chopper was a good sign. If it was searching for Jo, she must be at large. He checked his watch. Ten-thirteen. A little over forty-five minutes before the next broadcast. Richard left his lights off, and keeping clear of the spotlight, trawled the streets around the motel.

...

Jo cringed at the sound of the chopper. She was still a block from the motel and shaking with fatigue. Climbing fences and running through backyards was definitely not a recommended mode of travel. But when she'd been tempted to risk the footpath and had crept through to someone's front yard, she'd seen two cars cruising slowly in opposite directions. Agents were patrolling. That had been bad enough, but now the chopper had arrived, how was she supposed to stay hidden? The backyard theme for houses in this area was Spartan, the yards little more than tough grassy rectangles occasionally adorned with a straggly shrub. Oh Richard, she thought. Where are you? Are they holding you somewhere, or did you get away from the other agent? Are you waiting at the motel, wondering what's happened to me? I don't even know if I can get there.

Jo blinked back angry tears. Why had she suggested crossing at a major intersection instead of taking a longer, but safer route? And why the hell had Richard so meekly agreed to her stupid plan? Now she had no choice. She was out of time and would have to risk using the street before the helicopter came her way.

From the backyard she was in, Jo glanced towards the windows of the house. They were dark and carport was empty. Quickly she jogged down the driveway. Rather than a front fence, the owners had planted a row of agapanthus. These folks were obviously the gardeners of the street. Jo dashed to the agapanthus hedge and rolled under the strappy leaves. Lying on her stomach and trying not to think about the snails and spiders sharing her spot, she scanned the road.

Lights appeared and she ducked her head down, pulling the hood over. The car passed but she continued to lie, her muscles refusing to move other than to shiver in the biting cold. Come on Jo, she thought. You can't stay here forever. Get going! Stiffly she began rising and then froze. A van was coming slowly up the road without headlights. As it passed by, the streetlight briefly illuminated the lettering on its side – The Welcome Inn. Richard's motel! Richard had said he was going to try to get a van.

Jo leapt up and ran onto the road. Though the van was moving slowly, there was no way she'd catch it. Dropping to the gutter, she scraped up a handful of stones and sprinted forward, hurling them with all her might.

CHAPTER 36

An odd sound, like hailstones hitting the van, had Richard braking and checking his side mirror. Was that someone on the road? Jo! He leapt out and ran back. She was staggering and he caught her before she fell.

"Jo, my God, I've been so worried."

"Oh Richard." She gave a weak laugh but her arms wrapped around him in a stranglehold. "I thought I'd never see you again."

She smelt strongly of engine oil and was trembling from head to toe. Without hesitation he scooped her up and ran to the van. As he unlocked the back door, he spoke soothingly. "You're safe now. There's a blanket inside. I'll get you settled."

He lifted her in and followed, finding the blanket and wrapping it around her. Then he pushed the bike bag and his suitcase close to the wall to make a space where she could lie without rolling, and arranged the panniers as a pillow. Turning back, he sensed the panic in her stiffness, and her words reminded him of her ordeal in the boot.

"You're leaving me here?"

"Jo," he hugged her and spoke reassuringly. "We need to keep moving, but don't worry, there's plenty of room and air in this cabin. Try to sleep if you can. You're safe, and I'm getting us out of here."

He guided her into the space he'd created and she sank down, pulling the blanket around herself. Was she going to be all right? His fear was answered when she heaved up onto an elbow and said, "Richard?"

"Yes?"

"Try not to drive like a maniac this time."

He laughed and closed the doors. In the driver's cabin he started the engine and flipped on the headlights. Now they were just one of the many vans on the roads. Richard knew he had a silly smile on his face, which given what still lay ahead, was absurd, but at this moment he felt ready to tackle anything.

He was pleased with his choice of Murchison for the Hunter's eleven o'clock co-ordinates. It would look as if they were on their way to Bendigo. Instead, after the broadcast, they'd backtrack a little and take a minor road south, which would return them to the Goulburn Valley Highway. Ten minutes down the Highway was the Goulburn Weir turnoff, just north of Nagambie. The Lake Retreat was only five minutes along the Goulburn Weir Road, so if all went according to plan, less than half an hour after the broadcast they'd be holed up in a warm, comfortable room. That was the easy bit. In that warm, comfortable room would be Marilyn, and a tough sell.

Richard caught himself yawning. It had been a long day and it wasn't over yet. And after that three more days loomed. When the hell was he going to sleep? He understood now why Jo catnapped whenever she could, but twenty-minute snatches wouldn't substitute long for a proper night's rest. The Hunter and his agents, working in shifts, would always be fresh. It followed that if he and Jo used nothing more than a running and hiding strategy, they'd eventually be caught. Survival meant turning the tables on the Hunter, and he needed to work out how to do that before fatigue addled his brain.

A sign appeared and he turned off onto the Murchison-Violet Town road. Old bitumen, it was little more than a dark, narrow strip with crumbling edges. Eucalyptus trees crowded the sides and Richard's headlights picked out open paddocks, but no other cars. After twenty minutes he came to the Wahring-Murchison East crossroad. This was the road he would take south back to the highway after the broadcast, but now he crossed it, continuing west towards Murchison.

An occasional farmhouse began appearing and he kept his eyes peeled for a service station or roadhouse to pull into, but there was nothing. A wooden bridge brought him to another crossroad. On the far right corner was an old country hotel. A post office stood on the left. He'd reached Murchison.

Richard turned right, swinging into an angle parking spot in front of a launderette abutting the hotel. A bakery/teashop stood beside the launderette, and a few shops stretched beyond, but everything was closed and lifeless.

He walked to the back of the van and opened the doors. The sound woke Jo and she sat up, pulling the blanket around her shoulders. He leapt in to join her.

"Where are we?" She squinted at her watch.

"Murchison. We made good time. We have almost fifteen minutes before the broadcast. God it's cold back here! How are you coping?"

"The blanket helps."

She opened it up in invitation, and Richard hunkered down, putting one arm around her as he pulled the edge of the blanket over both of them. For a minute they sat in silence. Jo's head rested against his chest and Richard realized he was enjoying her warmth and closeness more that he probably should. He tried making small talk.

"How did your Uni interview go?"

"My what? Oh, that seems so long ago. I never actually *got* to the interview. Fitani intercepted me."

"I'm still finding it hard coming to terms with the idea that people from the future can communicate with us."

"Me too," said Jo. "I keep forgetting they're watching our every move, though that's probably not such a bad thing."

Richard squirmed inwardly, having also forgotten. He spoke bitterly. "Humanity must have really gone to the dogs if our descendants see nothing wrong with setting up murder games."

She surprised him with her next remark. "They have it pretty tough. It can't be easy living in silos on the edge of a nuclear wasteland, only able to use the clean land for food production."

"Bad, I agree, but still no excuse to take it out on *you*."

Jo gave a little laugh. "They don't see it that way. I and the Prey killed before me represent those responsible for their current state."

"The Prey killed *before* you?"

"Apparently *Play or Die* has been going for nine seasons."

"Well it's got to stop!" Richard shook his fist at the roof of the van. "Do you hear me? This is sick! You demean yourselves as a people behaving this way."

"You know Richard is right." Jo spoke earnestly, also looking towards their invisible audience. "Murder won't heal your wounds. You call it punishment but isn't it really self-indulgence? You're smart and creative, and your technology is advanced. You could be *solving* your problems instead of taking out your frustration on others."

Richard tightened his arm around Jo and looked into her eyes. "Well said, but will they listen?"

"Danny is their mouthpiece. As long as he continues to run the game, we have to assume they prefer controlling my life to taking control of their own."

"Perhaps there's nothing they *can* do about their lives."

"There's always something, and I have a feeling these people are being manipulated."

"By whom?"

"Their lives seem completely in the hands of the supposedly kindhearted Company they all work for. Every thirty years the land they've cleaned is planted out with food crops and their silo housing is relocated to the edges of the wastelands."

"So?"

"When Fitani showed me a holographic map of his production fields, a *vast* area was blurred out."

Richard gave an ironic laugh. "If *their* company is anything like the ones *we* have, that blur is covering Company holdings."

"Manufacturing facilities?"

"I doubt it. Why hide them? No, that's where you'll find the Company Execs living and frolicking."

"Surely not," said Jo, playing along. "That area's far more than is needed for just a few executives. The blur has to be a glitch in their software."

"So why don't they fix it? I thought you said these people were smart. Aren't their programmers up to the job?"

Jo gave his hand a warning squeeze under the blanket and changed the topic. "I don't suppose we've stopped anywhere near food? The burgers from this afternoon are long gone."

"Everything appears closed around here but I can take a look," Richard offered. "Maybe there's a store that will sell us a sandwich. Back in a tick."

Rising reluctantly from Jo's side, he relinquished the edge of the blanket. Then he leapt to the footpath and set off down the row of shops. They were all closed, but something else kept him walking – the need for a public toilet. All he found was a park, so he ducked in to relieve himself against a tree. Only when he'd finished did he remember this act had been seen by the viewers of the future. He clenched his teeth in embarrassment, understanding now what Jo had meant when she'd said it wasn't such a bad thing to forget about being watched.

On the way back, Richard became aware of a wailing sound, which rapidly increased to earsplitting volume. A police car swept off the bridge and turned, picking him up in its headlights. It sped down and came to a screeching halt beside him. The front window lowered and a voice said, "Stop there please, sir."

Richard faced the uniformed constable who had spoken, keeping his expression mild, though his heart was beating nineteen to the dozen.

"Is there a problem?"

"Bit late for an evening stroll." The voice had a hard note.

"I was actually trying to find a shop that was open, to get a snack." Richard always stuck to the truth whenever possible.

"Just passing through are you?"

"That's right."

"And your vehicle is?"

Richard pointed to his van parked near the unlit hotel, and the officer twisted to look back.

"Make your way to it sir. We'll follow you."

The car did a tight U-turn as Richard walked back, frantically trying to think of a story to give them. As he reached the van, the police car pulled into the parking spot alongside, and the two officers emerged. The one who'd spoken to him was young, perhaps in his late twenties, with a rugged build and set jaw. The driver was at least forty and carrying twice as much weight as he should have been. He ignored Richard and walked around the van, looking at the number plates and talking into a two-way radio.

The younger officer continued where he'd left off. "Sir can you tell me where you've come from and where are you going?"

Richard thought fast. "I've just come from Bendigo, where the van was in for repair. Now I'm on my way to Benalla. May I ask what this is all about, Constable?"

"Any reason why your van doors are open?" The young officer ignored his question.

"I had to get a map out of the back. I didn't see any urgency in closing the doors as I thought I was the only one here. I'll close them now," he offered, taking a step towards the van.

"Stay where you are sir."

The constable moved to block him, forcing his return to the footpath.

The older officer leaned into the van, shining a torch around. Richard held his breath.

"There's a suitcase in here."

"I'm staying overnight in Benalla," said Richard quickly. "I have to pick up some bedding supplies there first thing in the morning and get them back to the Welcome Inn in Shepparton before 9.30 a.m. or my bosses, Bev and Jeff Saunders, will want to know why."

The constable seemed to relax a little. "Your licence please."

Richard took out his wallet and passed the licence over.

"You're Richard Sayers?"

"Yes."

"This has a Melbourne address."

"Yes, I only moved to Shep a couple of months ago and haven't gotten around to changing it yet. My job at the Welcome Inn has been keeping me busy."

The constable raised his voice to speak to his colleague without turning his head.

"You got that registration yet Bruce?"

His colleague's radio crackled just then and they all heard the voice on the other side informing the officer that the van was registered to Bev and Jeff Saunders in Shepparton. The constable handed Richard his licence.

"Guess your story checks out. Sorry sir, we can't be too careful. We've had word a fugitive is on the loose in the area."

"Bloody hell! Is he dangerous?"

"It's actually a woman sir, but she could be with a man and they could be dangerous, so I suggest you get on your way. Don't pick up any hitchhikers."

"I won't," said Richard fervently. "Thanks for the warning."

Another wailing siren signaled the arrival of a second police car and a third siren could be heard in the distance, along with the sound of a helicopter approaching rapidly.

Richard appealed to the constable. "If I drive off now, they're all going to think *I'm* the fugitive."

"Don't worry, we'll let them know we've checked you out and they won't stop you. On your way now sir."

The constable wasn't taking no for an answer and Richard stepped to the back of the van and closed the doors, noting that both Jo and the blanket were missing. Where could she be? He had no choice but to leave and he couldn't even stop further down the road, or he'd again become the subject of suspicion, and next time they might check out his story more carefully. Fortunately this young constable had been too inexperienced to ask him to show the paperwork proving the car had just been repaired in Bendigo, or to make a phone call to the Welcome Inn to check they had an employee called Richard Sayers. It was unlikely he'd be so lucky a second time.

In heavy despair, Richard climbed into the driver's seat and started the engine. The older officer was talking into his radio and the younger was now walking to meet the second police car, which had pulled up nearby. A rustling noise from the floor of the passenger side nearly gave him a heart attack until the edge of a dark blanket flipped back and Jo's face grinned up at him.

Richard drew in a huge breath and relaxed weakly against the steering wheel. Then gathering himself, he backed out of the angle park and headed towards the intersection, indicating left.

"Stay where you are Jo," he said, trying not to move his lips. "They're all around us."

With a light heart, Richard drove back the way he'd come. The headlights of another police car speeding towards Murchison swept past, ignoring him and at the Wahring Murchison East crossroad, he turned right, beginning the six-kilometer drive to the Goulburn Valley Highway.

Jo's muffled voice drifted through the blanket.

"Can I get up now?"

"Safer to stay there. You can throw the blanket off, but keep it ready in case we're stopped."

The blanket was pushed away and Richard glanced down to see Jo curled up like a cat.

"Jo you're a sight for sore eyes! How on earth…?"

"Mainly luck. After you went off to look for some food… did you get anything by the way?"

"Sorry, I'll organize some grub at the resort."

"Good, I could eat a horse. What was I saying? Oh yes after you left, my alarm went off. The blonde wig was completely twisted around my money belt and I couldn't untangle it. I'd had my hood up when the female agent was chasing me, so they still don't know my hair's short and I wanted to keep it that way. Then I realized I had the answer in my hands – the blanket!

"I climbed out of the van and went around the corner of the hotel for the broadcast. The street was deserted so I put the whole blanket over myself. I can't tell you how weird it felt, standing like that. I kept expecting someone to walk by and yank off the blanket, but eleven o'clock came and went without any surprises. A minute after that I headed back to the van.

"As I got there I heard the siren and had to duck down behind the grill until the police car shot by. I could see you in its headlights and when they stopped to question you, I jumped into the front and covered myself with the blanket. I figured if the police decided to check out the van, they'd look in the back.

"Brilliant!" Richard smiled down at her. "And the great thing about being checked out by the first car on the scene, is they've radioed the others that this van's okay, so we should get to our destination unchallenged."

Nonetheless, he was relieved when they reached the Goulburn Valley Highway and were no longer the only vehicle on the road.

Jo shifted. "What I don't understand is how so many police cars arrived in Murchison so soon after the broadcast. I guess the Hunter has finally resorted to using the police, but Murchison doesn't even have its own *service* station, let alone a police station."

Richard thought about it. "If the Hunter's agents have started working with the police, they'd have told them you were in the Shepparton area. The police would have sent out roaming patrol cars and some were probably in the vicinity when word came through you were in Murchison."

"So now we're the subject of a police manhunt," said Jo thoughtfully.

There was nothing to say to that and they drove in silence. Six minutes later Richard turned onto the Goulburn Weir Road and followed it for a kilometer to the resort.

Slowing, he swung into the broad driveway and followed it past the front office to the luxury cabins generously spaced along the lake. Marilyn's red Hyundai Veloster was nowhere in sight. The cabin at the far end was dark, and its car space empty, so he backed into it, turning off lights and engine.

"We're here. It's safe to get up."

"I don't think I can move."

"Hang on, I'll come round the other side."

Richard opened Jo's door and saw her shiver when the icy breeze hit. He slipped his hands under her shoulders to ease her out and she began wriggling to assist. Suddenly she yelped and her leg spasm-ed in a cramp. The two fell backwards onto the ground in a tangle of limbs and he laughed as they got to their feet.

"No permanent damage?"

She smiled. "I guess not. That space may have been smaller than the boot, but at least it was warm, and I had company."

"Speaking of warm, let's get back in. Marilyn hasn't arrived yet."

He helped Jo into the passenger seat and closed the door. Then he jumped into the driver's side and started the engine to get the heater going.

"While I remember, here's your room key." Jo extracted it from a pocket of her money belt and then checked her watch. "It's eleven twenty-four. What's the plan?"

"That depends on Marilyn."

A familiar lump began to weigh down Jo's stomach. "Your *colleague?*"

"I guess I need to explain about that. We *are* colleagues, but it's true we've also had a casual thing going. Recently I realized it was rather more casual on my part than hers. I've been trying to work out how to end it without tears, but now…"

"Oh. Complicated." Jo spoke sympathetically, but her world had suddenly brightened. "And I noticed when you talked to her on the phone, you didn't mention me, so no doubt she's picturing a cozy rendezvous."

"Probably, which is why it might be better if I speak to her before she sees you."

"What are you going to say?"

"I… here she is!" He turned off the engine.

Jo watched as a sporty red coupe swept around the driveway and parked beside the third cabin down. A slim woman stepped out, taking a small overnight case from the boot before entering the cabin and closing the door behind her.

Richard retrieved the blanket from the floor and dropped it into Jo's lap.

"It should stay warm in here for a while, and I don't plan to be long, but just in case…"

She gave a theatrical sigh, but smiled at him. "Go sort things out."

CHAPTER 37

Melvin Briggs ground his teeth. That bitch had done it again. Without Fitani's presence, Jo and the man with her had made a direct appeal to the audience. They were *deliberately* trying to stir up the silo dwellers. The game had to be stopped immediately… but how to do it in a way that wouldn't backfire against The Company?

He'd not yet heard from Cedric or any of his other children. Were they all still too shocked from discovering what Jo had been saying? He opened a priority group call to the Morale Executive. The more heads on this, the better. The screen divided into a grid of sixteen squares – one for each member of the Executive. As the sections began lighting up, Melvin's jaw dropped in disbelief. Shock was not an emotion on any of the faces that appeared. The expressions before him ranged from sleepy to disgruntled, and not one of them belonged to his children or nieces or nephews!

Melvin recognized Cedric's Personal Assistant, and pounced. "Roberts, what is the meaning of this? Where is Cedric? And where," he bellowed at the sea of assistants blinking at him from the screen, "is the Morale Executive?"

Roberts cleared his throat and the others looked relieved that he had elected to speak. "The Executive is attending an important function this evening, Secretary Briggs," he said. "But they brought us in before they left and fully briefed us on what needed to be done. We are currently monitoring the progress of the game, along with tube and virtual discussion-room chatter."

Melvin was almost beyond words. "And this important function?"

"Why, the first ball of the new hunt season, of course," said Roberts.

When Melvin stared at him goggle-eyed, he added, "It's the most important calendar event of the month, apart from the CEO's birthday, but that's only for Directors and their families. All Secretarial families attend the hunt ball." Then, appearing to remember that Secretary Briggs was renowned for non-appearance at social events, he blushed.

"May I ask you all a question?" Melvin spoke in a deadly whisper, addressing the heads on the screen. "What if anything are you doing about the current situation apart from *monitoring* it?"

White faces stared mutely and Roberts spoke again. "We are recording any conversations that appear to be subversive..." He faded off.

"And have you made *many* of these recordings?" Melvin's voice was sarcastically polite.

"May we have a few minutes to check with our assistants, Secretary Briggs?" It was Roberts who spoke, but the others nodded nervously.

"By all means."

The squares on the screen greyed or were replaced by the Company Logo and Briggs sat in a daze. Was this how civilizations ended – with those in charge losing the ability to tell the difference between perks and real responsibilities?

He tried to concentrate on the problem at hand but his mind was filled with the twin images of the employees in their silos avidly following a human hunt, while young Company Executives attended a gala ball before riding to their own hunt in the tradition of the aristocracies of a bygone era.

In the years leading up to The Great Destruction, The Company, in preparation for the inevitable, had built vast subterranean refuges equipped with food stores, hydroponic farms, the most advanced electronic and scientific instruments, and many thousands of cryogenic vials of embryonic plant and animal life, to ensure Earth could be rapidly rebuilt once it was safe to return to the surface.

Following The Great Arising, after its newly gained blue collar workforce had been set to work cleaning the land and raising food crops, The Company had begun seeding small nature reserves in each Safe Place. Over the years as more cleaned land became available, they'd expanded the reserves and increased the variety of plants and animals within them. Not everything had thrived, but some of the animals had multiplied to an extent that called for regular culling. Bots had traditionally taken care of this but these days it was fashionable among the young set to go out on hunting parties and bring home game, which they cooked over roaring fires, and washed down with copious quantities of wine.

Cedric and his brothers and sisters on the Morale Executive, had apparently believed the hunt and its associated rituals took priority over preventing a potential revolution among the employees from coming to the boil.

Once again, Melvin ground his teeth. Part of his anger was self-directed. He'd obviously failed to impress upon his children the importance of their jobs, and why should they see it, when silo affairs had run smoothly with minimal intervention for a great many years? Look at the example *he* had set – often spending weeks at his country house, and only checking in remotely to ensure the few things needing to be done were being seen to. He knew other Secretaries in charge of various aspects of silo operations did even less.

Slowly the squares on his screen began lighting up again, with faces that now looked decidedly frightened.

"Sir." Roberts again spoke for them all. "I regret to report that a great deal of subversive dialogue is occurring among employees in Safe Places all over the world. Many are speaking of the need for accountability from The Company. Also it seems the employees have somehow gained access to historical records from the pre-Destruction Era."

"What!" cried Melvin. "How is this possible?"

"Unknown at the moment," said Roberts uncomfortably. "The data didn't come from our own historical archives. It's been years since they were accessed."

The Microwave Time Viewing technology, thought Melvin. The employees had pulled their own data from libraries of the past. Why had it never occurred to him they might use the Viewer this way? Because he'd trusted Fitani to safeguard it. Fitani had let him down.

Roberts was continuing. "Many of the employees are currently discussing modes of government. Some of the younger ones have begun quoting slogans such as 'No Taxation Without Representation', and asking why Secretarial and Director positions are only inheritable and unavailable to ordinary employees. Others want to know why they never hear from any Directors – just an occasional secretary of a Secretary." He swallowed and cleared his throat. "And there's one more thing, Sir."

"Spit it out Roberts."

"Some employees are talking about the blurred parts of the maps. They're openly speculating about what goes on in the areas devoted to Sacred Company Business."

Melvin Briggs frowned grimly. "Return to your duties," he said, and severed the connection.

As he sat staring at the blank communication screen, Melvin had never felt more alone. He considered putting a call through to Hastmeyer, his own boss, and Secretary to the CEO himself, but rejected the thought as soon as it formed. It would be a waste of time. Hastmeyer was entirely occupied in catering to the personal whims and foibles of the CEO and his family, and always left actual Company business to Melvin, his secretary.

Melvin punched in Fitani's access code and a Company message filled his screen: *Employee Danny Fitani is at work. His shift will end in three hours, thirty-two minutes.* Three and a half hours! So much could happen in that time, but it was unprecedented to interrupt an employee's work shift. Quickly Melvin accessed the game. What was going on at the moment?

Jo was sitting alone in a van. He noted with grim satisfaction that between them, the police and the Hunter's agents seemed to have her surrounded. Though they didn't yet know her exact location, they would have it at 2.00 a.m. and if she tried to break through their cordon before then, she'd *have* to be caught. Chances were good that soon after 2.00, Jo would be dead and the crisis over. But if by some freak misfortune she wasn't, he needed a plan.

Suddenly among the maelstrom of firings in Melvin's brain, a neural pathway flared more brightly. Incentive – *that* was the strategy he would use. And what was the greatest incentive for employees? Personal Points. *Play or Die* must be made too expensive for people to access and the blame laid at Fitani's door, not The Company's.

If Jo wasn't dead or in the Hunter's hands by 2.00 a.m. he would damn precedent and pull Fitani off his work shift an hour early. He'd tell him the CEO had decided to increase the rent on his blank Playroom, tenfold. The game show host would immediately be forced to raise the price of *Play or Die* beyond the reach of all but the wealthiest employees, and it wouldn't matter if *they* kept watching. The wealthy employees were happy with the status quo and would not be corrupted by Jo's ideas.

At the same time, the Employees' Entertainment Catalogue would advertise a once-in-a-lifetime, three-day-only drastic price drop on the most expensive entertainments. People would be left with the choice of spending their last Personal Points on *Play or Die*, or dropping it in favor of entertainments they'd never have a chance to try again. It was a no-brainer. People would leave *Play or Die* like a sinking ship and Jo and her subversive messages would be forgotten.

Melvin chuckled. Fitani wouldn't be too thrilled, but he'd get over it, and all was fair when survival was at stake.

...

Danny Fitani bent with the line and held his probe steady. Jo was turning his life into a nightmare. Had he not *told* her she was no longer to speak of The Company or the employees? Well, in truth he'd said she was not to ask questions about them, and that he would no longer discuss such matters with her, but it was the same thing! After she and Richard had indulged in their little diatribe, he'd half expected Secretary Briggs to appear and order the game's immediate cancellation. For the first time in his life he'd been happy to race off to the cloaking room and leave for the edge. Now he and the show would be safe for another four hours at least.

As he moved his probe along, Danny pondered the viewer-reaction to Jo's speech. It had been interesting. At first her Emoto Board tally had plummeted, as was to be expected. No one likes being manipulated and it was obvious Jo and Richard were trying to do just that. But almost immediately the points had started to build again. Were people actually falling for what she'd said?

Jo had called them murderers, as had other prey before her, and everyone knew that was not true. They were executioners and there was a big difference. Wasn't there? The punishment they were meting out was righteous but Jo had called it self-indulgent, saying that rather than putting all their energy into punishing others, they should be using it to find their own solutions. But there *were* no quick solutions. One day there'd be enough clean earth for the employees to stride out upon, but for now all they could do was keep working and wait until The Company announced that day had come.

Danny moved his probe again, and realized he'd had a lot of 'firsts' recently. Detestable as the four-hour shift at the edge was, this was the first time he actually dreaded the return to his tube. If Secretary Briggs' angry face wasn't waiting for him, a swarm of blinking message lights would be. And they wouldn't be the usual fun ones from fans and friends. Lately, those blinking lights heralded nothing but ulcers.

More than half of the message invasion would be from their younger demographic, the sixteen to twenty-five year olds, who in the past had been the most voracious for blood. Now, literally overnight, they'd begun viewing Jo as some kind of savior, dubbing her, 'The Fresh Pair of Eyes' and demanding that Fitani spare the Ancestor who had helped them see things for what they were. It was no doubt Jo's unexpected interest in them, which had caused these naïve youngsters to be swayed by what experienced employees, such as he, recognized as her baseless barbs against The Company.

The remaining message lights would be from the wealthier, over forties demographic. This group was baying for Jo's blood, accusing her of corrupting young employees and insisting she be terminated immediately. No, he definitely didn't want to go back to face those lights.

And on top of everything, someone, somehow had incredibly managed to tap into the *Fun 'n' Games* pipeline to Jo's era, collecting and spreading reams of historical information to all the Safe Places. The information was triggering unprecedented discussions, arguments and even impugning of The Company's motives.

A beep sounded and the line straightened and stretched together. How was it, Fitani wondered, popping the kinks in his shoulder blades, that people could be so easily swayed? The old image of Mother Company filled his mind. Though he knew she was just an avatar representation, thinking of her filled him with warmth. If only everyone knew this side of The Company, they wouldn't doubt she loved her employees and had devoted herself since 'The Great Arising' to their care and well-being.

Another beep sounded and he bent again, cursing the noisy stirrers who shouted down the defenders of The Company. The stirrers claimed The Company had a duty to provide specific information about the distribution of resources so that accurate projections could be made about when the cleaned land could finally be used for something other than primary production.

Others had started asking what role The Company had played *before* the Great Destruction, and why the Directors had waited underground for so long with technology that could have been used to help the survivors of the immediate aftermath. Why could they not all be content to accept that The Company had good and sufficient reasons for everything it did?

Jo, of course, was to blame for all this, trying to make The Company look bad. Clever, but it was just a trick. Surely people would see through it? Yet more and more were succumbing to her words, as the whole clothing thing was showing. In the beginning, the mimicking of Jo's outfits in some of their holographic styles had just been part of the fun. Then in the blink of an eye, it had turned serious. Now everywhere you looked, people who supported Jo or who were beginning to question The Company, were adopting the grey track pants and hoodie as their uniform. The rest found themselves shelling out Personal Points for increasingly extravagant holographic designs, in order to show their support for The Company. Where would it all end?

CHAPTER 38

At Richard's knock, Marilyn appeared looking fresh and animated. Her tailored fawn slacks and cream watered silk blouse made him marvel yet again at how much she'd changed since uni. Just two years ago she'd have gone naked rather than wear anything her parents would approve of. She brushed his cheek with a kiss, and the expensive perfume she'd recently begun wearing made his head swim.

"Come in, Rick. I've only just arrived."

"I know."

She led the way to a coffee table on which a silver bucket and a pair of champagne flutes stood. "Oh, have you been waiting for me darling? I would have been here sooner if it hadn't been for that damn police block."

"Police block?"

She turned and drew a quick breath. "My God, Rick, you're filthy. You look as though you've been in a fight."

"It's nothing. I'm okay. What's this about a police block?"

"Just out of Nagambie. They're stopping every car travelling south. The line of poor bastards waiting to get through stretches back half a kilometer or more. They weren't stopping cars coming up from Melbourne, but we were slowed down. On the bright side however…" she turned towards the coffee table. "The management of this wonderful resort appear to have left us some welcoming bubbly. And you look like you could use a drink. Shall I crack the bottle? … Rick?"

Richard forced his attention back to Marilyn, still shocked by her news. If he and Jo had gone just a few kilometers further down the highway they'd have been caught in the trap.

"Let's leave the champagne for the moment, Marilyn. I'm afraid tonight is more business than pleasure."

Her brow furrowed and then cleared. "Okay Rick, I guessed this wasn't *all* romantic spur-of-the-moment impulse. But you did promise to explain your missing car over a drink… and I have come *rather* a long way for you tonight."

The smile that followed this last sentence, with its little sting of emotional blackmail, would have been enough in the past to set him pouring champagne. Now, he resisted easily.

"Marilyn forget the drink. Someone's life is in danger and I need your help."

Her frown returned. "I'm not a field agent Richard. BEAM has people better suited for that sort of thing than me."

"Ordinarily I'd agree, but the situation is tricky. Jo doesn't trust our safe houses."

"Who's Joe?"

"You remember my Shepparton Community Leader?"

"Bill Warrington? We're currently investigating the two names you gave us in relation to his possible murder by the H Group."

"I got one of those names from Bill's files. The person who gave me access was Jo, his daughter."

"Ah." Marilyn sat on the couch, her expression hardening.

"She *is* in danger Marilyn. I swear to you."

Her eyes narrowed. "From the H Group? Doubtful. They'd hardly risk exposure trying to arrange her death so soon after her father's… unless they thought she had something *very* damaging on them. *Does* she have something very damaging on them?"

"I haven't been able to ascertain that yet. She's understandably shaken by the attempts on her life, but it's possible she has vital knowledge."

"Then hand her over to BEAM. They'll keep her safe and find out what it is she knows – if anything."

"She doesn't trust anyone except me and she's convinced the only way of staying safe is to keep moving. I'll need to stick with her for a while."

"*Stick* with her? Where is she now?"

"She's waiting outside in the van. I didn't want to bring her in before explaining the situation to you."

Marilyn stood stiffly. "Rick Sayers, your explanation so far hasn't been worth the breath you've used, but you can't leave the girl outside on a night like this. Go and get her immediately."

Richard squeezed her hands. "I knew we could count on you."

…

Marilyn paced the floor as she waited for Rick and the girl 'who trusted no one but him'. He'd tricked her into coming up and she should have known better. Something had smelt wrong from the start. Rick wasn't inclined to romantic gestures. Her grandmother's words of a year ago came to mind.

"That Rick boy – are you serious about him, or is he just part of this rebellion against your parents?"

At the time, Marilyn had bristled. "Why would you ask such a thing?"

"Calm down Marilyn, I'm not saying he's wrong for you…exactly. But maybe you could do better in a partner when it comes to achieving your goal."

That conversation, like so many with her grandmother, had begun with a question about her progress. Both women were hardheaded and goal-oriented. They could have clashed but instead had formed a strong bond.

Her father had made the mistake of trying to steer her, groom her to come into his business. In contrast, her grandmother always asked what *she* wanted to do, and then found ways to support her.

What *she* wanted to do, Marilyn had told her grandmother, was make the country a better place. While her mother waltzed off to cocktail parties and her father spent his time wheeling and dealing with the captains of industry, she planned to actually help people. Australia was supposed to be the 'lucky country' but the gap between the haves and have-nots told another story. Big business was dictating to governments, and no one seemed prepared to do anything about it.

"There's plenty of charity work you can do," her mother had said, as though charity ever got to the root of such problems. Marilyn had never been one to think small. Australia needed strategic planning and cutting-edge legislation, and she believed she had what it took to be a decision-maker. Her ultimate goal, revealed only to her grandmother, was no less than Prime Minister.

When her parents had finally, reluctantly decided that *perhaps* they could endure the idea of a politician in the family, Marilyn told them she'd joined the Labor Party. It had been the last straw and they'd parted ways.

But things hadn't gone to plan. In that conversation with her grandmother a year ago, Marilyn had admitted she wasn't on track with her goal.

"I don't understand why I'm not getting anywhere Gran," she'd said. "I'm doing everything right. I've been going to Party meetings since I started uni and I volunteer for the jobs no one wants. I have a Law/Political Science degree and they know I'm passionate and capable of hard work. I've shown them I can think on my feet, so why am I still being bypassed? Whenever an electorate position comes up I'm told I'm too inexperienced and haven't yet done my due diligence. Funny though – people my age who joined after me are being discussed as possible candidates."

"They don't trust you, Marilyn."

"Why? I've given them no reason to distrust me."

"The reason is in your blood – your private schooling, your moneyed background – they'll always be suspicious of that. I'm not saying advancing is impossible, but in the Labor Party it will always be harder for you than for members with working class backgrounds. And no matter how high you rise through the ranks, there'll be people in your Party, as well as among the voters, who will question what you're doing there."

"But the Labor Party is the closest fit to my personal philosophy. My background should be irrelevant."

"In an ideal world," her grandmother had said. "But you and I know the world is far from ideal. Reality is facing that and working with what you've got. Think about this. You want to be Prime Minister one day and I believe you'll get there. However, if you switch to the Liberals, it will happen a lot faster. You won't need to constantly prove yourself, your family connections will help fast track you through the ranks, and in the end, what does it matter whether you're with the left or the right as long as you're the leader? If you want to make things happen, you have to be the leader."

Those words had simmered for several weeks, until Steve Hardy, a relative newcomer, was endorsed for a vacancy in an electorate Marilyn had had her eye on.

In walking off her rage, she'd found herself wandering into a Liberal Party meeting, 'just to have a look'. There she'd bumped into some friends of her parents, who had welcomed her effusively. When she'd expressed surprise at their tolerance of her Labor Party membership, they'd laughed and quoted an old saying: *Anyone who is not a socialist at age 20 has no heart. Anyone who is still a socialist at age 40 has no head.*

One thing led to another and eventually Marilyn had resigned from the Labor Party and joined the Liberals. On hearing of this her parents had made overtures and fence mending had begun. Though she'd now been with the Liberals just ten months, Marilyn had made more progress with them than in her four years with the Labor Party.

Still, she had not yet told Rick about her change in political allegiance. Why not? Was she worried he wouldn't understand? Or was she more afraid of discovering he didn't feel strongly enough about her to care?

She'd never found Rick easy to read. The sex was good, but they rarely talked of personal things and he seemed only passingly interested in her political ambitions. Lately he'd cooled off even more. She'd put it down to the stress of his work, but was starting to wonder if her grandmother had been right and that it was time to look for a more suitable partner. Her mother, constantly introducing her friends' sons, would certainly be happy about that.

But Richard was her last tie to the idealistic person she'd once been, and Marilyn wasn't quite ready to cut that tie. Now, thinking of his trips to the Warrington farm over the last six months, she wondered if Jo had already begun the cutting.

...

Richard walked to the front passenger side of the van. Jo was leaning against the window wrapped in the blanket. Her eyes were closed but when he tapped lightly, she sat up, opening the door, and he slid in beside her.

"Bad news, I'm afraid."

"Marilyn hasn't taken things well?"

"What? No, no, she's just sent me to bring you in. The bad news is there's a police blockade a few kilometers down the road, which is stopping every car heading towards Melbourne."

"Shit!" Jo was wide-eyed. "If we'd gone any further we would have been caught in it. *Now* what do we do?"

"We could try changing direction, but chances are they'll have blocks set up on all the main roads out of Shepparton."

"And the Hunter and his agents no doubt have the lesser roads covered. So we're trapped here. At the two am broadcast they'll have us!"

The horror in her voice made Richard reflexively gather her up and hold her tightly to stop her trembling. "It's not over till it's over Jo," he whispered. "The next broadcast is more than two hours away, and now we have *three* heads to come up with a solution."

Jo took a shuddering breath and he felt warm air on his neck as she let it out slowly. "You're right. But it's hard not to panic."

He put his hands on her shoulders and gently pushed her back so he could look into her eyes. "You have more guts than anyone I know," he said truthfully. "And we *will* get through this. Now come on, before we freeze to death."

"What have you told Marilyn about me?" Jo asked as they walked to the cabin.

"She doesn't know the police blockade is for you. I've told her you're in danger, but I was vague on specifics, just implying the H Group was involved. Hopefully I can keep things focused on them. Say as little as possible and follow my lead."

...

When Marilyn opened the door, her first feeling was of relief. The filthy, bedraggled creature beside Richard was just a child. She quickly revised that assessment when the 'child', with quiet self-possession, offered her hand and thanked her for helping out.

Marilyn found herself responding automatically, spreading a magazine on the couch for Jo to sit on and offering to make tea, but the girl's large eyes, under-smudged with fatigue in the elfin face, had struck a familiar note and she suddenly realized why.

"Rick, come and help with the cups please," she said, and noticed his backward glance at the girl on the couch before he joined her in the tiny offset kitchen.

Under the clatter of crockery and running water, Marilyn found herself hissing. "What the hell are you playing at Rick? That girl on the couch is the fugitive, Kylie Marshall. I'll bet the roadblock I just came through is for her. Well, is it?"

She seemed to have caught him by surprise. Had he forgotten she would have seen the photo and prints he'd sent in earlier? But now he was straightening and speaking firmly.

"It's true the roadblock is for Kylie Marshall, but Marilyn, I swear to you the girl out there is Jo Warrington. I *know* Jo. I dealt with her father for months and she *is* Bill's daughter."

"The photo and prints you sent were hers?"

"Yes."

"Then why does the police database say they're Kylie Marshall's?"

"Kylie is a construct. Someone has managed to set up a false identity for Jo on the police database... You know the H Group has that kind of power."

She frowned. "But why would they do it? It would cause no more than a temporary inconvenience. Jo can surely gather sufficient documentation to prove who she is, quite apart from the statements of family and friends."

"True but such things take time to organize from a jail cell, and while locked up she'd be vulnerable to attack."

Marilyn regarded him thoughtfully, wondering what had happened to him and Jo. Had they really been attacked by the H Group? Their dishevelment was certainly more extreme than the after-effects of a romp in the hay.

"The H Group has never operated this way," she said, in a last appeal to get to the truth. "Why should they start now?"

"If not them, then who?" he threw back, and that she couldn't answer.

"What exactly is your plan Rick?" she finally asked. "If the girl won't accept assistance from BEAM and mystery assassins as well as the police are after her, what can *you* do to help?"

"My plan is to keep her moving and away from complications with the police, while BEAM investigates Brooks and Blatman. I believe they are key to this, so it's vital the investigation into them continues without a hiccup."

She sighed. "And what do you want from me?"

"I bribed Mikey at the Welcome Inn to let me borrow the motel's van, on the promise I'd have it back before eight am, when they'll need it for collecting supplies. I was hoping you'd return it for me, stay the night in my room and then take a rental car or train back to Melbourne in the morning."

"And my Veloster?" Though only a recent acquisition, in keeping with her new image, it had already become her baby.

"I'll take the best care of it, I swear. I just need to get Jo to Melbourne. When you arrive home you'll find it sitting contentedly in your garage, gleaming quietly." He finished with a grin and Marilyn shook her head.

"It had better be, and I'll want a proper explanation when this is all over."

"I owe you big time, Marilyn."

Yes, you do, she thought, but I wonder if you mean it.

They carried the steaming cups over to the sitting room, where Jo had replaced the champagne with an opened packet of peanuts from the bar fridge.

"It's not much," she said, addressing Richard. "And I know you promised me a meal when we arrived, but with everything that's happening, we should keep a low profile here. My pannier pack has some cheese, fruit and a chocolate bar we can add to this."

Richard slurped some coffee and put his cup down. "I'll get the panniers out of the van, along with the rest of our gear."

Marilyn watched his retreating back. He was seldom so obliging for her.

CHAPTER 39

When the door closed, Marilyn turned to Jo. "My boyfriend's a sucker for helping people in trouble. You're not his first lame duck and you won't be his last."

Jo met her gaze. "I'm grateful he's willing to help."

"How exactly *has* he been helping? You two look like you've been in a war together... or *something*."

"I *feel* like we've been in a war," said Jo. People are after me. If Richard hadn't stepped in I'd probably be dead by now. He thinks the H Group is involved."

Marilyn blinked. She didn't know what she'd been expecting. Maybe a protestation that Richard was just a friend, which she now knew wasn't true. She'd seen the way he'd looked at Jo tonight, and that had fired her determination to make it clear to this girl Rick was taken. She felt a jolt of surprise at her own reaction. Just minutes ago she'd been toying with the idea of looking for a new boyfriend and now here she was, overwhelmed by feelings of possessiveness for Rick. Giving someone up and having them taken away were two very different things.

As though reading her emotion, Jo blushed. "I realize this is an awkward situation," she said. "We don't know each other, and yet Richard has asked you to help me. I'd understand if you prefer not to."

"Well, he wouldn't have asked unless you were in real trouble," Marilyn heard herself saying. That was true. Richard's passion for righting wrongs had been what had drawn her to him in the first place. And what if Jo *were* nothing more than a damsel in distress? But no, looking at the blush still on the girl's face, Marilyn knew her first instinct had been correct. Jo had fallen for him.

That didn't mean once he'd got her to safety and all the excitement was over, things would stay that way. Most likely Rick would come to realize he had nothing in common with this simple farm girl and he'd return to Marilyn. That is, if she didn't blow it right now, by refusing to help. Her wisest strategy was to do her best for them, putting Richard in her debt.

Having come to that decision, she studied the girl thoughtfully. Jo looked exhausted. She smelt strongly of oil, and all manner of filth clung to her stained clothing. Though she'd obviously been through hell, she was keeping her cool, and Marilyn could not suppress a trickle of admiration.

"How are you planning to get through the roadblock?" she asked.

Jo seemed startled by her new attitude. "We haven't figured that out yet," she admitted. "Richard thought you might have some ideas."

"*What* did I think?" The door had opened and Richard stood there, laden with luggage. He dropped the gear on the floor and brought the pannier pack over to Jo.

Marilyn answered. "Apparently you thought I'd have some ideas for getting through the roadblock."

Richard looked sheepish. "You're a great ideas person, Marilyn."

Yes, she thought. You *should* feel guilty for what you're putting me through. He headed off to the kitchenette for plates and a knife and Marilyn wracked her brains for an idea that would impress him.

Jo pulled three oranges, a wrapped block of cheese, and a chocolate bar from the pannier bags and when Richard returned with the plates, laid them out.

"The photo on the police database," Marilyn said, looking at Jo. "It shows Kylie Marshall with shoulder length hair, so your short style will help. They'll expect you to be travelling alone..."

"Alone or with a man," said Richard, bringing Marilyn's narrowed gaze upon him.

"They know you're *helping* her! If BEAM's been compromised..."

"They don't know anything," he said quickly. "But given that she's been so hard to track down, they might easily surmise she has an accomplice, and who would a young drug addict most likely have helping her than a boyfriend?"

Marilyn considered the statement. "In that case, Jo will have to travel with a woman. And the two women will have to look as far removed from street drug life as possible."

Richard's jaw dropped. "I can't ask you to do that Marilyn. If you're caught you'll be charged with aiding a fugitive."

She warmed to this sign of his concern for her, and smiled. "Then we'd better make sure I'm not caught. And as far as aiding a fugitive, such a charge would have to be dropped after Jo proved she wasn't Kylie Marshall, would it not?"

"True, but before then..."

"Things could get sticky, yes, so let's maximize our chances of sailing unchallenged through that block."

"How?" Jo said.

Marilyn spoke decisively. "You'll be my sister. We're a similar size and I have an outfit with me that will look very cute on you. A little makeup to cover that pallor and something to darken your hair and we could easily pass for relatives."

"You're right," said Richard. "This could work!"

So much for his concern for me, Marilyn thought, and ignoring him, turned to Jo. "Toning down that blonde hair will be tricky."

"I could get some mud from the lake," Richard suggested.

She and Jo just looked at him.

"Okay, you two work out the details. I'll pack our gear into the Veloster."

As Marilyn tossed him her car keys, Jo jumped up and headed for the kitchenette. "I have an idea. How about a coffee rinse?"

"That could work," said Marilyn, joining her. "Let's see how many sachets they've left us."

By the time Richard returned, she was stirring a cup of concentrated brown sludge, surrounded by a flurry of opened coffee sachets.

"Jo's taking a shower," she told him. "I'll go and help her with this rinse in a minute."

"Will it do the trick, do you think?"

"Hope so. I'm tempted to add a little mascara, but anything that looks fake will only draw attention. I think we'll stick with this."

"Marilyn, about the logistics of this operation…"

"What logistics?" she said, having thought of a way of keeping Rick and Jo apart while he was packing the car. "I'll drive Jo to Melbourne. You can return the van to Shepparton yourself and come down by train in the morning."

He shook his head. "Too dangerous. Someone *does* want Jo dead and anyone with her will be in the firing line. All you need to do is get her through the roadblock and into Nagambie. Once there, turn into a side street. I'll follow in the van and we can swap over. You return the van to the Welcome Inn as we planned, and I'll take Jo on to Melbourne."

"You seem very keen to be the one with Jo."

"Marilyn, I *am* the field agent."

She laughed. "Come on Richard. We both know the most dangerous thing you've ever done is squash a centipede on your way up the steps of a farmhouse. Your skills are your gift of the gab, getting farmers to trust you."

"All the same, what would you do if someone started shooting at you?"

She studied his face and realized he was serious. She wasn't about to risk her life for this girl. "Very well, which street shall we turn into?"

"Can I borrow your phone?"

Marilyn handed it over and Richard brought up a map of Nagambie.

"Vine Street will do," he said, showing her the map. "The street on the left there, after you get into Nagambie."

She took back the phone. "Okay, and while we're working on logistics, you'd better give me the motel key and tell me where to leave the van."

Richard passed over his room key, along with the one Jo had returned. "These are for the motel room. There's a shed behind the units where they keep the van. I can't thank you enough for this Marilyn, and since I'm going to be forever indebted to you, can I add one further request?"

He pulled out the Commodore keys. "Before you leave Shepparton tomorrow, could you drop these in at the local car rental branch and tell them their Commodore is at the Mooroopna golf course, under a large grevillea bush? The bush is near the maintenance road off Park Street."

Numbly she took the keys. "What on Earth?"

"Long story, but don't try to pick up the car yourself. Get the hire company to send someone and add the cost to their bill. The car will have some scratches so BEAM may also be up for the excess charge on the insurance. If my handler asks you what's going on, just say I've told you it's all related to the H Group, and that I'll be sending in a report soon."

"You'd better. That kind of message won't satisfy them for long."

"I know."

"Rick, the more I hear about all this, the less I like it."

"Just try to make sure everyone possible stays on the Brooks and Blatman investigation. If you can do that…"

"Yes, I know, you'll be eternally grateful."

Apart from his gratitude, Marilyn decided it was time for a little reminder of what he'd be losing if he chose Jo. Casually she stripped to her lacy underwear, and having gained his full attention, slowly removed it too, before picking up the cup of concentrated coffee.

"Dyeing," she said, as she strolled to the bathroom, "is an operation best performed without clothing."

...

Richard washed his face at the kitchen sink, trying to negate the effect of Marilyn's striptease by imagining her reaction on learning it had been witnessed by an avid audience. He returned to the couch to wait for the two women and as the sound of running water drifted from the bathroom, he stretched out and closed his eyes.

"Wake up Rick, no rest for the wicked."

He sat up quickly, checking his watch. Twenty minutes to one. The girls had taken around forty minutes, but as he turned his attention to them, he was impressed. Marilyn was re-attired in the slacks and cream blouse and Jo looked stunning in tight black pants with short ankle boots. The long dusty pink top she wore accentuated her new coppery hair color.

Marilyn handed Jo a soft grey and pink wool scarf and a thin black belt.

"You might want to try these with that outfit," she said.

As Jo added the final touches, Richard marveled at the transformation. Both women were exquisitely made up and looked like a couple of wealthy yuppies ready to take on the world.

"Never dye your hair with coffee," laughed Jo. "What a nightmare! Who would have thought it could be so sticky and yet so drying at the same time?"

"We had to add conditioner just to be able to pull a comb through her hair, and it diluted the color, so we didn't dare rinse in case we lost it all."

Marilyn tossed Jo a plastic shower cap that had been provided by the resort. "Don't you dare lean on the headrest until we're through the roadblock and then before you do, put this on," she instructed. "I don't want coffee stains on my upholstery!"

Jo caught it and grinned. "Yes ma'am."

Richard noted the easy banter between them with relief. The hair project seemed to have created a bond.

"Ready to go?" he asked.

"Ready." Jo picked up a bulging plastic bag and at his raised eyebrow, gave a laugh. "It's a bin liner from the bathroom," she said. "I needed something to carry the filthy track pants and hoodie."

"Come on little sister," said Marilyn. "Let's be off." She passed her overnight case to Richard. "This needs to go in the van."

Outside, Richard handed Marilyn her keys. "I'll be right behind you. Good luck."

He headed towards the van with Marilyn's overnight case and the two women climbed into the Veloster. Jo dropped the bag of old clothes under her feet and Marilyn pulled out.

With her head-bowed to avoid the headrest, Jo sat immersed in her own thoughts as they negotiated the lake road. When the highway came up the two glanced at each other and simultaneously took a deep breath.

"What's our story?" Jo asked.

"I'm me," said Marilyn. "And you're my little sister, Claire, doing first year Arts at Uni. You've been on a mid semester break, and we've just treated ourselves to a week together at the Lake Retreat. We've had a great time visiting wineries, sightseeing, indulging in day spas and going for walks along the lake. Now we're heading home, as all good things must come to an end... What do you think?"

"I love it! All we have to do is look relaxed and happy – even enjoying the adventure of a roadblock in the middle of the night, and they'll pass us through without a second glance."

"That's the plan," said Marilyn. "And that is where we wait." She nodded to a brightly lit string of traffic cones, at the head of which police officers were directing cars to join a queue.

As they pulled up behind the last car, Jo lowered the window and leant out to peer down the line. Then she raised the window to shut out the cold night air and announced, "There's about a dozen cars ahead of us."

"How did you and Rick get caught up in this mess?"

Jo stiffened. Where was Marilyn going with this? "He heard of my father's death and came to the farm to offer his condolences. Luckily he was there when attempts were made on my life."

But Marilyn's next words were sympathetic. "I'm sorry about your father. Rick said he was a good man."

"He was, but now I realize how protective he also was. He discouraged me from sitting in on their talks when Richard came around, saying I'd find machinery chitchat boring, but now I find machinery was not what they were talking about at all."

"Your father never told you about the H Group?"

"No, and I have to say this whole global conspiracy to take over orchards sounds a bit paranoid."

"Perhaps, but you only have to look at history's examples to see we've always had those who strive for power – warlords fighting for territory, dictators, religious and elected leaders. Now it's the businessmen's turn. Already retail giants sell much of what the world buys, but ultimate power resides in the control of primary industry."

"Don't we have anti-monopoly laws to prevent that kind of thing?"

"We do, but laws are only as good as the governments that enforce them and governments are made up of politicians, who have their own power bases to defend. I know. I'm involved in politics myself. The links connecting apparently independent companies in the world today can be hard to find. Campaign contributions discourage politicians from looking."

"So BEAM looks for those links?"

"That's right. It's how we discovered the H Group and their purpose."

"But their plan – surely it would take years, hundreds of years to achieve."

"Years, yes, but not as long as you'd imagine when the plan is organized by a group already immensely wealthy and powerful."

The line of waiting cars crept forward.

"Well I don't see any evidence of them in Shep. The cannery owns some large orchards, but there are still plenty of smaller independent farmers."

"Like Mitch and Fran Davies?"

"Okay, they sold up, but their orchard was bought by a school teacher who came into an inheritance."

"So it appears, but this is a classic H Group technique for acquiring farms without resistance. BEAM investigated the schoolteacher and found he'd purchased the orchard under a business name. That business was a subsidiary of a larger business, which in turn had links through other businesses, to a company we know is controlled by the H Group."

"Are you saying the teacher is a member of the H Group?"

"No, of course not. Just one of their stooges. He *was* a real teacher, but perhaps he was disillusioned and ready to jump at any deal that would change his life. Someone offered him that deal. Act as the front man in the purchase of a farm and stay on it for a few years pretending to be a farmer. Over that time he'd receive funds to keep the farm in good order and running smoothly. To the community, it would look like our ex schoolteacher had a profitable farm even when he was selling his apples for next to nothing.

"The buyer waiting in the wings for *your* farm is another H Group stooge. With each fake farmer that moves in, pressure on the real farmers increases, since they can't drop their prices that low."

"We may have one fake farmer, but the rest are real and no one intends to sell up," said Jo.

"Unless they're offered enough incentive. With the squeeze from the supermarkets, it's getting harder for farmers to make a decent profit, is it not? They complain but as long as there appear to be independent farmers doing okay, people will always say the complainers just aren't working hard or efficiently enough.

"There's only so long anyone will put up with working like a dog just to stay above the breadline, so one by one they'll sell to 'buyers' who come along with a reasonable offer, until all the independents have been replaced by stooges. Once that's happens, the stooges will all sell up to a single company, and there'll be no real farmers left to make a fuss. The company they sell to will openly join all the orchards and use mass production techniques along with its new strong bargaining power to make a good profit. In each community it's a different company, but all of them have hidden connections to the H Group."

Jo's head was spinning. "For such a conspiracy to work, wouldn't the supermarkets need to be in on it?"

"Supermarkets can be manipulated like anyone else. It's in their own interests to keep their buy prices low, so they'll always offer primary producers as little as possible. If the price they offer is too low, the farmers will refuse to sell. During such an event, the farmers will have no income and the supermarkets won't have enough stock. The winner will be the one who can hold out the longest.

"This is where the H Group comes in. Their principals have large holdings in supermarket chains around the world. Through the boardrooms they keep the pressure on to continually cut buy-prices, and try to ensure that if say, orange growers in one area are not selling, other supermarkets will on-sell their oranges to the supermarket in that area cheaply for a short time, enabling them to hold out until the local farmers concede. If local farmers are able to co-operate and support each other for long enough, their supermarkets usually give in and the farmers are able to continue to make a reasonable living."

"That's what Dad was trying to organize."

"Yes, with Rick's assistance. We have ways of helping to support farmers through such holdouts, and when a farming community wins its battle with the supermarkets, the H Group lets go and moves on to more susceptible communities. Meanwhile, BEAM has gained more evidence about their operations."

"Richard believes the H Group is responsible for my father's death."

"He does, but I don't think it's likely. In rare instances they've been known to use murder, but only when there was a threat of discovery. They're experts at covering their tracks. That's why BEAM moves so carefully and quietly. When we've gathered sufficient evidence, we'll release it all at once to the world and there will be no doubt in anyone's mind who the principals of the H Group are and what they're up to. It'll be impossible for them to pull a vanishing trick only to re-emerge in a different form later on."

"But if you can pin an actual murder on them, you could go to press earlier?"

"It would certainly help and it's why we're actively investigating the names Rick gave us, but don't get your hopes up. There's no proof yet that your father's death was anything other than an accident."

Jo said nothing. The line had edged forward during their conversation and now only three cars were ahead of them. She could see the couple in the front car talking to police officers standing on either side. A third officer was lifting the boot lid. Her stomach knotted and she noticed her fists were likewise clenched. She felt as far removed from a carefree student returning from a wonderful holiday, as it was possible to be.

Marilyn had also gone quiet and Jo could see her knuckles above the steering wheel.

"We need to try and loosen up," Jo said. "Do you like singing?"

"It's not something I feel like doing right now."

"But it will take our minds off what's coming up, and wouldn't it help our story if we were singing together when they got to us?"

"What do you suggest?"

"Just something simple that we can harmonize on or sing in rounds, to show we have a tie – that we really are sisters, mucking around and having a ball."

"Okay, how about Frere Jacques?"

Jo began singing it and Marilyn joined in. It was a weak effort on both parts, but it broke the ice and Marilyn began again more strongly. Jo let two bars pass and then she began, the result being a pleasant round, which they continued for a while, increasingly louder and more laughingly.

"Okay, enough," said Marilyn, and started Row, Row, Row Your Boat. Jo joined in and they continued the round laughing and clapping until flashlights shining in from each side caught them by surprise. They lowered their windows and smiled up at the shadowed faces of two police officers – a young female on Jo's side and an older male on Marilyn's.

The male spoke. "Turn off your engine please."

"Good evening." Marilyn turned off the engine and shaded her eyes from the light. "Or perhaps I should say good morning."

The officer responded with a single word. "Licence."

Marilyn produced her driver's licence and passing it over, exclaimed, "You poor things, you must be so cold. Is this just an exercise or is there a reason for the roadblock?"

"We're looking for a fugitive," began the female officer, but the male cut her off.

"You're Marilyn Gibson?"

"I am."

"What's your address?"

Marilyn reeled it off while he checked it on her licence.

"Date of birth?"

She likewise passed this test.

"Who's your passenger?" he said, returning the licence.

"This is my sister, Claire."

Jo waved to him and then the policewoman on her side drew her attention asking, "Do you have some ID you can show me?"

"Sorry, I left my student card at home." Jo shaded her eyes from the flashlight, and with her feet, pushed the plastic bag on the floor, further forward under the dash. "I'm on a semester break and my wonderful big sister has just shouted me to a week at the Lake Retreat. We had the *best* time!"

A knocking sounded on their boot and the policeman on Marilyn's side told her to release the boot catch.

"You must have some kind of identification," the policewoman insisted.

"Of *course* I do," laughed Jo. "*Marilyn's* my identification. Marilyn, tell this nice police officer who I am."

Marilyn looked across to the policewoman and rolled her eyes. "Claire can be a bit trying at times, but there's no harm in her."

"Did you say you were looking for a fugitive?" Jo tried to divert the policewoman from the ID question. "Has he escaped from jail?"

The constable cast an anxious glance at her superior.

"Nothing for you to worry about," he said.

The boot lid slammed and a third officer called out, "Vacationers' luggage."

The senior policeman spoke. "Drive on."

"Thank you," Marilyn said, but the three officers were already on their way to the next car.

The girls raised their windows and Marilyn started the engine, easing slowly around the barricade before gently accelerating down the highway. For a few seconds they sat numbly, and then Jo swiveled to observe the receding lights of the roadblock and gave a whoop. "We did it!"

Marilyn flashed her a grin and took one hand off the wheel to slap Jo's in a triumphant high five. "*That*," she said, "was scary."

"You're telling me, but we were brilliant! Marilyn, I can never thank you enough for all this. You've been amazing."

"Well I have to admit, you helped me rise to the occasion." She laughed. "I'll never be able to hear Row Your Boat again without thinking of tonight."

She turned into Vine Street and cutting the engine, flipped off the headlights. The sudden stillness quietened the mood and Marilyn came to a realization.

She liked Jo. And she'd been hanging onto Richard for too long. Her grandmother was right. Rick had been part of her rebellion. They'd both got something out of the relationship, but there'd never been any real love. If she wanted to move forward, she had to let go of that last piece of the past.

Her words came softly. "I'm giving Rick up."

Jo twisted, but it was too dark to see what lay in her eyes.

Marilyn continued more strongly. "We've had a good run, but I'm about to travel a different road and it wouldn't help either of us if he came with me."

She was glad Jo stayed silent. The van's headlights appeared and pulled in behind them. Impulsively Marilyn took Jo's hands and squeezed them. "He's yours if you want him. Good luck."

She opened her door and stepped out to meet Richard. As they exchanged car keys, Marilyn smiled. "Make sure you look after my baby." Then she glanced back at Jo. "And keep *her* safe."

Richard gave her a hug. "I will… to both."

CHAPTER 40

Danny Fitani sat alone in the transport vehicle, red helmet on his lap. He'd been released from his work shift an hour early! His hands trembled. It was unheard of. The cycle was immutable... and yet here he was. It could only be bad news. They were about to tell him to cancel the show. And then what of the extra hour? The prison silo? Fitani felt a wash of shame and fear. He'd been an exemplary employee all his life. Surely they wouldn't send him there?

The transport rumbled to the middle of no-man's-land and stopped. A virtual screen appeared and Secretary Melvin Briggs glared at him.

"Fitani, you've let me down. You've let The Company down. You've let the employees down."

Danny opened his mouth but no words came out. He tried again but only managed a squeak. The Secretary sat silently, watching him squirm.

"Sir," he finally got out. "Secretary Briggs."

"If you have something to say for yourself, man, then say it."

"It's true the Prey spoke on the forbidden subject, but it happened so quickly and I wasn't there at the time to stop her."

"The CEO is most disturbed," Briggs pronounced somberly. "He mentioned cancellation and punishment. I risked his anger to speak on your behalf."

"Secretary Briggs," Fitani was flabbergasted. "I... thank you, I..."

"Do not thank me yet. You have disappointed me greatly, Fitani. I entrusted you with the Microwave Time Viewing technology and you used it to obtain and spread subversive literature among the employees."

"No," Fitani cried. "It wasn't me! Someone hacked into our pipeline to the past. By the time our programmers discovered and blocked the hack, it was too late."

Though he gave no indication of it, Melvin was relieved. Fitani had been sloppy in not sufficiently safeguarding the technology, but at least he'd not personally been involved in the dissemination of the histories. He was still trustworthy.

"Then you've chosen your team badly," said Melvin. "You assured me you had the best programmers."

"I do, I did, I…"

"Enough. Your lack of control over both the game and the technology has resulted in a great number of employees becoming confused, upset and even unhappy with The Company. Do you accept responsibility for this?"

Fitani gulped and nodded miserably.

"You have been remiss, but I have assured the CEO that your heart is in the right place and you are a Company man all the way."

"Yes," Fitani spoke eagerly. "I am."

"Now you need to prove it to the CEO."

"How?"

"I persuaded the CEO that cancelling the game outright would not be good for The Company. It would give Jo's words the appearance of truth, causing needless extra distress among the employees."

Melvin waited, but Fitani was hanging on his words and not about to interrupt. "The CEO has therefore decided you must continue to broadcast *Play or Die*, and that your penalty shall be financial. Beginning immediately, the rental on your studio Playroom has been raised tenfold. You are likewise required to raise *Play or Die's* hourly access fee to two hundred Personal Points."

"Two hundred Personal Points! But that's far beyond the reach of most employees."

"Would there be enough wealthy employees willing to pay, to enable you to keep the show going?"

"Maybe… just, but…"

"Do you wish to show the CEO your loyalty?"

"Yes of course, b…"

"Then I suggest you adhere to his wishes. Pay the penalty rental by putting up your prices. The CEO doesn't mind if only a few people can afford to access *Play or Die,* as long as access is possible."

"But the employees will blame *me*," Fitani protested. "They could storm the studio!"

Melvin was surprised Fitani had found the courage to object. It was a concern, as it meant the mood of the employees was even uglier than he'd realized.

"If the CEO feels he has less than your full loyalty, he might well go back to his first idea of a more physical punishment," said Melvin. He knew Fitani's abandonment by his mother had left him with a terror of being isolated. Just the suggestion of the prison silo should be enough to bring him into line. It was.

"I'll pay the new rental," said Fitani quickly. "And put up the price of *Play or Die*. The CEO has my complete loyalty."

Melvin smiled and threw in some softeners. "It will only be for the next three days. After that your rental will revert to the usual rate. And during that three-day period, The Company will drastically reduce prices on the most expensive entertainments. You needn't worry about employees storming your studio. They'll be too busy taking advantage of all the new bargains."

...

Angela Karpin had been asleep for only two hours when the message siren woke her. Blearily she checked the clock. What was going on? She had another six hours of Tube-Time and she'd left a 'Do not Disturb' message linked to her access code. A message siren overrode such instructions, but was for emergencies only. Her children! Angela accepted the call and her partner's face appeared.

"Collis? What's happened? Are Ben and Sandra okay?"

"They're fine Angela. Sorry, I didn't mean to scare you. It's just that everyone's wanting to know what's going on. Fitani's incommunicado and you had a 'Do not Disturb' on your access code."

She rubbed her eyes. "Fitani's on work shift right now and *I'm* trying to get some sleep."

"Then who put the price up?"

"What?"

"Try accessing *Play or Die* – not through your direct line but through the employee catalogue."

Angela called it up and was in the process of dismissing the usual rental window by touching the 'I accept the fee' icon, when she froze. At twenty Personal Points per hour, *Play or Die* was quite expensive, but such was its popularity that most employees were prepared to pay that, even if it meant settling, over the days of the broadcast, for basic foods, and spending more time on Playroom activities that earned points rather than used them.

The number she was staring at now was not 20. It was 200. The fee had increased ten times! It had to be a mistake. Only the *very* wealthy could afford two hundred Personal Point per hour. Stunned, Angela touched the 'No I don't accept' icon and immediately a bright and blaring advertisement took its place. For three days only, access to the five most expensive entertainments had been cut to twenty Personal Points per hour. Numbly she looked up at Collis.

"The only one with authority to change the *Play or Die* price is Fitani, and he can't do it from the edge. Someone must have hacked us. Let me investigate and I'll call you back."

Collis nodded and disconnected but before she had a chance to do anything, a second priority siren sounded and she accepted the call.

"Danny! But your work shift doesn't finish for another..." Angela checked the time, "thirty-five minutes. How..."

He gave a weak smile. "I'm sitting in a transport in the middle of no-man's-land. I'm hoping when my work shift is over it will take me to my own silo and not the prison one. At the moment I'm able to make calls out, but just as if I were still on work shift, no one can contact me."

Angela machine-gunned the questions, "What? How could that be? Are you under arrest? Collis just called. Someone's hacked in and changed the access price of *Play or Die*. Is this something to do with that?"

Again, Fitani produced a watery smile. "I was pulled off the work shift early to be censured by Secretary Briggs on behalf of the CEO."

Angela gasped and then frowned uncertainly. "Is this a stunt?"

"No stunt, Angela. Listen, I could be cut off at any time. I was the one who changed the access price of *Play or Die*." He ignored her second gasp and continued. "It seems I'm in big trouble."

Angela had never seen Fitani so shaken and unsure of himself. "Are you talking about Jo breaking the new rule?"

"There's that, but The Company is also upset about the breach of our pipeline and the distribution of those history files to the employees. It's caused... well you know what it's caused. Chaos."

Angela bit her lip. "Danny, I'm so sorry..."

"You weren't in the studio Playroom at time," he said. "If you had been, the hackers would never have succeeded. And now that we've made the pipeline hack-proof, it won't happen again."

Except, thought Angela, for that little back door I left in, and felt her face reddening.

Fitani saw it and hastened to reassure her. "Don't worry about it Angela. No one's mistake-proof. You still have my confidence, but now I have to win back the confidence of the CEO. My penalty for the trouble I've caused is having the rental on the studio Playroom increased tenfold."

"What? Danny, we can't..."

"Don't worry, I'll make up any shortfall in payments to our people out of my own pocket. It's only for the next three days, but you see why I've had to put up the access price of *Play or Die*. I just hope it doesn't result in my dangling from a rope like those effigies we burn each season." He gave a weak laugh.

Angela spoke firmly. "It won't come to that Danny. You concentrate on being the perfect game show host. I'll see what I can do from here."

She disconnected and lay thinking. The world was changing by the minute. Employees now knew that in the past there'd been many types of governments. Some had operated like The Company, while others had used chosen representatives of the people, who could be changed through elections. They'd learnt that many of the first democratic governments had been hard fought for, and if enough people wanted the same thing, they could get it by standing together and demanding – fighting if necessary. Angela could see why The Company wouldn't want employees knowing that.

Now they'd pulled Fitani off his work shift to censure him! It was unheard of. *And* they'd forced him to put *Play or Die* out of the reach of ordinary employees. If they were *that* worried about what Jo was saying, the employees needed to hear it.

She put a call through to Collis.

"Well my darling?" His eyes twinkled and she marveled that after all this time his smile could still melt her. "Price glitch now straightened out?"

She shook her head. "Afraid not. Turns out the price is correct."

"But that's outrageous! What's Fitani thinking? Has he become so greedy he believes people will pay *anything* to watch *Play or Die*?"

Angela chose her words carefully. She didn't want to get Fitani into even more trouble. "I suspect The Company may have influenced his decision."

"Why?"

"Perhaps Jo's words hold more truth than we thought?"

Collis stared at her for a second. "Do you really believe that?"

"I'm starting to."

"It's a big step from saying The Company isn't giving us enough information, to accusing them of actual dishonesty."

"Yes, Collis, it is. But if putting *Play or Die* beyond the ordinary person's reach is all Fitani's idea, why is The Company helping? They've just slashed the prices on the top five entertainments for... well what do you know, three days only – exactly the time remaining for the hunt, if Jo manages to keep staying alive."

Collis frowned. "If The Company doesn't want us watching *Play or Die* because they have something to hide, then we *have* to find a way to watch it."

Angela nodded. "I agree, and I have an idea, but first we need to bring people together. I'm going to post a topic in the main virtual discussion room. How does this sound for a title: "What are we going to do about the *Play or Die* price hike?"

He grinned. "That should bring them in. I'll start sending word around."

Ten minutes later avatars filled the discussion room and voices were breaking out everywhere.

"What's Fitani playing at?"

"That guy's got way too big for his boots."

"He can't just put the price up like that in the middle of a show, can he?"

"I say we put *him* up on the end of a rope!"

"Better yet, let's storm the *Fun 'n' Games* Playroom and demand they return the rental price of *Play or Die* to twenty Personal Points."

This last comment came from Gunter, who resided in a northern Safe Place. It met with instant approval and when people in her own Safe Place began volunteering for the storming group, Angela spoke up.

"Let's say a group *does* goes calling on the *Fun 'n' Games* Playroom and Fitani still won't reduce the price. What then, violence? People trying that would be enveloped in black clouds and easily overcome. All they'd achieve would be disruption to the shooting and broadcasting of *Play or Die*, which isn't what we want at all."

Gunter glowered. "Do you have a better idea?"

"As it happens, I do," said Angela, and waited for the room to grow quiet. "How does this sound? Each Safe Place chooses someone. Let's call that person the 'Get-around'. The Get-around pays the access fee for *Play or Die* and rents a blank Playroom, where they put up a virtual viewing screen to display the show. The Get-around then charges a nominal fee to any employee who wants to access the screen. The viewers' fees will cover the Get-around's costs."

"Far more than cover them!" said Gunter. "Each Safe Place will have thousands of viewers. Your Get-arounds will be making a fortune."

"The aim isn't to make anyone rich," said Angela quickly, but to give people access to *Play or Die* at a low cost. We could build in safeguards to ensure the Get-arounds don't profit from this."

"How?" said Gunter.

Sue-li from an eastern Safe Place broke in excitedly. "All we need to do is create a holding fund. Those wanting to access the virtual screen would pay their Personal Points into the fund. The Get-arounds would be authorized to withdraw enough Points from the fund to cover their costs and no more."

"I could create a program to do that," cried Angela. "I'd set it up in such a way that everyone would be able to see what Points were being paid into the Fund and what the Get-arounds were withdrawing. Any leftover points at the end could be divided amongst those who'd made payments."

Some animated discussion followed, but not everyone liked the idea. Anton, from Angela's own Safe Place, summed up the main drawback. "Those paying to watch the show on a virtual screen wouldn't be able to send in their responses to Jo's actions. Only the Get-arounds would have access to the Emoto Board."

"Then we need a way for the Get-around's responses to represent the whole Safe Place," said Collis. "All the Emoto Board does is collect responses and average them out to a point score. So all *we* have to do, is get viewers to send their own score to their Get-around."

Collis waved away the cries of derision and the rush of questions. "Let me finish. "Say that every 15 minutes, those watching *Play or Die* on a Get-around's screen, send a score between -10 and 10 to a computer program set up for the Get-around. The program would average the submitted scores and display a single number. If the number was below -4, the Get-around would concentrate on radiating disapproval to the Emoto Board. From -4 to 4, the Get-around would stay calmly neutral and if the number were 5 or more, would radiate approval. That way, the Get-around in each Safe Place would vote for all of us."

There was a rush of comments and Vicky Kwong spoke above the rest to point out a problem. "If we did that, there's no way each Safe Place could have just one Get-around. We'd need at least four watching on six hours shifts, in order to continuously cover the game. And the Get-arounds would have to be people of great integrity, who had sufficient control over themselves to be able to send an emotional message that might be different from what they personally felt."

"It's doable," Collis insisted, "if we select the right people."

"Who decides who the right people are?" asked Anton, and a silence fell upon the discussion room.

"Fellow employees," cut in Harold, a little pompously, "have we not just been reading about how the Ancestors resolved such dilemmas? Let us *all* decide! Let those who believe they would make good Get-arounds prepare a one-minute holo-speech explaining why they should be selected. And let each Safe Place *vote* for their Get-arounds."

This time the chatter was enthusiastic and the plan was agreed. As time was tight, employees who wished to nominate themselves as Get-arounds were given a mere hour to create and submit a one-minute holo-speech explaining why people should vote for them. Such was the excitement this generated, that people sent message sirens to wake up friends in tube sleep and by the end of the hour, every Safe Place had a dozen or more holo-speeches registered.

Now an hour and a half was given for people to review the speeches and vote for one person. At the end of that time the computer would tally the votes and announce each Safe Place's top four. These would become the Get-arounds. Employees about to go to Work-Time objected that this would not allow them to vote, but time constraints overrode their objections and the 90-minute timeframe stood.

Never before had employees taken an active hand in important decision-making affecting their own lives, and the newfound power set them afire. Those who had begun tuning into the cut-price alternative entertainments abandoned them in favor of avidly examining the holo-speeches and casting their votes.

By Jo's 5.00 a.m. coordinates broadcast, each Safe Place had a blank Playroom screening *Play or Die,* and four elected Get-arounds working in shifts to send responses to the Emoto Board in line with their viewers' wishes.

The employees had lost only three hours of the show. These covered the time after Jo and Richard had passed successfully through the police roadblock, and included the 2.00 a.m. broadcast. Though it was likely nothing much had happened in those hours, it was always possible the Hunter had found Jo, so unprecedented numbers flocked to rent access to the Get-arounds' viewing screens at the low, low price of five Personal Points per hour.

...

Melvin Briggs left his conversation with Fitani feeling decidedly better. Jo's recent sermon to the employees urging them to take control of their lives would be the last speech from her they would hear. By the time the bots brought in his breakfast, the employees would have forgotten *Play or Die* and be totally immersed in the new cut-price entertainments.

It had been a long stressful day, but Melvin had won out, and he rewarded himself with a relaxing bath before preparing for bed. As he lowered himself onto the soft mattress, he could not resist one last eavesdrop on the main employee discussion room to see how they were reacting to the new price.

Now, as his wife lay sleeping, Melvin sat bolt upright in his viewing headset, shocked to the core. The very thing he'd sought to prevent was happening. A rebellion was in progress. Employees were plotting to subvert the price hike! Their plan seemed elaborate, involving organizing elections, payments into holding funds and collecting and tabulating feedback scores, to enable individuals to influence the Emoto Board for a large group. These were all tasks that professionals such as the Secretarial staff of any Safe Place would take weeks to organize.

Melvin actually let out a chuckle when he realized that in their enthusiasm the employees had bitten off far more than they could chew. When it all fell in a heap, they'd disperse to their own individual pursuits and think twice about joining any future call to unite.

But as the minutes went by it become apparent that the tasks were not only within their means but were being completed at an extraordinary rate. It was as though in not knowing how long such things *should* take, they were uninhibited by psychological barriers. Melvin watched mesmerized, as working smoothly without fuss, the employees completed everything they'd set out to do, regaining access to the game at exactly 5.00 a.m.

Stunned and disbelieving, he took off his headset and slipped beneath the covers, lying rigidly with his eyes open. Was there anything left he could do? In his mind he saw the employees as a huge cauldron coming rapidly to the boil, and the flame underneath was *Play or Die*.

If he could find a way of quenching that flame, he might stop the cauldron from boiling over and avert a disaster. If not... he couldn't bring himself to imagine the consequences. But how could he quench it? To close down the broadcast now would be like throwing kerosene on the flames. The anger triggered would be enough to start the very revolt against The Company he was trying to prevent.

His only hope was to keep making it harder for the employees to access the game. He could do that in his own Safe Place, by raising the rental price of every blank Playroom to a point that made watching *Play or Die*, even secondhand, too expensive for the employees. The trouble was, they'd simply access a screening in one of the other Safe Places. No, to make this work, the rental price of every blank Playroom in every Safe Place on Earth, would have to be raised.

Briggs had no control over the Secretaries of the other Safe Places and knew from past experience that trying to influence them was a minefield. Those he counted as friends would no doubt go along, but others would be recalcitrant as a matter of course. After all, who was Briggs – a mere secretary to a Secretary, residing in a distant Safe Place, to tell *them* what to do? It was inevitable there'd be holdouts, and the scheme wouldn't work without the cooperation of every Safe Place.

Nothing short of a directive from the CEO himself would make the Secretaries in the other Safe Places toe the line, and knowing his chances of swinging that, Melvin's heart sank. Still, he could think of no alternative. He closed his eyes. First thing in the morning he would call his boss, Julian Hastmeyer, Secretary to the CEO.

...

Danny Fitani heaved a thankful sigh when the transport finally returned him to his own silo. He now had twelve hours of safety in his tube before having to face the wrath of the employees. But on arriving, he was amazed at the lack of blinking message lights. Why wasn't everyone after his blood? A call to Angela provided the reason.

Fitani's relief that the viewers had circumvented the price hike gradually gave way to a feeling of betrayal. The Company had thrown him to the wolves – he, their most loyal employee. Why had they treated him so? They couldn't really be worried about Jo's lies and misdirection. There must be another reason.

Cradled in the comfort of his smart mat, Fitani gave the matter deep thought. Mother Company had supported and loved him when he'd been a child and he knew of no others who had received such personalized attention from her. She obviously believed he was special – destined for great things. He thought he'd repaid that belief by developing his showmanship skills and bringing joy to the employees.

Obviously she had expected far more, and he had failed her. The 'betrayal' was her way of telling him so. Fitani was filled with a sense of horror. She mustn't abandon him. He would make amends. He would show her he was worthy. But how? She'd been expecting something of him. The Company must have been leaving me hints, he thought. What hints have I missed?

Gradually a phrase began repeating in his mind – 'Sacred Company Business'. The blurred areas – they were the only things that ever changed! He slapped the side of his head. How *could* I have been so blind? For hundreds of years, under our very noses, The Company has been expanding the blurs and no one's ever realized this was a message. It has to be what I was chosen for.

He thought back to The Great Arising. When the first employees had given up their homes in the centers of the Safe Places, The Company had promised they would always be able to view their lands. Company technicians had set up the first computer networks in the silos, which had included surveillance software enabling silo dwellers to look upon their lands at any time.

In each Safe Place, however, one section was blurred out – the area where Company Executives lived and performed their sacred work, and which must never be disturbed by prying eyes.

As time went on, employees had gained their own skills, and twice, curious individuals had tried to crack the programming blurring the area devoted to Sacred Company Business. In each case an electrical shock had been sent back though the computer, instantly frying the transgressor. The lesson had been learnt and to this day, the taboo on the blurred areas remained strong.

Since the first network installation, silo computer systems had been upgraded countless times, and for many generations employees had looked after the upgrading themselves. The one exception had been the land surveillance software. This resided on a separate, sealed circuit and was still maintained by Company Executives logging in remotely. The reason now was clear.

Company Executives had courage and intelligence. Anyone aspiring to those ranks needed to show they had sufficient of both. All these years, The Company had been waiting for employees to prove themselves worthy of promotion by passing a test they'd increasingly pushed into view – the blurred areas. They *wanted* the employees to break the programming!

Are we ready, Fitani wondered, or are the programming skills of the Executives still superior? No, he was confident the pupils had surpassed the masters. We can prove our intelligence, he thought, but what of our courage? It had been hundreds of years since anyone had been prepared to risk their lives trying to crack the land surveillance software.

Fitani finally understood his task. This was what Mother Company had prepared him for. The 'people' skills she'd encouraged him to hone – the ability to inspire and organize – had been all for one great purpose. He was to rouse the employees and guide them in moving to the next level.

CHAPTER 41

In her blonde wig, Jo shivered under the streetlamp. It was bitterly cold and her skin crawled in the filthy track pants and hoodie, but as her watch changed to 5.00 a.m. she smiled for the camera. She had a bolt-hole. At 5.01 she jogged down the dark block to Richard's place, stripped off her gear and climbed into bed. Richard's soft snores floated across from the sofa in the next room, and with a little sigh of regret at his gallantry, Jo fell back to sleep.

Now at 7.58, she was standing exactly where she'd been for the 5.00 a.m. posting, hoping the Hunter had placed his agents in a radius three hours away. This time the sun, not a streetlamp shone down and Jo watched her breath misting in the crisp morning air. Thirty seconds after eight o'clock, she turned and jogged towards the house. She was halfway back when the red Veloster coasted up beside her.

Richard peeled himself off the plastic bin-liner covering the driver's seat and climbed out. He held the door open and Jo took his place, removing the encrusted hoodie and wig to transform from the waist up into a neat, auburn haired businesswoman, driving to work.

Richard rested his forearms on the opened window. "I've set the car's navigation system to guide you to Marilyn's place in Carlton, but if anything goes wrong, her address is on that piece of paper in the Melway." He pointed to the Melbourne street directory on the passenger seat.

Jo smiled. "I'll be fine. Gotta go. Not safe to hang around."

It was a risk showing her face so close to where her coordinates had been broadcast twice in a row, but they needed Richard's car.

He stood back. "See you in twenty minutes."

Jo pulled out and drove down the quiet street to the main road. No one stopped her. She turned left and merged with the morning traffic. Soft winter sunlight streamed through the window and she marveled at her lightness of heart. Well, why shouldn't I feel this way, she thought. I've reached day three in good shape. I'm on my way to a new refuge at Marilyn's apartment, and I've picked up a guardian angel... or is that a white knight? Jo felt the corners of her mouth lifting at the clichés. With Richard helping, could the impossible become possible? Could she bring her father's murderers to justice *and* survive the game?

She drifted into a daydream about possibilities with Richard that were unconnected to either. A red light brought the traffic to a halt and the navigation system told her to turn right at the next street. She flipped on the radio, discovering the news broadcast was over, but some up-beat music was playing and she let it carry her along.

...

At the house, Richard collected the belongings they'd brought in the night before, even remembering to retrieve the laptops they'd left charging in the kitchen. Amazing what a few good hours of sleep could do to revitalize the brain cells. He piled their gear into the boot of his dark silver Camry, and added some extra items before leaving. Now as he crawled along with the traffic, Richard reviewed the plan he'd worked out the night before. It wasn't a great one, but it gave them a chance to put the Hunter on ice, so it was worth a try. He hoped the team working on Brooks and Blatman had been making progress. He'd check his email when he got to Marilyn's.

...

Jo turned into the steep driveway leading to the parking under Marilyn's building, and pulled into the space marked '54'. She grabbed the wig and greasy hoodie from the floor and retrieved her bike bag and helmet from the boot. The pannier pack was at Richard's and she hoped he'd remember to bring it.

Richard had told her Marilyn rented the luxury fifth floor apartment cheaply from a rich grandmother, but if he hadn't said Marilyn lived alone, Jo would have assumed she had a roommate. A pale granite-topped island bench with bar stools separated a modern kitchen from the dining/living area and it was there the furnishings deviated sharply from what she'd been expecting.

Cheap student bookshelves – planks laid between cinder blocks, were set up against a wall. A saggy, second-hand couch sat in front of a small television set, and there was no dining table.

Jo crossed to the shelves. Plenty of law books, along with some fiction – mainly Russian writers like Dostoevsky, Chekov and Tolstoy. She'd expected political titles – Marilyn had told her she was involved in politics, but the ones on these shelves all had communist or socialist themes, which didn't fit what Jo imagined Marilyn's views to be. Across the room, near the French windows, a new red leather settee with matching armchairs, circled an elegant coffee table. Now *that's* a Marilyn setting, Jo thought.

She stepped out through the French windows onto the balcony and drank in the green park below. A woman with a baby in a pram strolled along one of the paths, calling in a half-hearted way to the toddler racing ahead, to come back to mummy. Jo sighed. How wonderful not to have a care in the world.

The doorbell snapped her back to reality and she opened to Richard carrying her pannier pack in one hand and the pants and boots from Marilyn's outfit in the other.

"You made it alright then," he smiled.

She returned his grin. "No problem."

"I have an idea for the 11.00 a.m. broadcast. You'll need to wear last night's roadblock outfit under the track pants and hoodie."

"Let me wash this gunk out of my hair before I do anything else. It marks things I brush against and every time I move my head I get a whiff of stale coffee."

Richard laughed. "Go ahead and I'll get breakfast started."

Jo reached out to relieve him of the items and then leaned forward impulsively and kissed him. His eyes widened and he broke into a smile. She blushed and headed for the bathroom.

Twenty minutes later, a confident Jo emerged. A vigorous washing had taken out the stale coffee smell and left her hair with attractive coppery highlights. She'd added a touch of makeup from Marilyn's supply, and now fully dressed in her roadblock outfit, felt fresh and sexy. Jo had also been delighted to discover that the bathroom held a compact washer/drier, and her track pants and hoodie were now undergoing a heavy-duty wash.

Delicious smells and the musical introduction of the news broadcast drew her to the kitchen. The newsreader's opening story, reported in a tone of grave concern, was not of roadblocks or the police hunt for Kylie Marshall, but of a local football hero's failure to convince the tribunal not to suspend him for three matches. This was followed by the announcement that a national poll had shown Australians now put global warming at number seven on their list of important issues, where it had fallen from first.

Richard laughed. "That's what a long cold winter will do for you."

"I wonder if any of the issues from one to six included overpopulation," mused Jo.

"I think we both know the answer to that one," he said. "Your future people are right in saying most of our world refuses to even consider that issue."

"Well, right now all I'm considering is breakfast. I don't know how much longer I can hold out."

"Just as well it's ready then."

He pulled out a bar stool at the granite bench and poured her an orange juice. As she drank, Richard opened the oven and extracted two warmed plates, which he put down at the places he'd set. Diving in again, he removed two more plates, both laden. One held a stack of pancakes and the other, fried tomatoes, eggs and rashers of bacon.

"Dig in."

Jo needed no second invitation. She helped herself to a couple of pancakes, buttered the top one and added a fried egg, some bacon and a tomato.

"This is wonderful," she said around a mouthful.

Richard, who was making inroads into his own pancakes and eggs, nodded. "I didn't realize how hungry being on the run makes you. Tea?"

"Lovely! I've gone right off coffee after smelling it in my hair all night."

The teapot he picked up was delicate and appeared to be silver, but the mugs he poured into were large and colorful. Jo almost made a comment about how strangely contradictory Marilyn's belongings were, but decided she didn't want to bring Marilyn into the conversation. Instead she added milk from the jug Richard had put on the bench.

"I take my hat off to whoever trained you Rick."

"I prefer Richard," he said with a self-conscious smile. And I guess the thanks go to my mother, who showed me a few tricks while declaring that no son of hers would grow up to be helpless in the kitchen."

"You have brothers?"

"Actually no, I'm an only child, like you."

"You must be close to your parents."

"I was."

The reply was peremptory and he lowered his head to his food. Jo was bewildered. What did that mean? Had there been a falling out, or were his parents no longer alive? Obviously this wasn't where he'd intended the conversation to go, but right now he seemed like a little boy lost, and her heart went out to him.

Tentatively she asked, "Do they live elsewhere?"

"My mother lives interstate with her new husband," he replied shortly. "We've been out of contact for several years."

"And your father?" her voice was soft.

Richard continued to eat his breakfast and at the point when Jo decided he wasn't going to answer, said quietly into his plate, "There was an incident. It's not something I like to talk about… have ever talked about, really."

"Richard, I understand. I've also lost my father." Her voice trembled a little on the last words and he looked up, the tightness in his face changing to concern.

"Jo, I'm sorry. I didn't mean to open the wound."

"I wasn't able to talk it over with my aunt," said Jo. "I hardly know her and she never got on with Dad anyway. When I told her Dad's death couldn't have been an accident, she said I was deluded. My friends were much more sympathetic, but they obviously also believed the coroner.

"For the last few weeks I've just felt like raging. Dad and I were close, and his death was so unfair. Now I know that he was murdered I intend to make sure his killers don't get away with it."

She lifted her eyes to Richard's. "Was the incident with your dad anything like that?"

Richard took a deep breath and let it out in a long sigh, his shoulders slumping. "Yes and no. My Dad's death was also unexpected and could be laid at the door of others, but they didn't kill him directly. He took care of that himself."

"Oh, Richard." Jo began to reach out but he'd picked up the teapot and was pouring, his gaze fixed intently on the steaming liquid running into his mug.

"When I was a kid, Mum and Dad owned a wholesale plant nursery." He spoke to the stream. "They had a handful of employees and grew all kinds of plants. It was only a small business but they loved being their own bosses, and felt they were creating something for me."

He sipped from his mug, looking into the middle distance. "I'd sometimes travel with Dad in the truck when he went selling to the retail nurseries. Not so long ago there were dozens of little nurseries, and the owners would always come out and chat with us as they selected plants to buy. They all said Dad's were the healthiest of all, which made me feel so proud."

He looked at Jo and smiled. "Mum and Dad used to formulate their own special potting mixes for each variety they grew, and they were meticulous in cleaning up dead leaves and guarding against insect and fungal attacks. You can't let those jobs get away from you in the nursery business. The retailers always bought something, and by the time we'd done the rounds, the truck would be empty and Dad would have a notepad full of orders for next time.

"In recent years though, things changed. Big supermarket-style nurseries began opening up and the little guys couldn't compete. Some were absorbed, others closed down. For my parents, it became easier at first. The big nurseries had big orders, but only wanted one or two varieties. My folks ended up growing nothing but azaleas for a single company. I think a lot of the joy went out of the business for them after that.

"Then the squeeze began. The company took everything my parents could produce but began dropping the unit price they were prepared to pay. Mum and Dad gradually had to let their employees go and ended up laboring twelve hours a day to keep up with a demand that paid little more than the bills."

He looked across to Jo and she nodded. "I know what you're talking about. It's the same thing in the orchard industry."

Richard put his cup down. "I'd just finished school at the time and was heading off to university. They'd managed to keep from me just how desperate things were and even tried to help out with my fees. Then the company they'd been dealing with told them they'd just signed up a huge azalea wholesaler in New South Wales. This wholesaler had a vast automated setup and plants grow faster there too, because of the warmer climate. My parents were informed that as valued clients, the company would continue to buy from them if they could match the price of the NSW supplier. Turned out this was 30% less than their current price.

"Dad was in his mid forties, too late to start afresh. He and Mum had labored for twenty years in their nursery and had nothing to show for it. Mum went into the potting shed one day to find Dad hanging from a roof beam. Within a space of six months, she'd sold the nursery, married a barrister and moved to Sydney. It was as though that part of her life had never happened. All those years she and Dad had worked side-by-side had just been wiped from the slate.

"I couldn't dismiss it all the way she had. I was angry with myself for not having realized how bad things had got, angry with Dad for having taken the easy way out and angry with Mum for getting on with her life. But most of all, I was angry at the multinational giants sweeping the Earth and destroying the lives of little people like us, people just trying to make a living from our own small businesses."

"Richard, that's so awful."

"I felt as though I'd lost my whole life," he admitted. "Overnight the nursery was gone and in their own ways each of my parents had left me. Now with some perspective I can understand their actions and not take them personally. They were only human after all, but I can never forgive the goliaths. In their quests to continually expand and spread their control, they don't just destroy lives, they reduce everyone's options."

"But is there any stopping them?" she asked.

"I don't know, but at least with vigilance and organized resistance we can slow them down."

"Richard thank you for telling me this," said Jo. "Now I understand the choices you've made, including why you've been prepared to help me. I realize how hard it must have been for you to talk about it."

He smiled and squeezed her hand. An aching to draw him in overwhelmed Jo, and she tightened her hand on his. They moved together.

"Don't mind me," said a voice. "Go for the big smooch."

For a split second their eyes remained locked, then each stepped back and turned to face Fitani.

"Ahh, how disappointing," he responded.

"Business before pleasure," said Richard with a tight smile.

"Well then," Fitani bowed towards Jo. "What is your business?"

Jo appraised him thoughtfully. He wore a severely cut suit of a shiny rust-colored hue matching his hair. The Company logo stitched on the breast pocket was electric blue, along with the ruffled shirt beneath his jacket and the curled toes on the ends of his shoes.

"I prefer this outfit to your last," she said.

Surprisingly, Fitani didn't preen, but merely nodded. He looked tired and Jo couldn't help but remark, "Dear me, I haven't been keeping you up have I?"

"Touché my dear. It's true that few prey last this long. You've been running my crew quite ragged, but more people than ever before are watching the show. You and the Hunter are certainly giving everyone their Points' worth. So, what would you like to ask me today?"

"As I was driving here this morning," said Jo, "I started feeling for the first time, that I had a chance of surviving this game, and then I thought, what's the point of getting through five days of *Play or Die* if the whole world ends on day six. So what I want to know is, how long from now until The Great Destruction occurs?"

Fitani looked at her solemnly. "You needn't worry about day six … or day seven."

Then he doubled over with laughter holding his knees. "Oh you should *see* your faces! Relax, I'm joshing you. From your point of view the Great Destruction won't occur for another seventy-eight years."

"You're wasted as a game host," Richard gritted. "You should be running your own comedy show." He stiffened and grabbed Jo's arm. "I know what's been disturbing me about that guy's outfits."

Jo wrinkled her brow. "What do you mean? Is there anything *not* disturbing about his outfits?"

"True, but I was talking about the logo. Something about it has been niggling at me. Wait a minute."

Richard opened his laptop on the bench and started it up, while Fitani wandered around the apartment, humming an annoying little tune and eyeing the furnishings.

"Here, check this out."

Jo peered over his shoulder at an official looking document filling the screen.

"What is it?"

"A prospectus. All listed companies are required to produce one, outlining their purpose and general operations. This is the H Group's. They describe themselves as a small investment company, specializing in conservative investments for a select clientele. Most of their shareholders have no idea what's really going on, but they're happy to receive regular dividends and they give the H Group an air of legitimacy. Look at their logo on the cover page."

"A fancy H," said Jo. "Yes, it *does* look similar…" she leaned closer. "Except the serifs on Danny's are extended into elaborate curlicues."

"Things change over time. The logo on this prospectus could easily evolve to become the logo on Danny's jacket." He spoke grimly and Jo stared at him in horror.

"If that's true, it means BEAM will fail to bring down the H Group. They'll end up not only controlling this world but the next one too!"

"It *may* just be a coincidence," Richard growled, and Jo straightened up.

"Well, there's one way to find out… Danny," she called to the host who was circling the red leather settee critically, like a snob at an art show. "I'm ready to ask my second question."

Fitani strolled over. "Yes?"

"There's a small company in our time called the H Group. It appears to be innocuous, but has disguised tendrils into companies and businesses all over the world. Richard's organization, BEAM, has collected evidence that the H Group intends to take over the world's primary industry, with the ultimate aim of controlling all commerce. He can provide you with the evidence he's collected to make it quicker for you to identify them.

"My question is, when The Great Destruction occurs in seventy-eight years time, will the H Group still be in existence?"

Fitani's jaw dropped. "How on earth do you imagine such a ludicrous question will help you to escape the clutches of the Hunter?"

"*Richard* has helped me to escape the clutches of the Hunter, so by way of repayment, this question is for him," Jo replied calmly.

Fitani sighed and turned to Richard. "Show me what you've collected."

"The evidence is in encrypted files on non-networked computers at BEAM headquarters," said Richard. He gave the address of the building.

Fitani tilted his head and his image froze for a second. "Got it."

"But the computers aren't connected to any network."

"Trust me."

"The encryption…"

Fitani laughed and then turned to Jo. "This is a lot of information and links to corroborate and track through seventy-eight years," he said. "It'll take my team a while. I'll get back to you with your answer as soon at they get back to me."

"Fine," Jo agreed.

Agitatedly, Richard took a step towards the game show host. "How long is it likely to take?"

Fitani regarded him coolly. "As long as it takes."

Richard made a sound of disgust and moved to the French windows. "I need some air."

CHAPTER 42

Closing the glass doors behind him, Richard moved to the balcony rail. The people in the park below registered only as blurs. He felt sick. In just seventy-eight years the world would end. It was no time at all.

He'd had such dreams for humanity. He'd pictured the people of Earth becoming wise, finding ways to travel between stars, settling on other worlds and making humankind immortal. Instead they were going to blow themselves up in seventy-eight years. If he had children and grandchildren, they would die before their time – either in a nuclear explosion or worse, from starvation or radiation poisoning. Only a few remnants of humanity would struggle and survive in places untouched by the devastation. And their fate – enslavement by the very company he'd failed to defeat.

Richard's head spun and he leaned dizzily against the rail. What was the point in going on? Never had he been so close to understanding his father's actions. But there was Jo, and now he knew she felt for him what he felt for her. *She* was the point in going on.

He straightened and sucked in a huge lungful of air. Jo needed him and it was the only thing that mattered right now. He turned and walked back into the room to see her pushing her notepad into a pannier bag. The game show host was nowhere in sight.

"Where's Fitani?"

"Gone."

"What about your third question?"

"I've asked it." A blush was rising to her cheeks.

"Jo, my plan – I needed to know where the Hunter was. Is that what you asked him?"

"Sorry, it was something personal. Nothing that can help us right now."

"But we could have turned the tables on the Hunter – caught him by surprise."

Her look of contrition melted his frustration and he sat and took her hands. "It's okay. It would have been good to take the battle to the Hunter, but waiting for him to come to us will do."

"Go on."

"You've told me the Hunter likes to operate independently from his troops. That works in our favor. When he's on his own we can snatch him. If we tie him up in my apartment, he won't be able to communicate with his agents and you'll be safe until the game is over."

Jo frowned doubtfully. "It sounds terribly risky. Not only does he have a lot of agents, he's smart and *very* intuitive."

"And hopefully by now, very *tired*," Richard argued. "Don't forget, he's been chasing you all this time as well as working out strategies and coordinating his troops. No doubt he's had some sleeping time, but he sounds like a 'hands-on' sort of person who wouldn't want to leave things to others for long."

"You're right about that. And his modus operandi so far has been to deploy agents to cover the most likely places I'd be, while he tries to anticipate unconventional moves on my part and peels off to follow his hunches. If he sticks with that strategy and he *is* getting tired, it might just be possible to catch him by himself with his guard down."

"You agree it's worth a try then?"

"What exactly did you have in mind?"

Richard checked his watch. It was close to ten. "At quarter to eleven, you'll walk to the cafe down the road from here. You'll be in your photography outfit with Marilyn's clothes underneath and you'll go to a table and order a coffee. I'll follow in my car, but when I come in I'll sit at a different table.

"After the 11.00 a.m. broadcast you'll go to the restroom, strip off the track pants, hoodie and wig, and walk out looking totally different. Then you'll return to the apartment and sit tight. I'll stay in the cafe until the Hunter shows up. When he leaves, I'll follow him. As soon as I get the opportunity I'll knock him out and bundle him into the boot of my car. I grabbed a roll of duct tape from my house this morning, for that purpose. I'll bind him while he's unconscious, drive him home and…"

"And what? Heave a bound man out of your car and carry him into your house without anyone seeing? And if by some miracle you do manage that, what then? Chain him up in your nonexistent basement? How are you planning to keep him constrained for two and a half days?"

He shrugged impatiently. "I'll think of something. The main thing is to get him under our control."

"Richard this plan has so many holes in it I can't even begin to count them." Jo felt her throat tightening. "What if someone sees you attacking the Hunter and calls the police? You could end up in jail charged with assault and kidnapping. Or what if the Hunter's agents are near and they grab you? As time goes by and you fail to contact me I'll be dying a thousand deaths wondering what's happened to you."

Richard reached into his pocket and pulled out a small phone. "Here's something else I grabbed from home this morning. It's an untraceable phone. BEAM has a supply of them for emergency communication with our Community Leaders. I also changed the SIM card in my own phone, since at nine this morning the Hunter will have learnt my identity."

Jo's eyes widened. "Learnt your identity? Then if he sees you in the cafe he'll recognize you!"

"Not if I hide behind a newspaper." He pushed the phone towards Jo.

"You want me to *call* if I don't hear from you? How will that help if you're captured? They'd hardly leave you with a phone. Richard this is not going to work. We need to think of something else."

"Well we can't keep running. The more time the Hunter has to corner us, the more likely he is to succeed. Unless you can think of something better, I want to try this."

Jo stood abruptly and began pacing the apartment. Richard stayed where he was, watching her. Finally she came to stand in front of him. "I've thought of something that could make your plan a little less dangerous."

He waited.

"Do you have the *Find my iPhone* feature enabled?"

"I don't think so."

Jo sat beside him. "I can set it up for you. Then you can log into your iCloud account with a computer and have your phone's location displayed on a Google map. Here's my deal – and it's the only way I'll go along with this plan.

"You hide your iPhone somewhere on your person and put the untraceable phone in your pocket or any obvious place. If the Hunter's agents do catch you, they'll take *that* phone and I'll be able to find you by tracking your iPhone on my laptop. God knows what I'll do about it, but at least I'll know where you are."

Richard laughed and Jo gave him a punch on the arm. "That's my condition. Take it or leave it."

"Okay, okay. Set it up for me. I need to go check my email."

"Give me your iPhone."

He handed it over and went to retrieve his laptop. Both were soon engrossed in their separate activities.

Richard's first priority was the report on Brooks and Blatman. It had arrived with an email, attached as an encrypted file. He frowned as he read it.

This was not good. He typed a few queries and instructions, encrypted them and sent them off, noticing that Jo was approaching with her laptop.

"I need your username and password."

"My username is SayersR," he said, typing it in. "I'll change my password to something you can remember." His mouth twisted wryly. "How about Fitani?"

Jo laughed. "That'll do."

"While I'm at it, I'll set that as the password for my laptop too, in case you need to use it."

Jo left him to finish up, and headed off to clear away the breakfast things. When he finally shut the computer lid she pointed to the two phones she'd left on the coffee table.

Dutifully he scooped them up and dropped the cheap untraceable phone into his pocket as he wandered off to the bathroom. Where to hide the iPhone? A knife sheath was strapped to his calf, but he wasn't about to substitute a phone for his knife. Finally with a shrug, he slipped the phone down the front of his jocks, thankful he'd ignored society's dire warnings about wearing tight underwear. And as far as any radiation from the phone, he thought with grim irony, bring it on. Starting a family is no longer on my list of things to do.

He returned to the living area and saw Jo had donned the now clean track pants and hoodie, and combed out the blonde wig. By her feet sat a glossy cardboard carry bag emblazoned with the name of a women's clothing store.

She looked up and smiled. "I found this in a drawer of plastic bags. It's perfect for carrying my quick-change clothing. So I'm all set."

He checked his watch. "We have about twenty minutes before we need to leave. Let me bring you up-to-date on the Brooks and Blatman investigation."

"You've had word?"

"I've just received their preliminary report, which will probably also be the last, but it paints a clear enough picture. It seems that for some months Simon Brooks has made larger withdrawals on his accounts than alimony to his first wife, a new home for his second, and the private school fees for his kids, have warranted."

She looked at him questioningly.

"Gambling. Apparently he has a penchant for horses, dogs – anything that runs. A few months ago he took out a second mortgage on their new home, and has had trouble with the payments. A little while back he resorted to loan sharks."

"I don't get it. How would killing Dad help his situation?"

"This, I'm sorry to say, is just the kind of scenario the H Group excels in sniffing out and using to its advantage. With their influence on the boards of supermarket chains, they pull a few strings. Suddenly a substantial bonus is dangled in front of Brooks, conditional upon his being able to close a deal with the Shepparton fruit growers at the new reduced buy prices. Brooks would be desperate for that bonus and quite aware the only thing between him and it was your father. With your dad out of the picture, the other farmers would soon crumble and sign."

"But there's a big difference between wishing someone dead and actually organizing it," Jo objected. "Brooks is a white-collar executive. What would he know about hit men?"

"Probably not a lot, but the same can't be said for the unsavory money lenders he's in deep with, and it's odds on one of them would have given him Blatman's contact details if it meant speeding up Brooks' repayment."

"So the H Group's laughing. With Dad's death the Shepparton farmers will cave in to the supermarkets and reduce their profit margins to almost zero. They'll be ripe for the picking and the H Group will send in its stooges to buy them up. Even if Brooks is caught for the murder, he's just a Supermarket employee with a gambling addiction. The H Group is in the clear."

Richard nodded. "That's exactly the way they operate – by manipulating others. Their own hands stay clean and they scavenge from the mess left behind."

Jo sat down, appalled and sick. "And Brooks has got away with it – unless we can tie him to Blatman. Even then we'd have to prove Blatman sabotaged the tree shaker in order to murder Dad."

Richard sighed. "I'm afraid there's more bad news. He lifted the lid of his laptop and pressed a key to wake it up. The address Fitani gave us for Blatman is the home of a man called Graham Hodges. He's a thirty-two year old part-time postal worker, employed by Australia Post for the last twelve years." He turned the laptop so she could see the photo BEAM had sent him. "Graham Hodges has a clean record. Not a single complaint."

Richard waited as Jo peered at the very ordinary looking man in a postie uniform. "I guess Fitani steered you wrong."

"No!" Her response was immediate and unequivocal. "Danny may be a lot of things, but as far as *Play or Die* is concerned, he's a stickler for the rules."

She pointed at the screen. "If that man lives at the address Danny gave us then he is Morris Blatman. When you think about it, a postie is a great part-time job for a hit man. He'd be able to set up postboxes under fake names to manage communication with clients, and with his official vest and scooter he could go practically anywhere. Who pays attention to a postman? If he has to occasionally dump a sack of letters at his house to give himself time to perform a hit, he can deliver them on his next day off with no one the wiser.

"I'll bet you his home is far better than the average part-time postie's, and what about his car? Get your agents to check out his standard of living and keep watching his movements. Eventually they're bound to catch him trying to kill someone. Then at least we'll be able to put *him* behind bars."

Richard cleared his throat uncomfortably. "Jo I think you have the wrong idea about BEAM. We're not affiliated with the police or any law enforcement agency. Our sole purpose is to protect small business where we can, from unscrupulous moves by the big guys. Currently we're doing our best to bring down the worst big guy of all – the H Group. When I told them we might be able to lay your father's death directly at their door, my bosses were happy to give me some leeway in deploying our resources, but now that it's obvious we can't pin a murder on them, those agents will be called off and used elsewhere, probably already have been, and I'll be expected to come in and make a full report before being sent off to another posting."

Jo's expression of hope died and her shoulders slumped.

Richard hastened to reassure her. "Don't worry, I'm not going anywhere. Even if I have to quit my job, I'm seeing you through this game. And later we might be able to do something about Blatman ourselves. At least we know his real name and where he lives."

Jo looked up, her face set. "You're right about BEAM. Thanks to them I've learnt things I could never have discovered by myself, but I can't expect them to go on solving my problems. And it's not fair to drag *you* along any more either."

She stood up. "Richard, you'll never know how grateful …" Her voice cracked and she swallowed. "But it's time we went our separate ways. You've risked your life enough. If you were killed trying to help me, I'd never…"

Again her voice broke and he stepped towards her but she held her arm out stiffly. "When you told me you suspected the H Group of murdering my father, I had no qualms about accepting your help. After all, you were the one who'd got him involved with them. But I know Dad. Even without you or any knowledge of the H Group, he would have put up a fight against the supermarket chain and the end result would have been the same.

"You don't owe me anything Richard and I don't want you risking your life any more."

She gave a little laugh. "Don't worry. I was surviving the game before you came along, and I'll keep on surviving. I'm tough. I'm going to the cafe by myself for the broadcast, and afterwards I'll return to collect my gear. Please don't be here."

Richard ached to gather her up but he could see the effort it was costing Jo to take this stand and he couldn't break her defenses and pride.

He nodded. "If that's what you want. Marilyn's not likely to be here when you get back either. Knowing her, she'll go straight to the office when she arrives in Melbourne, so just leave the key on the bench for her."

Jo gave him a weak smile. "Thank you."

Richard forced himself to stay put and nodded again. "Good luck Jo."

She picked up the bag, turned and left the apartment. As soon as the door closed behind her Richard turned to his laptop, created a new text file, and typed a few words. Then he left the computer on the coffee table and eased open the apartment door, peering down the hall. The lift doors were just closing.

He raced to the stairwell and leapt down the stairs, exiting at the ground floor. Through the front glass doors he saw Jo reach the footpath and turn to walk towards the shops and cafes of Lygon Street.

His Camry was angle parked in front and Richard debated whether to take it or follow Jo on foot, but he couldn't risk the Hunter making a getaway by car, so with an eye on her progress, he hopped into the Camry and started the engine. When she reached the end of the block, he backed out and followed slowly in her wake.

...

Jo walked unseeing past the shops and restaurants and reached the cafe at 10.55. She walked in, found a table and ordered a double-shot black. She needed it. Her ebullience of the morning was gone. She was on her own again, and though it felt as though she'd been cut adrift in space, she didn't regret her decision.

The sudden prospect of losing Richard's support when he told her BEAM might recall him had made her realize the truth. What she felt for him went deep. If keeping Richard close got him killed, she would never be able to live with herself.

The look on his face when she'd told him they had to part ways had nearly crumbled her resolve, and she'd been grateful and relieved when he hadn't argued. Now she could concentrate on the job of getting through the next two and a half days with a clear conscience.

CHAPTER 43

Angela wiped the back of her hand across her eyes. All her life she'd been taught Ancestors were selfish, but Jo had just done the most unselfish thing possible. This final action above all, proved she did not deserve to die. Angela glanced around the studio Playroom and saw others surreptitiously blowing noses. No one here wanted Jo's death. She was a hero. And she was right. This was a game of murder, not justice. It belittled them and was distracting them from solving their own problems.

Fitani wasn't going to do anything about it. He was already being harassed by messages from employees urging that he either save or kill Jo, and the stress was showing. Instead of sending his avatar to the studio Playroom after his most recent interaction with Jo, he'd placed a 'Do Not Disturb' on his access code and was ignoring all calls to his tube.

The time had again come to take things into her own hands. The Company wouldn't like it, but The Company, Angela now realized, was one of the problems the employees would have to solve. Quietly, she slipped from the studio Playroom.

...

Julian Hastmeyer was annoyed. Being Secretary to the CEO was more than a full time job. While others might envy his exalted position, he alone knew the work involved. And now his own secretary, Melvin Briggs, normally a most reliable chap, was insisting on taking up some of his time to discuss a matter of utmost importance. Utmost importance? What could be more important than ensuring the success of the biggest event of the year?

For weeks all the children, nephews, nieces and cousins on his staff had been helping to prepare for it – the CEO's 82nd birthday party. Of course this year's extravaganza would not compete with the absolute spectacle he'd orchestrated two years ago. Back then Directors from every Safe Place had attended for a full month of festivities. Nevertheless an eighty-second birthday was important, and deserving of all the efforts being put into it.

At this very moment Julian's eldest son, and heir apparent, was organizing the beauty pageant winners. These lovelies were the cream of the daughters from Secretarial families in every Safe Place. Julian touched the thumbnail on his screen to view the crystal bathhouse, where they fluttered around in their scanty outfits, readying themselves to pamper the CEO when he entered for his bath. No doubt the girls were all very excited, for by the end of the day the most favored one would remain, living a life of status and luxury on the CEO's estate and maybe if she played her cards right, even becoming his twenty-third wife.

Julian leant back in his contoured leather chair and changed the view to the preparations occurring in the pleasure gardens. Banquet tables garlanded with flowers were being set up and he could see Suzanne, his fourth daughter, instructing several dozen minor cousins already dressed in their waiter uniforms – no bots for this occasion, in their duties. Silver trays laden with wine glasses and a variety of stimulants and relaxants stood to hand, and the finest musicians among the secretarial families were tuning their instruments and engaging in last minute rehearsals. It was a great honor to be chosen to play at the CEO's birthday party, bringing much status to one's family.

Quickly Julian scanned the other areas of activity – the bustling kitchens, the entertainments already being enjoyed by some early rising guests, and gave a satisfied sigh. Perhaps he would be able to spare five minutes for Melvin's matter of utmost importance.

...

Fitani finally bit the bullet and sent his avatar to the studio Playroom, glad for the first time he wasn't visiting in person. Immediately voices bombarded him.

"What the hell, Danny?"

"Are you out of your mind?"

"Why did you make *Play or Die* so expensive?"

"Are you aware hundreds of thousands of viewers are now watching the show secondhand and not paying us a single Personal Point?"

Fitani's avatar held up his hands. "I owe you all an explanation, and that's what I'm here for."

"We're listening," said an angry voice.

"What I'm about to tell you is in the strictest confidence." He paused, and now the room grew silent. "The price hike wasn't my idea, but I had to go along because it was what The Company wanted."

Exclamations and questions broke out immediately, and once again Fitani raised his hands. "The Company also wanted it to appear that the increase *was* my idea, so we can't tell the viewers it's not."

"There could only be one reason for that," Justin said angrily. "Jo's been telling the truth and The Company is trying to stop employees from hearing it!"

"There *is* another possible reason." Fitani spoke soothingly. "Let's not be too quick to condemn our savior and support for so many hundreds of years."

"What's the other reason?" said Mavis.

"That The Company is simply being over-protective. I've thought about it and realized they must still see the employees as children – as the naïve survivors they rescued in The Great Arising. That's the reason they've never included us in their decision-making. No one wants children interfering in adult matters. They've forgotten it's been hundreds of years since we were savages – that we've grown, become educated, and have high-level skills and knowledge to offer. All we need to do is show our worthiness, and they'll lift the veil from their operations and welcome us into the Executive ranks."

"How are we supposed to show our worthiness?" asked Garal.

All eyes turned to Fitani. "By passing a test, which has been here, waiting for us all along," he said.

"Enough riddles, Danny," Justin growled. "What test?"

"The blurred areas devoted to Sacred Company Business. Only by breaking through The Company's programming, will we prove that we have the skills, intelligence and courage needed for inclusion into the Executive."

The team stared at Fitani. The programmers in the room had heard Richard wonder aloud whether the employees had the skills to remove the blur, and it had rankled them. Their loss of revenue from the overpricing of *Play or Die* was added incentive. Some of them believed Fitani's theory, that removing the blur was a coming-of-age test. Others simply decided that if The Company refused to become more transparent in its operations, it was time the employees forced that transparency, and found out what the blurred areas were hiding. Either way, every member of the programming team was soon regarding it as a duty to crack the land surveillance software.

· · ·

Sitting at the terminal, Angela laced her fingers and applied pressure until she felt a satisfying crack. Where to start? The Hunter had to die. It was the only way to stop him, but how to arrange it? *Play or Die* had used a professional assassin a couple of seasons back, when a Hunter had failed to bag her Prey in five days, but contacting the same assassin using *Play or Die*'s protocols would show Fitani he had a traitor within. She had to use someone else. Unfortunately employing a hit man wasn't easy. The first contact was always through a referral. Her head came up. Of course, Morris Blatman. They had a record of the protocols Simon Brooks had used when he'd ordered the hit on Jo's father. She'd use the same protocols and Blatman would think Brooks was ordering another hit.

After Angela's distribution of the histories, Fitani had ordered his team of programmers to make the Microwave Time Viewing technology 'hack-proof'. During the process, Angela had created her own backdoor into the pipeline. Guilt had nagged her at the time, but now she was glad she'd done it. There would be no evidence of her break-in. The only worry still left was whether her hit man would get to the Hunter, before the Hunter got to Jo.

. . .

Melvin Briggs found himself stammering in the face of Julian Hastmeyer's impatient expression.

"Sir, I know it sounds incredible but the latest broadcast of *Play or Die* is stirring up the employees. There are rumblings of discontent. If we don't act immediately, I fear for the consequences."

"The consequences?" Hastmeyer imbued the word with the utmost disdain. "If you *really* want to talk consequences, try interrupting the CEO on the morning of his birthday as he takes his bath with a dozen of the most luscious beauties in the land. Now *that* would entail consequences."

"He doesn't have to be involved. All you'd need to do is issue an edict in the CEO's name, that effective immediately and for the next three days, Directors of all Safe Places must tax virtual access to their blank Playrooms at a rate of 200 Personal Points per hour per person accessing."

Hastmeyer's forehead creased. "And this would make the employees happy?"

Melvin gulped. "No, but it would reduce their incentive for watching *Play or Die*. Secretary Hastmeyer, it is absolutely imperative that the employees be diverted from this dangerous game! The longer they watch it, the worse it gets. They need to be refocused onto something else as quickly as possible."

The Secretary's frown deepened. "Let me see if I've got this right. You want me, in the CEO's name, without having consulted him, to issue an edict which will irritate the other Directors and anger the employees, because you have failed in your job of keeping them happy."

Melvin paled and drew breath.

"Think, before you answer that," Hastmeyer warned.

Melvin thought. If he insisted that Hastmeyer follow his recommendation, it would be tantamount to admitting his own failure, which would be the end of his job. Hastmeyer would certainly accept the seriousness of the situation if Melvin was prepared to make such a sacrifice, and he'd issue the edict, thereby probably saving The Company's neck.

But now Melvin began asking himself whether it really *was* necessary. Losing his job was no small thing. His reputation would be blackened and rather than appointing one of his sons to take his place, the CEO might decide it was time for another family to take on the role the Briggs family had held for generations. Should that occur, his wife and children and their children would suffer the disgrace for years to come. No one would understand his sacrifice and it might be for naught anyway. Jo was possibly dead already and the game over. Or perhaps the employees would naturally tire of ranting against The Company and turn back to the everyday things in their lives.

If he backtracked right now and assured Hastmeyer he could solve the problem without the Secretary's intervention, it was possible there'd be no dire consequences at all. On the other hand he might be signing The Company's death warrant. Melvin twisted in an agony of indecision and then lowered his eyes.

"Perhaps the edict is a bit premature. I believe I may be able to find another solution."

Hastmeyer smiled. "Good man. I knew I could rely on you. Was there anything else?"

"No Sir, just to extend my best wishes to the CEO on this important day."

. . .

Many hundreds of years into Jo's future, a morning went by during which: two thousand white-suited figures toiled over a rectangle of ground in front of them; executives snored in their beds, rode to hounds or in the case of a few smug guests, swam in sparkling warmed pools or strolled to play croquet on the exquisite lawns of the most powerful man in the world; thousands of ordinary people slumbered in hexagonal tubes while thousands more engaged in a myriad of diverse activities, all within the confines of a series of silos; a young woman used Microwave Time Viewing technology to make contact with a man from the past; a group of programmers tested an idea, frying a number of computer components, but escaping any hurt themselves; some technicians pieced together an unsavory puzzle and disbelieving the result, started again from scratch; many thousands followed the story of a girl living in a world far removed from their own; and a frightened secretary of a Secretary stared fixedly out at trees and pastures as he rocked in a chair on the verandah of his country house, waiting to see if the world he knew was about to end.

CHAPTER 44

Just after eleven, Jo stood in the cafe's toilet cubicle, stripping off track pants and hoodie. This was the third broadcast placing her in central Melbourne, so the Hunter's agents could arrive any minute. She thrust her photography gear into the carry bag, and emerging in her sleek yuppie outfit, left the cafe. Though it was hard to resist the adrenaline urge to hurry, Jo made herself stroll casually up the street.

From his nearby parking spot, Richard watched her walk away. She appeared carefree and confident and her courage bolstered his own. He slipped inside, selected a morning paper from the rack provided for patrons, and grabbed a table as someone stood to go.

The cafe was doing a brisk business, serving mainly women breaking a busy morning's shopping. A few students from Melbourne University also appeared to be forsaking lectures in favor of getting a java hit. Richard ordered a latté and settled back behind the paper.

It was all too obvious when the agents arrived some five minutes later. Three men and a woman strode in purposefully, spreading out to scan the tables. The woman walked through to the ladies room and came out seconds later shaking her head. The four then converged upon the counter, where one of the males held up a photo and seemed to be demanding that the frantically busy girl at the coffee machine stop to look at it.

Between frothing milk and nodding to a waiter calling a new order across to her, the girl cast a quick glance at the photo and shrugged her shoulders. The four went into a huddle and then spread out again, homing in on waiters and waitresses. Richard smiled at the annoyed headshakes they were getting and when they started hassling the patrons with their photos, two of the waiters stepped over angrily and ushered them out of the cafe.

Richard half rose. Had one of the men been the Hunter? All had hair, though that was easy enough to fake. In the end he sat again, his gut persuading him to wait a little longer. For all that, he nearly missed the Hunter when he did come in, initially writing him off as another student. In jeans and a faded cloth cap over a black stubble haircut, the young man sauntered to a free table within earshot, and clicked his fingers to summon a waitress.

Perhaps it was the arrogant body language that tweaked Richard's radar, but confirmation came when the man twisted to give his order, and revealed the tip of a tattoo at the base of his neck.

Richard held the newspaper up, apparently engrossed in one of the articles, but listening attentively. The waitress had returned with the Hunter's coffee and he could hear her objecting to being paid on the spot.

"All payments are at the counter, sir."

The voice that replied was honey-smooth, overshadowed with a slightly affected accent. "This fifty isn't for the coffee. It's your tip if you have time to sit for a second and answer a question."

The scraping of a chair indicated her ready cooperation.

"About fifteen minutes ago, a girl with long blonde hair in grey track pants…"

An exasperated sigh. "Not again! I'll tell you what I told the others. I did see a girl like that come in around eleven, but I didn't serve her. I was busy. Things were hectic at that time. They're starting to calm down now, but…"

"Forget that girl, she's not important. What I want to know is whether you saw *any* girl leaving the cafe that you hadn't noticed coming in."

There was a surprised, "Hmm! Now you come to mention it, I *did*. I remember wondering which table the girl had been sitting at, because she seemed to appear out of nowhere."

"Could you describe her?"

"About my height with short reddish-blonde hair. She was wearing black pants with a long pink top. Oh, and a gorgeous pink and charcoal scarf to die for."

"Did you see which way she went?"

"She turned right, up the hill."

A rustle and renewed chair scraping signaled the transaction had been completed, but Richard remained where he was, turning a page and thanking the gods that Jo had had a ten minute head start. She should be back at Marilyn's by now. The Hunter began talking again and it was soon clear he was on the phone giving Jo's new description to someone and outlining a specific perimeter of operations.

Richard began regretting the plan to return to Marilyn's place. Agents would be closing in on that area with an updated description of Jo. He had to call as soon as possible and warn her. She would not be pleased he'd failed to abide by her wishes, but if she'd read his note, she'd know that already. Standing, he kept his back to the Hunter as he edged around the tables to the cash register on the counter. As he left the cafe, he could still hear the Hunter talking.

Richard slipped into his car and keeping one eye on the doorway, pressed the numbers for Marilyn's apartment on the cheap phone. No one picked up – not surprising as Jo would be reluctant to answer Marilyn's phone, and eventually the answering machine kicked in. Jo should be there right now to hear his message but as Marilyn would hear it too, he decided on a cryptic approach.

"His people have your new description and are closing in. He's wearing jeans and a cap, and now has black stubble hair. Stay put until I call."

The faded cap appeared in the doorway and Richard twisted around, pretending to be getting something from the back seat. When he turned back, the Hunter was climbing into a Passat parked three spaces down.

Quickly Richard added, "He's driving a black VW Passat," before closing the connection and dropping the phone into his pocket. He risked another glance at the car. Had the Hunter seen his face? The man was starting the engine and checking his rearview mirror. He cast no glance in Richard's direction.

When he drove off, Richard followed, trying to keep some distance between himself and the Passat, but the volume of vehicles on the road made it hard to keep the car in sight, and he couldn't afford to drop too far behind. On the plus side, the heavy traffic also made a tailing car less noticeable, and the Hunter would be concentrating on trying to find Jo.

Richard noted that while he'd directed his troops to cordon off the northern area, he himself was circling and weaving in and out of streets to the south. Obviously the Hunter was expecting Jo to double-back and was hoping to chance upon her. This made following tricky, but at least he wasn't travelling fast.

The thought had barely crossed his mind when the Hunter accelerated through an intersection as the light turned red. Richard, two cars behind, was stuck. He leant out of the window and spotted the Passat turning between two buildings about a hundred meters down the road.

When the light turned green, he sped to the spot – a narrow lane, and turned into it. Immediately he saw the black car, parked at the far end. It was blocking most of the lane except for a small passage on its right.

Richard pulled up behind it. The Passat was empty. The Hunter had taken off on foot. Jumping out, he thumbed the remote lock on his keys, and dropped them into his pocket as he ran. From a niche at the side, a leg extended. As he fell, Richard sensed a looming shape before something solid hit the back of his head.

A splitting headache combined with a feeling of suffocation made Richard reflexively attempt to gasp. He couldn't do it and panic brought him quickly to full consciousness. He was lying cramped in a dark place, dragging air heavily in through his nose. His mouth was held shut by something wide and strong, which seemed to be wound tightly around his whole head.

The duct tape, he thought. Hoist by my own petard. He struggled and discovered tape bound his ankles and that his wrists were fastened behind his back. He tried to dispel the panic by concentrating on his surroundings. They were dark, cramped and rocking. He was a prisoner in a car boot – exactly what he'd planned for the Hunter.

Jo hadn't been kidding when she'd warned him the Hunter was smart. Was this the end then? Was the Hunter about to drive him off a cliff or leave him somewhere he wouldn't be found until it was too late? With his hands taped behind him, Richard could reach neither phone nor the knife at his calf, and his struggles only increased the need for oxygen and heightened the terrifying sensation of suffocation. Pain lanced through his head, adding to the surreal nightmare.

...

Jo reached the apartment without incident and immediately changed into her cycling outfit. She left Marilyn's clothes folded on her bed, and was unzipping the bike bag when the phone rang. She started, half expecting Marilyn to enter the room and answer it. The phone continued to ring. Ignore it, Jo thought, struggling to extract the bike from its carry case. Finally the answering machine kicked in and she froze at Richard's voice.

"His people have your new description and are closing in. He's wearing jeans and a cap, and now has black stubble hair. Stay put until I call." There was a pause and then the words, "He's driving a black VW Passat." The connection clicked off.

She should have known. Richard's agreement to part ways had been too ready. He must have followed her to the cafe. The open laptop on the coffee table now registered on her consciousness and Jo walked over and pressed a key to wake it up. In the password field she typed 'Fitani'. Six words leapt out at her. *Sorry love, we're in this together.*

Tears welled, and between guilt and relief, a little spark of hope began jumping. Jo closed the laptop. She couldn't leave now. If Richard was following the Hunter with the aim of capturing him, it would be a while before he called back.

She checked her watch. 11.20 a.m. For the first time since the game began, she was at a loose end but dismissed all thought of taking a nap. Worrying about Richard would make sleeping impossible. Instead she threw herself into a tried and true remedy. Tidying up always reduced her to an unthinking trance-like state and this was exactly the kind of mental break she needed. The morning's dishes were still on the draining rack. Jo walked over and put them away. Then she carefully wiped every inch of bench, cooktop and sink, restoring the kitchen to its previous immaculate state.

A familiar cough broke through her daze. Turning, she felt her mouth drop. Fitani was wearing the same outfit as before! How could he have forgotten to change? His face was grave, almost haggard.

"Danny, you look terrible." She moved into the living room and sat in an armchair. "What's wrong?"

The host materialized opposite on the red settee.

"I have your answer about the H Group. Sorry it took so long, but my technicians could not believe what they found and nor could I. We've triple-checked, but it always comes out the same." He opened his mouth and closed it, for the first time at a loss for words.

Guessing why, Jo knew Danny's audience would soon be in the same state of shock. She spoke quietly. "I think I know what you're finding so hard to say. BEAM's attempts to destroy the H Group will fail."

The host nodded and cleared his throat. "The people running your H Group are nasty, very nasty. Over the next seventy-eight years their increasingly devious and immoral machinations will enable them to take control of your world's primary industry. As they grow stronger they will worry less about keeping their links and tactics hidden and will come to control first primary industry and ultimately all commerce that matters.

"In building their power they will use deception, bribery, blackmail and murder, rolling over any who stand in their way. They *want* the world's population to keep expanding because more mouths require more goods and services, which means more gold for their coffers."

"So you're saying when my people finally blow themselves up, they will be the only company still operating."

Fitani nodded, drawing a shaky breath. "The H Group epitomizes all that is worst in the Ancestors – greed, selfishness and unthinking rapaciousness to the point of influencing world governments to encourage procreation in a world already grossly overpopulated." His voice faded away.

Jo prompted gently. "And when the H Group realizes that the world they've been exploiting is about to self-destruct?"

Fitani hung his head. "They will make preparations to save themselves. They will build vast underground bunkers, equipped to house and feed their families and the families of their most valuable servants over the many years of the nuclear winter and its aftermath. The rest of the world they will leave to its own devices."

Jo waited. It was not for her to say what must now be said.

Fitani drew breath. "As I tell you this fact, so I announce it to the rest of my world. The H Group is… The Company. For hundreds of years we have toiled for and given our loyalty to those we have most despised."

With an effort he straightened and his voice became firm. "However, I urge my people *not* to lose faith. I believe that *shame* at the part they played in bringing about The Great Destruction, caused the H Group – The Company, to repent and change its ways. I believe that in saving the survivors and helping us to rebuild our Earth over all these years, The Company has tried to make amends. I urge my people not to lose their faith in our great Company."

Jo was frowning. "Danny, what you say may be true, but for your people, I suspect faith alone will no longer be enough."

To her surprise, Fitani stood proudly. "Faith alone will not be required. I will soon be able to provide proof of what I say."

"How is that possible?"

"It's possible because of the blurred areas. They are proof The Company seeks redemption. There is a reason why the blur in every Safe Place has grown so much over the years. Each one is hiding a great gift that The Company Executives have been building for our world.

"For hundreds of years the Executives have toiled, preparing these gifts to demonstrate their true repentance. Perhaps they are not quite ready to reveal, but for the sake of all, they must now be shown lest our love and faith in our Company be lost.

"I therefore announce that my team's programmers have been working on breaking the security protocols of the land surveillance software and are close to success. Soon The Company's gifts will be revealed and all will know that our savior is as good and beneficent as we have always believed."

His speech ended, Fitani turned solemnly to Jo. "I have answered your question and become the stronger for it."

Bowing, he disappeared.

CHAPTER 45

The car stopped and as a door thunked, Richard felt his heart racing. A pop, and the boot lid rose. Blinding daylight flooded in, silhouetting the shape of the Hunter. He stood for a second and then bent forward, showing white teeth.

"Richard Sayers, I presume? Fortunately not as bright as you think, since you fell right into my trap. You should have stuck to selling farming machinery."

Casually the Hunter held up a thick metal bar about thirty centimeters long.

"How's your head?"

He tossed the bar into the air and caught it, rotating it back and forth between his fingers before bringing one end to rap smartly against Richard's collarbone. There was an audible crack and the Hunter chuckled as the duct tape muffled Richard's involuntary cry.

"Perhaps you're wondering how I set the trap."

The bar, now vertical in the Hunter's fist, jabbed viciously into Richard's thigh. As he clenched his teeth, the other end cracked against his kneecap, and he jerked in agony.

The Hunter spoke calmly. "I said to myself, if I were the boyfriend, what would *I* do to save my darling from the nasty Hunter?"

He reached forward and seized Richard's lapel, chuckling again as his victim flinched, but merely flapping his jacket open, finding the phone and transferring it to his own pocket. Next he found Richard's wallet and tucking the bar under one arm, examined the driver's licence inside and nodded.

"I'd probably say, this Hunter fellow needs to be put on ice and no doubt I'd then ask my dear darling girlfriend for tips on the Hunter's strategy."

He pocketed the wallet and raised the bar.

"No doubt my girlfriend, that wily little bitch, would have told me the Hunter liked to send his troops to cover the most likely options, while he worked the outside possibilities alone, and this would have sounded ideal for catching him. How am I doing so far Ricky?"

The bar circled and Richard closed his eyes, but not knowing where it would land was worse than following its mesmerizing path, and his lids sprang open of their own volition.

"Naturally I expected you to be waiting for me at the next broadcast point and on entering the cafe I immediately guessed you were the one holding the newspaper so high. I made sure to take a nearby table so you could hear me talking and know you'd found me. I'd already picked out an ambush spot – that handy little alley near this car park. All I needed was for you to follow me."

The bar delivered a smack on the anklebone. Water welled in Richard's eyes and he swallowed the liquid building at the back of his nose.

The Hunter laughed. "Did you think I hadn't seen you when I walked out of the cafe? And then what fun we had driving all around Carlton together. Unfortunately I couldn't allow it to go on for too long. I do have Prey to catch you know."

The Hunter held one end of the bar between thumb and forefinger and started it swinging to and fro.

"Once I'd knocked you out in the alley and lifted your car keys, I opened your boot to stuff you in. Imagine my pleasure at the surprise you'd left me – duct tape! I'd planned on breaking your legs to stop you from escaping, but duct tape allows a more leisurely approach. Far preferable to draw out one's pleasure, don't you think?"

The metal tip caressed Richard's cheek.

"I then drove your car to the rooftop of the nearby car park, which is where we are now. They have long-term parking up here, so we're pretty much undisturbed."

The bar snaked down to the broken collarbone and pressed. Richard groaned, rolling back onto his bound hands, and the metal flicked in a quick jab to the groin.

Tears and mucus filled Richard's eyes and nose and the Hunter watched silently for a few minutes as his victim writhed, choking and gulping. When Richard finally regained control of his breathing, the Hunter leant forward and spoke in confidential tones.

"I've enjoyed this a great deal," he breathed. "So much more satisfying than playing with the neighborhood cats. Of course I have to be careful not to get too carried away and kill you – at least before I bag my Prey. The game has strict rules in that regard. Mind you, once Jo's dead, the game will be over and I'll take my money *and* my little plaything." He gave a carefree tap to the injured kneecap. "And we can have a delightful time finishing our own personal game."

He reached for the boot lid. "I'll let you have fun thinking about that while I'm killing Jo. Oh, did you think I'd be asking you where she was? No need. Though my agents found your house empty at 9.30, I believe it will contain your girlfriend very soon. However, should she fail to turn up, and I've learnt the hard way not to underestimate that little bitch, then I'll be right back for part two of our play date."

The boot lid slammed, leaving Richard locked in a sea of pain but thankful to Jo that at least the brunt of the Hunter's groin shot had been taken by the iPhone.

...

Jo paced the living room. Not a word from Richard and it was eleven-forty. He could still be following the Hunter, waiting for an opportunity to nab him, but she had a bad feeling.

She opened her laptop and logged into Richard's iCloud account, telling it to find his iPhone. A Google map appeared, with a blue pin dropped on Leicester Street. Jo zoomed to see the street was lined with what looked like the backs of old factories. Interspersed were occasional newer buildings, and a multi-storied car park. A center-parking strip divided the road.

Assuming Richard was travelling along Leicester, she waited a few minutes before clicking the *Find my iPhone* button again. The blue pin was in the same place. Could this mean the capture was happening there right now? Was Richard lifting an unconscious Hunter into his car? If so, the phone's next location would be on route to, if not right at, Richard's house.

Jo walked out onto the balcony and forced herself to wait three long minutes before returning to try again. The location point hadn't moved. What did this mean? Had the detection software stopped working?

Seriously worried, she began running possibilities through her mind. Perhaps in his struggle with the Hunter, Richard had dropped his phone in the street and not noticed. He could be home right now, calmly binding the Hunter to a chair and congratulating himself on a smooth operation.

Not daring to call his iPhone for fear of jeopardizing the situation if something *had* gone wrong, Jo used the online white pages to find Richard's home phone, and lifting Marilyn's handset, called the number. The ring tone sounded, repeating endlessly before she heard his calm voice saying, "This is Richard."

"Richard," she slumped in relief. "Did..."

"Sorry I can't answer your call right now. Please leave a message and I'll get back to you."

A long beep sounded. In despair she left a message. "Richard, it's me. Please call as soon as you get in. I'm worried."

It was now close to noon and Jo set the iPhone search software to do its thing again. A message appeared stating the phone could not be located. What was going on? She swore. If only Richard had kept his promise to stay out of it, she'd now be cycling across Melbourne, with no greater concern than where to be for the next broadcast. Funny how worry was relative.

Finally she admitted to herself that something was badly wrong, and tried to visualize a scenario in which the Hunter had captured Richard. What would he do with him? Given that Richard's car would be handy, the logical thing would be to lock him in the boot. His dead phone was a concern, but probably only meant the Hunter had found and destroyed it. He wouldn't dare murder Richard, knowing that doing so would end the game and cause an assassin to be sent after him.

Richard's car was probably parked on Leicester Street right now with its unconscious owner inside. What model did he drive? Her only glimpse had been when they'd pulled into his driveway last night, soon after two am. Their headlights had lit up the back of the vehicle under the carport, but in her exhausted state, Jo had merely registered it to be of medium size and dark silver in color. Dozens of such cars were probably parked along Leicester Street.

It was time to call in the big guns. Waking up Richard's laptop, she connected to the Internet and opened his mail program. His latest emails had encrypted attachments but it wasn't the messages she wanted, it was the address they'd been sent from.

She hit the reply button, and typed, "URGENT This is Jo Warrington. Richard Sayers' life is in danger! He is somewhere on Leicester Street in Carlton, possibly locked in the boot of his car. I am going there now dressed in a cyclist's outfit. Please help!"

She clicked the "top priority" checkbox and sent the email. Then picking up her own laptop, Jo took a last look at the map on the screen before closing the lid and pushing it into a pannier bag. She assembled her bike, attached the pannier, and putting on her helmet and sunglasses, headed for the door.

The hallway was empty as Jo wheeled the bike into the lift and pressed the button for the basement. If the Hunter had agents nearby it would be better for her to emerge from the driveway than to attract attention by wheeling a bike out through the front doors. No one stopped Jo as she cycled to Lygon Street and turned south. At Queensberry, she made a right turn and cycled to Leicester. There she turned left towards the car park she'd seen on the map.

The whole trip had taken less than ten minutes and now Jo began a slow reconnaissance of the street, weaving back and forth to knock on the boots of silver cars parked by the curb and in the center-parking strip. No one responded to her knocks and eventually she drew level with the multi-storied car park – an ideal place, she realized, for hiding a car with Richard in it.

Jo cycled slowly past, noticing the automated barrier arms across the entryways. No personnel to remember who went in and out. She braked and jumped off the bike, wheeling it around one of the arms. Inside, the cavernous ground floor was filled with cars.

What now? Should I start knocking on car boots? There are so many and this is only the ground floor. Think, she told herself. If the Hunter *did* bring Richard's car here, where would he park it? Surely not on a level that gets a lot of use, like this one. How high is the car park?

Jo looked around and saw an elevator in a side wall. She cycled across to it and pushed the call button. When the doors opened she would learn how many stories needed to be searched. As she waited for the lift to descend, one car exited and another pulled up to the entry barrier. The box near the driver's window poked out a cheeky white tongue, and an arm extended to grab it.

Suddenly Jo found herself paying attention. The car was a jet black VW – a Passat! Standing by the lift she was in full view if the driver decided to turn his head but luckily he was intent upon his own business and when the barrier lifted, he accelerated to the up-ramp.

The elevator doors opened. Jo placed one hand across the cavity and leant out to watch the Passat as it wound higher and higher. Eventually she could no longer make out its progress. Her first impulse was to jump on her bike and cycle as far away from the Hunter as she could, but what if he had Richard in his car?

She stepped into the lift and looked at the buttons. There were six levels above the ground floor, the sixth being the rooftop. Levels "5" and "Rooftop" had the words "Long-term parking" beside them. Long-term parking! That would be ideal for the Hunter.

On impulse Jo pressed Rooftop, and the lift began a ponderous jerky ascent. Her heart pounded and her fingers squeezed the handlebars during the interminable trip. The doors finally, slowly opened onto a wide expanse of concrete. Few cars were parked up here. People probably preferred not to expose their vehicles to the elements for long periods.

Holding the doors open, Jo cautiously peered around them. On her left, about fifty meters down, a black Passat was parked beside a dark silver Camry. Both were backed into the short wall.

As she watched, the Passat driver emerged, and even at this distance she could see his jeans and cap. He appeared to be carrying a stick of some kind as he walked around to the boot of the Camry. Before lifting it, he looked up to scan the rooftop and she jerked back.

Now as she stood holding her hand against the door cavity, Jo wondered what was going on. The silver Camry had to be Richard's car, and likely he was trapped in the boot right now. But why was the Hunter wasting time checking on Richard when he should be looking for her? He couldn't be intending to kill him – he knew the rules of *Play or Die*. With a shiver of fright, Jo realized. He was planning to torture Richard to get her location.

She peered out again. The boot of the Camry was open and the Hunter was bending beneath the lid.

"Hey!" she yelled, waving one hand, while keeping the lift door retracted with the other. "Here I am! It's *me* you want."

The figure froze momentarily and then began a galloping run towards her. Jo stepped back into the lift, frantically thumbing the ground floor button and sobbing with relief when the slow-moving doors closed before the Hunter reached them.

During the sluggish journey to the bottom, Jo's mind raced, but her uppermost thought was, lead him away. Someone in BEAM must have read her email by now, so *her* job was clear – get the Hunter as far from Richard as possible so the BEAM agents had time to find and rescue him.

For a split second she wondered if the Hunter would phone his detectives and order them to move Richard. But no, he wouldn't want them knowing he'd locked an innocent person into the boot of a car. Richard would stay right there until either his own people found him or the Hunter returned, and if she had her way, BEAM would get there first.

The lift doors opened to the sounds of screeching tires and roaring engine. As Jo ran out with her bike she saw the Passat speeding down a ramp only one floor above. She raced to the entrance and was weaving around the barrier arm when it turned into the final stretch and accelerated towards her.

Jo turned right onto the footpath. Out of sight of the Hunter, she spun a hundred and eighty degrees, and waited with one foot on the pedal. The Passat smashed through the flimsy barrier arm and swept right with a squeal of tires. As soon as it had cleared the entrance, Jo was on her bike cycling fast back across the entrance and on towards Victoria Street.

When the Hunter realized Jo's feint, he threw the Passat into a screeching U-turn, swiping cars parked in the middle and along the curb, but during his maneuver, Jo reached the main road. Her heart sank.

Though Leicester Street was empty of traffic, Victoria was full. Trams, trucks and cars sped past. There was no way to cross. Turning left into Victoria Street wouldn't work. The Hunter would simply follow and no doubt succeed in 'accidentally' hitting and killing her.

She heard a roar. He was coming down. Spinning around, she turned her back on Victoria and cycled up Leicester Street's second lane with the center strip of cars between herself and the Hunter. As he reached the end, the Hunter swept around through the clear zone and accelerated towards her, but Jo squeezed back between the parked cars to the other lane and cycled up it a short distance before stopping with one foot on the ground.

To get into *her* lane, the Hunter would have to drive a hundred meters up to where the center parking ended at the next clear zone and make a U-turn.

Alternatively he could pull up level with her and try jumping out and running between the parked cars to catch her, but he'd be on foot and she had her bike.

The Hunter seemed to be having the same thoughts and he slowed to a crawl, pulling up within calling distance. He flashed her a grin through the barrier of cars between them.

"Touché Jo. But how long do you think you can keep this up?"

She declined to answer and spinning her bike towards Victoria Street, began cycling in that direction. To her dismay, the Hunter did not continue up the street to the clear zone, but simply reversed, staying level with her. Again she turned tightly and cycled north. In his lane, the Hunter kept abreast. He was right, she couldn't keep this up, but if she left the protection of the central strip of cars, he'd be on her in a flash.

She stopped and turned to face him through the parked cars.

"Is there anything I can do to persuade you to call this off?"

The Hunter threw back his head and laughed. "You think you can offer me something of greater value than fifty million dollars? You *do* place a high price on your virtue."

"I was thinking more of an appeal to your decency. The fifty million would be blood money. Do you think you could live with yourself afterwards?"

Again the Hunter burst into laughter, and Jo saw actual tears of mirth rolling down his cheeks. Taking advantage of his temporary blindness, she stood on her pedals and cycled hard, but with barely a pause, the Passat was once more abreast, and Jo could see the end of the center-parking strip coming up.

A feeling of exhaustion and lethargy settled upon her. What was the point in continuing to cycle up and down this lane? The end had arrived and the Hunter had won. It was time to stop and accept her fate. But the thought of Richard trapped in the boot of his car kept her going. Once she was dead, there would be no barrier to the Hunter killing Richard. And he would probably do that rather than leave a vengeful boyfriend on the loose to track him down.

Jo made a tight U-turn and headed down the lane, ignoring the Hunter's car reversing parallel with her. She would try a blind dash over Victoria Street. If by some miracle she got safely across that wide, busy road, she'd lead him on a merry dance through the market she'd seen on the other side. If she didn't make it, being hit by a car or tram was no worse than what the Hunter planned. And if he didn't kill her himself, he would forfeit his prize, so at least he wouldn't profit by her death.

Twenty meters before the end, Jo realized there was a way she could buy Richard some extra time and stopped. The Hunter drew level and grinned at her.

"Give up?"

She'd stay here, keeping him talking as long as possible. The minute he got tired of it and leapt from his car, she'd make her suicide run across Victoria Street.

"I've just thought of a way to beat you." Jo returned his grin.

"This I have to hear."

"I arrange to die by a hand other than yours."

"A lose/lose situation."

"Correct. I die, but you miss out on your prize."

"And how do you plan to find someone to perform this deed within the next ten seconds?"

Jo glanced involuntarily towards Victoria Street and the Hunter immediately understood.

"Try that," he said quickly, "and your boyfriend will suffer for it."

Jo went cold.

"Dear Richard and I have already had such fun together, and pain is an item in endless store. Tell you what, I'll do you a deal. You join me in the car right now and I promise two things. Your death will be quick, and I'll leave Richard alone. On the other hand should you succeed in killing yourself, I give you my guarantee that your boyfriend's death will be as protracted and agonizing as I can make it, and I do pride myself on a certain expertise in that area."

Jo wobbled in a sudden wave of dizziness and her stomach heaved. Time did a strange shift and she found herself floating in a slowed-down world, aware, though from a state of supreme detachment, of events occurring around her. A car drove past her, signaling left. A postman travelled up the Hunter's side of the road on his motorized scooter, and a woman, fishing in her handbag, began crossing towards the car park. Near her front wheel a couple of little sparrows pecked at a squashed piece of piecrust. How cute they were, and so bold to be scavenging in such a dangerous location.

Jo felt herself dismounting from the bike. The sparrows flew off as she pushed it between the parked cars. Numbly she leant it against a center parking meter and took a step towards him. The Hunter, grinning, watched her coming. Behind him, the postman had driven right up to the front passenger window. Seeing Jo, he began turning away. Blatman! The face from Richard's laptop. Her father's assassin.

"Murderer," Jo screamed, running around the front of the Passat. Wobbling, the postman kicked his bike into gear, but she threw herself at him, vaguely aware of the Hunter also leaping from the passenger door. The bike went over and all three landed on the road.

In a blind rage Jo went for Blatman. As she raked his face her ears rang with screams and she realized they were coming from her. A hard fist hit her in the stomach and she collapsed onto the bike. Two bodies struggled beside her and a boot kicked sharply against her arm. She rolled, trying to get out of the way. On the road in front of her was a gun. She blinked and stared at it stupidly. The end had a long cylinder. A silencer?

A hand grasped her leg and she threw out her arm to grab the gun as she was dragged along the road. Twisting she looked up into the snarling face of the Hunter. As he threw himself at her, she squeezed the trigger. The snarl froze and he dropped heavily on top of her.

Almost immediately he was kicked off and the fluorescent jacket of the postman loomed. His swinging foot struck the gun from her hand and she heard him curse as it skidded under a parked car. A siren wailed into the street and Jo she could see the dilemma in his eyes. She lifted her knees and raised her fists. Killing her would be no quick thing. He turned and ran. She closed her eyes.

"Jo Warrington? Are you Jo?"

Strong hands were lifting her to a sitting position. The earsplitting wailing abruptly cut off and she raised her head to see a large man squatting beside her.

"Are you all right?" he said. "I'm from BEAM."

Two police cars, their lights flashing, had boxed in the black Passat and a little distance away an ambulance stood waiting. Men were coming towards her with a trolley and Jo began to object before she realized it was for the Hunter.

"Blatman!" she said.

The man looked at her questioningly.

"The postman – he's an assassin."

The man looked at the Hunter's body. "He did that? Don't worry, he didn't get away. The police caught him."

Jo frowned. "I don't understand. He *was* going for the Hunter, but the game has two and half more days to run. They wouldn't send an assassin unless the Hunter had killed an innocent... Oh God. Richard!"

"We found him. He's been taken away in an ambulance."

"Is he..." she couldn't finish the words.

"I haven't seen him myself, but my associates tell me his injuries are not life threatening. He'll be okay."

Tears spilled from her eyes and the man squatting opposite, reached out a tentative hand. "Are you hurt?"

She smiled through the blur. "No."

. . .

In a bright private room eight stories above a teeming city, Richard sat in a hospital bed. His arm was in a sling and a cage kept the blankets off his lower body, but he was loaded with analgesics and feeling no pain. Outside the open door, the sounds of nurses talking and teacarts clinking were reassuring in their normality.

He smiled up at Jo who sat in the chair beside him, holding his hand.

"You are truly amazing," he said. "Are you sure you're okay?"

"I'm relieved it's over. I don't think reality's set in yet." She shuddered. "I was just about to get into the Hunter's car. If the sight of Blatman hadn't turned me into some kind of a mad thing, I'd be dead right now."

He squeezed her hand. "It's the Hunter who's dead. We're safe."

"I killed him," said Jo, in wonder. "My session with the police is going to be a long one. At the moment they think I was an innocent bystander, but they'll soon realize I was the shooter."

"Yes, in self-defense against a very nasty specimen. They know what the Hunter did to me and it's clear there was a hit man going after *him*. The gun you killed him with was Blatman's. It'll all work out."

Jo squeezed his hand. "I hope you're right."

"What I don't understand is why Fitani would set an assassin onto the Hunter before the five days were up."

"Maybe he killed someone in the course of getting to me."

Richard frowned. "Seems unlikely. He was a careful operator."

"Can you think of another explanation?"

"Jo, what if your words finally got through to Fitani, and he decided to stop the game?"

She shook her head. "I can't see him breaking his own rules. Bumping off the Hunter without reason wouldn't be sporting. If Fitani really *did* decide to call things off, he'd more likely offer a consolation prize – say five million instead of fifty."

"Do you think the Hunter would have accepted that?"

Jo remembered the delight on his face when he thought he had her. "No, he enjoyed the game too much. I'm guessing it woke something in him, and even after killing me, he wouldn't have stopped. With his prize money he could have found ways to hide from the law while he went on an endless murdering spree."

"I'm sure you're right." Richard had his own memories of the Hunter, which were going to take some time to fade. His eyes drifted to the young dark-haired woman watching them from the foot of his bed. She had neither picked up his chart, nor wheeled in a tea trolley. They were expecting to be interviewed by the police, but this woman's grey track pants and hoodie were definitely not police issue.

"Can I help you?" he asked.

Jo spun to face her and the woman gave them a tentative smile.

"Hi. I'm Angela, from Danny Fitani's time. I'm glad you got the Hunter yourself, Jo, but I'm the one who sent the assassin."

"Why?" Jo breathed.

"You freed my people." There was a vitality behind her words. "You showed us honor, courage and truth. We can never thank you enough."

Richard frowned. "Where's Fitani?"

"In the thick of the revolution." Angela smiled. "He's our greatest convert."

"So," Jo remembered her last conversation with the host. "The blurred areas did not clear to reveal a great gift?"

The girl gave a short laugh. "Oh, there was a gift all right, but not one the Executives ever intended for us. On the backs of our labor, they'd created a paradise for themselves – kilometers of parks and gardens. Even great treed forests teeming with wildlife. And mansions – huge spreading edifices, occupying hectares of precious land and Jo, the people they housed!"

Her face filled with disgust as she spat out the words. "Great fat leeches. Parasites, wallowing in their wealth. They spent their lives eating and drinking and engaging in endless unproductive and unsavory entertainments. When we saw how we'd been used, a great revolution began. Tubes were unlocked and black clouds disabled. People rushed from their silos to the fields, crushing crops underfoot."

"And you marched on the Executives?" Richard asked, jubilant to learn the H Group would finally meet their Waterloo.

"The Executives live a great many kilometers from the silos," said Angela. "We quickly discovered that holographic clothing protects from neither cold winds nor from stones and sticks underfoot."

Richard whistled. "They've kept you naked as babes in those silos. Before your revolution can begin you'll need to clothe yourselves and organize transport and weapons."

Angela nodded. "It is what we are doing right now."

Jo broke in. "What are you planning to do with the Executives when you reach them? And what will become of your lives in the silos?"

"These questions are also being discussed. In a way it's been good we weren't able to blindly converge on The Company. When we act it will be as one, and wanton destruction and chaos will be avoided."

Richard couldn't suppress a laugh. "A revolution by committee!"

"Yes." Angela smiled, not understanding the irony. "And it's moving fast. Already several manufacturing silos have been turned over to producing clothing and transport, and plans for improving our lifestyles are being developed. Many approve of Jo's idea of using the parks and wilderness areas for resorts, and we are already adjusting our cycles to incorporate daily outdoor time, including weekends and holidays."

Richard was incredulous. "It sounds like you plan to go on living in the silos."

"Why wouldn't we? They are a comfortable and efficient way to house the great many thousands in each Safe Place and to keep our resources to hand. All we've wanted is the freedom to stride out over our land and now everyone will be able to do this."

Jo spoke warmly. "I'm so glad your people finally have their freedom. I've come to see them as my people too. We're all part of humanity and the future is now brighter for everyone."

Angela smiled. "Yes, thanks to you, Jo, and in answer to your earlier question about what will be done with the Executives, many Employees started by demanding their blood, but now opinion seems to be swaying in favor of bringing them into the silos. They can work for their points like everyone else and do their bit to keep our new world moving forward."

She cleared her throat and spoke solemnly. "Jo, our society owes you a great debt. You will not be forgotten among my people. We have done what we can to assist in getting your life back to normal. The false Kylie Marshal identity has been erased from all storage devices and the detective agencies working for the Hunter have been paid off and informed that the baby has been returned to its grandfather.

As our final tribute to you, we have dismantled the Microwave Time Viewer and passed a law banning any interaction with the past. From now on our energies will be focused on the present and the future. Good-bye and good luck."

She faded and Richard turned to Jo. "It's over," he smiled.

"Almost," said Jo. "There's still Simon Brooks. We have to prove he hired Blatman to murder my father."

Richard tightened his fingers on hers. "We'll do it together... if you still want my help."

"Oh Richard." Jo leaned across the bed, trying to avoid his injuries and began a long, slow kiss.

He put his good arm around her and pulled her close. When they finally surfaced, Jo laughed. "I've been wanting to do that for so long."

He looked into her eyes and spoke quietly. "Jo, before we go any further I need to be upfront with you. Our world will end horribly in seventy-eight years. I won't be responsible for bringing children into it."

She surprised him with a wistful smile. "I agree. As it turns out, I can't have children, but even if I could, I wouldn't, knowing what we now know."

He reached for her hand. "At least we also know that humanity again has hope. The H Group *will* be defeated and the Earth will be repaired. We couldn't ask for more – except for Brooks and Blatman being brought to justice," he grinned.

"Well we won't be short of funds while we're working on that," said Jo, returning his smile.

"We won't?"

"Remember my last question to Fitani?"

"The personal one?"

She blushed. "I've seen enough movies to know I'd be mad not to take advantage of having access to the future. Why should the Hunter be the only one to benefit financially? I asked for the winning lotto numbers in this Saturday's twenty million dollar draw."

Richard laughed. "Now there's a girl with her feet on the ground."

"Well, money buys a lot of things. For one, I'll be able to hire my own detectives to help get evidence on Blatman and Brooks."

"Wait a minute," Richard became animated. "Morris Blatman's now in custody for attempted murder. The police investigation should discover he's a hit man. That could be incentive for him to admit to your father's murder and give up Simon Brooks for a reduced prison sentence."

"Richard, if you're right, this may all soon be over."

Jo's eyes sparkled as she stretched across the bed to reach his lips.

ABOUT THE AUTHOR

Jen Cole is a primary school teacher, who specializes in computing.
Over the years, she has written a number of software programs for
her students, including *TTAPS* – a touch-typing program,
which has sold around Australia.

Play or Die, her first novel, was begun in 2007 and completed in 2009.
It then languished and was polished until publication in 2012.
Jen is now working on her next novel and has written a number of short
stories for adults and children, two of which are scheduled to be published by
Penguin Australia in 2013.

www.ingramcontent.com/pod-product-compliance
Lightning Source LLC
Chambersburg PA
CBHW070841250626

47159CB00003B/876